May Agnes Fleming

Sharing Her Crime

A novel

May Agnes Fleming

Sharing Her Crime
A novel

ISBN/EAN: 9783337027407

Printed in Europe, USA, Canada, Australia, Japan

Cover: Foto ©Andreas Hilbeck / pixelio.de

More available books at **www.hansebooks.com**

SHARING HER CRIME.

A Novel.

BY

MAY AGNES FLEMING,

AUTHOR OF

"GUY EARLSCOURT'S WIFE," "A TERRIBLE SECRET," "SILENT AND TRUE,"
"A WONDERFUL WOMAN," "LOST FOR A WOMAN,"
"ONE NIGHT'S MYSTERY," "A MAD MARRIAGE,"
ETC., ETC.

"A perfect woman, nobly planned,
To warn, to comfort, and command;
And yet a spirit still and bright,
With something of an angel light."

NEW YORK:
Copyright, 1882, by
G. W. Carleton & Co., Publishers.
LONDON: S. LOW & CO.
MDCCCLXXXIII.

Stereotyped by
SAMUEL STODDER,
00 ANN STREET, N. Y.

TROW
PRINTING AND BOOK BINDING CO.,
N. Y.

CONTENTS

CONTENTS.

SHARING HER CRIME.

CHAPTER I.

THE PLOTTERS.

> " 'Tis a woman hard of feature,
>   Old, and void of all good nature.
>   'Tis an ugly, envious shrew, ·
>   Railing forever at me and you."—POPE.

IT was Christmas Eve. All day long crowds of gayly dressed people had walked the streets, basking in the bright wintry sunshine. Sleigh after sleigh went dashing past, with merrily jingling bells, freighted with rosy cheeks, and bright eyes, and youthful faces, all aglow with happiness.

But the sun must set on Christmas Eve, as on all other days; and redly, threateningly, angrily, he sank down in the far west. Dark, sullen clouds came rolling ominously over the heavens; the wind blew piercingly cold, accompanied with a thin, drizzling rain that froze ere it fell.

Gradually the streets were deserted as the storm in-

[7]

creased in fury ; but the Yule logs were piled high, the curtains drawn, and every house, *save one*, in the handsome street to which my story leads me, was all aglow, all ablaze with light.

In a lull of the storm the sounds of music and merry-making would rise and swell on the air, as light feet tripped merrily amid the mazes of the dance ; or a silvery peal of laughter would break easily on the wayfarer's ear. The reflection of the light through the crimson curtains shed a warm, rosy glow over the snowy ground, brightening the gloom of that stormy winter's night.

But rising dark, grim, and gloomy amid those gayly lighted mansions, stood a large, quaint building of dark-red sandstone. It stood by itself, spectral, shadowy, and grand. No ray of light came from the gloomy windows that seemed to be hermetically sealed. All around was stern, black, and forbidding.

And yet—yes, from one solitary window there *did* stream a long, thin line of light. But even this did not look bright and cheerful like the rest ; it had a cold, yellowish glare, making the utter blackness of the rest of the mansion blacker still by contrast.

The room from which the light issued was high and lofty. The uncarpeted floor was of black polished oak, as also were the wainscoting and mantel. The walls were covered with landscape paper, representing the hideous Dance of Death, in all its variety of frightful forms. The high windows were hung with heavy green damask, now black with dirt and age. A large circular table of black marble stood in one shadowy corner, and a dark, hard sofa, so long and black that it resembled a coffin, stood in the other.

A smoldering sea-coal fire, the only cheerful thing in that gloomy room, struggled for life in the wide, yawning chimney. Now it would die away, enveloping the apartment in gloom, and anon flame fitfully up, until the ghostly shadows on the wall would seem like a train of ghastly specters flitting by in the darkness. The elm trees in front of the house trailed their long arms against the window with a sound inexpressibly dreary ; and the driving hail beat clamorously, as if for admittance.

On either side of the fire-place stood two large easy-chairs, cushioned with deep crimson velvet. In these, facing each other, sat two persons—a man and a woman —the only occupants of the room.

The woman was tall, straight, and stiff, and seemingly about fifty years of age, Her dress was a rustling black satin, with a small crape handkerchief fastened on her bosom with a magnificent diamond pin. Her hands, still small and white, were flashing with jewels as they lay quietly folded in her lap. A widow's cap rested on her head, which was alternately streaked with gray and jet. But her face—so stern, so rigid, no one could look upon it without a feeling of fear. The lips—so thin that she seemed to have no lips at all—were compressed with a look of unswerving determination. Her forehead was low and retreating, with thick black eyebrows meeting across the long, sharp nose, with a look at once haughty and sinister. And from under those midnight brows glittered and gleamed a pair of eyes so small, so sharp and keen—with such a look of cold, searching, *steely* brightness—that the boldest gaze might well quail before them. On that grim, hard face no trace of womanly feeling seemed ever to have lingered—all was stern, harsh, and freezingly cold. She sat rigidly erect in her chair, with her needle-like eyes riveted immovably on the face of her companion, who shifted with evident uneasiness beneath her uncompromising stare.

He was a man of forty, or thereabouts, so small of

1*

stature that, standing side by side, he could scarcely have reached the woman's shoulder. But, notwithstanding his diminutive size, his limbs were disproportionately large for his body, giving him the appearance of being all legs and arms. His little, round bullet-head was set on a prodigiously thick, bull-like neck ; and his hair, short, and bristling up over his head, gave him very much the look of the sun, as pictured in the almanacs.

This prepossessing gentleman was arrayed in an immaculate suit of black, with a spotless white dickey, bristling with starch and dignity, and a most excruciating cravat. Half a dozen rings garnished his claw-like hands, and a prodigious quantity of watch-chain dangled from his vest. The worthy twain were engaged in deep and earnest conversation.

"Well, doctor," said the lady, in a cold, measured tone, that was evidently habitual, "no doubt you are wondering why I sent for you in such haste to-night."

"I never wonder, madam," said the doctor, in a pompous tone—which, considering his size, was quite imposing. "No doubt you have some excellent reason for sending for me, which, if necessary for me to know, you will explain."

"You are right, doctor," said the lady, with a grim sort of smile. "I *have* an excellent reason for sending for you. You are fond of money, I know."

"Why, madam, although it is the root of all evil——"

"Tush, man ! There is no need for Satan to quote Scripture just now," she interrupted with a sneer. "Say, doctor, what would you do to earn five hundred dollars to-night ?"

"Five hundred dollars ?" said the doctor, his small eyes sparkling, while a gleam of satisfaction lighted up his withered face.

"Yes," said the lady, "and if well done, I may double the sum. What would you do for such a price?"

"Rather ask me what I would *not* do."

"Well, the job is an easy one. 'Tis but to——"
She paused, and fixed her eyes on his face with such a wild sort of gleam that, involuntarily, he quailed before her.

"Pray go on, madam. I'm all attention," he said, almost fearing to break the dismal silence. "'Tis but to—*what?*"

"Make away with—a woman and child!"

"Murder them?" said the doctor, involuntarily recoiling.

"Do not use that word!" she said, sharply. "Coward! do you really blanch and draw back! Methought one of your profession would not hesitate to send a patient to heaven."

"But, madam," said the startled doctor, "you know the penalty which the law awards for murder."

"Oh, I perceive," said the woman, scornfully, "it is not the crime you are thinking of, but your own precious neck. Fear not, my good friend ; there is no danger of its ever being discovered."

"But, my *dear* madam," said the doctor, glancing uneasily at the stern, bitter face before him, "I have not the nerve, the strength, nor the——"

"*Courage!*" she broke in, passionately. "Oh, craven —weak, chicken-hearted, miserable craven ! Go, then— leave me, and I will do it myself. You dare not betray me—you *could* not without bringing your neck to the halter—so I fear you not. Oh, coward! coward ! why did not heaven make *me* a man ?"

In her fierce outburst of passion she arose to her feet, and her tall figure loomed up like some unnaturally large, dark shadow. The man quailed in fear before her.

"Go !" she said, fiercely, pointing to the door, " You have refused to *share my crime.*   Go ! poor cowardly poltroon ! but remember, Madge Oranmore never forgives nor forgets !"

"But, my dear Mrs. Oranmore, just listen to me one moment," said the doctor, alarmed by this threat. " I have not refused, I only objected. If you will have the goodness to explain—to tell me what I must do, I will—see about it."

" See about it !" hastily interrupted the lady. " You *can* do it—it is in your power; and yes, or no, must be your answer, immediately."

" But——"

" No buts, sir. I will not have them. If you answer yes, one thousand dollars and my future patronage shall be yours. If you say no, yonder is the door ; and once you have crossed the threshold, beware ! Now, Doctor Wiseman, I await your reply."

She seated herself again in her chair; and, folding her hands in her lap, fixed her hawk-like eyes on his face, with her keen, searching gaze. His eyes were bent in troubled thought on the floor. Not that the crime appalled him ; but if detected—*that* was the rub. Doctor Wiseman was, as his name implies, a man of sense, with an exceedingly accommodating conscience, that would stretch *ad libitum*, and never troubled him with any such nonsense as remorse. But if it were discovered ! With rather unpleasant vividness, the vision of a hangman and halter arose before him, and he involuntarily loosened his cravat. Still, one thousand dollars *were* tempting. Doctor Nicholas Wiseman had never been so perplexed in his life.

" Well, doctor, well," impatiently broke in the lady, "have you decided—*yes* or *no?*"

"Yes," said the doctor, driven to desperation by her sneering tone.

"'Tis well," she replied, with a mocking smile, "I knew you were too sensible a man to refuse. After all, 'tis but a moment's work, and all is over."

"Will you be good enough to give me the explanation now, madam?" said the doctor, almost shuddering at the cold, unfeeling tone in which she spoke.

"Certainly. You are aware, doctor, that when I married my late husband, Mr. Oranmore, he was a widower with one son, then three years old."

"I am aware of that fact, madam."

"Well, you also know that when this child, Alfred, was five years of age, *my* son, Barry, was born."

"Yes, madam."

"Perhaps you think it unnecessary for me to go so far back, doctor, but I wish everything to be perfectly understood. Well, these two boys grew up together, were sent to school and college together, and treated in every way alike, *outwardly*; but, of course, when at home, Barry was treated best. Alfred Oranmore had all the pride of his English forefathers, and scorned to complain; but I could see, in his flashing eyes and curling lips, that every slight was noticed. Mr. Oranmore never interfered with me in my household arrangements, nor did his son ever complain to him; though, if he had, Mr. Oranmore had too much good sense to mention it to *me*."

The lady compressed her lips with stately dignity, and the doctor looked down with something as near a smile as his wrinkled lips could wear. *He* knew very well Mr. Oranmore would not have interfered; for never after his marriage had the poor man dared to call his soul his own. The lady, however, did not perceive the smile, and went on:

"When Barry left college, he expressed a desire to travel for two or three years on the Continent ; and I readily gave him permission, for Mr. Oranmore was then dead. Alfred was studying law, and I knew his dearest wish was to travel ; but, as a matter of course, it was out of the question for *him* to go. I told him I could not afford it, that it would cost a great deal to pay Barry's expenses, and that he must give up all idea of it. Barry went, and Alfred staid ; though, as things afterward turned out, it would have been better had I allowed him to go."

Her eyes flashed, and her brows knit with rising anger, as she continued ;

"You know old Magnus Erliston—Squire Erliston, as they call him. You know also how very wealthy he is reputed to be—owning, besides the magnificent estate of Mount Sunset, a goodly portion of the village of St. Mark's. Well, Squire Erliston has two daughters, to the eldest of whom, in accordance with the will of his father (from whom he received the property), Mount Sunset Hall will descend. Before my husband's death, I caused him to will his whole property to my son Barry, leaving Alfred penniless. Barry's fortune, therefore, is large, though far from being as enormous as that Esther Erliston was to have. Well, the squire and I agreed that, as soon as Barry returned from Europe they should be married, and thus unite the estates of Oranmore and Erliston. Neither Barry nor Esther, with the usual absurdity of youth, would agree to this arrangement ; but, of course, their objection mattered little. I knew I could easily manage Barry by the power of my stronger will ; and the squire, who is rough and blustering, could, without much difficulty, frighten Esther into compliance— when all our schemes were suddenly frustrated by that meddler, that busy-body, Alfred Oranmore."

She paused, and again her eyes gleamed with concentrated hatred and passion.

" He went to Mount Sunset, and by some means met Esther Erliston. Being what romantic writers would call one of 'nature's princes,' he easily succeeded in making a fool of her ; they eloped, were married secretly, and Squire Erliston woke up one morning to learn that his dainty heiress had abandoned papa for the arms of a *beggar*, and was, as the wife of a penniless lawyer, residing in the goodly city of Washington.

" Pretty Esther doubtless imagined that she had only to throw herself at papa's feet and bathe them with her tears, to be received with open arms. But the young lady found herself slightly mistaken. Squire Erliston stamped, and raged, and swore, and frightened every one in St. Mark's out of their wits ; and then, calming down, 'vowed a vow' never to see or acknowledge his daughter more. Esther was then eighteen. If she lived to reach her majority, Mount Sunset would be hers in spite of him. But the squire had vowed that before she should get it, he would burn Sunset Hall to the ground and plow the land with salt. Now, doctor, I heard that, and set myself to work. Squire Erliston has a younger daughter ; and I knew that, if Esther died, that younger daughter would become heiress to all the property, and she would then be just as good a wife for Barry as her sister. Well, I resolved that Esther should no longer stand in my way, that she should never live to reach her majority. Start not, doctor, I see that you do not yet know Madge Oranmore."

She looked like a very fiend, as she sat smiling grimly at him from her seat.

" Fortune favored me," she continued. " Alfred Oranmore, with two or three other young men, going out one day for a sail, was overtaken by a sudden squall—they knew little about managing a boat, and all on board were drowned. I read it in the papers and set out for Washington. After much difficulty I discovered Esther in a wretched boarding-house; for, after her husband's death, all their property was taken for debt. She did not know me, and I had little difficulty in persuading her to accompany me. home. Three days ago we arrived. I caused a report to be circulated at Washington that the wife of the late Alfred Oranmore had died in great poverty and destitution. The story found its way into the papers; I sent one containing the account of her death to Squire Erliston; so all trouble in that quarter is over."

"And *Esther ?*" said the doctor, in a husky whisper.

"Of her we will speak by and by," said the lady, with a wave of her hand; "at present I must say a few words of my son Barry. Three weeks ago he returned home; but has, from some inexplicable cause, refused to reside here. He boards now in a distant quarter of the city. Doctor, what says the world about this—is there any reason given ?"

"Well, yes, madam," said the doctor, with evident reluctance.

"And what is it, may I ask ?"

"I fear, madam, you will be offended."

"'Sdeath ! man, go on !" she broke in passionately. "What sayeth the far-seeing, all-wise world of him ?"

"'Tis said he has brought a wife with him from Europe, whom he wishes to conceal."

"Ha ! ha !" laughed the lady, scornfully. "Yes, I heard it too—a barefooted bog-trotter, forsooth ! But 'tis false, doctor ! false, I tell you ! You must contradict the report everywhere you hear it. That any one should dare to say that my son—my proud, handsome Barry—would marry a potato-eating Biddy ! Oh ! but for my indignation I could laugh at the utter absurdity."

But the fierce gleam of her eye, and the passionate clenching of her hand, bespoke her in anything but a laughing humor.

"I would not for worlds this report should reach Lizzie Erliston," she said, somewhat more calmly. "And speaking of her brings me back to her sister. Doctor, Esther Oranmore lies in yonder room."

He startled slightly, and glanced uneasily in the direction, but said nothing.

"Doctor," continued Mrs. Oranmore, in a low, stern, impressive voice, while her piercing eyes seemed reading his very soul, "*she must never live to see the sun rise again!*"

"Madam!" he exclaimed, recoiling suddenly.

"You hear me, doctor, and you *must* obey. She must not live to see Christmas morning dawn."

"Would you have me murder her?" he inquired, in a voice quivering between fear and horror.

"If you will call it by that name, yes," she replied, still keeping her blazing eyes fixed immovably on his face. "She and her child must die."

"Her child!"

"Yes, come and see it. The night of its birth must be that of its death."

She rose, and making a motion for him to follow her, led the way from the apartment. Opening a heavy oaken door, she ushered him into a dim bed-room, furnished with a lounge, a square bedstead, whose dark drapery gave it the appearance of a hearse, and a small table covered with bottles and glasses. Going to the lounge, she pointed to something wrapped in a large shawl. He bent down, and the faint wail of an infant met his ear.

"*She* is yonder," said the lady, pointing to the bed ; "examine these bottles ; she will ask you for a drink, *give* it to her—you understand ! Remember, you have promised." And before he could speak, she glided from the room.

CHAPTER II.

THE DEATH OF ESTHER.

> "What shrieking spirit in that bloody room
>   Its mortal frame hath violently quitted ?
> Across the moonbeam, with a sudden gleam,
>   A ghostly shadow flitted."—HOOD.

OR a moment he stood still, stunned and bewildered. Understand? Yes, he understood her too well.

He approached the bed, and softly drew back the heavy, dark curtains. Lying there, in a troubled sleep, lay a young girl, whose face was whiter than the pillow which supported her. Her long hair streamed in wild disorder over her shoulders, and added to the wanness of her pale face.

She moaned and turned restlessly on her pillow, and opened a pair of large, wild eyes, and fixed them on the unprepossessing face bending over her. With lips and eyes opened with terror, she lay gazing, until he said, in as gentle a voice as he could assume ;

"Do not be afraid of me—I am the doctor. Can I do anything for you, child ?"

"Yes, yes," she replied, faintly ; "give me a drink."

He turned hastily toward the table, feeling so giddy he could scarcely stand. A tiny vial, containing a clear, colorless liquid, attracted his eye. He took it up and examined it, and setting his teeth hard together, poured its contents into a glass. Then filling it with water he approached the bed, and raising her head, pressed it to her lips. His hand trembled so he spilt it on the quilt. The young girl lifted her wild, troubled eyes, and fixed them on his face with a gaze so long and steady that his own fell beneath it.

"Drink !" he said, hoarsely, still pressing it to her lips.

Without a word she obeyed, draining it to the last drop. Then laying her back on the pillow, he drew the curtain and left the room.

Mrs. Oranmore was sitting, as she had sat all the evening, stern and upright in her chair. She lifted her keen eyes as he entered, and encountered a face so pallid and ghastly that she almost started. Doctor Wiseman tottered rather than walked to a seat.

"Well ?" she said, inquiringly.

"Well," he replied, hoarsely, "I have obeyed you."

"That *is* well. But pray, Doctor Wiseman, take a glass of wine ; you are positively trembling like a whipped schoolboy. Go to the sideboard ; nay, do not hesitate ; *it* is not poisoned."

Her withering sneer did more toward reviving him than any wine could have done. His excitement was gradually cooling down beneath those calm, steady eyes, bent so contemptuously upon him.

He drank a glass of wine, and resumed his seat before the fire, watching sullenly the dying embers.

"Well, you have performed your task ?"

"I have, madam, and earned my reward."

"Not quite, doctor ; the infant is yet to be disposed of."

"Must it die, too ?"

"Yes, but not here. You must remove it, in any way you please, but death is the safest, the surest."

"And why not here?"

"Because I do not wish it," she answered, haughtily; "that is enough for you, sirrah! You must take the child away to-night."

"What shall I do with it?"

"Dolt! blockhead! have you no brains?" she said, passionately. "Are you aware ten minutes' walk will bring you to the sea-side? Do you know the waves refuse nothing, and tell no tales? Never hesitate, man! You have gone too far to draw back. Think of the reward; one thousand dollars for ten minutes' work! Tush, doctor! I protest, you're trembling like a nervous girl."

"Is it not enough to make one tremble?" retorted the doctor, roused to something like passion by her deriding tone; "two murders in one night—is that *nothing?*"

"Pshaw! no—a sickly girl and a puling child more or less in the world is no great loss. Hark!" she added, rising suddenly, as a wild, piercing shriek of more than mortal agony broke from the room where Esther lay. "Did you hear that?"

Hear it! The man's face was horribly ghastly and livid, as shriek after shriek, wild, piercing, and shrill with anguish, burst upon his ear. Great drops of perspiration stood on his brow—his teeth chattered as though by an ague fit, and he trembled so perceptibly that he was forced to grasp the chair for support.

Not so the woman. She stood calm, listening with perfect composure to the agonizing cries, that were growing fainter and fainter each moment.

"It is well none of the servants are in this end of the house," she said, quietly; "or those loud screams would

be overheard, and might give rise to disagreeable remarks."

Receiving no answer from her companion, she turned
to him, and seeing the look of horror on his ghastly
face, her lip curled with involuntary scorn. It was
strange she could stand there so unmoved, knowing herself to be a murderess, with the dying cries of her victim
still ringing in her ears.

They ceased at last—died away in a low, despairing
moan, and then all grew still. The deep, solemn silence
was more appalling than her shrieks had been, for they
well knew they were stilled forever in death.

"All is over!" said Mrs. Oranmore, drawing a deep
breath.

"Yes," was the answer, in a voice so hoarse and unnatural, that it seemed to issue from the jaws of death.

Again she looked at him, and again the mocking
smile curled her lip.

"Doctor," she said, quietly, "you are a greater
coward than I ever took you to be. I am going in now
to see her—you had better follow me, if you are not
afraid."

How sardonic was the smile which accompanied these
words. Stunned, terrified as he was, it stung him, and
he started after her from the room.

They entered the chamber of the invalid. Mrs.
Oranmore walked to the bed, drew back the curtains, and
disclosed a frightful spectacle.

Half sitting, half lying, in a strange, distorted attitude
she had thrown herself into in her dying agony, her lips
swollen and purple, her eyes protruding, her hair torn
fiercely out by the roots, as she had clutched it in her
fierce anguish, was Esther.

The straining eyeballs were ghastly to look upon—

the once beautiful face was now swollen and hideous, as she lay stark dead in that lonely room.

Moment after moment passed away, while the murderers stood silently gazing on their victim. The deep silence of midnight was around—nothing was heard save the occasional drifting of the snow against the windows.

A stern, grave smile hovered on the lips of Mrs. Oranmore, as she gazed on the convulsed face of the dead girl. Drawing the quilt at last over her, she turned away, saying, mockingly :

" Where now, Esther Oranmore, is the beauty of which you were so proud ? This stark form and ghastly face is now all that remains of the beauty and heiress of Squire Erliston. Such shall be the fate, sooner or later, of all who dare to thwart me."

Her eyes flamed upon the shrinking man beside her, with an expression that made him quake. A grim smile of self-satisfied power broke over her dark face as she observed it, and her voice had a steely tone of command, as she said :

" Now for the child. It must be immediately disposed of."

" And *she?*" said the doctor, pointing to the bed.

" I shall attend to that."

" If you like, madam, I will save you the trouble."

" No, sir," she replied, sharply ; "though in life my enemy, her remains shall never be given up to the dissecting-knife. I have not forgotten she is a gentleman's daughter, and as such she shall be interred. Now you may go. Wrap the child in this, and—*return without her !*"

" You shall be obeyed, madam," said Doctor Wiseman, catching the infection of her reckless spirit. He stooped and raised the infant, who was still in a deep sleep.

Muffling it carefully in the shawl, he followed the lady from the room, and cautiously quitted the house.

The storm had now passed away ; the piercing wind had died out, and the midnight moon sailed in unclouded majesty through the deep blue sky, studded with myriads of burning stars.

The cool night air restored him completely to himself.

Holding the still sleeping infant closer in his arms, he hurried on, until he stood on the sloping bank commanding a view of the bay.

The tide was rising. The waves came splashing in on the beach—the white foam gleaming coldly brilliant in the moonlight. The waters beyond looked cold, and sluggish, and dark—moaning in a strange, dreary way as they swept over the rocks. How *could* he commit the slumbering infant to those merciless waves ? Depraved and guilty as he was, he hesitated. It lay so confidingly in his arms, slumbering so sweetly, that his heart smote him. Yet it must be done.

He descended carefully to the beach, and laying his living bundle on the snowy sands, stood like Hagar, a distance off, to see it die.

In less than ten minutes, he knew, the waves would have washed it far away.

As he stood, with set teeth and folded arms, the merry jingle of approaching sleigh-bells broke upon his startled ear. They were evidently approaching the place where he stood. Moved by a sudden impulse of terror, he turned and fled from the spot.

Guilt is ever cowardly. He sped on, scarcely knowing whither he went, until in his blind haste he ran against a watchman.

The unexpected shock sent both rolling over in the snow, which considerably cooled the fever in Doctor

Wiseman's blood. The indignant "guardian of night," with an exclamation which wouldn't look well in print, laid hold of the doctor's collar. But there was vigor in Doctor Wiseman's dwarfed body, and strength in his long, lean arms; and with a violent effort he wrenched himself free from the policeman's tenacious grasp, and fled.

"Charley" started in pursuit, and seeing he would soon be overtaken, the doctor suddenly darted into the high, dark portico of an imposing-looking house, and soon had the satisfaction of beholding the angry watchman tear past like a comet, in full pursuit.

CHAPTER III.

THE ASTROLOGER.

" He fed on poisons, and they had no power,
　　But were a kind of nutriment ; he lived
　　Through that which had been death to many men.
　　To him the book of night was opened wide,
　　And voices from the deep abyss revealed
　　A marvel and a secret."—BYRON.

AVING assured himself that all danger was past, Doctor Wiseman was about to start from the building, when a sudden moonbeam fell on the polished door-plate, and he started back to see the name it revealed.

"The astrologer, Ali Hamed !" he exclaimed. "Now what foul fiend has driven me to his accursed den to-night ? 'Tis said he can read the future ; and surely no man ever needed to know it more than I. Can it be that the hand of destiny has driven me here, to show me what is yet to come. Well, it is useless going home or attempting to sleep to-night; so, Ali Hamed, I shall try what your magical black art can do for me."

He rang the bell sharply, but moment after moment passed, and no one came. Losing all patience, he again rang a deafening peal, which echoed and re-echoed through the house.

Presently the sound of footsteps clattering down stairs struck his ear, and in a moment more the door was cautiously opened, and a dark, swarthy face protruded through the opening. Seeing but one, he stood aside to allow him to enter, and then securely locked and bolted the door.

"The astrologer, Ali Hamed, resides here?" said the doctor.

Accustomed to visitors at all hours of the day and night, the man betrayed no surprise at the unreasonable time he had taken to inquire, but answered quietly in the affirmative.

"Can I see him?"

"I think so; step in here one moment, and I wil see."

He ushered Dr. Wiseman into a small and plainly furnished parlor, while he again went up stairs. In a few moments he reappeared, and, bidding his visitor follow him, led the way up the long staircase through a spacious suite of apartments, and finally into a long, dark room, where the astrologer usually received visitors.

The doctor glanced around with intense curiosity, not unmingled with awe. The floor was painted black, and the walls were hung with dark tapestry, covered with all manner of cabalistic figures. Skulls, crucibles, magic mirrors, tame serpents, vipers, and all

2

manner of hideous things were scattered profusely around.

While the doctor still stood contemplating the strange things around him, the door opened and the astrologer himself entered. He was an imposing-looking personage, tall and majestic, with grave, Asiatic features, and arrayed with Eastern magnificence. He bent his head with grave dignity in return to the doctor's profound bow, and stood for a few moments silently regarding him.

"You would know the future?" said the astrologer, at length, in his slow, impressive voice.

"Such is my business here to-night."

"You would have your horoscope cast, probably?"

"Yes."

"Then give me the day and hour of your birth, and return to-morrow morning."

"No, I cannot wait until then; I must know all to-night."

The astrologer bowed, and after many tedious preliminaries, directed the doctor to quit the room until he should send for him. Dr. Wiseman then entered one of the long suite of apartments through which he had passed, and seated himself in a state of feverish anxiety to hear the result. Some time elapsed ere the swarthy individual who had admitted him presented himself at the door and announced that the astrologer was ready to receive him.

Dr. Wiseman found Ali Hamed standing beside a smoking caldron, with his cross-bones, and lizards, and mystic figures around him, awaiting his entrance.

Not much given to credulity, the doctor determined to test his skill before placing implicit belief in his predictions; and therefore, bluntly announcing his skepticism, he demanded to know something of the past.

"You are a widower, with one child," said the astrologer, calmly.

The doctor bowed assent.

"You are not rich, but avaricious; there is nothing you would not do for money. You are liked by none; by nature you are treacherous, cunning, and unscrupulous; your hands are dyed, and your heart is black with crime; you——"

"Enough!" interrupted the doctor, turning as pale as his saffron visage would permit; "no more of the past. What has the future in store for me?"

"A life of disgrace, and death *on the scaffold!*"

A suppressed cry of horror burst from the white lips of the doctor, who reeled as if struck by some sudden blow.

"To-night," continued the astrologer, unheeding the interruption, "*a child has been born whose destiny shall be united with yours through life; some strange, mystic tie will bind you together for a time. But the hand of this child will yet bring your head to the halter.*"

He paused. Dr. Wiseman stood stiff, rooted to the ground with horror.

"Such is your future; you may go," said the Egyptian, waving his hand.

With his blood freezing in his veins, with hands trembling and lips palsied with horror, he quitted the house. An hour had scarcely passed since his entrance; but that hour seemed to have added ten years to his age. He felt not the cold, keen air as he slowly moved along, every sense paralyzed by the appalling prediction he had just heard.

"Die on the scaffold!" His crime deserved it. But the bare thought made his blood run cold. And through a child born that night he was to perish! Was it the child of Esther Oranmore? Oh, absurd! it had been swept far away by the waves long ere this. Whose, then, could it be? There were more children born this Christmas Eve than that one; but how could any one ever know what he had done? No one knew of it but Mrs. Oranmore; and he well knew she would never tell.

He plunged blindly onward through the heaps of drifted snow, heeding not, caring not, whither his steps wended. Once or twice he met a watchman going his rounds, and he shrank away like the guilty thing that he was, dreading lest the word "*murder*" should be stamped on his brow. He thought with cowardly terror of the coming day, when every eye, he fancied, would turn upon him with a look of suspicion.

Involuntarily he wandered to the sea-shore, and stood on the bank where he had been one hour before. The waves were dashing now almost to his feet; no trace of any living thing was to be seen around.

"It *has* perished, then!" he exclaimed, with a feeling of intense relief. "I knew it! I knew it! *It*, then, is not the child which is to cause my death. But, pshaw! why do I credit all that *soi-disant* prophet told me! Yet he spoke so truly of the past, I cannot avoid believing him. Perish on the scaffold! Heavens! if I felt sure of it, I would go mad. Ha! what is that? Can it be the ghastly white face of a child?"

He leaned over and bent down to see, but nothing met his eye save the white caps of the waves.

"Fool that I am!" he exclaimed, turning away impatiently. "Well might stony Madam Oranmore deem me a coward did she see me now. I will hasten back to her, and report the success of my mission."

He turned away, and strode in the direction of her house as fast as he could walk over the frozen ground, quite unconscious of what was at that same moment passing in another quarter of the city on that same eventful night.

CHAPTER IV.

BARRY ORANMORE.

——" Pray for the dead—
Why for the dead, who are at rest?
Pray for the living, in whose breast
The struggle between right and wrong
Is raging, terrible and strong."—LONGFELLOW.

T was a luxuriously furnished apartment. A thick, soft carpet, where blue violets peeped from glowing green leaves so naturally that one involuntarily stooped to cull them, covered the floor. Rare old paintings adorned the wall, and the cornices were fretted with gold. The heavy crimson curtains shut out the sound of the wintry wind, and a glowing coal fire shed a living, radiant glow over everything around. The air was redolent of intoxicating perfume, breathing of summer and sunshine. On the marble-topped center-table stood bottles and glasses, a cigar-case, a smoking-cap, and a pair of elegant, silver-mounted pistols. It was evidently a gentleman's room, judging by the disorder. A beautiful marble Flora stood in one corner, arrayed in a gaudy dressing-gown, and opposite stood a dainty little Peri adorned with a beaver hat. Jupiter himself was there, with a violin suspended gracefully around his neck, and Cupid was leaning against the wall, heels uppermost, with bent bow, evidently taking deliberate aim at the flies on the ceiling.

Among the many exquisite paintings hanging on the wall, there was one of surpassing beauty; it represented a bleak hill-side, with a flock of sheep grazing on the scanty herbage, a lowering, troubled sky above; and one could almost see the fitful gusts of wind sighing over the gray hill-tops. Standing erect was a young girl—a mere child in years—her long golden hair streaming wildly in the breeze, her straw hat swinging in her hand, her fair, bright face and large blue eyes raised with mingled shyness and sauciness to a horseman bending over her, as if speaking. His fiery steed seemed pawing with impatience ; but his rider held him with a firm hand. He was a tall, slight youth, with raven black hair and eyes, and a dark, handsome face. There was a wild look about the dark horseman and darker steed, reminding one of the Black Horseman of the Hartz Mountains. Underneath was written, in a dashing masculine hand, " The first meeting." There was something strikingly, vividly life-like in the whole scene ; even the characters— the slender girl, with her pretty, piquant face, and the handsome, graceful rider—were more like living beings than creations of fancy.

And—yes, standing by the fire, his arm resting on the mantel, his eyes fixed on the hearth, stood the original of the picture. The same tall, superb form ; the same clear olive complexion ; the same curling locks of jet, and black eyes of fire ; the same firm, proud mouth, shaded by a thick black mustache—there he stood, his eyes riveted on the glowing coals, his brow knit as though in deep and painful thought. Now and then the muscles of his face would twitch, and his white hands involuntarily clench at some passing thought.

At intervals the noise of doors shutting and opening would reach his ear, and he would start as though he had received a galvanic shock, and listen for a moment intently. Nothing could be heard but the crackling of the fire at such times, and again he would relapse into gloomy musing.

'What a fool I have been !" he exclaimed, at length

between his clenched teeth, as he shook back with fierce impatience his glossy hair, " to burden myself with this girl ! Dolt, idiot that I was, to allow myself to be bewitched by her blue eyes and yellow hair ! What demon could have possessed me to make her my wife? My wife ! Just fancy me presenting that little blushing, shrinking Galway girl as my wife to my lady mother, or to that princess of coquettes, Lizzie Erliston ! I wish to heaven I had blown my brains out instead of putting my head into such a confounded noose—making myself the laughing-stock of all my gallant friends and lady acquaintances ! No, by heaven ! they shall never laugh at Barry Oranmore. Eveleen shall be sent back to her friends. They will be glad enough to get her on any terms ; and she will soon forget me, and be happy tending her sheep once more. And yet—and yet—poor Eveleen !" he said, suddenly, pausing before the picture, while his dark eyes filled with a softer light, and his voice assumed a gentler tone ; " she loves me so well yet —far more than I do her. I hardly like the thought of sending her away ; but it cannot be helped. My mother's purse is running low, I fear ; Erliston's coffers must replenish it. Yes, there is no help for it ; Eveleen must go, and I must marry little Lizzie. Poor child ; she left home, and friends, and all for me ; and it *does* seem a villainous act in me to desert her for another. But go she must ; there is no alternative."

He was walking up and down in his intense excitement—sometimes pausing suddenly for a few moments, and then walking on faster than before. Thus half an hour passed, during which he seemed to have formed some determination ; for his mouth grew stern, and his clear eyes cold and calm, as he once more leaned against the mantel, and fell into thought.

Presently the door opened and a woman entered. She

was a stout, corpulent person, with coarse, bloated face, and small, bleared eyes. As she entered, she cast an affectionate glance toward the brandy bottle on the table —a glance which said plainly she would have no objection to trying its quality. She was arrayed for the street, with a large cloak enveloping her ample person, and a warm quilted hood tied over her substantial double chin.

"Well, sir, I'll be movin', I reckon," said the woman, adjusting her cloak. "The young lady's doing very nicely, and the baby's sleeping like an angel. So they'll get along very well to-night without me."

The young man started at the sound of her voice, and, looking up, said carelessly :

"Oh, it's you, is it? Are you for leaving?"

"Yes, sir ; it's time I was home and to bed. I ain't used to bein' up late nights now—don't agree with my constitution; it's sorter delicate. Shouldn't wonder if I was fallin' into a decline."

The quizzical dark eyes of the young man surveyed the rotund person before him, and in spite of himself he burst out laughing.

"Well, now, if you was in a decline yourself, you'd laugh t'other side of your mouth, I reckon," said the offended matron. "S'pose you think it's very funny laughing at a poor, lone 'oman, without chick nor child. But I can tell you——"

"Ten thousand pardons, madam, for my offense," he interrupted, courteously, though there was still a wicked twinkle in his eye. "Pray sit down for a moment; I have something to say to you."

"Well, now, it don't seem exactly right to sit here with you at this hour of the night. Howsomever, I will, to oblige you," and the worthy dame placed her ample frame in a cushioned elbow-chair.

"Perhaps this argument may aid in overcoming your scruples," said the young man, filling her a glass of wine, and throwing himself on a lounge ; "and now to business. You are a widow ?"

"Yes, sir. My blessed husband died a martyr to his country—died in the discharge of his duty. He was a custom-house officer, and felt it his duty always to examine liquors before destroying them. Well, one day he took too much, caught the devil-rum tremendous, and left me a disconsolate widder. The coroner of the jury set onto him, and——"

"There, there ! never mind particulars. You have no children ?"

"No," said the old woman stiffly, rather offended by his unceremonious interruption.

"If you were well paid, you would have no objection to taking one and bringing it up as your own ?" said the young man, speaking quietly, though there was a look of restless anxiety in his fine eyes.

"Well, no ; I'd have no objection, if——" and here she slapped her pocket expressively, by way of finishing the sentence.

"Money shall be no object ; but remember, the world must think it is your own—*I* am never to be troubled about it more."

"All right—I understand," said the nurse, nodding her head sagely. "S'pose it's the little one in there ?"

"It is. Can you take it away now ?"

"To-night ?"

"Yes."

"But laws ! ain't it too cold and stormy. Better wait till to-morrow."

"No," was the quick and peremptory answer. "To-night, now, within this very hour, it must be removed ; and I am never to hear of it more."

2*

"And the poor young lady ? Seems sorter hard, now
don't it ?" she'll take on wonderfully, I'm feared."

A spasm of pain passed over his handsome face, and
for a moment he was silent. Then, looking up, he said,
with brief sternness :

"It cannot be helped. You must go without disturbing her, and I will break the news to her myself.
Here is my purse for the present. What is your address ?"

The woman gave it.

"Very well, you shall hear from me regularly ; but
should we ever meet again, in the street or elsewhere, you
are not to know me, and you must forget all that has
transpired to-night."

"Hum !" said the fat widow, doubtfully.

"And now you had better depart. The storm has almost ceased, and the night is passing away. Is Ev—is
my wife awake ?"

"No ; I left her sleeping."

"So much the better. You can take *it* with you without disturbing her. Go."

The buxom widow arose and quitted the room. Oranmore lay on a lounge, rigidly motionless, his face hidden
by his hand. A fierce storm was raging in his breast—
"the struggle between right and wrong." Pride and
ambition struggled with love and remorse, but the fear
of the world conquered : and when the old woman re-
entered, bearing a sleeping infant in her arms, he looked
up as composedly as herself.

"Pretty little dear," said the widow, wrapping the
child in a thick woolen shawl, " how nicely she sleeps !
Very image of her mother, and she's the beautifulest
girl I ever saw in my life. I gave her some paregoric
to make her sleep till I go home. Well, good-night, sir.
Our business is over."

"Yes, good-night. Remember the secret; forget what has transpired to-night, and your fortune is made. You will care for *it* "—and he pointed to the child—"as though it were your own."

"Be sure I will, dear little duck. Who could help liking such a sweet, pretty darling? I s'pose you'll come to see it sometimes, sir?"

"No. You can send me word of its welfare now and then. Go, madam, go."

The widow turned to leave the room, and, unobserved by the young man, who had once more thrown himself on his face on the sofa, she seized a well-filled brandy-flask and concealed it beneath her shawl.

Quitting the house, she walked as rapidly as her bulksome proportions would permit over the snowy ground. The road leading to her home lay in the direction of the sea-shore; and, as she reached the beach, she was thoroughly chilled by the cold, in spite of her warm wrappings.

"It's as cold as the Arctic Ocean, and I've heerd say that's the coldest country in the world. A drop of comfort won't come amiss just now. Lucky I thought on't. This little monkey's as sound as a top. It's my 'pinion that young gent's no better than he ought to be, to treat such a lovely young lady in this fashion. Well, it's no business of mine, so's I'm well paid. Lor! I hope I hain't gin it too much paregoric; wouldn't for anything 'twould die. S'pose I'd get no more tin then. That's prime," she added, placing the flask to her lips and draining a long draught.

As the powerful fumes of the brandy arose to her head, the worthy lady's senses became rather confused; and, falling rather than sitting on the bank, the child, muffled like a mummy in its plaid, rolled from her arms into a snow-wreath. At the same moment the loud ring-

ing of bells and the cry of " Fire ! fire !" fell upon her
ear. It roused her ; and, in the excitement of the moment forgetting her little charge, she sprang up as well
as she could, and, by a strange fascination, was soon involuntarily drawn away to mingle with the crowd, who
were hurrying in the direction of her abode.

Scarcely five minutes before, Dr. Wiseman had quitted
that very spot : and there, within a few yards of each
other, the two unconscious infants lay, little knowing
how singularly their future lives were to be united—little
dreaming how fatal an influence *one* of them was yet to
wield over *him.*

Some time after, when the flames were extinguished
and the crowd had quitted the streets for their beds—
when the unbroken silence of coming morning had fallen
over the city—the widow returned to seek for her child.

But she sought in vain ; the rising tide had swept
over the bank, and was again retreating sullenly to the
sea.

Sobered by terror and remorse, the wretched woman
trod up and down the dreary, deserted snowy beach
until morning broke ; but she sought and searched in
vain. The child was gone.

CHAPTER V.

MOUNT SUNSET HALL,

"A jolly place, 'twas said, in days of old."—WORDSWORTH.

HE jingle of the approaching sleigh-bells, which had frightened Dr. Wiseman from the beach, had been unheard by the drunken nurse; but ten minutes after she had left, a sleigh came slowly along the narrow, slippery path.

It contained but two persons. One was an elderly woman, wrapped and muffled in furs. A round, rosy, cheery face beamed out from a black velvet bonnet, and two small, twinkling, merry gray eyes, lit up the pleasantest countenance in the world.

Her companion, who sat in the driver's seat, was a tall, jolly-looking darkey, with a pair of huge, rolling eyes, looking like a couple of snow-drifts in a black ground. A towering fur cap ornamented the place where the "wool ought to grow," and was the only portion of this son of darkness which·could be discovered for his voluminous wrappings.

The path was wet, slippery, and dangerous in the extreme. The horses were restive, and a single false step would have overturned them into the water.

"Missus Scour, if you please, missus, you'd better git out," said the negro, reining in the horses, in evident alarm; "this yer's the wussest road I'se ever trabeled. These wishious brutes 'll spill me and you, and the sleigh, and then the Lor only knows what'll ever become of us."

"Do you think there's any danger, Jupiter?" said Mrs. Gower (for such was the name her sable attendant had transformed into *Scour*), in a voice of alarm.

"This road's sort o' 'spicious anyhow," replied Jupiter. "I'd 'vise you, Missus Scour, mum, to get out and walk till we is past this yer beach. 'Sides the snow, this yer funnelly beach is full o' holes, an' if we got upsot inter one of 'em, ole marse might whistle for you and me, and the sleigh arter that !"

With much difficulty, and with any amount of whoaing, Jupiter managed to stop the sleigh, and assisted stout Mrs. Gower to alight. This was no easy job, for that worthy lady was rather unwieldy, and panted like a stranded porpoise, as she slowly plunged through the wet snow-drifts.

Suddenly, above the jingling sleigh-bells, the wail of an infant met her ear. She paused in amazement, and looked around. Again she heard it—this time seemingly at her feet. She looked down and beheld a small, dark bundle, lying amid the deep snow.

Once more the piteous cry met her ear, and stooping down, she raised the little dark object in her arms.

Unfolding the shawl, she beheld the infant whose cries had first arrested her ear.

"Good heavens ! a baby exposed to this weather— left here to perish !" exclaimed good Mrs. Gower, in horror. "Poor little thing, it's half frozen. Who could have done so unnatural a deed ?"

"Laws ! Missus Scour, what ye got dar ?" inquired Jupiter.

"A baby, Jupe ! A poor little helpless infant whom some unnatural wretch has left here to die !" exclaimed Mrs. Gower, with more indignation than she had ever before felt in her life.

"Good Lor! so 'tis!   What you gwine to do wid it, Missus Scour, mum?"

"Do with it?" said Mrs. Gower, looking at him in surprise.   "Why, take it with me, of course.   You wouldn't have me leave the poor infant here to perish, would you?"

"'Deed, Missus Scour, I wouldn't bring it 'long ef I was you.   Jes' 'flect how tarin' mad ole marse 'll be 'bout it.   Don't never want to see no babies roun'.   Deed, honey, you'd better take my 'vice an' leave it whar it was," said Jupiter.

"What?   Leave it here to die.   I'm ashamed of you, Jupiter," said the old lady, rebukingly.

"But Lor! Missus Scour! ole marse 'll trow it out de winder fust thing.   Shouldn't be s'prised, nudder, ef he'd wollop me for bringing it.   Jes' 'flect upon it, Missus Scour, nobody can't put no 'pendence onto him, de forsooken ole sinner.   Trowed his 'fernal ole stick at me, t'other day, and like to knock my brains out, jes' for nothin' at all.   'Deed, honey, I wouldn't try sich a 'sper-riment, no how."

"Now, Jupiter, you needn't say another word.   My mind's made up, and I'm going to keep this child, let 'ole marse' rage as he will.   I'm just as sure as I can be, that the Lord sent it to me, to-night, as a Christmas gift, in place of my poor, dear Aurora, that he took to heaven," said good Mrs. Gower, folding the wailing infant closer still to her warm, motherly bosom.

"Sartin, missus, in course you knows best, but ef you'd only 'flect.   'Pears to me, ole marse 'll tar roun worser dan ever, when he sees it, and discharge you in you 'sponsible ole age o' life 'count of it."

"And if he *does* discharge me, Jupiter, after twenty years' service, I have enough to support myself and this little one to the end of my life, thank the Lord!" said

Mrs. Gower, her honest, ruddy face all aglow with generous enthusiasm.

"Well, I s'pose 'taint no sorter use talking," said Jupiter, with a sigh, as he gathered up the reins; "but ef anything happens, jes 'member I 'vised you of it 'forehand. Here we is on de road now, so you'd better get in ef you's agoin' to take de little 'un wid you."

With considerable squeezing, and much panting, and some groaning, good Mrs. Gower was assisted into the sleigh, and muffled up in the buffalo robes.

Wrapping the child in her warm, fur-lined mantle, to protect it from the chill night air, they sped merrily along over the hard, frozen ground.

Christmas morning dawned bright, sunshiny, and warm. The occupants of the sleigh had long since left the city behind them, and were now driving along the more open country. The keen, frosty air deepened the rosy glow on Mrs. Gower's good-humored face. Warmly protected from the cold, the baby lay sleeping sweetly in her arms, and even Jupiter's sable face relaxed into a grin as he whistled " Coal Black Rose."

The sun was about three hours high when they drew up before a solitary inn. And here Jupiter assisted Mrs. Gower into the house, while he himself looked after his horses.

Mrs. Gower was shown by the hostess into the parlor, where a huge wood-fire roared up the wide chimney. Removing the large shawl that enveloped it, Mrs. Gower turned for the first time to examine her prize.

It did not differ much from other babies, save in being the tiniest little creature that ever was seen ; with small, pretty features, and an unusual profusion of brown hair. As it awoke, it disclosed a pair of large blue eyes—rather vacant-looking, it must be confessed— and immediately set up a most vigorous squealing. Small as it was, it evidently possessed lungs that would not have disgraced a newsboy, and seemed bent upon fully exercising them ; for in spite of Mrs. Gower's cooing and kissing, it cried and screamed "and would not be comforted."

"Poor little dear, it's so hungry," said the good old lady, rocking it gently. "What a pretty little darling it is. I'm *sure* it looks like little Aurora !"

"What is the matter with baby ?" inquired the hostess, at this moment entering.

"It's hungry, poor thing. Bring in some warm milk, please," replied Mrs. Gower.

The milk was brought, and baby, like a sensible child, as it doubtless was, did ample justice to it. Then rolling it up in the shawl, Mrs. Gower placed it in the rocking-chair, and left it to its own reflections, while she sat down to a comfortable breakfast of fragrant coffee, hot rolls, and fried ham.

When breakfast was over Jupiter brought round the horses and sleigh, and Mrs. Gower entered, holding her prize, and they drove off.

It was noon when they reached the end of their long journey, and entered the little village of St. Mark's. Sloping upward from the bay on one side, and encircled by a dense primeval forest on the other, the village stood. St. Mark's was a great place in the eyes of its inhabitants, and considered by them the only spot on the globe fit for rational beings to live in. It was rather an unpretending-looking place, though, to strangers, who sometimes came from the city to spend the hot summer months there, in preference to any fashionable watering-place. It contained a church, a school-house, a lecture-room, a post-office, and an inn.

But the principal building, and pride of the village, was Mount Sunset Hall. It stood upon a sloping eminence, which the villagers dignified with the title of hill, but which in reality was no such thing. The hall itself was a large, quaint, old mansion of gray stone, built in the Elizabethan style, with high turrets, peaked gables, and long, high windows. It was finely situated, commanding on one side a view of the entire village and the bay, and on the other the dark pine forest and far-spreading hills beyond. A carriage-path wound up toward the front, through an avenue of magnificent horse chestnuts, now bare and leafless. A wide porch, on which the sun seemed always shining, led into a long, high hall, flanked on each side by doors, opening into the separate apartments. A wide staircase of dark polished oak led to the upper chambers of the old mansion.

The owner of Sunset Hall was Squire Erliston, the one great man of the village, the supreme autocrat of St. Mark's. The squire was a rough, gruff, choleric old bear, before whom children and poultry and other inferior animals quaked in terror. He had been once given to high living and riotous excesses, and Sunset Hall had then been a place of drunkenness and debauchery. But these excssses at last brought on a dangerous disease, and for a long time his life was despaired of ; then the squire awoke to a sense of his situation, took a "pious streak "—as he called it himself—and registered a vow, that if it pleased Providence not to deprive the world in general, and St. Marks in particular, of so valuable an ornament as himself, he would eschew all his evil deeds and meditate seriously on his latter end. Whether his prayer was heard or not I cannot undertake to say ; but certain it is the squire recovered ; and, casting over in his mind the ways and means by which he could best do penance for his past sins, he resolved to go through a course of Solomon's Proverbs, and—get married. Deeming it best to make the greatest sacrifice first, he got married ; and, after the honeymoon was past, surprised his wife one day by taking down the huge family Bible left him by his father, and reading the first chapter. This he continued for a week—yawning fearfully all the time ; but after that he resolved to make his wife read them aloud to him, and thereby save him the trouble.

"For," said the squire sagely, "what's the use of having a wife if she can't make herself useful. 'A good wife's a crown to her husband,' as Solomon says."

So Mrs. Erliston was commanded each morning to read one of the chapters by way of morning prayers. The squire would stretch himself on a lounge, light a cigar, lay his head on her lap, and prepare to listen. But before the conclusion of the third verse Squire Erliston and his good resolutions would be as sound as one of the Seven Sleepers.

When his meek little wife would hint at this, her worthy liege lord would fly into a passion, and indignantly deny the assertion. *He* asleep, indeed ! Preposterous !—he had heard every word ! And, in proof of it, he vociferated every text he could remember, and insisted upon making Solomon the author of them all. This habit he had retained through life—often to the great amusement of his friends—setting the most absurd phrases down to the charge of the Wise Monarch. His wife died, leaving him with two daughters ; the fate of the eldest, Esther, is already known to the reader.

Up the carriage-road, in front, the sleigh containing our travelers drove. Good Mrs. Gower—who for many years had been Squire Erliston's housekeeper—alighted, and, passing through the long hall, entered a cheerful-looking apartment known as the "housekeeper's room."

Seating herself in an elbow-chair to recover her breath, Mrs. Gower laid the baby in her bed, and rang the bell. The summons was answered by a tidy little darkey, who rushed in all of a flutter.

"Laws! Missus Scour, I's' 'stonished, I is! Whar's de young 'un! Jupe say you fotch one from the city."

"So I did; there it is on the bed."

"Sakes alive, ain't it a mite of a critter! Gemini! what'll old marse say? Can't abide babies no how! 'spect he neber was a baby hisself!"

"Totty, you mustn't speak that way of your master. Remember, it's not respectful," said Mrs. Gower, rebukingly.

"Oh, I'll 'member of it—'specially when I's near him, and he's got a stick in his hand," said Totty, turning again to the baby, and eying it as one might some natural curiosity. "Good Lor! ain't it a funny little critter? What's its name, Miss Scour?"

"I intend calling it Aurora, after my poor little daughter," replied Mrs. Gower, tears filling her eyes.

"*Roarer!* Laws! ain't it funny? Heigh! dar's de bell. 'Spect it's for me," said Totty, running off.

In a few moments she reappeared; and, shoving her curly head and ebony phiz through the door, announced, in pompous tones, " dat marse wanted de honor ob a few moments' private specification wid Missus Scour in de parlor."

"Very well, Totty; stay in here and mind the baby until I come back," said Mrs. Gower, rising to obey.

Totty, nothing loth, seated herself by the bed and resumed the scrutiny of the baby. Whether that young lady remarked the impertinent stare of the darkey or not, it would be hard to say; for, having bent her whole heart and soul on the desperate and rather cannibal-like task of devouring her own little fists, she treated Totty with silent contempt.

Meantime, Mrs. Gower, with a look of firm determination, but with a heart which, it must be owned, throbbed faster than usual, approached the room wherein sat the lord and master of Sunset Hall. A gruff voice shouted : "Come in !" in reply to her "tapping at the chamber-door ;" and good Mrs. Gower, in fear and trembling, entered the awful presence.

In a large easy-chair in the middle of the floor—his feet supported by a high ottoman—reclined Squire Erliston. He was evidently about fifty years of age, below the middle size, stout and squarely built, and of ponderous proportions. His countenance was fat, purple, and bloated, as if from high living and strong drink ; and his short, thick, bull-like neck could not fail to bring before the mind of the beholder most unpleasant ideas of apoplexy. His little, round, popping eyes seemed in danger of starting from their sockets ; while the firm compression of his square mouth betokened an unusual degree of obstinacy.

"Good-morning, Mrs. Gower. Fine day, this ! Got home, I see. Shut the door !—shut the door !—draughts always bring on the gout ; so beware of 'em. Don't run into danger, or you'll perish in it, as Solomon says. There ! sit down, sit down, sit down !"

Repeating this request a very unnecessary number of times—for worthy Mrs. Gower had immediately taken a seat on entering—Squire Erliston adjusted his spectacles carefully on the bridge of his nose, and glanced severely at his housekeeper over the top of them. That good lady sat with her eyes fixed upon the carpet—her hands folded demurely in her lap—the very personification of mingled dignity and good-nature.

"Hem ! madam," began the squire.

"Yes, sir," replied Mrs. Gower, meekly.

"Jupe tells me—that is, he told me—I mean, ma'am,

the short and long of it is, you've brought a baby home with you—eh?"

"Yes, sir," replied the housekeeper.

"And how dare you, ma'am—how *dare* you bring such a thing here?" roared the squire, in a rage. "Don't you know I detest the whole persuasion under twelve years of age? Yes, ma'am! you know it; and yet you went and brought one here. 'The way of the transgressor is hard,' as Solomon says; and I'll make it confoundedly hard for you if you don't pitch the squalling brat this minute out of the window! D'ye hear that?"

"Yes, sir," replied Mrs. Gower, quietly.

"And why the deuce don't you go and do it, then—eh?"

"Because, Squire Erliston, I am resolved to keep the child," said Mrs. Gower, firmly.

"What! *what!* WHAT!" exclaimed the squire, speechless with mingled rage and astonishment at the audacious reply.

"Yes, sir," reiterated Mrs. Gower, resolutely. "I consider that child sent to me by Heaven, and I cannot part with it."

"Fudge! stuff! fiddlesticks! Sent to you by heaven, indeed! S'pose heaven ever dropped a young one on the beach? Likely story!"

"Well, I consider it the same thing. Some one left it on the beach, and heaven destined me to save it."

"Nonsense! no such thing! 'twas that stupid rascal, Jupe, making you get out. I'll horsewhip him within an inch of his life for it!" roared the old man, in a passion.

"I beg you will do no such thing, sir. It was no fault of Jupiter's. If you insist on its quitting the house, there remains but one course for me."

"Confound it, ma'am! you'd make a saint swear, as

Solomon says. Pray tell me what *is* that course you speak of ?"

" I must leave with it."

" What ?" exclaimed the squire, perfectly aghast with amazement.

" I must leave with it !" repeated Mrs. Gower, rising from her seat, and speaking quietly, but firmly.

" Sit down, ma'am—sit down, sit down ! Oh, Lord ! let me catch my breath ! Leave with it ! Just say that over again, will you ? I don't think I heard right."

" Your ears have not deceived you, Squire Erliston. I repeat it, if that child leaves, I leave, too !"

You should have seen Squire Erliston then, as he sat bolt upright, his little round eyes ready to pop from their sockets with consternation, staring at good Mrs. Gower much like a huge turkey gobbler. That good lady stood complacently waiting, with her hand on the handle of the door, for what was to come next.

She had not long wait ; for such a storm of rage burst upon her devoted head, that anybody else would have fled in dismay. But she, "good, easy soul," was quite accustomed to that sort of thing, and stood gazing upon him as serenely as a well-fed Biddy might on an enraged barn-yard chanticleer. And still the storm of abuse raged, interspersed with numerous quotations from Solomon—by way, doubtless, of impressing her that his wrath was righteous. And still Mrs. Gower stood serene and unruffled by his terrible denunciations, looking as placid as a mountain lake sleeping in the sunlight.

" Well, ma'am, well ; what do you think of your conduct *now ?*" exclaimed the squire, when the violence of his rage was somewhat exhausted.

" Just what I did before, sir."

" And what was that, eh ?—what was that ?"

"That I have done right, sir ; and that I will keep the child !"

"*You will ?*" thundered the squire, in an awful voice.

"Yes, sir !" replied Mrs. Gower, slightly appalled by his terrible look, but never flinching in her determination.

"You—you—you—abominable—female, you !" stammered the squire, unable to speak calmly, from rage. Then he added : "Well, well ! I won't get excited—no, ma'am.   You can keep the brat, ma'am !   But mind you, if it ever comes across me, I'll wring its neck for it as I would a chicken's !"

"Then I *may* keep the little darling ?" said good Mrs. Gower, gratefully.   "I am sure I am much obliged, and——"

"There ! there ! there !   Hold your tongue, ma'am ! Don't let me hear another word about it—the pest ! the plague !   Be off with you now, and send up dinner.   Let the turkey be overdone, or the pudding burned, at your peril !   'Better a stalled ox with quietness, than a dry morsel,' as Solomon says.   Hurry up there, and ring for Lizzie !"

Mrs. Gower hastened from the room, chuckling at having got over the difficulty so easily.   And from that day forth, little Aurora, as her kind benefactress called her, was domesticated at Mount Sunset Hall.

CHAPTER VI.

LIZZIE'S LOVER.

> "Fond girl! no saint nor angel he
> Who woocs thy young simplicity;
> But one of earth's impassioned sons,
> As warm in love, as fierce in ire,
> As the best heart whose current runs
> Full of the day-god's living fire."
> FIRE WORSHIPERS.

HE inn of St. Mark's was an old, brown, wooden house, with huge, unpainted shutters, and great oak doors, that in summer lay always invitingly open. It stood in the center of the village, with the forest stretching away behind, and the beach spreading out in front. Over the door swung a huge signboard, on which some rustic artist had endeavored to paint an eagle, but which, unfortunately, more closely resembled a frightened goose.

Within the "Eagle," as it was generally called, everything was spotlessly neat and clean; for the landlord's pretty daughter was the tidiest of housewives. The huge, oaken door in front, directly under the above-mentioned sign-board, opened into the bar-room, behind the counter of which the worthy host sat, in his huge leathern chair, from "early morn till dewy eve." Another door, at the farther end, opened into the "big parlor," the pine floor of which was scrubbed as white as human hands could make it; and the two high, square windows at either end absolutely glittered with cleanliness. The wooden chairs were polished till they shone, and never blazed a fire on a cleaner swept hearth than

3

that which now roared up the wide fire-place of the "Eagle."

It was a gusty January night. The wind came raw and cold over the distant hills, now rising fierce and high, and anon dying away in low, moaning sighs among the shivering trees. On the beach the waves came tramping inward, their dull, hollow voices booming like distant thunder on the ear.

But within the parlor of the "Eagle" the mirth and laughter were loud and boisterous. Gathered around the blazing fire, drinking, smoking, swearing, arguing, were fifteen or twenty men—drovers, farmers, fishermen, and loafers.

"This yer's what *I* calls comfortable," said a lusty drover, as he raised a foaming mug of ale to his lips and drained it to the last drop.

"I swan to man if it ain't a rouser of a night," said a rather good-looking young fellow, dressed in the coarse garb of a fisherman, as a sudden gust of wind and hail came driving against the windows.

"Better here than out on the bay to-night, eh, Jim?" said the drover, turning to the last speaker.

"Them's my sentiments," was the reply, as Jim filled his pipe.

"I reckon Jim hain't no objection to stayin' anywhere where Cassie is," remarked another, dryly.

"Who's taking my name in vain here?" called a clear, ringing voice, as a young girl, of some eighteen years of age, entered. Below the middle size, plump and round, with merry, black eyes, a complexion decidedly brown, full, red lips, overflowing with fun and good-nature— such was Cassie Fox, the pretty little hostess of the "Eagle."

Before any one could reply, an unusual noise in the bar-room fell upon their ears. The next moment, Sally,

the black maid-of-all-work, came into the " big parlor,"
with mouth and eyes agape.

" Laws, misses," she said, addressing Cassie, " dar's a
gemman—a rale big-bug—out'n de bar-room ; a 'specta-
ble, 'sponsible, 'greeable gemman, powerful hansom, wid
brack eyes an' har, an' a carpet-bag !"

" Sakes alive !" ejaculated Cassie, dropping the tray,
and turning to the looking-glass ; " he's handsome, and
—*my hair's awfully mussed!* Gracious ! what brings him
here, Sally ?"

" Got cotch in de storm ; 'deed he did, chile—heard
him tell marse so my own blessed self."

"Goodness !" again ejaculated the little hostess. " I'm
all in a flusterfication. Handsome ! dear, dear !—my
hair's all out of curl ! Black eyes !—I must unpin my
dress Nice hair ! Jim Loker, take your legs out of the
fire, nobody wants you to make andirons of 'em."

" Cass ! Cass, I say ! Come here, you Cass !"
called the voice of mine host from the bar-room.

Cassie bustled out of the room and entered the bar.
Old Giles Fox stood respectfully before the stranger, a
young man wrapped in a cloak, tall and handsome, with
a sort of dashing, reckless air, that well became him.

" Here, Cass," said her father, " this gentleman's going to stay all night. Show him into the best room, and
get supper ready. Be spry, now."

" Yes, sir," said Cassie, demurely, courtesying before
the handsome stranger, who glanced half carelessly,
half admiringly, at her pretty face. "This way, sir, if
you please."

The stranger followed her into the parlor, and encountered the battery of a score of eyes fixed full upon
him. He paused in the doorway and glanced around.

" Beg pardon," he said, in the refined tone of a gentleman, " but I thought this room was unoccupied. Can

I not have a private apartment?" he added, turning to Cassie.

"Oh, yes, to be sure," replied the little hostess; "step this way, sir," and Cassie ran up-stairs, followed by the new-comer, whose dark eyes had already made a deep impression in the susceptible heart of Cassie.

He threw himself into a chair before the fire and fixed his eyes thoughtfully on the glowing coals. Cassie, having placed his dripping cloak before the fire to dry, ran down stairs, where he could distinctly hear her shrill voice giving hasty orders to the servants.

Supper was at length brought in by Cassie, and the stranger fell to with the readiness of one to whom a long journey has given an appetite.

"There," he said at last, pushing back his chair. "I think I have done justice to your cookery, my dear—Cassie—isn't that what they call you?"

"Yes, sir; after Cassiopia, who was queen in furrin parts long ago. Efiofia, I think, was the name of the place," said Cassie, complacently.

"What?" said the stranger, repressing a laugh. "What do you say was the name of the place?"

"Efiofia!" repeated Cassie, with emphasis.

"Ethiopia! Oh, I understand! And who named you after that fair queen, who now resides among the stars?"

"Mother, of course, before she died," replied the namesake of that Ethiopian queen. "She read about her in some book, and named me accordingly."

The stranger smiled, and fixed his eyes steadily on the complacent face of Cassie, with an expression of mingled amusement and curiosity. There was a moment's pause, and then he asked:

"And what sort of place is St. Mark's—I mean, what sort of people are there in it?"

"Oh, pretty nice," replied Cassie; " most all like those you saw down stairs in the parlor."

"But, I mean the gentry."

"Oh, the big-bugs. Well, yes, there is some of 'em here. First, there's the squire——"

"Squire who?" interrupted the stranger, with a look of interest.

" Squire Erliston, of course ; he lives up there in a place called Mount Sunset."

"Yes?" said the young man, inquiringly.

"Yes," repeated Cassiopia, " with his daughter, Miss Lizzie."

" Has he only one daughter?"

"That's all, now. He had two ; but Miss Esther ran off with a wild young fellow, an' I've hearn tell as how they were both dead, poor things ! So powerful handsome as they were too—'specially him."

"And Miss Lizzie?"

"Oh, yes. Well, you see she ain't married—she's more sense. She's awful pretty, too, though she ain't a mite like Miss Esther was. Laws, she might have bin married dozens of times, I'm sure, if she'd have all the gents who want her. She's only been home for two or three months ; she was off somewhere to boardin'-school to larn to play the pianner and make picters and sich."

" And the papa of these interesting damsels, what is he like?" inquired the young man.

" He ?—sakes alive ! Why, he's the ugliest-tempered, crossest, hatefullest, disagreeablest old snapping-turtle ever you saw. He's as cross as two sticks, and as savage as a bear with a sore head. My stars and garters ! I'd sooner run a mile out of my way than meet him in the street."

" Whew ! pleasant, upon my word ! Are all your country magnates as amiable as Squire Erliston ?"

" There ain't many more, 'cepting Doctor Nick Wiseman, and that queer old witch, Miss Hagar."

" Has he any grown-up daughters?" inquired the
stranger, carelessly.

Cassie paused, and regarded him with a peculiar look
for an instant.

" Ahem !" she said, after a pause. " No; he's a
widderer, with only one child, a daughter, 'bout nine
months old, and a nevvy a year or so older. No, there
ain't no young ladies—I mean real ladies—in the village,
'cept Miss Lizzie Erliston."

He paid no attention to the meaning tone in which
this was spoken, and after lingering a few moments
longer, Cassie took her leave, inwardly wondering who
the handsome and inquisitive stranger could be.

" Praps this'll tell," said Cassie, as she lifted the
stranger's portmanteau, and examined it carefully for
name and initials. " Here it is, I declare !" she exclaimed, as her eyes fell on the letters " B. O.," inscribed
on the steel clasp. " B. O.- I wonder what them stands
for ! ' B O' *bo*. Shouldn't wonder if he was a beau.
Sakes alive ! what can his name be and what can he
want ? Well, I ain't likely to tell anybody, 'cause I
don't know myself. ' Has he got any grown-up darters ?' "
she muttered, as the young man's question came again to
her mind. " Maybe he's a fortin' hunter. I've hern tell
o' sich. Well, I hope Miss Lizzie won't have anything
to do with him if he is, and go throw herself away on a
graceless scamp like Miss Esther did. Well, I guess, if
he goes courtin' there, old Thunderclap will be in his
wool, and—O, massy on us !—if that Sally hain't let the
fire go dead out, while I was talkin' upstairs with ' B. O.'
Little black imp ! won't I give it to her ?"

The morning after the storm dawned clear and cold.
All traces of the preceding night's tempest had passed

away, and the sun shone forth brightly in a sky of clear, cloudless blue.

The handsome young stranger stood in the bar-room of the "Eagle," gazing from the open door at the bay, sparkling and flashing in the sun's light, and dotted all over with fishing-boats. Behind the counter sat worthy Giles Fox, smoking his pipe placidly. From the interior of the building came at intervals the voice of Cassie, scolding right and left at "You Sally" and "little black imp."

Suddenly the stranger beheld, emerging from a forest path on the right of the inn, a gentleman on horseback. He rode slowly, and the stranger observed that all the villagers he encountered saluted him respectfully, the men pulling off their hats, the women dropping profound courtesies, and the children, on their way to school, by scampering in evident alarm across meadows and fields.

As he drew rein before the inn-door, the stranger drew back. The old gentleman entered and approached the bar.

"Good-morning, Giles," he said, addressing the proprietor of the "Eagle" in a patronizing tone.

"Good-morning, squire—good-morning, sir. Fine day after the storm last night, said the host, rising.

"Great deal of damage done last night—great deal," said the old man, speaking rapidly, as was his custom : "one or two of the fishermen's huts down by the shore washed completely away. Yes, *sir—r!* Careless fools! Served 'em right. Always said it would happen—*I* knew it. 'Coming events cast their shadows afore,' as Solomon says."

The young stranger stepped forward and stood before him.

"Beg pardon, sir," he said, with a slight bow ; "have I the honor of addressing Squire Erliston ?"

"Yes, yes—to be sure you have ; that's me. Yes, *sir*. Who're you, eh ?—who're you ?" said the squire, staring at him with his round, bullet eyes.

"If Squire Erliston will glance over this, it will answer his question," said the young man, presenting a letter.

The squire held the letter in his hand, and stared at him a moment longer; then wiped his spectacles and adjusted them upon his nose, opened the letter, and began to read.

The stranger stood, in his usual careless manner, leaning against the counter, and watched him during its perusal.

"Lord bless me !" exclaimed the squire, as he finished the letter. "So you're the son of my old friend, Oranmore ? Who'd think it ? You weren't the size of a well-grown pup when I saw you last. And you're his son ? Well, well ! Give us your hand. 'Who knows what a day may bring forth ?' as Solomon says. I'd as soon have thought of seeing the Khan of Tartary here as you. Oranmore's son ! Well, well, well ! You're his very image —a trifle better-looking. And you're Barry Oranmore ? When did you come, eh ?—when did you come ?"

"Last night, sir."

"Last night, in all the storm ? Bless my soul ! Why didn't you come up to Mount Sunset ? Eh, sir ? Why didn't you come ?"

"Really, sir, I feared——"

"Pooh !—pshaw !—nonsense !—no, you did not. 'Innocence is bold ; but the guilty flee-eth when no one pursues,' as Solomon says. What were you afraid of ? S'pose everybody told you I was a demon incarnate— confound their impudence ! But I ain't ; no, *sir !* 'The devil's not as black as he's painted,' as Solomon says— or if he didn't say it, he ought to."

"Indeed, sir, I should be sorry to think of my father's old friend in any such way, I beg to assure you."

"No, you won't—haven't time. Come up to Mount Sunset—come, right off ! Must, sir—no excuse ; Liz 'll be delighted to see you. Come—come—come along !"

"Since you insist upon it, squire, I shall do myself the pleasure of accepting your invitation."

"Yes, yes—to besure you will !" again interrupted the impatient squire. "Bless my heart !—and you're little Barry. Well, well !"

"I am Barry, certainly," said the young man, smiling ; "but whether the adjective 'little' is well applied or not, I feel somewhat doubtful. I have a dim recollec- tion of measuring some six feet odd inches when I left home."

"Ha, ha, ha !—to be sure ! to be sure !" laughed the lusty old squire. "Little !—by Jove ! you're a head and shoulders taller than I am myself. Yes, sir—true as gospel. 'Bad weeds grow fast,' as Solomon says. Lord ! *won't* my Liz be astonished, though ?"

"I hope your daughter is quite well, squire."

"Well !—you'd better believe it. My daughter is *never* sick. No, sir ; got too much sense—specially Liz. Esther always *was* a simpleton—ran away, and all that, before she was out of her bibs and tuckers. Both died— knew they would. 'The days of the transgressors shall be short on the earth,' as Solomon says. But Liz has got her eye-teeth cut. Smart girl, my Liz."

"I anticipate great pleasure in making the acquaint- ance of Miss Erliston," said Oranmore, carelessly ; "her beauty and accomplishments have made her name famil- iar to me long ago."

"Yes, yes, Liz is good-looking—deucedly good-look- ing ; very like what I was at her age. Ah, you're laugh- ing, you rascal ! Well, I dare say I'm no beauty *now* ;

3* .

but never mind that at present. 'Handsome is as handsome does,' as Solomon says. Come, get your traps and
come along. Giles, fly round—we're in a hurry."

Thus adjured, Giles kindly consented to "fly round."
All was soon ready ; and, after giving orders to have his
portmanteau sent after him, young Oranmore mounted
his horse, and, accompanied by the squire, rode off
toward Mount Sunset Hall, the squire enlivening the
way by numerous quotations from Solomon.

On reaching the Hall, his host ushered him into the
parlor, where, seated at the piano, was the squire's
daughter, Lizzie, singing, by some singular coincidence :

> "There's somebody coming to marry me—
> There's somebody coming to woo."

Whether Miss Lizzie had seen that *somebody* coming
through the window, I cannot say.

She rose abruptly from her seat as they entered,
exclaiming :

"Oh, papa ! I'm so glad you have come."

Then, seeing the stranger, she drew back with the
prettiest affectation of embarrassment in the world.

Lizzie Erliston was pretty—decidedly pretty—with a
little round, graceful figure, snowy complexion, rosebud
lips, and sparkling, vivacious blue eyes. Graceful,
thoughtless, airy, dressy, and a most finished flirt was
little Lizzie.

"Mr. Oranmore, my daughter Liz ; Liz, Mr. Oranmore, son of my old friend. Fact ! Hurry up breakfast now—I'm starving."

"I am delighted to welcome the son of papa's friend,"
said Lizzie, courtesying to the handsome stranger, who
returned the salutation with easy gallantry.

Breakfast was brought in, and the trio, together with

worthy Mrs. Gower, were soon seated around the table.

"I am afraid, Mr. Oranmore, you will find it very dull here, after being accustomed to the gayety of city life. Our village is the quietest place in the world."

"Dull!" repeated Oranmore. "Did angels ever condescend to dwell on this earth. I should say they had taken up their abode in St. Mark's."

He fixed his large dark eyes on her face, and bowed with a look of such ardent yet respectful admiration as he spoke, that Lizzie blushed "celestial, rosy red," and thought it the prettiest speech she had ever heard.

"Fudge!" grunted the squire.

"Ah, Mr. Oranmore, I see you are a sad flatterer," said the little lady, smilingly, buttering another roll.

"Not so, Miss Erliston. Dare I speak what I think, I should indeed be deemed a flatterer," replied Oranmore, gallantly.

"Bah!" muttered the squire, with a look of intense disgust.

At this moment a child's shrill screams resounded in one of the rooms above, growing louder and louder each moment.

"There—that's Aurora! Just listen to the little wretch!" exclaimed Lizzie. "That child will be the death of us yet, with her horrid yells. Her lungs must be made of cast-iron, or something harder, for she is incessantly screaming."

The Squire darted an angry look at Mrs. Gower, who faltered out : She was very sorry—that she had told Totty to be sure and keep her quiet—that she didn't know what was the matter, she was sure——

"Ring the bell!" said the squire, savagely cutting her

short.　The summons was answered by the little darkey, Totty.

"Well, Totty, what's the natter?" said Lizzie., "Don't you hear the baby squalling there like a little tempest?　Why don't you attend to her?"

"Lor! Miss Lizzie, 'twan't none o' my fault—'deed 'twan't," said the little darkey.　"Miss Roarer's a-roarin' 'cause she can't put her feet in de sugar-bowl.　'Deed I can't 'vent her, to save my precious life.　Nobody can't do nothing wid dat 'ar little limb."

"I'll do something to *you* you won't like if you don't make her stop!" said the angry squire.　"Be off with you now; and, if I hear another word, I'll—I'll twist your neck for you!"

"Marse, I declare I can't stop her," said Totty, dodging in alarm toward the door.

"Be off!" thundered the squire, in a rage, hurling a hot roll at the black head of Totty, who adroitly dodged and vanished instanter.

"Of all diabolical inventions, young ones are the worst!" snappishly exclaimed Squire Erliston, bringing down his fist on the table.　"Pests! plagues! abominations!　Mrs. Gower, ma'am, if you don't give it a sleeping draught when it takes to yelling, I'll—I'll—I'll——"

"By the way, Mr. Oranmore, as you are from the city," broke in Lizzie, "perhaps you may have heard of some one there who has lost a child?"

"What—what did you say?—a child?" exclaimed Oranmore, starting so suddenly and looking so wild, that all looked at him in surprise.

"Yes.　But, dear me, how pale you look!　Are you ill?"

"Ill!　Oh, no; pray go on," said Oranmore, recovering himself by an effort.

"Well; last Christmas eve, Mrs. Gower was returning from the city, where she had been to make purchases, and taking the shore road, picked up an infant on the beach, and brought it home. It is a wonder no inquiries were made about it."

Barry Oranmore breathed freely again. It could not be *his* child, for he had seen the nurse before leaving the city; and she, fearing to lose her annuity, had told him the child was alive and well : therefore it must be another.

A week passed rapidly away at Sunset Hall. There were sails on the bay, and rides over the hills, and shady forest walks, and drives through the village, and long romantic rambles in the moonlight. And Lizzie Erliston was in love. Was *he?* She thought so sometimes when his deep, dark eyes would rest on her, and fill with softest languor as they wandered side by side. But, then, had she not discovered his restlessness, his evident longing to be away, though he still remained? Something in his conduct saddened and troubled her ; for she loved him as devotedly as it was in the power of a nature essentially shallow and selfish to love. But the dangerous spell of his voice and smile threw a glamour over her senses. She could almost have loved his very faults, had she known them. And, yielding herself to that witching spell, Lizzie Erliston, who had often caught others, at last found herself caught.

CHAPTER VII.

THE CYPRESS WREATH.

" Bride, upon thy marriage-day,
  Did the fluttering of thy breath
  Speak of joy or woe beneath?
  And the hue that went and came
  On thy cheek like waving flame,
  Flowed that crimson from the unrest,
  Or the gladness of thy breast?"—HEMANS.

"SQUIRE ERLISTON, can I have a few moments' private conversation with you this morning?" said Oranmore, as he sought the squire, whom Mrs. Gower was just helping to ensconce in his easy-chair.

"Certainly, certainly, my boy. Mrs. Gower, bring the rest of the pillows by and by. 'Time for everything,' as Solomon says. Clear out now, ma'am, while I attend to this young man's case."

Barry Oranmore stood in the middle of the floor, resting one hand lightly on the back of a chair. Squire Erliston, propped up in an easy-chair with pillows and cushions, and wearing an unusually benign expression of countenance—caused, probably, by Miss Aurora's extraordinary quietness on that morning.

"You have doubtless perceived, sir, my attentions to your daughter," went on the young man, in a tone that was almost careless. "Miss Lizzie, I am happy to say, returns my affection ; and, in short, sir, I have asked this interview to solicit your daughter's hand."

He bowed slightly, and stood awaiting a reply. The squire jumped from his seat, kicked one pillow to the other end of the room, waved another above his head, and shouted :

"Bless my soul ! it's just what I wanted ! Give us your hand, my dear boy. Solicit her hand ! Take it, take it, with all my heart. If she had a dozen of hands, you should have them all."

"I thank you sincerely, Squire Erliston. Believe me, it only needed your consent to our union to fill my cup of *happiness* to the brim."

His voice was low—almost scornful ; and the emphasis upon "happiness" was bitter, indeed. But the squire, in his delight, neither heeded nor noticed.

"The wedding must come off immediately, my dear fellow. We'll have a rousing one, and no mistake. I was afraid Liz might run off with some penniless scamp, as Esther did ; but now it's all right. Yes, the sooner the wedding comes off the better. 'He who giveth not his daughter in marriage, doeth well ; but he who giveth her doeth better,' as Solomon ought to know, seeing he had some thousands of 'em. Be off now, and arrange with Lizzie the day for the wedding, while I take a sleep. When it's all over, wake me up. There, go ! Mrs. Gower ! hallo ! Mrs. Gower, I say ! come here with the pillows."

Oranmore hurried out, while Mrs. Gower hurried in —he to tell Lizzie of the success of his mission, and she to prepare her master for the arms of Morpheus.

That day fortnight was fixed upon as their marriage-day. The Bishop of P—— was to visit St. Mark's, and during his advent in the village the nuptials were to be celebrated.

And such a busy place as Sunset Hall became after the important fact was announced ! Poor Mrs. Gower lost, perceptibly, fifty pounds of flesh, with running in and out, and up and down stairs. Old carpets and old servants were turned out, and new curtains and French cooks turned in. Carpets and custards, and ice-creams and Aurora's screams, and milliners and feathers, and flowers and flounces, and jellies and jams, and upholstery reigned supreme, until the squire swore by all the " fiends in flames " that it was worse than pandemonium, and rushed from the place in despair to seek refuge with Giles Fox, and smoke his pipe in peace at the " Eagle."

Barry Oranmore, finding his bride so busily engaged superintending jewels, and satins, and laces, as to be able to dispense with his services, mounted his horse each day, and seldom returned before night. And, amid all the bustle and confusion, no one noticed that he grew thinner and paler day after day ; nor the deep melancholy filling his dark eyes ; nor the bitter, self-scorning look his proud, handsome face ever wore. They knew not how he paced up and down his room, night after night, trying to still the sound of *one* voice that was ever mournfully calling his name. They knew not that when he quitted the brilliantly-lighted rooms, and plunged into the deep, dark forest, it was to shut out the sight of a sad, reproachful face, that ever haunted him, day and night.

Lizzie was in her glory, flitting about like a bird from morning till night. Such wonderful things as she had manufactured out of white satin and Mechlin lace, and such confusion as she caused—flying through the house, boxing the servants' ears, and lecturing Mrs. Gower and shaking Aurora—who had leave now to yell to her heart's content—and turning everything topsy-turvy, until the squire brought down his fist with a thump, and declared that though Solomon had said there was a time for everything, neither Solomon, nor any other man, could ever convince him that there was a time allotted for such a racket and rumpus as *that.*

But out of chaos, long ago, was brought forth order ; and the "eve before the bridal" everything in Sunset Hall was restored to peace and quietness once more. The rooms were perfectly dazzling with the glitter of new furniture and the blaze of myriads of lusters. And such a crowd as on the wedding night filled those splendid rooms ! There was Mrs. Gower, magnificent in brown velvet, preserved for state occasions like the present, with such a miraculous combination of white ribbons and lace on her head. There was the squire, edifying the public generally with copious extracts from Solomon and some that were *not* from Solomon. There was Mrs. Oranmore, grim and gray as ever, moving like the guilty shadow of a lost soul, through those gorgeous rooms and that glittering crowd, with the miserable feeling at her heart, that her only son was to be offered that night a sacrifice on the altar of her pride and ambition. There was Doctor Wiseman, all legs and arms, as usual, slinking among the guests. There was the bishop, a fat, pompous, oily-looking gentleman, in full canonicals, waiting to tie the Gordian knot.

There was a bustle near the door, a swaying to and fro of the crowd, and the bridal party entered. Every voice was instantaneously hushed, every eye was fixed upon them. How beautiful the bride looked, with her elegant robes and gleaming jewels, her downcast eyes, and rose-flushed cheeks, and half-smiling lips. The eyes of all the gentlemen present were fixed wistfully upon her. And the eyes of the ladies wandered to the bridegroom, with something very like a feeling of awe, as they saw how pale and cold he was looking—how different from any bridegroom they had ever seen before. Were his thoughts wandering to *another* bridal, in a land beyond the sea, with one for whose blue eyes and golden hair he would *then* willingly have surrendered fame, and wealth, and ambition ? And now, she who had left friends, and home, and country for his sake, was deserted for another. Yet still that unknown, penniless girl was dearer than all the world beside. Well might he look and feel unlike a bridegroom, with but one image filling his heart, but one name on his lips—" *Eveleen ! Eveleen !*"

But no one there could read the heart, throbbing so tumultuously beneath that cold, proud exterior. They passed through the long rooms—the bishop stood before them—the service began. To *him* it seemed like the service for the dead—to *her* it was the most delightful thing in the world. There was fluttering of fans, flirting of perfumed handkerchiefs, smiling lips and eyes, and

> " With decorum all things carried ;
> Miss smiled, and blushed, and then was—married."

The ceremony was over, and Lizzie Erliston was Lizzie Erliston no longer.

But just at that moment, when the crowd around were about to press forward to offer their congratulations, a loud, ringing footstep, that sounded as though shod with steel, was heard approaching. A moment more, and an uninvited guest stood among them. The tall, thin, sharp, angular figure of a woman past middle age, with a grim, weird, old-maidenish face ; a stiff, rustling dress of iron-gray ; a black net cap over her grizzled locks, and a tramp like that of a dragoon, completed the external of this rather unprepossessing figure.

All fell back and made way for her, while a murmur : " Miss Hagar ! What brings Miss Hagar here ?" passed through the room.

She advanced straight to where Lizzie stood, leaning proudly and fondly on the arm of Oranmore, and drawing forth a wreath of mingled cypress and dismal yew, laid it amid the orange blossoms on the head of the bride.

With a shriek of superstitious terror, Lizzie tore the ominous wreath from her head, and flung it on the floor. Heeding not the action, the woman raised her long, gaunt, fleshless arm like an inspired sibyl, and chanted in a voice so wild and dreary, that every heart stood still :

> " Oh, bride ! woe to thee !
> Ere the spring leaves deck the tree,
> Those locks you now with jewels twine
> Shall wear this cypress wreath of mine."

Then striding through the awe-struck crowd, she passed out and disappeared.

Faint and sick with terror, Lizzie hid her face in the arm that supported her. A moment's silence ensued, broken by the squire, who came stamping along, exclaiming :

"Hallo! what's the matter here ! Have either of these good people repented of their bargain, already. ' Better late than never,' as Solomon says."

"It was only my sister Hagar, who came here to predict fortunes, as usual," said Doctor Wiseman, with an uneasy attempt at a laugh, "and succeeded in scaring Miss Lizzie—Mrs. Oranmore, I mean—half out of her wits."

" Pooh ! pooh ! is that all.   Liz, don't be such a little fool ! There goes the music. Let every youngster be off, on penalty of death, to the dancing-room. ' Time to dance,' as Solomon says, and if it's not at weddings, I'd like to know when it is. Clear !"

Thus adjured, with a great deal of laughing and chatting, the company dispersed. The folding-doors flew open, and merry feet were soon tripping gayly to the music, and flirting, and laughing, and love-making, and ice-creams were soon at their height, and Lizzie, as she floated airily around the room in the waltz, soon forgot all about Miss Hagar's prediction. Barry Oranmore, by an effort, shook off his gloom, and laughed with the merriest, and waltzed with his bride, and the pretty bridemaids ; and all the time his heart was far away with that haunting shape that had stood by his side all the night.

*   *   *   *   *   *

A month had passed away. Their bridal tour had been a short one, and the newly wedded pair had returned to Sunset Hall. And Lizzie was at last beginning to open her eyes, and wonder what ailed her husband So silent, so absent, so restless, growing more and more so day after day. His long rides over the hills were now taken alone ; and he would only return to lie on a lounge in some darkened room, with his face hidden from view by his long, neglected locks. At first she pouted a little at this ; but seeing it produced no effect, she at last concluded to let him have his own way, and she would take hers. So evening after evening, while he lay alone, so still and motionless, in his darkened chamber, Lizzie frequented parties and *soirees*, giving plausible excuses for her husband's absence, and was the gayest of the gay.

One morning, returning with the gray dawn, from an unusually brilliant *soiree*, she inquired for her husband, and learned that, half an hour before, he had called for his horse and ridden off. This did not surprise her, for it had often happened so before ; so, without giving the matter a second thought, she flung herself on her bed, and fell fast asleep.

Half an hour after the sound of many feet, and a confused murmur of many voices below, fell on her ear.

Wondering what it could mean, she raised herself on

her elbow to listen, when the door was burst open ; and Totty, gray, gasping, horror-stricken, stood before her.

"Totty, what in the name of heaven is the matter !" exclaimed Lizzie, in surprise and alarm.

"Oh, missus! Oh, missus !" were the only words the frightened negress could utter.

"Merciful heaven ! what has happened ?" exclaimed Lizzie, springing to her feet, in undefined terror. "Totty, Totty, tell me, or I shall go and see."

"Oh, Miss Lizzie ! Oh, Miss Lizzie !" cried the girl, falling on her knees, "for de dear Lord's sake, don't go. Oh, Miss Lizzie, it's too drefful to tell ! It would kill you !"

With a wild cry, Lizzie snatched her robe from the clinging hands that held it, and fled from the room down the long staircase. There was a crowd round the parlor door ; all the servants were collected there, and inside she could see many of the neighbors gathered. She strove to force her way through the throng of appalled servants, who mechanically made way for her to pass.

"Keep her back—keep her back, I tell you," cried the voice of Dr. Wiseman, "would you kill her?"

A score of hands were extended to keep her back, but they were too late. She had entered, and a sight met her eyes that sent the blood curdling with horror to her heart. A wild, terrific shriek rang through the house, as she threw up both arms and fell, in strong convulsions, on the floor.

CHAPTER VIII.

GIPSY.

" A little, wild-eyed, tawny child,
A fairy sprite, untamed and wild,
Like to no one save herself,
A laughing, mocking, gipsy elf."

EAR after year glides away, and we wonder vaguely that they can have passed. On our way to the grave we may meet many troubles, but time obliterates them all, and we learn to laugh and talk as merrily again as though the grass was not growing between our face and one we could never love enough. But such is life.

Ten years have passed away at St. Mark's since the close of our last chapter ; ten years of dull, tedious monotony. The terrible sight that had met Lizzie Oranmore's eyes that morning, was the dead form of her young husband. He had been riding along at his usual reckless, headlong pace, and had been thrown from his horse and killed.

Under the greensward in the village church-yard, they laid his world-weary form to rest, with only the name inscribed on the cold, white marble to tell he had ever existed. And no one dreamed of the youthful romance that had darkened all the life of Barry Oranmore. Lying on the still heart, that had once beat so tumultuously, they found the miniature of a fair young face and a long tress of sunny hair. Wondering silently to whom they belonged, good Mrs. Gower laid them aside, little dreaming of what they were one day to discover.

Lizzie, with her usual impulsiveness, wept and sobbed for a time inconsolably. But it was not in her shallow, thoughtless nature to grieve long for any one ; and ere a year had passed, she laughed as gayly and sang as merrily as ever.

Sometimes, it may be, when her child—her boy—would look up in her face with the large dark eyes of him who had once stolen her girlish heart away, tears for a moment would weigh down her golden eyelashes ; but the next instant the passing memory was forgotten, and her laugh again rang out merry and clear.

And so the ten years had passed, and no change had taken place at Sunset Hall save that it was far from being the quiet place it had been formerly.

Has the reader forgotten Aurora, the little foundling of yelling notoriety? If so, it is no fault of hers, for that shrill-voiced young lady never allowed herself to be pushed aside to make room for any one. Those ten years at least made a change in her.

See her now, as she stands with her dog by her side, for a moment, to rest, in the quaint old porch fronting Sunset Hill. She has been romping with Lion this morning, and now, panting and breathless, she pauses for an instant to prepare for a fresh race. There she stands ! A little, slight, wiry, agile figure, a little thin, dark, but bright and sparkling face, with small, irregular features, never for a moment at rest. With a shower of short, crisp, dark curls streaming in the breeze, every shining ring dancing with life, and fire, and mirth, and mischief. And with such eyes, looking in her face you forgot every other feature gazing in those "bonny wells of brown," that seemed fairly scintillating wickedness. How they did dance, and flash, and sparkle, with youth, and glee, and irrepressible fun—albeit the darker flame that now and then leaped from their shining depths bespoke a wild, fierce spirit, untamed and daring, slumbering in her heart, quiet and unaroused as yet, but which would one day burst forth, scathing, blighting all on whom it fell.

And such is Aurora Gower. A wild, dark, elfish changeling, not at all pretty, but the most bewitching sprite withal, that ever kept a household in confusion. Continually getting into scrapes and making mischief, and doing deeds that would have been unpardonable in any one else, Aurora, in some mysterious way of her own, escaped censure, and the most extravagant actions were passed over with the remark, that it was "just like her—just what you might expect from a gipsy." Owing to her dark skin and wild habits, "Gipsy" was the name by which Mrs. Gower's *protegee* was universally known. With every one she was a favorite, for though always saucy, often impertinent, and invariably provoking, it was impossible to be angry with a little fairy of a creature whom they could almost hold up between their finger and thumb.

As for the burly old squire, he could as soon think of getting along without his brandy as without Gipsy. For though they continually quarreled, he abusing her unmercifully, and she retorting impudently, yet, when Gipsy at the end would flounce out in a towering passion, she was sure a few hours after to find a peace-offering from the old man, in the shape of a costly gift, lying on her table. After some coaxing she would consent to forgive him, and Squire Erliston and his little ward would smoke the calumet of peace (figuratively speaking); but, alas! for the short-lived truce—ere another hour the war of words would be raging "fast and furious" once more.

Good Mrs. Gower zealously strove to impress on the wayward elf a becoming respect for the head of the household ; and sometimes, in a fit of penitence, Aurora would promise "not to give Guardy any more bile," but being by nature woefully deficient in the bump of reverence, the promise had never been kept ; and at last the worthy housekeeper gave up the task in despair.

And so Aurora was left pretty much to follow her "own sweet will," and no one need wonder that she grew up the maddest, merriest elf that ever danced in the moonlight. At the age of eleven she could ride with the best horseman for miles around, hunt like a practiced sportsman, bring down a bird on the wing with her unerring bullet, and manage a boat with the smartest fisherman in St. Marks. Needle-work, dolls, and other amusements suitable for her age, she regarded with the utmost contempt, and with her curls streaming behind her, her hat swinging in her hand, she might be seen flying about the village from morning till night, always running, for she was too quick and impetuous to walk. In the stormiest weather, when the winds were highest and the sea roughest, she would leap into one of the fishermen's boats, and unheeding storm and danger, go out with them, in spite of commands and entreaties to the contrary, until danger and daring became with her second nature. But while Aurora has been standing for her picture the rest of the family have assembled in the breakfast-parlor of Mount Sunset Hall. Languidly stretched on a sofa lay Lizzie Oranmore. Those ten years have made no change in her ; just the same rose-leaf complexion, the same round, little graceful figure, the same coquettish airs and graces as when we saw her last. She might readily have been taken for the elder sister of her son, Louis, who stood by the window sketching the view before him.

There was a striking resemblance between Louis and his dead father ; the same clear, olive complexion, the same sable locks and bold black eyes, the same scornful, curving upper lip, and the same hot, rash, impetuous nature. But with all his fiery impetuosity he was candid, open and generous, the soul of honor and frankness, but with a nature which, according as it was trained, must be powerful for good or evil.

Sitting propped up in an easy-chair, with his gouty leg, swathed in flannel, stretched on two chairs, was the squire, looking in no very sweet frame of mind. The morning paper, yet damp from the press, lay before him; but the squire's attention would wander from it every moment to the door.

"Where's that little wretch this morning?" broke out the squire, at last, throwing down his paper impatiently.

"I really can't say," replied Lizzie, opening her eyes languidly. "I saw her racing over the hills this morning, with those dreadful dogs of hers. I expect she will be back soon."

"And we must wait for her ladyship!" growled the squire. "I'll cane her within an inch of her life if she doesn't learn to behave herself. 'Spare the child and spoil the rod,' as Solomon says."

"Here she comes!" exclaimed Louis, looking up. "Speak of Satan and he'll appear."

"Satan! She's no Satan, I'd have you know, you young jackanapes!" said the squire, angrily, for though always abusing the "little vixen," Aurora, himself, he would suffer no one else to do it.

"Look, look how she dashes along!" exclaimed Louis, with kindling eyes, unheeding the reproof. "There! she has leaped her pony over the gate, and now she is standing up in her saddle; and—bravo! well done, Gipsy! She has actually sprung over black Jupe's head in a flying leap."

While he spoke Gipsy came running up the lawn toward the house, singing, in a high, shrill voice, as she ran :

> " He died long, long ago, long ago—
>   He had no hair on the top of his head,
> The place where the wool ought to grow,
>   Lay down the shovel and the hoe-o-o,
>   Hang up——"

"Stop that, stop that, you vixen ! Stop it, I tell you, or I'll hang *you* up !" said the squire, angrily. "Where do you learn those vulgar doggerels ?"

" Make 'em up, Guardy—every one of 'em. Ain't I a genius ?"

" I don't believe it, you scapegrace."

" No wonder you don't, seeing there never was a genius in the family before ; but 'better late than never,' you know."

"None of your impertinence, miss. Give an account of yourself, if you please. Where were you this morning ? Answer me *that !*"

" Nowhere, sir."

" Don't tell stories, you little sinner. Where is nowhere ?"

" Over to Doctor Spider's."

" Gipsy, my dear, why will you persist in calling Doctor Wiseman nicknames ?" remonstrated Lizzie.

" Why, Aunt Liz, because he's just like a spider, for all the world—all legs," flippantly replied Gipsy.

" And what business had you there, monkey ? Didn't I tell you not to go ? I thought I told you *never* to go there !" said the squire, in rising wrath.

" Know it, Guardy, and that's just the reason I went."

" Because I forbade you, eh ?"

" Yes, sir."

"You—you—you disobedient little hussy, you! Aren't you ashamed of yourself?"

"Ashamed!—what of? I haven't got the gout in my leg."

"Gipsy, you dreadful child, hush!" said Lizzie, in alarm.

"Oh, let her go on! She's just as you taught her, madam. And as to you, Miss Gipsy, or Aurora, or whatever your name is, let me tell you, the gout is nothing to be ashamed of. It runs in the most respectable families, miss."

"Lord, Guardy! What a pity I can't have it, too, and help to keep up the respectability of the family!"

Louis turned to the window, and struggled violently with a laugh, which he endeavored to change into a cough, and the laugh and cough meeting, produced a choking sensation. This sent Gipsy to his aid, who, after administering sundry thumps on his back with her little closed fists, restored him to composure, and the squire returned to the charge.

"And now, to 'return to our mutton,' as Solomon says; or—hold on a minute—was it Solomon who said that?"

The squire paused, and placed his finger reflectively on the point of his nose, in deep thought; but being unable to decide, he looked up, and went on:

"Yes, miss, as I was saying, what took you over to Deep Dale so early this morning? Tell me that."

"Well, if I must, I must, I s'pose—so here goes."

"Hallo, Gipsy!" interrupted Louis. "Take care—you're making poetry."

"No, sir! I scorn the accusation!" said Gipsy, drawing herself up. "But, Guardy, since I *must* tell you, I went over to see—ahem!—Archie!"

"You did !" grunted Guardy. "Humph! humph! humph !"

"Don't take it so much to heart, Guardy. No use grieving—'specially as the grief might settle in your poor afflicted leg—limb, I mean."

"And may I ask, young lady, what you could possibly want with him ?" said the squire, sternly.

"Oh, fifty things ! He's my beau, you know."

"Your beau !—*your* beau !—your BEAU ! My conscience !"

"Yes, sir, we're engaged."

"You are? 'Oh, Jupiter,' as Solomon says. Pray, madam (for such I presume you consider yourself), when will you be twelve years old ?"

"Oh, as soon as I can. I don't want to be an old maid."

"So it seems, you confounded little Will-o'-the-wisp. And will you be good enough to inform us how this precious engagement came about ?" said the squire, with a savage frown.

"With pleasure, sir. You see, we went out to gather grapes in the wood one day, and we had a splendiferous time. And says I, ' Archie, ain't this nice ?'—and says he ' Yes'—and says I, ' Wouldn't it be nice if we'd get married?'—and says he, ' Yes'—and says I, '*Will* you have me, though ?'—and says he, ' Yes'—and says I——"

" ' Ain't we a precious pair of fools?' and says he, ' Yes,' " interrupted the squire, mimicking her. "Oh, you're a nice gal—you're a pretty young lady !"

"Yes, ain't I, now? You and I are of one opinion there, exactly. Ain't you proud of me ?"

"*Proud* of you, you barefaced little wretch ! I'd like to twist your neck for you !" thundered the squire.

"Better not, Guardy ; you'd be hung for *man-slaughter* if you did, you know."

" *You* don't call yourself a man, I hope !" said Louis.

" Well, if I don't, I'm a girl—which is a thousand times nicer. And speaking of girls, reminds me that Miss Hagar's got the dearest, darlingest, *beautifulest* little girl you ever set your eyes on."

" Miss Hagar ?" they all exclaimed in surprise.

" Yes, to be sure. Law ! you needn't look so astonished ; this is a free country. And why can't Miss Hagar have a little girl, if she wants to, as well as anybody else, I'd like to know ?" exclaimed Gipsy, rather indignantly.

" To be sure," said Louis, who took the same view of the case as Gipsy.

" Where did she get it ?—whose little girl is it ?" inquired Lizzie, slightly roused from her languor by the news.

. " Don't know, I'm sure ; nobody don't. She was off somewhere poking round all day yesterday, and came home at night with this little girl. Oh, Louis, she's such a dear little thing !"

" Is she ?" said Louis, absently.

" Yes, indeed—with a face like double-refined moonlight, and long, yellow hair, and blue eyes, and pink dress, and cheeks to match. She's twice as pretty as Minette ; and Miss Hagar's going to keep her, and teach her to tell fortunes, I expect."

" I wonder Dr. Wiseman allows Miss Hagar to fill the house with little beggars," said Lizzie.

" Oh, Spider's got nothing to do with it. Miss Hagar has money of her own, and can keep her if she likes. Pity if she'd have to ask permission of that 'thing of legs and arms,' everything she wants to do."

" Gipsy, my dear, you really must not speak so of Dr. Wiseman : it's positively shocking," said the highly-scandalized Mrs. Oranmore.

" Well, I don't care ; he *is* a ' thing of legs and arms.' There, now !"

" What's the little girl's name, Gipsy ?" inquired Louis.

" *Celeste*—isn't it pretty ? And she—oh, she's a darling, and no mistake. *Wouldn't* I marry her if I was a man—maybe I wouldn't."

" What's her other name ?"

" Got none—at least she said so ; and, as I didn't like to tell her she told a story, I asked Miss Hagar, and *she* told me to mind my own business ; yes, she actually did. Nobody minds how they talk to me. People haven't a bit of respect for me ; and I have to put up with *sass* from every one. I won't stand it much longer, either. There !"

" No, I wouldn't advise you to," said Louis. " Better *sit* down ; no use in standing it."

" Wiseman's a fool if he lets that crazy tramp, his sister, support beggars in his house," exclaimed the squire, in a threatening tone. " Lunatics like her should not be allowed to go at large. He has no business to permit it."

" I'd like to see him trying to stop it," said Gipsy. " I'd be in his wool."

" *You!*" said the squire, contemptuously. " What could a little Tom Thumb in petticoats, like you, do ?"

" Look here, now, Guardy, don't call a lady names. When you speak of Tom Thumb, you know, it's getting personal. What could I do ? Why, I'd set his house on fire some night about his ears, or some day, when out shooting, a bullet might strike him accidentally on purpose. It takes me to defend injured innocence," said Gipsy, getting up, and squaring-off in an attitude of defiance, as she exclaimed : " Come on, old Wiseman, I'm ready for you !"

"Well, I can't allow you to associate with beggars. You must never go to Deep Dale again. I can't countenance his proceedings. If he choose to make a fool of himself, it's no reason why I should do so too."

"None in the world, sir—especially as nature has saved you that trouble."

"You audacious little demon, you! what do you mean?"

"Ahem! I was just observing, sir, that it's time for breakfast," said Gipsy, demurely.

"Humph! humph! well, ring for Mrs. Gower, and hold your tongue."

"Sorry I can't oblige you, Guardy. But how can I hold my tongue and eat?"

"I wish I could find something to take the edge off it; it's altogether too sharp," growled the old man to himself.

Mrs. Gower, fat and good-natured as ever, entered at this moment; and, as they assembled round the table, the squire—who, though he generally got the worst of the argument, would never let Gipsy rest—again resumed the subject.

"Mind, monkey, you're not to go to Deep Dale again; I forbid you—positively forbid you."

"Lor! Guardy, you don't say so!"

"Don't be disrespectful, minx. If I'm your guardian, you shall obey me. You heard me say so before, didn't you?"

"Why, yes, I think so; but, then, you say so many things, a body can't be expected to remember them all. You *must* be talking, you know; and you might as well be saying that as anything else."

"But I am determined you shall obey me this time. Do you hear? At your peril, minion, *dare* to go there again!" thundered the squire.

"That very pretty, Guardy, won't you say it over again," replied the tantalizing elf.

"Gipsy! oh, Gipsy, my dear!" chanted the ladies Gower and Oranmore, in a horrified duet.

"You—you—you—little, yellow abomination you! You—you—skinny——"

"Squire Erliston," said Gipsy, drawing herself up with stately dignity, "let me remind you, you are getting to be personal. How would you like it if I called *you*—you—you red-faced old fright—you—you—you gouty-legged——"

"There! there! that'll do," hastily interrupted the squire, while a universal shout of laughter went round the table at the ludicrous manner in which the little imp mimicked his blustering tone. "There, there! don't say a word about it; but mind, if you dare to go to Dr. Wiseman's, you'll rue it. Mind that."

"All right, sir; let me help you to another roll," said Gipsy, with her sweetest smile, as she passed the plate to the old man, who looked, not only daggers, but bowie-knives at the very least.

4*

CHAPTER IX.

A STORM AT MOUNT SUNSET HALL.

> " At this Sir Knight grew high in wrath,
> And lifting hands and eyes up both,
> Three times he smote his stomach stout,
> From whence, at length, fierce words broke out."
>
> HUDIBRAS.

"TOTTY ! Totty ! I say, Totty, where are you ? I declare to screech, I never saw such a provoking darkey in my life. Nobody never can find her when she's wanted ! Totty ! Totty ! hallo, Totty ! I want you dreadfully, it's a matter of life and death ! If that girl doesn't pay more attention to me, I'll—I'll discharge her ; *I will*, so help me Jimmy Johnston ! Totty ! Totty-y-y !" So called and shouted Gipsy, as she flew in and out, and up and down stairs, banging doors after her with a noise that made the old house ring, and scolding at the top of her voice all the time.

"Laws ! Miss Roarer, here I is," said Totty, hurrying as fast as possible into the presence of the little virago, to get rid of the noise.

"Oh, it's a wonder you came ! I s'pose you'd rather be lounging down in the kitchen than 'tending to your mistress. How dare you go away, when you don't know what minute I may want you ? Hey ?"

"Good Lor ! Miss Roarer, I only went down to de kitchen to get my breakfas' 'long o' the res'. How you 'spec I's gwine to live 'thout eatin'? You allers *does* call jes' the contrariest time, allers——"

"Hold your tongue !" exclaimed her imperious little

mistress; "don't give me any of your *imperunce!* There, curl my hair, and put on my pretty purple riding-habit, and make me just as pretty as ever you can. Hurry up!"

"Make you pretty, indeed!" muttered the indignant Totty; "'deed, when de Lord couldn't do it, 'taint very likely I can. Come 'long and keep still, two or free minutes, if you can. I never knew such a res'less little critter in all my life."

While Gipsy was standing as quietly as her fidgety nature would allow, to have her hair curled, Mrs. Gower entered.

"Well, 'Rora, my dear, where are you going this morning, that you are dressing in your best?" said Mrs. Gower, glancing at the gay purple riding-habit—for dress was a thing Gipsy seldom troubled herself about.

"Why, aunty, where *would* I be going; over to Spider's, of course."

"Oh, Gipsy, my dear, .pray don't think of such a thing!" exclaimed the good woman, in a tone of alarm. "Your guardian will be dreadfully angry."

"Lor! aunty, I know that; there wouldn't be any fun in it if he wasn't," replied the elf.

"Oh, Aurora, child! you don't know what you're doing. Consider all he has done for you, and how ungrateful it is of you to disobey him in this manner. Now, he has set his heart on keeping you from Deep Dale (you know he never liked the doctor nor his family), and he will be terribly, frightfully angry if he finds you have disobeyed him. Ride over the hills, go out sailing or shooting, but do not go there."

Gipsy, who had been yawning fearfully during this address, now jerked herself away from Totty, and replied, impatiently:

"Well, *let* him get frightfully angry; I'll get 'frightfully angry' too, and so there will be a pair of us.' Do you s'pose I'd miss seeing that dear, sweet, little girl again, just because Guardy will stamp, and fume, and roar, and scare all mankind into fits? Not I, indeed. Let him come on, who's afraid," and Gipsy threw herself into a stage attitude, and shouted the words in a voice that was quite imposing, coming as it did from so small a body.

"Oh, Gipsy, child! consider," again began Mrs. Gower.

"Oh, aunty, dear! I won't consider, never did; don't agree with my constitution, no how you can fix it. Archie told me one day when I was doing something he considered a crazy trick, to 'consider.' Well, for his sake, I tried to, and before ten minutes, aunty, I felt symptoms of falling into a decline. There now!"

"Oh, my dear! my dear! you are incorrigible," sighed Mrs. Gower; "but what would you do if your guardian some day turned you out of doors? You have no claim on him, and he *might* do it, you know, in a fit of anger."

"If he did"—exclaimed Gipsy, springing up with flashing eyes.

"Well, and if he did, what would you do?"

"Why, I'd defy him to his face, and then I'd run off, and go to sea, and make my fortune, and come back, and marry you—no, I couldn't do that, but I'd marry Archie. Lor! I'd get along splendidly."

"Oh, Gipsy! Gipsy! rightly named Gipsy! how little you know what it is to be friendless in the world, you poor little fairy you! Now, child, be quiet, and talk sensibly to me for a few minutes."

"Oh, bother, aunty! I can't be quiet; and as to talking sensibly, why I rather think I am doing that just now. There, now—now do, please, bottle up that lecture you've got for me, and it'll keep, for I'm off!" And darting past them, she ran down stairs, through the long hall, and was flying toward the stables in a twinkling.

On her way she met our old friend, Jupiter.

"Hallo, Jupe! Oh, there you are! Go and saddle Mignonne *'mediately*. I want him; quick, now!"

"Why, Miss Roarer, honey, I'se sorry for ter diserblige yer, chile, but ole mas'r he tole me not to let yer get Minnin to-day," said Jupiter, looking rather uneasily at the dark, wild, little face, and large, lustrous eyes, in which a storm was fast brewing.

"Do you mean to say he told you not to let me have my pony?" she said, or rather hissed, through her tightly-clenched teeth.

"Jes' so, Miss Ro rer; he tell me so not ten minutes ago."

"Now, Jupiter, look here; you go right off and saddle Mignonne, or it'll be the worse for you. D'ye hear?"

"Miss Roarer, I 'clare for't I dassent. Mas'r'll half kill me."

"And I'll *whole* kill you if you don't," said Gipsy, with a wild flash of her black eyes, as she sprang lightly on a high stone bench, and raised her riding-whip over the head of the trembling darkey; "go, sir; go right off and do as I tell you!"

"Laws! I can't—'deed chile! I can't——"

Whack! whack! whack! with no gentle hand went the whip across his shoulders, interrupting his apology.

"There, you black rascal! will you dare to disobey your mistress again!" Whack! whack! whack! "If you don't bring Mignonne out this minute, I'll shoot you dead as a mackerel! There; does that argument overcome your scruples?" whack! whack! *whack!*

With something between a yell and a howl, poor

Jupiter sprung back, and commenced rubbing his afflicted back.

"Will you go?" demanded Gipsy, raising her whip once more.

"Yes ! yes ! Who ever did see such a 'bolical little limb as dat ar. Ole mas'r 'll kill me, I knows he will," whimpered poor Jupiter as he slunk away to the stables, closely followed by his vixenish little mistress, still poising the dangerous whip.

Mignonne, a small, black, fleet-footed, spirited Arabian, was led forth, pawing the ground and tossing his head, as impatient to be off, even, as his young mistress.

"That's right, Jupe," said Gipsy, as she sprang into the saddle and gathered up the reins ; "but mind, for the future, never dare to disobey *me*, no matter what anybody says. Mind, if you do, look out for a pistol-ball, some night, through your head."

Jupiter, who had not the slightest doubt but what the mad-headed little witch would do it as soon as not, began whimpering like a whipped school-boy. Between the Scylla of his master's wrath, and the Charybdis of his willful little mistress, poor Jupiter knew not which way to steer.

"Don't cry, Jupe—there's a good fellow," said Gipsy, touched by his distress. "Keep out of your master's sight till I come back, and I'll take all the blame upon myself. There, now—off we go, Mignonne !"

And waving her plumed hat above her head, with a shout of triumphant defiance as she passed the house, Gipsy went galloping down the road like a flash.

The sky, which all the morning had looked threatening, was rapidly growing darker and darker. About half an hour after the departure of Gipsy, the storm burst upon them in full fury. The wind howled fiercely through the forest, the rain fell in torrents, the lightning flashed in one continued sheet of blue electric flame, the thunder crashed peal upon peal, until heaven and earth seemed rending asunder.

The frightened inmates of Sunset Hall were huddled together, shivering with fear. The doors and windows were closed fast, and the servants, gray with terror, were cowering in alarm down in the kitchen.

"Lor' have massy 'pon us! who ever seed sich lightnin'? 'Pears as though all de worl' was 'luminated, and de las' day come!" said Jupiter, his teeth chattering with terror.

"An' Miss Roarer, she's out in all de storm, an' ole mas'r don't know it," said Totty. "She *would* go, spite of all Missus Scour said. I 'clare to man, that dat ar rampin', tarryfyin' little limb's 'nuff to drive one clar 'stracted. I ain't no peace night nor day 'long o' her capers. Dar!"

"Won't we cotch it when mas'r finds out she's gone," said a cunning-looking, curly-headed little darkey, whom Gipsy had nicknamed Bob-o-link, with something like a chuckle,; "good Lor! jes' see ole mas'r a swearin' an' tearin' round', an' kickin' de dogs an' niggers, an' smashin' de res' ob de furnitur'. Oh, Lor!" And evidently overcome by the ludicrous scene which fancy had conjured up, Bob-o-link threw himself back, and went off into a perfect convulsion of laughter, to the horror of the rest.

While this discussion was going on below stairs, a far different scene was enacting above.

At the first burst of the storm, Lizzie and Mrs. Gower hastened in affright to the parlor, where the squire was peacefully snoring in his arm-chair, and Louis was still finishing his sketch.

The noise and bustle of their entrance aroused the squire from his slumbers, and after sundry short snorts

he woke up, and seeing the state of affairs, his first inquiry was for Gipsy.

"Where's that little abomination, now?" he abruptly
demanded, in a tone that denoted his temper was not im-
proved by the sudden breaking up of his nap.

All were silent. Mrs. Gower through fear, and the
others through ignorance.

"Where is she? where is she, I say?" thundered the
squire. "Doesn't somebody know?"

"Most likely up stairs somewhere," said Louis. "Shall
I go and see?"

"No, you sha'n't 'go and see.' It's the duty of the
women there to look after her, but they don't do it. She
might be lost, or murdered, or killed, fifty times a day,
for all they care. 'Who trusteth in the ungodly shall
be deceived,' as Solomon says. Ring that bell."

Louis obeyed ; and in a few minutes Totty, quaking
with terror, made her appearance.

"Where's your young mistress? Where's Miss
Gipsy, eh?" demanded the squire, in an awful voice.

"Deed, mas'r, she's rode off. I couldn't stop her
nohow, 'deed——"

"Rode off!" shouted the squire, as, forgetful of his
gouty leg, he sprang to his feet ; "rode off in this storm ?
Villains! wretches! demons! I'll murder every one of
you! Out in this storm! Good Lord! Clear out,
every living soul of you, and if one of you return without her, I'll—I'll blow his brains out!" roared the old
man, purple with rage.

"Why, grandfather," said Louis, while the rest
cowered with fear, "it is not likely Gipsy is out exposed
to the storm. There are many places of shelter well-
known to her among the hills, and there she will stay
until this hurricane is over. It would be impossible for

any one to find her now, even though they could ride through this storm."

"Silence!" thundered the squire; "they must find her! Here, Jupe, Jake, Bob, and the rest of you, mount, and off in search of Miss Aurora over the hills, and at the peril of your life, return without her. Be off! go! vanish! and mind ye, be sure to bring her home."

"Law! mas'r, Miss Roarer ain't over de hills. She's gone over to Deep Dale," said Totty.

"WHAT!" exclaimed the squire, pausing in his rage, aghast, thunder-struck at the news.

"'Deed, Lord knows, mas'r, I couldn't stop her."

"You—you—you—diabolical imp you!" roared the old man, seizing his crutch, and hurling it at her head, as Totty, in mortal alarm, dodged and fled from the room. "Oh, the little demon! the little wretch! won't I pay her for this, when I get hold of her! the—the disobedient, ungrateful, undutiful hussy! I'll cane her within an inch of her life! I'll lock her up on bread and water! I'll keep her in the house day and night! I'll— oh, Lord, my leg," he exclaimed, with a groan, as he fell back, powerless, between rage and despair, in his seat.

Mrs. Gower and Lizzie, still quaking with terror, drew farther into the corner to escape his notice, while Louis bent still lower over his drawing to hide a smile that was breaking over his face.

At this moment a fresh burst of rain and wind shook the doors and windows of the old house, and with it the squire's rage broke out afresh.

"Call Jupe! Be off, Louis, and tell him to ride over to Deep Dale this instant, and bring that little fiend home! And tell him if he doesn't return with her in less than half an hour, I'll break every bone in his body! Go!"

Louis accordingly repaired to the kitchen and delivered the order to poor Jupiter—who, bemoaning his hard fate in being obliged to serve so whimsical a master, was forced to set out in the storm in search of the oapricious Gipsy.

Half an hour, three-quarters passed, and then Jupiter, soaking with rain, and reeking with sweat, came galloping back ; but like young Lochinvar, immortalized in the song :

"He rode unattended and rode all alone,"

and gray, and shaking, and trembling with fear and expectation of the "wrath which was to come," he presented himself before his master.

"Well, sir, where's Miss Gipsy?" shouted the old man, as he entered.

"Mas'r, I couldn't bring her, to save my precious life ; she wouldn't come, nohow. I tell her you wanted her in a desprit hurry ; and she said, s'posin' you waited till your hurry was over. I said you tole me not to come home 'thout her ; and she said, very well, I might stay all night, if I liked, 'cause she warn't comin' home till to-morrer. I tole her you was t'arin' mad ; and she said, you'd better have patience, and smoke your pipe. I couldn't do nothin' 'tall with her, so I left, an' come back, an' dat's all." And without waiting for the burst of wrath which he saw coming, Jupiter beat a precipitate retreat to the lower regions.

You should have seen the wrath of Squire Erliston then. How he stamped, and raged, and swore, and threatened, until he nearly frightened Lizzie into hysterics, used as she was to his fits of passion. And then, at last, when utterly exhausted, he ordered the servants to go and prepare a large, empty room, which had long been unused, as a prison for Gipsy, upon her return.

Everything was taken out of it, and here the squire vowed she should remain until she had learned to obey him for the future. Then, relapsing into sulky silence, he sat down, "nursing his wrath to keep it warm," until the return of the little delinquent.

CHAPTER X.

MISS HAGAR.

" Let me gaze for a moment, that ere I die,
  I may read thee, lady, a prophecy :
  That brow may beam in glory awhile,
  That cheek may bloom, and that lip may smile ;
  But clouds shall darken that brow of snow,
  And sorrows blight tha' bosom's glow."
                    —L. DAVISON.

EANTIME, while the squire was throwing the household of Sunset Hall into terror and consternation, the object of his wrath was enjoying herself with audacious coolness at Deep Dale.

The family of Doctor Nicholas Wiseman consisted of one daughter, a year or two older than Gipsy, a nephew called Archie Rivers, and a maiden step-sister, Miss Hagar Dedley. The doctor, who was naturally grasping and avaricious, would not have burdened himself with the care of those two had it been anything out of his own pocket. The parents of Archie Rivers had been tolerably wealthy, and at their death had left him quite a fortune, and amply remunerated the doctor for taking charge of him until he should be of age. Miss Hagar had a slender income, sufficient for her wants, and was permitted a room in his house as long as she should continue to take care of herself.

Deep Dale had once been the residence of a wealthy and aristocratic family, but had by some unknown means passed from their hands to those of Doctor Wiseman.

It was, as its name implied, a long, deep, sloping dale, with the forest of St. Mark's towering darkly behind, and a wide, grassy lawn sloping down from the front. The house itself was a long, low, irregular mansion of gray sandstone, with a quaint, pleasant, old-fashioned look.

Evening was now approaching. The curtains were drawn, the lamps lighted, and the family assembled in the plainly, almost scantily, furnished sitting-room.

By the fire, in a large leathern arm-chair, sat our old acquaintance, the doctor, with one long, lean leg crossed over the other, one eye closed, and the other fixed so intently on the floor that he seemed to be counting the threads in the carpet. Years have done anything but add to his charms, his face never looked so much like yellow parchment as it did then, his arms and legs were longer and skinnier-looking than ever, and altogether, a more unprepossessing face could hardly have been discovered.

By the table, knitting, sat Miss Hagar. Her tall, thin figure, and grave, solemn face, made her look almost majestic, as, with her lips firmly compressed, she knit away in grim silence. Unlike other spinsters, she neither petted dogs nor cats, but had a most unaccountable mania for fortune-telling, and had been, for years, the seeress and sibyl of the whole neighborhood.

In a distant corner of the room sat the little *protegee* of Miss Hagar, with Gipsy on one side of her, and Archie Rivers on the other, regarding her as though she were some sort of natural curiosity. And, truly, a more lovely child could scarcely have been found.

She appeared to be about the same age as Gipsy, but was taller and more graceful, with a beautifully rounded figure, not plump, like that of most children, but slender and elegant, and lithe as a willow wand. A small, fair, sweet face, with long, golden hair, and soft, dreamy eyes of blue, and a smile like an angel's.

Such was Celeste!

Such a contrast as she was to Gipsy, as she sat with her little white hands folded in her lap, the long golden lashes falling shyly over the blue eyes ; her low, sweet voice and timid manner, so still and gentle ; and her elfish companion, with her dark, bright face, her eager, sparkling, restless eyes, her short, sable locks, and her every motion so quick and startling, as to make one nervous watching her.

Archie Rivers, a merry, good-looking lad, with roguish blue eyes and a laughing face, sat, alternately watching the fair, downcast face of Celeste, and the piquant, gipsyish countenance of the other.

At the table sat Minnette Wiseman, a proud, superb-looking girl of twelve. Her long, jet-black hair fell in glossy braids over her shoulders ; her elbows rested on the table ; her chin supported by her hands ; her large, glittering black eyes fixed on Celeste, with a look of fixed dislike and jealousy that was never to die out during life.

"And so you have no other name but Celeste," said Gipsy, trying to peer under the drooping lashes resting on the blue-veined cheek. "Now, if that isn't funny ! Everybody has two names but you—even *me.* I have two names."

"Yes, Gipsy Gower. There is something odd and elfinish in the very name," said Archie, laughing.

"Elfinish? It's no such thing. It's a great deal prettier than yours, Archie Rivers ! And where did you live before you came here, Celeste?" continued Gipsy, returning to the charge.

"With Aunt Katie," replied Celeste, softly.

"And where is she now?" went on Gipsy.

"Dead!" said the child, while her lip trembled, and a tear fell on the little brown hand lying on her own.

"Do tell! and I've made you cry, too. Now, if that ain't too bad. Do you know, Celeste, I never cried in my life?"

"Oh, what a fib!" exclaimed Archie. "You were the horridest young one to cry ever I heard in my life. You did nothing but yell and roar from morning till night."

"I don't believe it! I don't believe it!" inignantly exclaimed Gipsy. "I'm sure I was too sensible a baby to do anything of the kind. Anyway, I have never cried since I can remember. And as to fear—were you ever afraid?" she asked, suddenly, of Celeste.

"Oh, yes—often."

Did you ever? Why, you look afraid now. Are you?"

"Yes."

"My! What of?"

"Of *you*," said Celeste, shrinking back, shyly, from her impetuous little questioner.

"Oh, my stars and garters! Afraid of *me*, and after I've been so quiet and good with her all the evening!" ejaculated Gipsy; while Archie, who was blessed with a lively sense of the ridiculous, leaned back and laughed heartily.

"Well, after that I'm never going to believe there's anything but ingratitude in *this* world," said Gipsy, with an emphasis on the "*this*" which seemed to denote she *had* met with gratitude in another.

But tears filled the gentle eyes of Celeste, as she looked up, and said :

"Oh, I hope you're not angry with me. I didn't mean to offend you, I'm sure. I'm *so* sorry."

"Oh, it's no matter. Nobody minds what they say to me. I'm used to it. But it's so funny you should be afraid. Why, I never was afraid in my life."

"That's true enough, anyway," said Archie, with an assenting nod.

"There's Guardy now. Oh! won't he be awful when I get home—but laws! who cares! I'll pay him off for it, if he makes a fuss. I sha'n't be in his debt long, that's one comfort."

"Do you remember how dolefully Jupiter looked as he came in for you, all dripping wet; and when you told him you wouldn't go, he——" and overcome by the ludicrous recollection, Master Archie again fell back in a paroxysm of laughter.

"What a fellow you are to laugh, Archie!" remarked Gipsy. "You astonish me, I declare. Do you laugh much, Celeste?"

"No, not much."

"That's right—I don't laugh much either—I'm too dignified, you know ; but somehow I make other people laugh. There's Archie now, for everlasting laughing ; but Minnette—do you know I never saw her laugh yet— that is, really laugh. She smiles sometimes ; not a pleasant smile either, but a scornful smile like. I say, Minnette," she added, raising her voice, "what is the reason you never laugh?'

"None of your business," rudely replied Minnette.

"The Lord never intended her face for a smiling one," said Miss Hagar, breaking in, suddenly. "And you, you poor little wild eaglet, who, a moment ago, boasted you had never wept, you shall yet shed tears of blood. The bird has its eyes put out with red-hot iron before it can be made to sing sweetly ; and so you, too, poor bird, must be blinded, even though you should flutter and beat yourself to death, trying to break through the bars of your cage."

"Humph ! I'd like to see them trying to put my eyes out," said Gipsy. "I guess I'd make them sing, and on the wrong side of their mouths, too—at least, I think I should !"

"Oh, Miss Hagar, tell us our fortunes—you haven't done so this long time," exclaimed Archie, jumping up. "Here is Gipsy wants to know hers, and Celeste's, too ; and as for me, I know the future must have something splendid in store for so clever a fellow, and I'm anxious to know it beforehand."

"Don't be too anxious," said Miss Hagar, fixing her gloomy eyes prophetically on his eager, happy face ; "troubles are soon enough when they come, without wishing to forestall them."

"Why, Miss Hagar, you don't mean to say I'm to have troubles?" cried Archie, laughing. "If they do come, I'll laugh in their face, and cry, 'Never surrender.' I don't believe, though, my troubles will be very heavy."

"Yes, the heaviest troubles that man can ever know shall be thine," said the oracle, in her deep, gloomy voice. "The day will come when despair, instead of laughter, will fill your beaming eyes ; when the smile shall have left your lip, and the hue of health will give place to the dusky glow of the grave. Yes, the day will come when the wrong you may not quell shall cling to you like a garment of flame, crushing and overwhelming you and all you love, in its fiery, burning shame. The day will come when one for whom you would give your life shall desert you for your deadliest enemy, and leave

you to despair and woe.   Such is the fate I have read in
the stars for you."

"La ! Archie, what a nice time you're going to have,"
said the incorrigible Gipsy, breaking the impressive
silence that followed the sibyl's words—" when all that
comes to pass !   It will be as good as a play to you."

"Miss Hagar must have sat up all last night getting
that pretty speech by heart," said Minnette, fixing her
mocking black eyes on the face of the spinster.   " How
well she repeated it !   She'd make her fortune on the
stage as a tragedy queen."

"Scoffer !" said the sibyl, turning her prophetic eyes
on the deriding face of the speaker, while her face darkened, and her stern mouth grew sterner still.   "One day
that iron heart of thine shall melt ; that heart, which, as
yet, is sealed with granite, shall feel every fiber drawn
out by the roots, to be cast at your feet quivering and
bleeding, unvalued and uncared for.   Come hither, and
let me read your future in your eyes."

"No, no !" said Minnette, shaking back, scornfully,
her glossy black hair.   " Prate your old prophecies to
the fools who believe you.   I'll not be among the number."

"Unbeliever, I heed it not !" said Miss Hagar as she
rose slowly to her feet ; and the light of inspiration
gathered in her eyes of gray, as, swaying to and fro, she
chanted, in a wild, dirge-like tone :

> "Beware ! beware ! for the time will come—
> A blighted heart, a ruined home.
> In the dim future I foresee
> A fate far worse than death for thee."

Her eyes were still riveted on the deriding face and
bold, bright eyes, that, in spite of all their boldness,
quailed before her steady gaze.

5

"Good-gracious, Miss Hagar, if you haven't nearly frightened this little atomy into fits!" said Gipsy. "I declare, of all the little cowards ever was, she's the greatest! Now, if I thought it wouldn't scare the life out of her, I'd have my fortune told. If everybody else is going to have such pretty things happen to them, I don't see why I shouldn't, too."

"Come here, then, and let me read thy fate," said Miss Hagar. "The spirit is upon me to-night, and it may never come more."

"All right. Archie, stop grinning and 'tend this little scary thing. Now, go ahead, Miss Hagar."

The seeress looked down solemnly into the dark, piquant little face upturned so gravely to her own; into the wicked brown eyes, twinkling and glittering with such insufferable mischief and mirth; and, bending her tall body down, she again chanted, in her dreary tone:

> "Thou wast doomed from thy birth, oh, ill-fated child;
> Like thy birthnight, thy life shall be stormy and wild;
> There is blood on thine hand, there is death in thine eye,
> And the one who best loves thee, *by thee shall he die!*"

"Whew! if that ain't pleasant! I always knew I'd be the death of somebody!" exclaimed Gipsy. "Wonder who it is going to be? Shouldn't be s'prised if 'twas Jupiter. I've been threatening to send him to Jericho ever since I can remember. La! if it comes true, won't Minette, and Archie and I be in a ' state of mind' one of these days! I say, Celeste, come over here, and let's have a little more of the horrible. I begin to like it."

"Yes, go, Celeste, go," said Archie, lifting her off her seat.

But Celeste, with a stifled cry of terror, covered her face with her hands, and shrank back.

"Coward !" exclaimed Minnette, with a scornful flash of her black eyes.

"Little goose !" said Gipsy, rather contemptuously ; "what are you afraid of ? Go ! it won't hurt you."

"Oh, no, no !—no, no !—no, no !" cried the child, crouching farther back in terror. "It's too dreadful. I can't listen to such awful things."

"Let her stay," said Miss Hagar, seating herself moodily. "Time enough for her—poor, trembling dove ! —to know the future when its storm-clouds gather darkly over her head. Let her alone. One day you may all think of my words to-night."

"There ! there ! don't make a fool of yourself any longer, Hagar," impatiently broke in the doctor. " Leave the little simpletons in peace, and don't bother their brains with such stuff."

"Stuff !" repeated Miss Hagar, her eyes kindling with indignation. "Take care ; lest I tell *you* a fate more awful still. I speak as I am inspired ; and no mortal man shall hinder me."

"Well, croak away," said her brother, angrily, "but never again in my presence. I never knew such an old fool !" he muttered to himself in a lower tone.

He started back almost in terror, as he ceased ; for standing by his side, with her eyes fairly blazing upon him with a wild, intense gaze, was the elfish Gipsy. She looked so like some golden sprite—so small and dark, with such an insufferable light in her burning eyes— that he actually shrank in superstitious terror from her.

Without a word, she glided away, and joined Archie in the corner, who was doing his best to cheer and amuse the timid Celeste.

During the rest of the evening, Gipsy was unusually silent and still ; and her little face would at times wear a puzzled, thoughtful look, all unused to it.

"What in the world's got into you, Gipsy?" asked Archie, at length, in surprise. "What are you looking so solemn about?"

"Archie," she said, looking up solemnly in his face, "am I *possessed?*"

"Possessed! Why, yes, I should say you were—possessed by the very spirit of mischief!"

"Oh, Archie, it's not that. Don't you know it tells in the Bible about people being possessed with demons? Now, Archie, do you think I am?"

"What a question! No; of course not, you little goose. Why?"

"Because when *he*," pointing to the doctor, "said what he did, I just felt as if something within me was forcing me to catch him by the throat and kill him. And, Archie, I could hardly keep from doing it; and I do believe I'm possessed."

This answer seemed to Master Archie so comical that he went off into another roar of laughter; and in the midst of it, he rolled off his seat upon the floor—which event added to his paroxysm of delight.

The doctor growled out certain anathemas at this ill-timed mirth, and ordered Master Rivers off to bed. Then Miss Hagar folded up her work, and taking Celeste with her, sought her own room, where a little trundle-bed had been prepared for the child. And Minnette—who, much against her will, was to share her room with Gipsy, for whom she had no particular love—got up and lit the night-lamp, and, followed, by the willful fay, betook herself to rest.

The next morning dawned clear, sunshiny and bright. Immediately after breakfast, Gipsy mounted Mignonne, and set out to encounter the storm which she knew awaited her at Sunset Hall.

CHAPTER XI.

GIPSY OUTWITS THE SQUIRE.

"Then on his cheek the flush of rage
O'ercame the ashen hue of age ;
Fierce he broke forth ; ' And dar'st thou, then,
To beard the lion in his den,
The Douglas in his hall ?' "—MARMION.

GIPSY rode along, singing gayly, and thinking, with an inward chuckle, of the towering rage which " Guardy" must be in. As she entered the yard she encountered Jupiter, who looked upon her with eyes full of fear and warning.

" Hallo, Jupe ! I see you haven't ' shuffled off this mortal coil' yet, as Louis says. I suppose you got a blowing up last night, for coming home without me, eh ?"

" Miss Roarer, honey, for mussy sake, don't 'front mas'r to-day," exclaimed Jupiter, with upraised hands and eyes ; " dar's no tellin' what he might do, chile. I 'vises you to go to bed an' say you's sick, or somefin, caze he'd jes' as lief kill you as not, he's so t'arin' mad."

" Nonsense, you old simpleton ! Do you think I'd tell such a lie ? Let him rage ; I'll rage too, and keep him in countenance."

" Miss Roarer, if you does, dar'll be bloodshed, and den I'll be took up for all—I knows dar will," said poor Jupiter, in a whimpering tone. " Dis comes' o' livin' with ladies what ain't ladies, and old gen'lemen what's got de old boy's temper in dem."

" Why, you old good-for-nothing, do you mean to say I'm not a lady !" exclaimed Gipsy, indignantly.

"Jes' so, Miss Roarer, I don't care ef yer does whip me—dar ! S'pose a lady, a *real* lady, would go for to shoot a poor nigger what ain't a doing no harm to nobody, or go ridin' out all hours ob de night as *you* do. No ! stands to reason, dey wouldn't, an' dat's de trufe now, ef I *is* a good-for-nothin'.   Dar !"

"You aggravating old Jupiter, you, I'll *dar* you if you give me any more of your impudence," said Gipsy, flourishing her whip over her head.

"Miss Roarer," began Jupiter, adroitly ducking his head to avoid a blow.

"Silence, sir !   Don't 'Miss Roarer' me.   Keep your advice till it's called for, and take Mignonne off to the stables, an' rub him down well ; and if you leave one speck of dust on him, I'll leave you to guess what I'll do to you."   And so saying, Gipsy gathered up her riding-habit in her hand, and ran up the broad step, singing at the top of her voice :

"Oh ! whistle and I'll come to you, my lad,
Oh ! whistle and I'll come to you, my lad ;
Though Guardy and aunty, an' a' should go mad,
Just whistle an' I'll come to you, my lad."

"Gipsy, Gipsy, hush, child !   Your guardian is dreadfully angry with you, and will punish you very severely, I'm afraid," said Mrs. Gower, suddenly appearing from the dining-room.   "This reckless levity will make matters worse if he hears you.   Oh, Gipsy, how could you do such an outrageous thing ?"

"La, aunty ! I haven't done any 'outrageous thing' that I know of."

"Oh, child ! you know it was very wrong, *very* wrong, of you, indeed, to stay at Deep Dale all night against his express commands."

"Now, aunty, I don't see anything very wrong at all about it. I only wanted to have a little fun."

"Fun! Oh! you provoking little goose! he'll punish you very severely, I'm certain."

"Well, let him, then. I don't care. I'll pay him off for it some time—see if I don't. What do you s'pose he'll do to me, aunty? Have me tried by court-martial, or hold a coroner's inquest on top of me, or what?"

"He is going to lock you up in that old lumber-room, up in the attic, and keep you there on bread and water, he says."

"Well, now, I'll leave it to everybody, if that isn't barbarous. It's just the way the stony-hearted fathers in the story-books do to their daughters, when they fall in love, and then their beaus come, filled with love and rope-ladders, and off they go through the window. I say, aunty, is there any chance for me to get through the window?"

"No, indeed, they are fastened outside with wooden shutters and iron bolts. There is no chance of escape, so you had best be very good and penitent, and beg his pardon, and perhaps he may forgive you."

"Beg his pardon! Ha! ha! ha! aunty, I like that, wouldn't Archie laugh if he heard it. Just fancy *me*, Gipsy Gower, down on my knees before him, whimpering and snuffling, and a tear in each eye, like a small potato, and begging his serene highness to forgive me, and I'll never do it again. Oh! goodness gracious, just fancy what a scene it would be!"

"You provoking little minx! I am sure any other little girl would beg her guardian's pardon, when she knew she did wrong."

"But I *don't* know that I've did wrong. On the contrary, I know I've did *right;* and I'm going to do it over again, the first chance—there!"

"Oh, Gipsy!—child—you are perfectly incorrigible. I despair of ever being able to do anything with you. As I told you before, I shouldn't be surprised if your guardian turned you out of doors for your conduct."

"And as I told *you* before, aunty, I would not want better fun. Archie Rivers is going to West Point soon, and I'll go with him, and 'do my country some service' in the next war."

"If he turned you out, Gipsy, it would break my heart," said Mrs. Gower, plaintively.

"Yes, and I suppose it would break mine too, but I luckily don't happen to have a heart," said Gipsy, who never by any chance could, as she called it, "do the sentimental." "However, aunty, let's live in the sublime hope that you'll break the necks of two or three hundred chickens and geese, before you break your own heart yet. And I protest, here comes Guardy, stamping and fuming up the lawn. Clear out, aunty, for I expect he'll hurl the whole of the Proverbs of Solomon at my head, and one of 'em might chance to hit you. Go, aunty, I want to fight my own battles; and if I don't come off with drums beating and colors flying, it'll be a caution ! Hooray !"

And Gipsy waved her plumed hat above her head, and whirled round the room in a defiant waltz.

She was suddenly interrupted by the entrance of the squire, who, thrusting both hands into his coat pockets, stood flaming with rage before her; whereupon Gipsy, plunging her hands into the pockets of her riding-habit, planted both feet firmly on the ground, and confronted him with a dignified frown, and an awful expression of countenance generally, and to his amazement, burst out with :

"You unprincipled, abandoned, benighted, befuddled old gentleman ! how dare you have the impudence, the effrontery, the brazenness, the impertinence, the—the—everything-else! to show your face to me after your outrageous, your unheard-of, your monstrous, your—yes, I will say it—diabolical conduct yesterday! Yes, sir! I repeat it, sir—I'm amazed at your effrontery, after sending a poor, unfortunate, friendless, degenerate son of Africa through the tremendous rain, the roaring lightning, the flashing thunder, the silent winds, in search of me, to stand there, looking no more ashamed of yourself than if you weren't a fair blot on the foul face of creation! Answer me, old gentleman, and forever afterward hold thy peace!"

"You abominable little wretch! You incarnate little fiend, you! You impish little imp, you! I'll thrash you within an inch of your life!" roared the old man, purple with rage.

"Look out, Guardy, you'll completely founder the English language, if you don't take care," interrupted Gipsy.

"You impudent little vixen! I'll make you repent yesterday's conduct," thundered the squire, catching her by the shoulder and shaking her till she was breathless.

"Loo—loo—look here, old gentleman, do—do—don't you try that again!" stuttered Gipsy, panting for breath, and wrenching herself, by a powerful jerk, free from his grasp.

"Why didn't you come home when I sent for you? Answer me that, or I won't leave a sound bone in your body. Now, then!"

"Well, Guardy, to tell the truth, it was because I didn't choose to. Now, then!"

"You—you—you incomparable little impudence, I'll fairly murder you!" shouted the squire, raising his hand in his rage to strike her a blow, which would assuredly

5*

have killed her; but Gipsy adroitly dodged, and his hand fell with stunning force on the hall table.

With something between a howl and a yell, he started after her as she ran screaming with laughter; and seizing her in a corner, where she had sunk down exhausted and powerless with her inward convulsions, he shook her until he could shake her no longer.

"I'll lock you up! I'll turn you out of doors! I'll thrash you while I am able to stand over you! No, I won't thrash a woman in my own house, but I'll lock you up and starve you to death. I'll be hanged if I don't!"

"You'll be hanged if you do, you mean."

"Come along; we'll see what effect hunger and solitary confinement will have on your high spirits, my lady," said the squire, seizing her by the arm and dragging her along.

"Guardy, if you do, my ghost 'll haunt you every night, just as sure as shooting," said Gipsy, solemnly.

"What do I care about you or your ghost! Come along. 'The unrighteous shall not live out half their days,' as Solomon says; therefore it's according to Scripture, and no fault of mine if you don't live long."

"Solomon was never locked up in a garret," said Gipsy, thrusting her knuckles in her eyes and beginning to sob, "and he don't know anything about it. It's real hateful of you to lock me up—now! But it's just like you, you always were an ugly old wretch every way." Sob, sob, sob.

"That's right, talk away! You can talk and scold as much as you like to the four bare walls presently," said the squire, dragging her along.

"You're a hateful old monster! I wish you were far enough—I just do! and I don't care if I'm taken up for defamation of character—so, there! Boo, hoo—a hoo—

a hoo," sobbed, and wept, and scolded Gipsy, as the squire, inwardly chuckling, led her to her place of captivity.

They reached it at length ; a large empty room without a single article of furniture, even without a chair. It was quite dark, too, for the windows were both nailed up, and the room was situated in the remotest portion of the building, where, let poor Gipsy cry and scream as she pleased, she could not be heard.

On entering her prison, Gipsy ceased her sobs for a moment to glance around, and her blank look of dismay at the aspect of her prison, threw the squire into a fit of laughter.

"So," he chuckled, "you're caught at last. Now, here you may stay till night, and I hope by that time I'll have taken a little of the mischief out of you."

"And I'll have nothing to pass the time," wept Gipsy. "Mayn't I go down stairs and get a book ?"

"Ha ! ha ! ha ! No. I rather think you mayn't. Perhaps I may bring you up one by and by," said the squire, never stopping to think how Gipsy was to read in the dark.

"Look up there on that shelf, I can't reach ; there's one, I think," said Gipsy, whose keen eye had caught sight of an old newspaper lying on the spot indicated.

The squire made a step forward to reach it, and like an arrow sped from a bow, at the same instant, Gipsy darted across the room, out through the open door. Ere the squire could turn round, he heard the door slam to, and he was caught in his own trap, while a triumphant shout, a delighted "hurrah !" reached his ear from without.

The squire rushed frantically to the door, and shook, and pulled, and swore, and threatened and shouted, to all of which Gipsy answered by tantalizingly asking him whether he'd come out now, or wait till she let him. Then, finding threats of no avail, he betook himself to coaxing ; and wheedled, and persuaded, and promised, and flattered, but equally in vain, for Gipsy replied that she wouldn't if she could, couldn't if she would, for that she had thrown the key as far as she could pitch it, out of the window, among the shrubs in the garden—where, as she wasn't in the habit of looking for needles in haystacks, she thought it quite useless searching for it ; and ended by delivering him a lecture on the virtue of patience and the beauty of Christian resignation   And after exhorting him to improve his temper, if possible, during his confinement, as she was going over to spend the day at Dr. Spider's and teach Miss Hagar's little girl to ride, she went off and left him, stamping, and swearing, and foaming, in a manner quite awful to listen to.

True to her word, Gipsy privately sought the stables, saddled Mignonne herself, and rode off, without being observed, to spend the day at Deep Dale.   The absence of the squire was noticed ; but it was supposed he had ridden off on business after locking up Gipsy, and therefore it created no surprise.   As he had positively forbidden any one in the house to go near her prison, no one went ; and it was only when Gipsy returned home late at night that she learned, to her surprise and alarm, he had not yet been liberated.   The door was forced open by Jupiter, and the squire was found lying on the floor, having raged himself into a state that quite prevented him from "murdering" Gipsy as he had threatened.   Two or three days elapsed before " Richard " became "himself again ;" and night and day Gipsy hovered over his bedside—the quietest, the most attentive little nurse that ever was seen, quite unalarmed by his throwing the pillow, the gruel and pill-boxes at her head every time she appeared in his sight.

CHAPTER XII.

. THE TIGRESS AND THE DOVE.

" Oh, wanton malice—deathful sport—
Could ye not spare my all?
But mark my words, on thy cold heart
A fiery doom shall fall."

N the golden glow of the morning, Minnette Wiseman stood at the door, gazing out—not watching the radiant beauties of nature—not listening to the sweet singing of the birds—not watching the waves flashing and glittering in the sunlight—but nursing her own dark, fathomless thoughts.

From the first moment of the coming of Celeste she had hated her, with a deep, intense hatred, that was destined to be the one ruling passion of her life. She was jealous of her beauty, angry to see her so petted and caressed by every one, but too proud to betray it.

Pride and jealousy were her predominant passions; you could see them in the haughty poise of her superb little head, in the dusky fire smoldering in her glittering black eyes, in the scornful, curling upper lip, in the erect carriage and proud step. In spite of her beauty no one seemed to like Minnette, and she liked no one.

Among her schoolmates her superior talents won their admiration, but her eagle ambition to surpass them all soon turned admiration into dislike. But Minnette went haughtily on her way, living in the unknown world of her dark, sullen thoughts, despising both them and the love she might have won.

A week had passed since the coming of Celeste.

Miss Hagar, feeling she was not competent to undertake the instruction of such a shy, sensitive little creature, wished to send her to school. The school to which Minnette and Gipsy went (sometimes) was two miles distant, and taught by the Sisters of Charity. Miss Hagar would have sent her there, but there was no one she could go with. She mentioned this difficulty to her brother.

"Can't she go with Minnette?" said the latter, impatiently.

"No, she sha'n't," said the amiable Minnette. "I'll have no such whimpering cry-baby tagging after me. Let Madam Hagar go with her darling herself if she likes."

"Just what I expected from you," said Miss Hagar, looking gloomingly in the sullen face before her. "If the Lord doesn't punish you one day for your hatred and hard-heartedness, it'll be because some of his creatures will do it for him. Take my word for it."

"I don't care for you or your threats," said Minnette, angrily ; "and I *do* hate your pet, old Miss Hagar, and I'll make everybody else hate her if I can, too."

"Minnette, hold your tongue," called her father, angry at being interrupted in his reading.

Minnette left the room, first casting a glance full of dislike and contempt on Celeste, who sat in a remote corner, her hands over her face, while the tears she struggled bravely to suppress fell in bright drops through her taper fingers. Sob after sob swelled the bosom of the sensitive child, on whose gentle heart the cruel words of Minnette had fallen with crushing weight. Dr. Wiseman, after a few moments, too, left the room, and Celeste, in her dark corner, wept unseen and uncared for.

Suddenly a light footstep entering the room startled

her. Her hands were gently removed from her tear-stained face, while a spirited voice exclaimed :

"Hallo! Sissy! what's the matter? Has that kite-heart, Minnette, been mocking you?"

"No-o-o!" faltered Celeste, looking up through her tears into the bright face of Archie Rivers.

"What's the case, then? Something's wrong, I know. Tell me, like a good little girl, and I'll see if I can't help you," said Archie, resolutely retaining the hands with which she struggled to cover her face.

"Miss Hagar wants to send me to school, and I've no one to go with. Minnette doesn't like to be troubled with——"

"Oh, I see it all! Minnette's been showing her angelic temper, and won't let you go with her, eh?"

"Ye-e-es," sobbed Celeste, trying bravely not to cry.

"Well, never mind, birdie! I have to pass the Sisters' school every day on my way to the academy, and I'll take care of you, if you'll go with me. Will you?" he said, looking doubtfully into her little, shrinking face.

"I—I think so," said Celeste, rather hesitatingly. "I will be a trouble, though, I'm afraid."

"Not you!" exclaimed Archie, gayly. "I'll be your true knight and champion now, and by and by you'll be my little wife. Won't you?"

"No-o-o, I don't like to," said Celeste, timidly.

Archie seemed to think this answer so remarkably funny that he gave way to a perfect shout of laughter. Then, perceiving the sensitive little creature on the verge of crying again, he stopped short by an effort, and said, apologetically :

"There! don't cry, sis : I wasn't laughing at you. I say, Miss Hagar," he added, springing abruptly to his feet as that ancient lady entered, " mayn't I bring Celeste to school? I'll 'tend to her as carefully as if she was my daughter. See if I don't."

A grim sort of smile relaxed the rigid muscles of Miss Hagar's iron face as she glanced benignly at his merry, thoughtless face over the top of her spectacles.

"Yes, she may go with you, and the Lord will bless you for your good, kind heart," she said, laying her hand fondly on his curly head.

Archie, throwing up his cap in the exuberance of his glee, said :

"Run and get ready, sis, and come along."

"No; wait until to-morrow," said Miss Hagar. "She cannot go to-day."

"All right; to-morrow, then, you've to make your *debut* in the school of St. Mark's. I say, Miss Hagar, what shall we call her? not your name—Dedley's too dismal."

"No ; call her Pearl—she *is* a pearl," said Miss Hagar, while her voice became as gentle as *such* a voice could.

"Very well, Celeste. Pearl then be it. And so, Celeste, be ready bright and early to-morrow morning, and we'll go by Sunset Hall, and call for Gipsy and Louis. By the way, you haven't seen Louis yet, have you ?"

"No," said Celeste.

"Oh, then, you must see him, decidedly, to-morrow. But mind, you mustn't go and like him better than you do me, because he's better-looking. I tell you what, little sis, he's a capital fellow, and *so* clever ; he's ahead of every fellow in the academy, and beats *me* all to smash. because I'm not clever at anything except riding and shooting, and I'm his equal in those branches. So now I'm off—good-bye !"

And with a spring and a jump, Archie was out of the room and dashing along the road at a tremendous rate.

The next morning Celeste, with a beating heart, set out with Archie for school. How pretty she looked in her white muslin dress, her white sunbonnet covering her golden curls—a perfect little pearl !

Archie, having paid her a shower of compliments, took her by the hand and set out with her for Sunset Hall. At the gate Celeste halted, and no persuasions could induce her to enter.

"No, no ; I'll wait here until you come back. Please let me," she said, pleadingly.

"Oh, well, then, I won't be long," said Archie, rushing frantically up the lawn and bursting like a whirlwind into the hall door.

In a few moments he reappeared, accompanied by Louis.

"Look, old fellow ! there she is at the gate. Isn't she a beauty ?" said Archie.

Louis stopped and gazed, transfixed by the radiant vision before him. In her floating, snowy robes, golden hair, her sweet, angel-like face, on which the morning sunshine rested like a glory, she was indeed lovely, bewildering, dazzling.

"How beautiful ! how radiant ! how splendid ! Archie, she is as pretty as an angel !" burst forth Louis, impetuously.

"Ha, ha ha ! a decided case of love at first sight. Come along and I'll introduce you," exclaimed Archie.

Having presented the admiring Louis to Celeste, who, after the first shy glance, never raised her eyes, he informed her that Gipsy had gone out riding early in the morning, and they were forced to go without her.

"Celeste, you must sit to me for your portrait," said Louis, impulsively, as they walked along.

"I don't know," said Celeste, shrinking closer to

Archie, whom she had learned to trust in like an old friend.

"I'm sketching the 'Madonna in the Temple' for Sister Mary, and your sweet, holy, calm face will do exactly for a model," said Louis.

"That's a compliment, sis," said Archie, pinching her cheek; "you'd better sit. Hallo! if that isn't Gipsy's bugle! And here she comes, as usual, flying like the wind. If she doesn't break her neck some day, it will be a wonder."

As he spoke, the clear, sweet notes of a bugle resounded musically among the hills above them; and the next moment the spirited little Arabian, Mignonne, came dashing at a break-neck pace down the rocks, with Gipsy on his back, a fowling-piece slung over her shoulder, and sitting her horse as easily as though she were in an easy-chair. With a wild "tally-ho!" she cleared a yawning chasm at a bound, and reined her horse in so suddenly that he nearly fell back on his haunches. The next instant she was beside them, laughing at Celeste, who clung, pale with fear, to Archie.

"What luck this morning, Diana?" exclaimed Archie.

"Pretty well for two hours. Look!" said Gipsy, displaying a well-filled game-bag.

"Did you kill those birds?" inquired Celeste, lifting her eyes in fear, not unmixed with horror, to the sparkling face of the young huntress.

"To be sure! There! don't look so horror-struck. I declare if the little coward doesn't look as if she thought me a demon," said Gipsy, laughing at Celeste's sorrowful face. "Look! do you see that bird away up there, like a speck in the sky?· Well, now watch me bring it down;" and Gipsy, fixing her eagle eye on the distant speck, took deliberate aim.

"Oh, don't—don't!" cried Celeste, in an agony of terror; but ere the words were well uttered, they were lost in the sharp crack of her little rifle.

Wounded and bleeding, the bird began rapidly to fall, and, with a wild shriek, Celeste threw up her arms, and fell to the ground.

"Good gracious! if I haven't scared the life out of Celeste!" exclaimed Gipsy, in dismay, as Archie raised her, pale and trembling, in his arms.

"What a timid little creature!" thought Louis, as he watched her, clinging convulsively to Archie.

"Oh, the bird! the poor bird!" said Celeste, bursting into tears.

Gipsy laughed outright, and pointing to a tree near at hand, said:

"There, Louis, the bird has lodged in that tree; go and get it for her."

Louis darted off to search the tree, and Gipsy, stooping down, said, rather impatiently:

"Now, Celeste, don't be such a little goose! What harm is it to shoot a bird?—everybody does it."

"I don't think it's right; it's so cruel. Please don't do it any more," said Celeste, pleadingly.

"Can't promise, dear? *I* must do something to keep me out of mischief. But here comes Louis. Well, is it dead?"

"No," said Louis, "but badly wounded. However, I'll take care of it; and if it recovers, Celeste, you shall have it for a pet."

"Oh, thank you! you're *so* good," said Celeste, giving him such a radiant look of gratitude that it quite overcame the gravity of Master Rivers, who fell back, roaring with laughter.

Celeste and Gipsy stood a little apart, conversing, and the boys sat watching them.

"I say, Louis, what do you think of her ?" said Archie, pointing to Celeste.

"I think she is perfectly bewitching—the loveliest creature I ever beheld," replied Louis, regarding her with the eye of an artist. "She reminds me of a lily—a dove, so fair, and white, and gentle."

"And Gipsy, what does *she* remind you of ?"

"Oh ! of a young Amazon, or a queen eaglet of the mountains, so wild and untamed."

"And Minnette, what is she like ?"

"Like a tigress, more than anything else I can think of just now," said Louis, laughing ; "beautiful, but rather dangerous when aroused."

"Aroused ! I don't think she could be aroused, she is made of marble."

"Not she. As Miss Hagar says, the day will come when she will, she must feel ; every one does sometime in his life. What does Scott say :

> " ' Hearts are not flint, and flints are rent ;
> Hearts are not steel, and steel is bent.' "

"Well, if you take to poetry, you'll keep us here all day," said Archie, rising. "Good-bye, Gipsy ; come along Celeste !"

*   *   *   *   *   *   *

True to promise, Louis adopted the wounded bird ; and under his skillful hands it soon recovered and was presented to Celeste. She would have set it free, but Louis said : "No ; keep it for my sake, Celeste." And so Celeste kept it ; and no words can tell how she grew to love that bird. It hung in a cage in her chamber, and her greatest pleasure was in attending it. Minnette hated the very sight of it. That it belonged to Celeste would have been enough to make her hate it ; but added to that, it had been given her by Louis Oranmore, the only living being Minnette had ever tried to please ; and jealousy added tenfold to her hatred.

Seeing the bird hanging, one day, out in the sunshine, she opened the cage-door, and, with the most fiendish and deliberate malice, twisted its neck, and then, going to Celeste, pointed to it with malignant triumph sparkling in her bold, black eyes.

Poor Celeste ! She took the dead and mangled body of her pretty favorite in her lap, and sitting down, wept the bitterest tears she had ever shed in her life. Let no one smile at her childish grief ; who has been without them ? I remember distinctly the saddest tears that ever I shed were over the remains of a beloved kitten, stoned to death. And through all the troubles of after years, that first deep grief never was forgotten.

While she was still sobbing as if her heart would break, a pair of strong arms were thrown around her, and the eager, handsome face of Louis was bending over her.

"Why, Celeste, what in the world are all those tears for ?" he inquired, pushing the disheveled golden hair off her wet cheek.

"Oh, Louis, my bird ! my poor bird !" she cried, hiding her face on his shoulder, in a fresh burst of grief.

"What ! it's dead, is it ?" said Louis, taking it up. "Did the cat get at it ?"

"No, no ; it wasn't the cat ; it was—it was——"

"*Who?*" said Louis, while his dark eyes flashed. "Did any one dare to kill it ? Did Minnette, that young tigress——"

"Oh, Louis ! don't, don't ! You mustn't call her such dreadful names !" said Celeste, placing her hand over his mouth. "I don't think she meant it ; don't be angry with her, please ; it's so dreadful !"

"You little angel!" he said, smoothing gently her fair hair; "no, for your sake I'll not. Never mind, don't cry; I'll get you another, twice as pretty as that!"

"No, Louis; I don't want any more! I'd rather have the dear birds free! And now, will you—will you bury poor birdie?" said Celeste, almost choking in her effort to be "good and not cry."

"Yes; here's a nice spot, under the rose-bush," said Louis; "and I'll get a tombstone and write a nice epitaph. And you must console yourself with the belief that it's happy in the bird's heaven, if there is such a place," added Louis, as he placed poor "Birdie" in its last resting-place.

Half an hour after, Celeste sought the presence of Minnette. She found her sitting by the window, her chin resting on her hand, as was her habit, gazing out. She did not turn round as Celeste entered; but the latter went up softly, and, placing her hand on hers, said gently:

"Minnette, I'm afraid you're angry with me? I'm very sorry; please forgive me?"

Minnette shook her roughly off, exclaiming:

"Don't bother me, you little whining thing! Go out of this!"

"Yes; but only say you forgive me, first! Indeed, indeed, Minnette, I didn't mean to offend you. I want to love you, if you'll let me!"

"Love!" exclaimed Minnette, springing fiercely to her feet, her black eyes gleaming like fire. "You artful little hypocrite! You consummate little cheat? Don't talk to me of love! Didn't I see you in the garden, with your arms around Louis Oranmore, in a way for which you ought to be ashamed of yourself—complaining to him of my wickedness and cruelty in killing the bird he gave you. And yet, after turning him against me, you come here, and tell me you love me! Begone, you miserable little beggar! I hate the very sight of you!"

Her face was convulsed with passion. With a cry of terror, Celeste fled from the room to weep alone in her own chamber, while Minnette sat by the window, watching the stars come out in their splendor, one by one, with the germs of that jealousy taking deep root in her soul, that would grow and bear fruit for evermore!

CHAPTER XIII.

GIPSY ASTONISHES THE NATIVES.

"What mighty mischief glads her now?"—FIRE WORSHIPERS.

MONG the villagers of St. Mark's, the mad-headed, wild-eyed, fearless Gipsy Gower was a universal favorite. Not one among them but had received from her warm heart and generous hand some service. The squire furnished his "imp" plentifully with pocket-money, which was invariably bestowed with careless generosity upon the poor of the parish; but given in a way that precluded all thanks. Sometimes the door would be thrust open with such violence as to wake the inmates, thinking a troop of horse was about to favor them with a visit, and her purse flung into the middle of the floor; and away she would ride like a flash. But on these occasions they were never at a loss to know the donor. If, on her next visit, they began to thank her for her gift,

Gipsy indignantly denied all knowledge of it, and positively refused to listen to them.

Dr. Wiseman, who was a pretty extensive land-owner, had several tenants in the remotest part of the village, whom he forced to pay an exorbitant rent, giving them to understand that unless they paid it on the very day it came due, out they must go! One evening, about dusk, Gipsy, who had been riding out, was overtaken by a storm of wind and rain, and sought shelter in one of the cottages.

On entering she found the whole family in deep distress. The head of the family sat gazing moodily at the fire: his wife, surrounded by her children, was weeping; and they, following her example, had set up a clamorous cry.

"Why, what's up now? What's the matter, Mrs. Brown?" inquired Gipsy, in surprise.

"Oh, Miss Gipsy! is it you? Sit down. Alas, it's the last time we can ever ask you!" said the woman, with a fresh burst of tears.

"Why, are you going to turn me out the next time I come?" said Gipsy, taking the proffered seat.

"Heaven forbid we'd ever turn you out, Miss Gipsy, after all you've done for us!" said the woman; "but after to-night we'll no longer have a roof to shelter us."

"You won't, eh? Do you intend to set fire to this old shanty, and burn it down?" inquired Gipsy.

"No, no; but Dr. Wiseman was here for his rent (this is pay-day, you know), and we haven't a cent in the house to give him. Mr. Brown's been sick mostly all summer, and all we could make it took to feed the children. And now Dr. Wiseman says he'll turn us out, to starve or beg, to-morrow," replied the woman through her tears.

"The old sinner!" exclaimed Gipsy, through her

hard-closed teeth. "Did you ask him to give you time to pay?"

"Yes, I went on my knees, and begged him to spare us for a few months, and we would pay him every cent; but he wouldn't. He said he would give us until to-morrow morning, and if we didn't have it then, out we must go."

For a moment Gipsy was silent, compressing her lips to keep down her fiery wrath, while the woman wept more passionately than ever.

"Have his other tenants paid him?" inquired Gipsy, at length.

"Yes, all but us."

"When did he start for home?"

"Not five minutes ago?"

"Which way did he take?" said Gipsy, springing to her feet, and beginning to examine her pistols.

"He went over the hills," said the man at the fire, speaking now for the first time; "I heard them say he was afraid to be robbed if he went round by the road, as he had all the money he got from the tenants with him."

"All right, then, Mrs. Brown, my dear woman. Keep up heart; and if some good fairy gets you out of this scrape, don't say a word about it. Good night."

"You had better not venture alone in the storm," said Mrs. Brown, anxiously; "one of the boys will go with you."

"Thank you, there's no necesstiy. I feel safer on Mignonne's back than with all the boys that ever afflicted the world for its sins for a body-guard. So mind my words, 'hold on to the last,' as the shoemaker said, and don't despair."

The last words were lost in the storm of wind and rain, as she opened the door. Springing on the back of Mignonne, she turned his head in the direction of the hills, and sped over the ground as rapidly as her fleet-footed Arabian could carry her.

Through the night, and wind, and rain, over the dangerous hilly path jogged Dr. Wiseman. He scarcely felt the storm, for a talisman in the shape of a well-filled pocket-book lay pressed to his avaricious heart. His mare, a raw-boned old brute, as ugly as her master, walked along slowly, manifesting a sublime contempt for storm and wind that would have done the heart of a philosopher good. What her thoughts were about it, would be hard to say; but her master's ran on money, robbers, highwaymen, and other such "knights of the road."

"There are many desperate characters in the village who know I have a large sum of money about me, and who would no more mind waylaying, robbing, and perhaps murdering me, than I would of turning the Brown's out to-morrow. Luckily, however, they'll think I've taken the village road," said the doctor to himself, in a sort of soliloquy, "and so I'll escape them. But this road is a dismal one, and seems just the place for a rendezvous of robbers. Now, if a highwayman were to step up from behind one of these rocks, and cry——"

"Your money or your life!" cried a deep, sepulchral voice at his ear, with such startling suddenness that, with an exclamation of horror and fear, the doctor nearly fell from his seat.

Recovering himself, he strove to see the robber, but in the deep darkness and beating rain it was impossible. But though he couldn't see, he could hear, and the sharp click of a pistol distinctly met his ear.

"Your money or your life!" repeated the low, hoarse voice, in an imperious tone.

For reply, the doctor, rendered desperate by the fear

of losing his money, drew a pistol and fired. As it flashed, he saw for a moment a horse standing before him, but the rider seemed to have lain flat down, for no man was there. Ere he could draw his second pistol, his horse was grasped by the bridle-rein, and the cold muzzle of a pistol was pressed to his temple.

"Your money or your life!" cried a fierce, excited voice that terror alone prevented him from recognizing. "Deliver up your money, old man, or this instant you shall die."

"Oh, spare my life!" cried the wretched doctor, in an agony of terror, for the cold ring of steel still pressed his temple like the deadly fang of a serpent. "Spare my life, for God's sake, and you shall have all! I'm a poor man, but you shall have it."

"Quick, then," was the imperious rejoinder, as the doctor fumbled in his pockets, and at last, with a deep groan of despair, surrendered the plump pocket-book to the daring outlaw.

"That is all I have; now let me go," cried the miserable doctor.

"Yes; but first you must solemnly swear never to speak to man, woman, or child of what has occurred to-night. Swear by your own miserable soul!"

"I swear!" groaned the unhappy doctor.

"And lest you should be tempted to commit perjury, and break your oath, let me tell you that the very first attempt to do so will be followed by instant *death*. Mind! I will watch you day and night, dog your steps like a blood-hound, and if you dare to breathe it to living mortal, that moment will be your last."

"I'll never mention it! I'll never speak of it. Oh, let me go," implored the agonized Galen.

"Very well, then. I have the honor to wish you

good-night. If you don't ride straight home, I'll send a bullet through your head."

And with this cheering assurance the robber put spurs to the horse, and rode off in the direction opposite to that leading to Deep Dale.

Little need was there to exhort the terror-stricken doctor to ride straight home. Never before had the spavined old mare fled over the ground with the velocity she did that night, and Doctor Wiseman did not breathe freely until he was double-locked in his own room.

The Browns paid their rent the next day, and would no longer remain tenants of the doctor. If he suspected any one, the robber's threat caused him prudently to remain silent; but his wretched look was an unfailing subject of mirth for Gipsy Gower for a month after, and the cunning twinkle of her eye said as plainly as words :

"I know, but I won't tell."

One day, Gipsy fell into deeper disgrace with the squire than had ever occurred before. In fact, it was quite an outrageous thing, and the only apology I can offer for her is, that she meant no harm.

The Bishop of B., Senator Long, and a number of distinguished gentlemen and ladies from the city had come to St. Mark's to spend a few days. Squire Erliston, as a matter of course, immediately called to see his friends, and a few days after gave a large dinner-party, to which they were all invited.

The important day for the dinner-party arrived. Lizzie was up in her room, dressing. Mrs. Gower was superintending affairs in the dining-room. The squire, in full dress, sat alone, awaiting his friends. As he sat, sleep overpowered him, and unconsciously he sank into a profound slumber.

While he was snoring in peace, little dreaming of the

fate awaiting him, that little imp of mischief, Gipsy, entered. One glance sufficed, and across her fertile brain there shot a demoniacal project of mischief, while her whole form became instinct, and her wicked eyes scintillated with fun.

Quitting the room, she returned presently with a box of lampblack in one hand, and the mustard-pot in the other.

"Now, Guardy, you keep still a little while till I turn you into an Indian chief, and here goes for your war-paint."

So saying, the little wretch drew a streak of mustard across his nose, following it by a similar one of lampblack. And so she continued until his whole face was covered with alternate stripes of yellow and black, scarcely able to repress a shout of laughter as she worked, at the unspeakably ludicrous appearance he presented.

Having exhausted her supply of paint, Gipsy stepped to the door to survey her work, and unable longer to restrain a roar of laughter, fled to her room, quivering with the anticipation of the fun to come.

Scarcely had she quitted the room when the door was flung open, and, in pompous tones, the servant announced :

" De Right Reveren' Bishop of B., de Hon'ble Senator Long and Mrs. Long."

And the whole party, half a dozen in number, entered the apartment.

The noise awoke the squire; and a most musical snore was mercilessly interrupted, and ended in a hysterical snort. Starting to his feet with an expression of countenance that utterly repudiated the idea of his having been asleep, he advanced with extended hand toward the bishop. That high functionary drew back for a moment aghast, and glanced at his companions in horror. Human nature could stand it no longer, and a universal shout of laughter resounded through the room.

"Eh? What? Lord bless me, what's the matter?" said the squire, turning his face from one to another, inwardly wondering if they had all gone mad. "What are you laughing at?"

A fresh roar of laughter from the whole party answered this, as they all pressed their hands to their sides, utterly unable to stop. Seeing this, the squire at last began grinning with sympathy, thereby adding so much to the ludicrousness of his appearance, that some threw themselves on the floor, some on chairs and sofas, in perfect convulsions.

"What the deuce is it?" repeated the squire, at last losing patience. "Will you oblige me by telling me what the matter is?"

"My dear sir," began the bishop, in tremulous tones.

The squire turned his painted face eagerly toward the speaker. In vain he attempted to proceed, it was not in human nature to withstand that face, and the bishop fell back in a paroxysm that threatened never to end.

It was a scene for an artist. The row of convulsed faces around, pausing for a moment breathlessly, but breaking forth louder than ever the minute their eyes again fell upon him. And there sat the squire with his black and yellow face, turning in dismay from one to another, his round bullet-eyes ready to pop from their sockets.

At this moment the door opened, and Lizzie, Louis, and Mrs. Gower, followed by all the servants in the house, attracted by the noise, burst into the room. The moment their eyes fell on the squire, who had started to his feet to address them, their looks of surprise vanishsd, and, as if by one accord, shout after shout of laughter broke from all. In vain did the squire stamp, and fume, and demand to know what was the matter; his only answer was a fresh explosion of mirth.

At last, in despair, Mrs. Gower managed to point to a mirror opposite. The squire rushed frantically to the spot, and then paused, transfixed, aghast with horror. Turning slowly round, he confronted his guests with such a look of blank, utter dismay, that all the laughter previous was nothing to the universal roar which followed that despairing glance. Then bursting out with : " It's that fiend !—that demon incarnate !—that little Jezebel has done this," he rushed from the room in search of her.

Gipsy, attracted by the laughter, had ventured cautiously to descend the stairs. The squire perceived her, as like a flash she turned to fly. With one galvanic bound he sprang up the stairs, seized her by the shoulder, shouting :

" By Heaven ! I'll pay you for this when they go !"

Then opening an adjoining door, he thrust her in, turned the key, put it in his pocket, and rushed out of the house into the yard, where, by the friendly aid of soap and hot water, and some hard scrubbing, he managed to make himself once more look like a Christian.

Then, returning to his guests—who by this time had laughed themselves into such a state that they could laugh no longer—he dispersed the servants with sundry kicks and cuffs, and proceeded to explain, as well as he was able, how it came about. Politeness forced the party to make every effort to maintain their gravity, but more than once, while seated in solemn conclave round the dinner-table, the recollection of the old man's ludicrous appearance would prove too much for flesh and blood—and, leaning back, they would laugh until the tears stood in their eyes. Their example proving contagious, the whole party would join in, to the great mortification of the squire—who inwardly vowed that Gipsy should pay dearly for every additional laugh.

But for the squire to reckon without Gipsy was rather a hazardous experiment. Seldom did that young lady find herself in a position from which her genius would not extricate her—as the squire found to his cost in the present instance.

Gipsy's first sensation at finding herself for the first time really a prisoner was one of intense mortification, followed by indignation ; and her thoughts ran somewhat after the following fashion :

"The mean old thing !—to lock me up here just because I applied a little mustard outside instead of inside! Never mind ; if I don't fix him for it, it'll be a wonder. So you'll pay me for this, will you, Guardy? Ah ! but you ain't sure of me yet, you see. If I don't outwit you yet, my name's not Gipsy Roarer Gower ! Now, Gipsy, my dear, set your wits to work, and get yourself out of this black hole of a prison."

Going to the window, she looked out. The sight would have appalled any one else ; but it did not intimidate Gipsy. The room she was in was on the third story, at a dizzy height from the ground. She looked around for a rope to descend ; but none did the room contain. What was she to do? Gipsy raised herself on one toe to consider.

Suddenly her eye fell on a new suit of broadcloth her guardian had brought home only the day before. She did not hesitate an instant.

To her great delight she found a pair of scissors in her pocket ; and, taking the coat and unmentionables from the wall where they hung, she sat down and diligently fell to work cutting them into long strips. Fifteen minutes passed, and nothing remained of Guardy's new clothes but a long black knotted string—which, to her great delight, she found would reach easily to the ground.

Fastening it to the window-sill securely, she began to descend, and in ten minutes she stood once more on *terra firma.*

Going to the stables, she saddled Mignonne and led him to the front gate, where she left him standing. Then, with unheard-of audacity, she entered the hall, opened the dining-room door, and thrusting in her wicked little head, she exclaimed exultingly :

"I say, Guardy, you can 'pay' me any time at your leisure, and I'll give you a receipt in full."

Then, I am sorry to say, making a hideous grimace, she turned to fly ; but the squire jumped from his seat—overturning the bishop and Mrs. Senator Long in his violent haste—and shouting, "Stop her! stop her!" rushed after her from the room.

But he was too late, and she leaped upon Mignonne's back and was off. Waving her hat in the air in a defiant "hurra !" she dashed down the road and disappeared.

Amazement and rage were struggling in the breast of the squire. Doubting whether it was all a delusion, he rushed up stairs to the room. The door was still fast ; and, burning with impatience, he opened it. And there he found the window wide open, and his new suit converted into a rope, which still dangled, as if in exultation from the window. And the mystery was solved.

What the squire said and did there, it is useless to say. The reader knows his remarks were anything but edifying ; and even the august presence of the over-turned bishop could not prevent him from hurling a torrent of invectives against the unfortunate Gipsy. Never had Squire Erliston been so angry in his life.

6*

Inwardly vowing that she should repent what she had done, the squire "bided his time"—little dreaming how bitterly he was destined to repent that vow.

CHAPTER XIV.

THE MOONLIGHT FLITTING.

"Oh, when she's angry, she is keen and shrewd ;
She was a vixen when she went to school,
And though she is but little, she is fierce."

HE moonlight was falling brightly on the lawn, and shimmering like silver sheen on the leaves of the horse-chestnuts, as Gipsy rode home. The company had just dispersed, and the squire was about to retire, when the clatter of horse's hoofs on the graveled path made him start up and hasten out to the porch. And there he beheld the audacious Gipsy riding fearlessly toward him, shouting at the top of her lungs some wild chorus, of which he only caught the words :

"You must place in my coffin a bottle of red,
And say a good fellow is gone."

"If I don't pay her off before I sleep to-night !" muttered the squire, between his clenched teeth. "I'll put an end to her pranks, or know for why."

Gipsy leaped lightly from her horse, and resigning him to Jupiter, ran up the steps, and encountered the purple face and blazing eyes of her angry guardian.

"Good-evening, Guardy!" was her salute. "Nice night!"

"Stop!" said the squire, catching her by the arm as she was about to run past—"stop! I've an account to settle with you, my lady!"

"Oh, any time at your convenience, Squire Erliston; I'll not be hard on you."

"Silence, Miss Impertinence! You have the impudence of Satan to face me after what you have done!"

"Now, Guardy, don't be unreasonable, but look at the matter in its proper light. All fashionable people paint."

"Silence!" exclaimed the squire, in a voice hoarse with rage. "Silence! before I brain you, you little villain! You have made me the laughing-stock of the country for miles around. I can never dare to show my face after what has occurred, without being jeered and mocked at. And all through you—the creature of my bounty—the miserable little wretch who would have been a common street-beggar if I had not clothed, and fed, and educated you!—through you, you brazen-faced, good-for-nothing little pauper, whom I would have kicked out long ago to the workhouse where you belong, if I had not feared the opinion of the world. Begone from my sight, before I am tempted to brain you!"

His face was perfectly livid with the storm of passion into which he had wrought himself. As he ceased, he raised his hand and brutally struck her a blow that sent her reeling across the room.

Then all the demon in her fiery nature was aroused. With the shriek of a wounded panther, she leaped toward him, with clenched hands, blazing eyes, hardground teeth, ghastly face, convulsed brow, and eyes that fairly scintillated sparks of fire. She looked a perfect little fiend, as she glared upon him, quivering in every nerve with frenzied passion.

The old sinner drew back appalled, frightened into calmness by that dark, fierce face. For a moment she expected she would spring at his throat like a tigress and strangle him. But, with a long, wild cry, she clasped her hands above her head, and fled swiftly upstairs, disappearing like some elfin sprite in the darkness beyond.

"Good Lord!" muttered the squire, wiping the drops of terror off his face. "What a perfect little devil! Did ever any one see such a look on a human face before! It's my opinion she's allied to Old Nick, and will carry me off some night in a brimstone of cloud and fire—I mean a fire of cloud and brimstone. Good gracious! I'm palpitating like a hysterical girl. I never got such a fright in my life. I vow it's a danger to go to bed with that desperate little limb in the house. I shouldn't wonder if she set the place on fire about our ears and burned us all in our beds, or cut our throats, or something. She looked wild and crazy enough to do it. Well, I reckon, I'll be more careful how I chastise her for the future, that's certain."

So saying, the squire took his night-lamp and went off to bed, taking the precaution to double lock his door, lest the "little imp" should take it into her head to carry him off bodily during the night.

No such catastrophe occurred, however, and when the squire went down to breakfast, he found everything going on as usual. Lizzie lay on a lounge, immersed in the pages of a novel, and Louis sat by the window busily sketching, as was his custom.

"I say, Lizzie, have you seen anything of Gipsy this morning?" he inquired, as he entered.

"No, papa."

"I'd rather think she rode off before any of us were

up this morning," said Louis, raising his head. " Mignonne is not in the stable."

This was nothing unusual, so without waiting for her, the family sat down to breakfast.

But half an hour after, Totty came running in alarm to Mrs. Gower, to say Miss Gipsy's bed had not been slept in all night. This fact was self-evident; and the worthy housekeeper sought out the squire to learn whether Gipsy had returned home the night before.

"Yes, yes, to be sure she did. 'Night brings home all stragglers,' as Solomon says. Why?"

"Because she has not slept in her bed the livelong night."

"No!" shouted the squire, springing from his seat, as if some one had speared him. "Lord bless me! where can she have gone?"

"Ah, Squire Erliston, you do not think anything has happened to the dear child, do you?" said Mrs. Gower, clasping her hands.

"Fiddle-de-dee, woman, of course not. She's gone back to Deep Dale, I'll lay a wager. Oh, here comes young Rivers, now we'll know."

"Archie, my dear," said Mrs. Gower, as that young gentleman entered the room, "did Gipsy go back to Deep Dale last night?"

"Go back! Why, of course she didn't."

"Oh, Squire Erliston, you hear that. Oh, where can that crazy creature have gone?" exclaimed Mrs. Gower, twisting her fingers in distress.

"Why, what's wrong? Where is Gipsy?" asked Archie, in surprise.

"Oh, I don't know. She came home late last night, and must have gone away somewhere, for she never went to bed at all. Oh, I am sure she has been killed, or drowned, or shot, or something ! I always knew it would happen," and Mrs. Gower fairly began to cry.

"Knew what would happen ?" said Archie, perplexed and alarmed.

"Something or other. I always said it; and now my words have come true," replied Mrs. Gower sobbing.

"Mrs. Gower, ma'am, allow me to tell you, you're a fool !" broke out the squire. "Most likely she didn't feel sleepy, and rode off before you were out of your bed this morning, just like the young minx. Ring the bell, and we'll see what time she started."

Archie obeyed, and Totty made her appearance.

"Tott," said the master, "be off with you, and send Jupiter here immediately."

Totty ducked her wooly head by way of reply, as she ran off, and presently Jupiter made his appearance in evident trouble.

"Jupe, you black rascal, what time did Gipsy ride off this morning ?" asked the squire.

"Please, mas'r, it warn't dis mornin' she rid off," said Jupiter, holding the door ajar, in order that he might retreat if his master grew violent

"What do you mean, sir?" roared his master, in rising terror.

"'Deed, mas'r, I couldn't stop the young wixen—de young lady, I mean—she don't mind me, no how, she don't."

"Nor anybody else, for that matter," groaned the squire, inwardly.

"You see, mas'r, arter she come home, I tuk Minnon inter de stable, and 'gan rubbin' him down, 'caze he was all in a foam she done rid him so hard. Well, 'bout half an hour arter, as I was goin' to bed, I hears a noise in de yard, an' when I looks out, dar was Miss Gipsy takin' de horse out again. 'Deed she was, mas'r, an' 'fore I could get out she war gone—'twan't no fault of mine."

"Oh, Gipsy! Gipsy!" shouted the squire, jumping to his legs and stamping up and down the floor in an agony of remorse and sorrow. "And I've driven you from home, old monster that I am! I'm a brute! an alligator! a crocodile! a wretched old wretch! a miserable, forsaken old sinner! and I'll knock down any man that dare say to the contrary! Oh, Gipsy, my dear little plague! where are you now? My darling little wild eaglet! friendless in the wide world!" Here catching sight of Jupiter still standing in the door-way, he rushed upon him and shook him until the unfortunate darkey's jaws chattered like a pair of castanets. "As for you, you black rascal! I have a good mind to break every bone in your worthless skin. Why didn't you wake me up, sir, when you saw her going, eh? Answer me that!"

"Mas'r—ma—ma—mas'r," stuttered poor Jupiter, half strangled, "'deed de Lord knows I was 'fraid to 'sturb ye. Ma—ma—ma—mas'r ——"

"Silence, sir! Up with you and mount—let every man, woman, and child in the place be off in search of her. And Mrs. Gower, ma'am, do you stop snuffling there. 'No use crying for spilled milk,' as Solomon says. We'll have her home and soundly thrashed before night, or my name's not Magnus Theodoric Erliston. Ha! there! Louis! Archie! the rest of you, mount and off! And Mrs. Gower, ma'am, do you run out and saddle my horse, and bring him round while I draw on my boots."

"Squire Erliston," sobbed the poor old lady, "you know very well I can't saddle your horse. Oh, Gipsy! Gipsy!" she added, with a fresh burst of tears.

"Well, fly and tell some of the rest, then. Women are such worthless creatures—good for nothing but crying. There they go, with Louis and young Rivers at their head, to scour the country. 'In the days when we went gipsying,' as Solomon says. I do believe that little minx will be the death of me yet—I know she will ! I'm losing flesh ; I'm losing temper ; I'm losing cash ! I'm losing rest, and losing patience every day. She'll bring my gray hairs in sorrow to the grave, as Solomon says, only I happen to wear a wig, Ah ! there's my horse. Now for it ! Gipsy Gower, you little torment, you, *won't* I tell you a piece of my mind when I catch you !"

But the squire was destined not to catch her ; for, though they continued the search for the lost one until night, no trace of her could be found. All that could be learned of her was from an innkeeper in a neighboring town, some twenty miles distant. He said a young girl answering the description given of Gipsy had arrived there about daylight, and, after taking a hasty breakfast, had left her horse—which was utterly exhausted by the pace with which she had ridden him—and started in the mail coach for the city.

Mignonne was led home, and as it was too late to go farther that day the tired horsemen returned, silent and dispirited, homeward. The next day the search was renewed, and the driver of the mail-coach questioned concerning the little fugitive. He could throw but little light on the subject ; she accompanied him as far as the city, where she paid her fare and left him. And that was all he knew.

Placards were posted up, and rewards offered ; the police were put upon her track ; but all in vain. And at last all hope was given up, and the lost child was resigned to her fate.

One day, about three weeks after her flight, the postman brought a letter for Mrs. Gower. One glance at the superscription, and with a cry of joy she tore it open, for it was in the light, careless hand of Gipsy. It ran as follows :

"My Dear, Darling Aunty :—I suppose you have had great times up at Sunset Hall since I made a moonlight flitting of it. I wish I had been there to see the fun. I suppose Guardy stamped and roared, and blew up Jupiter, and blessed *me*—after his old style. Well, you know, aunty, I just couldn't help it. Guardy was getting so unbearable there was no standing him, and so I'm going to take Gipsy Gower under my own especial patronage, and make a good girl of her. Don't be angry, now, aunty, because I'll take precious good care of myself—see if I don't. Tell Guardy not to make a fuss, for fear it might bring on the gout, and tell him not to keep searching for me, for if he hunts till he's black in the face he won't find me. Remember me to Aunt Liz, and Louis, and Celeste, and—and *Archie*. Tell Archie not to fall in love with anybody else ; if he does he may look out for a squall from your own little   Gipsy."

This characteristic letter, instead of comforting the family, plunged them into still deeper trouble on her account. Mrs. Gower wept for her darling unceasingly, and would not be comforted ; Lizzie sighed and yawned, and lay on her lounge from morning till night, looking drearier than ever ; and the servants went in silence and sadness about their daily business, heaving a sigh and shedding a tear over every memento that recalled poor Gipsy. Now that she was gone they found how dearly they loved her, in spite of all the scrapes and troubles she had ever cost them.

A dull, heavy, stagnant silence hung over the mansion from morning till night. There was no more banging of doors, and flying in and out, and up and down stairs, and scolding, and shouting, and singing all in one burst, now. The squire was blue-molding—fairly "running to seed," as he mournfully expressed it—for want of his little torment.

No one missed the merry little elf more than the lusty old squire, who sighed like a furnace, and sat undisturbed in his own arm-chair from one week's end to the other. Sometimes Louis would bring over Celeste, who had nearly wept her gentle eyes out for the loss of her friend, to comfort him, and the fair, loving little creature would nestle on a stool at his feet and lay her golden head in his lap, and go to sleep. And the squire would caress her fair, silken curls with his great, rough hands, and pat her white, dimpling shoulders, and turn away with a half groan ; for she was not Gipsy !

As for poor Archie, he took to wandering in the woods and shooting unoffending birds and rabbits, because it was Gipsy's favorite sport, and looked as doleful as though he had lost every friend in the world.

"Fall in love with any one else," indeed ! Master Archie scorned the idea, and began to have sundry visions of joining the monks of La Trappe as soon as he grew old enough. This and his other threats of going to sea, of enlisting, of killing somebody,.by way of relieving his spirits, kept poor Celeste trembling with fear for him from morning till night. And in her own gentle way she would put her arms round his neck and cry on his shoulder, and beg of him not to say such naughty things, for that Gipsy would come back yet— she *knew* that she would.

But Minnette, who didn't care a straw whether Gipsy ever came back or not, would laugh her short, deriding laugh, and advise him to become a Sister of Charity at once. And Celeste said *she* would be one when she grew up, and then she would be always near to comfort him. And Minnette's taunts always sent poor Archie off to the woods in a more heart-broken state of mind than ever before.

CHAPTER XV.

THE " STAR OF THE VALLEY."

> ——" Face and figure of a child,
> Though too calm, you think, and tender,
> For the childhood you would lend her."—BROWNING.

HE winter was now drawing on. The short, bleak November days had come, with their chill winds and frosty mornings. Miss Hagar looked at the slight, delicate form and pale little face of her *protegee*, and began to talk of keeping her at home, instead of sending her to school during the winter months.

Celeste listened, and never dreamed of opposing her wishes, but stole away by herself, and shed the first selfish tears that had ever fallen from her eyes in her life. It was so pleasant in school, among so many happy young faces, and with the holy, gentle-voiced Sisters of Charity, and so unspeakably lonesome at home, with nothing to do but look out of the window at gray hills and leafless trees, and listen to the dreary sighing of the wind. Therefore Celeste grieved in silence, and strove to keep back the tears when in Miss Hagar's presence, lest she should think her an ungrateful, dissatisfied little girl.

One morning, however, as Miss Hagar entered the

deserted parlor, she found Celeste sitting in the chimney-corner, her face hidden in her hands, sobbing gently to herself. A little surprised at this, for the child seemed always smiling and happy before her, Miss Hagar took her on her knee, and asked what was the matter.

"Nothing," replied Celeste, though her cheek glowed crimson red, as she felt she was not speaking the truth.

"People don't cry for nothing, child!" said the aged spinster, severely. "*What's the matter?*"

"Please, Miss Hagar, I'm so naughty, but—but—I don't want to leave school."

"Don't want to leave school? Why, child, you'd freeze to death going to school in the winter."

"But Minnette goes," pleaded Celeste.

"Minnette's not like you, little lily. She's strong and hardy, and doesn't mind the cold; it only brings living roses to her cheeks; but *you*, little whiff of down that you are, you'd blow away with the first winter breeze."

Celeste had no reply to make to this. She only hung down her head, and tried very hard to swallow a choking sensation in her throat.

At this moment Archie burst in, in his usual boisterous manner, all aglow with snow-balling Louis. Master Rivers seemed in very good condition, notwithstanding the loss of Gipsy; though I rather think he would have been induced to knock any one down who would tell him he had forgotten her.

"What! in trouble again, little sis? Who's been bothering you now? Just give me a hint, and I'll invite them not to do it again."

"Why, the little simpleton is crying because I won't let her freeze herself to death going to school all winter!" said Miss Hagar.

"Oh, that's it—is it? Dry up your tears, then, Birdie; there's 'balm in Gilead' for you. Yesterday, that good-natured old savage, Squire Erliston, hearing me tell Louis that Celeste could not go to school owing to the distance, immediately insisted that we should all use his family sleigh for the winter. Now, Miss Hagar, see how those radiant smiles chase her tears away. We'll nestle you up in the buffalo robes, and dash off to school with you every morning to the music of the jingling sleigh-bells. Eh, puss? won't it be glorious?"

"What's that?" said Minnette, entering suddenly.

"Why, Squire Erliston has given his sleigh up to Pussy here to take her to school, and perhaps we'll take you if you're not cross, though the squire has no particular love for you."

"Thank you for nothing," said Minnette, scornfully; "but I wouldn't go if you did ask me. Before I'd be such a baby!" she added, glancing contemptuously at Celeste.

And Minnette was as good as her word, positively refusing even the stormiest mornings to go in the sleigh. Archie exhausted all his eloquence, and Celeste pleaded tearfully, offering to stay at home and let her take her place; but Minnette answered all their entreaties by a sullen "I won't." Even when Louis, the only living being to whom her high, stubborn will would bend, pleaded with her to come, she only turned away, and said, in a tone *very* gentle for her :

"No, Louis, don't ask me ; I can't go. Why should I ? I'm no trembling little coward like Celeste. I *love* the winter !—yes, twice as well as the summer ! The summer is too still, and warm, and serene for me ! But the winter, with its maddening winds and howling storms, and white, frosty ground and piercing cold breeze, sends the blood bounding like lightning through every vein in my body, until I fly along, scarcely touching the ground beneath me ! Louis, walking alone through the drifted snow, I feel no cold; but in your warm sleigh beside *her*, my heart would feel like ice !"

" Strange, wild girl that you are ! Why do you dislike Celeste so much ?"

" I don't know. I never liked any one in my life—at least not more than *one*. Do *you* like her ?" she said, lifting her eyes, glancing with dusky fire, to his face.

" Like her !" he exclaimed, shaking back his short, black curls, while his full, dark eye kindled—" like that lovely little creature ! that gentle little dove ! that sweet little fairy ! beautiful as an angel ! radiant as a poet's dream ! bewitching as an Eastern houri ! Like her ! Oh, Minnette !"

She paused for a moment, and fixed her gleaming eyes on the bright, handsome face, sparkling with boy-ish enthusiasm ; then, without a word, turned away, and fled from his sight.

And from that moment her hatred of Celeste re-doubled tenfold in its intensity. Every opportunity of wounding and insulting the sensitive heart of the gentle child was seized ; but every insult was borne with patience—every taunt and sarcasm met with meek silence, that only exasperated her merciless tormentor more and more. Sometimes Celeste would feel rising in her bosom a feeling of dislike and indignation toward her persecutor ; and then, filled with remorse, she would kneel in the chapel and meekly pray for a better spirit, and always rise strengthened and hopeful, to encounter her arch-enemy, with her taunting words and deriding black eyes.

One last incident, displaying forcibly their different dispositions, and I have done with the *children*, Minnette and Celeste, forever.

The Sisters had purchased a beautiful new statue of the Madonna, and placed it in the refectory until it could be properly fixed in the chapel. The children were repeatedly forbidden to enter the refectory while it was there, lest it should accidentally be broken.

One day, the Sisters had given a *conge*, and their pupils were out playing noisily in the large garden and grounds attached to the convent. Minnette, who never liked to mingle in a crowd, selected three of the boldest spirits present, and proposed they should play "Puss in the corner" by themselves.

"Oh! we can't here in this great big place," was the reply; "besides, the other girls will be sure to join us."

"Let us go into the class-room, then," said the adventurous Minnette.

"Sister Mary Stanislaus is sweeping out the class-room, and she won't let us," said one of the girls.

"Well, then, there's the refectory," persisted Minnette.

"Oh! we daren't go there! Mother Vincent would be dreadfully angry. You know the new statue is there!" said the girls, aghast at the very idea.

"Such cowards!" exclaimed Minnette, her lip curling and her eye flashing. "I wish Gipsy Gower were here. *She* would not be afraid."

"*I* ain't a coward! I'll go!" cried one, following the daring Minnette, who had already started for the forbidden room. The others, yielding to their bolder spirit, followed after, and soon were wildly romping in the refectory.

Suddenly, Minnette, in her haste, rushed against the shelf where the statue stood. Down it came, with a loud crash, shivered into a thousand fragments.

The four girls stood pale, aghast with terror. Even Minnette's heart for a moment ceased to beat, as she gazed on the broken pieces of the exquisite statue. It was but for a moment; all her presence of mind returned, as she breathlessly exclaimed :

"Sister will be here in a moment and catch us. Let us run out and join the other girls, and she'll never know who did it."

In an instant they were rushing pell-mell from the room. Minnette was the last, and as she went out her eye fell upon Celeste coming along the passage. A project for gratifying her hatred immediately flashed across her mind. Seizing Celeste by the arm she thrust her into the refectory, closed the door, and fled, just as the Sister, startled by the noise, came running to the spot.

She opened the door! There stood Celeste, pale and trembling, gazing in horror on the ruins at her feet.

An involuntary shriek from Sister Stanislaus brought all the nuns and pupils in alarm to the spot. Celeste had entered the forbidden room—had, by some accident, broken the beautiful and costly statue; that was a fact self-evident to all. She did not attempt to deny it—her trembling lips could frame no words, while the *real* culprits stood boldly by, silent and unsuspected.

Celeste was led away to appear before " Mother Vincent," and answer the heavy charge brought against her. She well knew how it all happened, and could very easily have cleared herself ; but she had just been reading a lecture on humility and self-denial, and heroically resolved to bear the blame sooner than charge Minnette. " Minnette will hate me worse than ever if I tell," she thought; "and I must try and get her to like me. Besides, I deserve punishment, for I felt dreadfully bad and naughty, when she made the girls laugh at me this morning."

So Celeste met the charge only by silence, and sobs, and tears ; and Mother Vincent, leading her into the class-room, where all the girls and teachers were assembled, administered a public reproof.

" Had it been any of the other girls," she said, " she would not have felt surprised ; but Celeste was such a good girl generally, she was indeed surprised and grieved. It was not for the loss of the statue she cared most— though *that* could scarcely be replaced—but so glaring an act of disobedience as entering the refectory could not go unpunished.   Therefore, Sister Mary Joseph would lead Celeste off and leave her by herself until school was dismissed, as a warning to be more obedient in future."

And Celeste, with her fair face flushed with shame— her bosom heaving with sobs as though her gentle heart would break—was led away to the now unforbidden refectory, and left alone in her deep sorrow.   The real culprits sat silent and uneasy, starting guiltily when a low, suppressed sob would now and then reach their ear. But Minnette, with her black eyes blazing with triumph, her cheeks crimson with excitement, sat bold and undaunted, proud and rejoicing in her victory.

That evening one of the girls, unable to endure the stings of conscience, went to the Mother. Superior and nobly confessed the whole.   The good lady listened amazed, but silent.   Celeste was released, brought before her, and confronted with Minnette.

" Why did you tell this falsehood, Minnette ?" said the justly indignant lady, turning to her.

"I told no falsehood, madam," she said, boldly, though her cheek glowed like fire, and her falcon eye fell beneath the keen, steady gaze of the other.

" You *acted* a falsehood, then, which is quite as bad," said Mother Vincent ; "and I am pained beyond measure to find so artful and wicked a disposition in one so young.   And you, my child," she added, drawing Celeste

7

toward her and caressing her golden head; "why did you suffer this wrong in silence?"

"Because I deserved it, Mother; I didn't like Minnette this morning," she answered, dropping her pale face sadly.

A glance that might have killed her, it was so dazzlingly, intensely angry, shot from the lightning eyes of Minnette.

After a few brief words, both were dismissed. The sleigh stopped to take up Celeste, and Minnette walked proudly and sullenly home.

When she reached the house she found Celeste standing in the door-way, with Louis beside her, twining her golden curls over his fingers. All the evil passions in Minnette's nature were aroused at the sight. Springing upon her, fairly screaming with rage, she raised her clenched hand and struck her a blow that felled her to the ground. Then darting past, she flew like a flash up the polished oaken staircase, and locked herself in her own room; but not until the wild cry of Louis at the demoniac act reached her ear, turning her very blood to gall.

He sprang forward, and raised Celeste up. She had struck on a sharp icicle as she fell, and the golden hair clung to her face clotted with the flowing blood. Pale and senseless, like a broken lily, she lay in his arms, as, with a heart ready to burst with anguish, Louis bore her into the house and laid her on a sofa. His cry brought Miss Hagar to the spot. She stood in the door-way, and with her usual calmness surveyed the scene. Celeste lay without life or motion on the sofa, and Louis bent over her, chafing her cold hands, and calling her by every tender and endearing name.

"Some of Minnette's handiwork," she said, coming forward; " poor little white dove, that vulture would tear out your very heart if she could. But my words will come true, and some day she will find out she has a heart herself, when it is torn quivering and bleeding in strong agony from the roots."

"Oh, Miss Hagar, do you think she is dead?" cried Louis, his brave, strong heart swelling and throbbing in an agony of grief.

"No; I hope not. Ring the bell," was her answer.

Louis obeyed; and having dispatched the servant who answered it for the doctor, she proceeded to wash the blood from the wound. Doctor Wiseman came in with the utmost indifference; listened to the story, said it was "just like Minnette;" thought it ten chances to one whether she would ever recover; gave a few general directions as to how she was to be treated, and went off to sip his coffee and read the newspaper.

Louis' indignation knew no bounds.

"Leave this detestable old house," he exclaimed impetuously, to Miss Hagar; "take Celeste over to Sunset Hall, and live with us. Grandfather is rough, but kind and generous; and you and poor little Celeste will be warmly welcomed. *Do* come, Miss Hagar."

"No, Louis," said Miss Hagar, shaking her head. "I thank you for your kind offer; but I cannot be dependent on anybody. No; I cannot go."

"But, good heavens! Miss Hagar, will you stay and let that hawk-heart Minnette kill this poor, gentle little soul, who is more like an angel than a living child."

"No," said Miss Hagar; "there is a cottage belonging to me about half a mile from here, at a place called Little Valley. You know it, of course. Well, I shall have it furnished; and as soon as Celeste recovers, if she ever *does* recover, poor child, I shall go there. Thank the Lord! I'm able to support myself; and there she will be beyond the power of Minnette."

"Beyond the power of Minnette," thought Louis, as he walked homeward. "Will she *ever* be beyond the power of that mad girl? What can have made her hate that angelic little creature so, I wonder?"

Ah, Louis! Ten years from hence will *you* need to ask that question?

The indignation of all at Sunset Hall at hearing of Minnette's outrageous conduct was extreme. The squire was sure that "bedeviled tigress would never die in bed." Mrs. Gower's fat bosom swelled with indignation, and even Lizzie managed to drawl out "it was positively too bad." And immediately after hearing it Mrs. Gower ordered out the sleigh, and loading it with delicacies for the little sufferer, set out for Deep Dale, where she found her raving in the delirium of a brain fever.

Days and weeks passed ere Celeste rose from her bed, pale and weak, and frailer than ever. Minnette, with proud, cold scorn, met the reproachful glances of those around her; and never betrayed, by word or act, the slightest interest in the sufferer. Only once, when Celeste for the first time entered the parlor, supported by Louis, did she start; and the blood swept in a crimson tide to her face, dyeing her very temples fiery red. She turned aside her head; but Celeste went over, and taking her unwilling hand, said, gently:

"Dear Minnette, how glad I am to see you once more. It seems such a long time since we met. Why did you not come to see me when I was sick?"

"You had more agreeable company," said Minnette, in a low, cold voice, glaring her fierce eyes at Louis as she arose. "Excuse me," and she passed haughtily from the room.

Miss Hagar's Valley Cottage was now ready for her reception; and as soon as Celeste could bear to be removed they quitted Deep Dale. Celeste shed a few tears as she bade good-bye to the doctor and Minnette, but they were speedily turned to smiles as Louis gayly lifted her in his arms and placed her in the sleigh beside Archie. Then, seating himself on the other side of her, he shouted a merry adieu to Minnette, who seemed neither to see nor hear him as she leaned, cold and still, against the door. Miss Hagar took her seat in front with the driver; and off the whole party dashed.

As the spring advanced the roses once more bloomed upon the pale cheeks of Celeste; and the fair " Star of the Valley," as Master Louis had poetically named her, was known far and wide. Celeste had never been so happy before in her life. Every day brought Louis or Archie to the cottage, with books, flowers, or pictures, or something to present their " star" with. And as yet Celeste loved them both alike, just as she did Miss Hagar, just as she did Mrs. Gower. Though weeks and months passed away, Minnette never came near them. Sometimes Celeste went with the boys to see her; but her reception was always so cold and chilling that, fearing her visits displeased her, she at last desisted altogether.

'And Minnette, strange girl that she was, lived her own life in secret. She sat in her own room, silent and alone, the livelong day; for after that eventful morning on which the statue was broken, she would go to school no more. With her chin leaning on her hand, she would sit for hours with her glittering black eyes fixed on the fire, thinking and thinking, while the doctor sat silently reading by himself, until finally Master Archie, with a jaw-splitting yawn, declared that he *would* go and be a Sister of Charity if they'd take him ; for of all the old tombs ever he heard of, Deep Dale beat them hollow.

CHAPTER XVI.

OUR GIPSY.

" Leaping spirits bright as air,
Dancing heart untouched by care,
Sparkling eye and laughing brow,
And mirthful cheek of joyous glow."

N the spring Louis and Archie were to go to New York and enter college. The squire, who was dying by inches of the inaction at Sunset Hall, resolved to accompany them; and Lizzie, rousing herself from her indolence, also resolved to accompany them. Doctor Wiseman intended sending Minnette to boarding-school, and Miss Hagar offered to send Celeste, likewise, if she would go; but Celeste pleaded to remain and go to the Sisters; and as it happened to be just what Miss Hagar wished, she consented.

The evening before that fixed for the departure of the boys was spent by them at the Valley Cottage. Archie was in unusually boisterous spirits, and laughed till he made the house ring. Louis, on the contrary, was silent and grave, thinking sadly of leaving home and of parting with his friends.

Celeste, who always caught her tone from those around her, was one moment all smiles at one gay sally of Archie's, and the next sighing softly as her eye fell upon the grief-bowed young head of Louis. Miss Hagar sat by the fire knitting, as stiff, and solemn, and grave as usual.

" It will be a year—twelve whole months—before we all meet again," said Louis, with a sigh.

"Oh, dear !" said Celeste, her eyes filling with tears ; "it will be *so* lonesome. It seems to me the time will never pass."

"Oh, it will pass—never fear," said Archie, in the confident tone of one who knows he is asserting a fact ; "and we'll come back young collegians—decidedly fast young men—*Mirabile dictu*—that's Latin—and I'll marry you, sis. Oh, I forgot Gipsy."

Here Archie's face suddenly fell to a formidable length, and he heaved a sigh that would have inflated a balloon.

"Oh, if Gipsy were here it wouldn't be a bit lonesome—I mean, not so much. Minnette's going away, too," said Celeste, sadly.

"Well, you needn't care for her, I'm sure," said Archie, gruffly. "She's as sharp as a bottle of cayenne pepper, and as sour as an unripe crab-apple. For my part, I'm glad to be out of the way of her dagger-tongue."

"Oh, Archie, please don't," said Celeste, gently. "How do you know but she likes you now, after all ?"

"Likes me ? Oh, that's too good. Hold me, somebody, or I'll split !" exclaimed Archie, going off into an inextinguishable fit of laughter at the very idea.

Louis rose and went to the door ; Celeste followed him, leaving Archie to recover from his laughter and expatiate to Miss Hagar on the pleasures and prospects he hoped to enjoy in Gotham.

It was a beautiful moonlight night. The bright May moon shed a shower of silvery glory over the cottage, and bathed them in its refulgent light.

"Oh, Louis, what is the matter ?" said Celeste, laying her hand on his arm. "Are you so sorry for leaving home ?"

"I don't care for that, Celeste ; I am sorry to leave you."

"But it's only for a year. I will be here when you come back."

"Will you, Celeste ?"

"Why, yes, Louis, of course I will."

"Oh, no, you won't, Celeste. There will be something here taller and more womanly, who will talk and act like a young lady, and whom I will call Miss Pearl ; but the little, gentle Celeste will be here no longer."

"Well, won't it be the same with you ?" said Celeste, with an arch smile. "Something will come back taller and more manly, who will talk and act like a young gentleman, and whom I must call Mr. Oranmore, I suppose. But the Louis who brings me pretty books, and calls me 'the Star of the Valley,' I will never see again."

"Oh, Celeste, you know better than that. Will you think of me sometimes when I am gone ?"

"Oh, yes, always. What a strange question ! Why, I never thought of asking you to think of me, though you are going among so many strangers, who will make you forget all your old friends."

"You know I couldn't forget any of my old friends, Celeste, much less you. I shall think of you, and Miss Hagar, and Mrs. Gower, and—yes, and poor Gipsy every day. See, I have brought you a parting gift, Celeste, for your celestial little neck."

So saying, he drew out a little gold chain and cross, and threw it over the graceful neck that bent to receive it.

"Oh, thank you, dear Louis. I shall prize your gift so much. How kind and thoughtful of you ! I wish I had something to give you in return."

"One of your curls will do."

"Will it? Oh, then you shall have it."

So saying, she drew out a tiny pair of scissors and

severed a long, shining ring of gold from her bright little head.

"Hallo! what's this? Exchanging true lovers' tokens, by all that's tender! Ha, ha, ha!" shouted Master Rivers, appearing suddenly, and roaring with laughter.

"Confound you!" muttered Louis, giving him a shake. "And now I must go and bid Miss Hagar good-bye. Archie, go off and bring the gig round. Celeste, stay here; I'll be with you again in a minute."

So saying, Louis entered the cottage, shook hands with the hoary spinster, who bade him be a good boy, and not bring back any city habits. Then going to the door, where Celeste still stood looking on her cross, and closing her eyes to force back the tears that were fast gathering in them, he took her in his arms and said:

"And now good-bye, little darling. Don't quite forget Louis."

"Oh, Louis," was all she could say, as she clung to his neck and sobbed on his shoulder.

He compressed his lips and resolutely unclasped her clinging arms; then pressing his lips to her fair brow, he leaped into the gig, seized the reins, and, in his excitement, dashed off, quite forgetting Archie, who had lingered to say good-bye to Celeste.

Archie rushed after him, shouting "Stop thief! stop thief!" until Louis, discovering his mistake, pulled up, and admitted that wronged and justly-indignant young gentleman.

"Now for Deep Dale, to bid good-bye to Minnette and Old Nick," said Archie, irreverently, "and then hie for Sunset Hall."

"Yes, poor Celeste," said Louis, with a sigh, evidently forgetting he had a companion; whereupon Archie again went into convulsions of laughter, kicking

7*

up his heels and snapping his fingers in an ectasy of delight. Louis found his example so contagious, that—after trying for a few moments to preserve his gravity—he, too, was forced to join in his uproarious mirth.

On their arrival at Deep Dale they found the doctor in his study. Louis bade him a formal farewell; and having learned that Minnette was in the parlor, he went down to seek her, accompanied by Archie.

She sat in her usual attitude, gazing intently out of the window at the cold moonlight. She looked up as they entered, and started violently as she perceived who were her visitors.

"Well, Minnette, we've come to bid you good-bye,' said Archie, gayly, throwing his arms round her neck and imprinting a cousinly salute on her cheek. "Good-bye for twelve months, and then hie for home and a happy meeting. Louis, I leave you to make your adieux to Minnette, while I make mine to old Suse, down in the kitchen. Mind, Minnette, don't give him one of your curls, as I saw another little girl do awhile ago, unless he gives you a gold cross and chain in return for it—he gave her one." And with a mischievous laugh, Archie clattered down stairs, taking half the staircase at a bound.

She drew herself back and up; and the hand she had half extended to meet his was withdrawn, as, with a cold formal bow, she said:

"Farewell! I wish you a safe journey and a happy return."

"And nothing more! Oh, Minnette! Is it thus old friends, who have known each other from childhood, are to part? Just think, we may never meet again!"

"*Do you care?*" she asked, in a softened voice.

"Care! Of course I do. Won't you shake hands,

Minnette! You're not half as sorry to let me go as little Celeste was."

"Oh, no; I don't lose so much. I have no books, nor flowers, nor visits, nor gold crosses to lose by your absence," she said, sarcastically—her face, that had softened for a moment, growing cold and hard at the mention of her name. "Good-bye Louis, and—I wish you all success and happiness."

The hand she extended was cold as ice. He pressed it between his, and gazed sadly into the clear, bright eyes that defiantly met his own.

"Come, Louis, don't stay there all night!" called Archie, impatiently. "Old Suse has been hugging and kissing me till I was half smothered, down there in the kitchen ; and it didn't take her half the time it does you two. Come along."

"Good-bye! good-bye!" said Louis, waving his hand to Minnette, who followed him to the door; and the next moment they were dashing along at break-neck speed toward Sunset Hall.

The moonlight that night fell on Celeste, kneeling in her own little room, praying for Louis and Archie, and sobbing in unrestrained grief whenever her eye fell upon the bright gold cross—*his* parting gift. Appropriate gift from one who seemed destined to never lay aught but *crosses* upon her!

It fell upon Minnette, sitting still by the window, with a face as cold and white as the moonlight on which she gazed. She did not love Louis Oranmore ; but she admired him—liked him better than any one else she knew, perhaps, because he was handsome. But she hated Celeste ; and his evident preference for her kindled up the flames of jealousy in her passionate soul, until she could have killed her without remorse.

The next morning the gay party set out for New

York; and in due course of time they reached that city, and put up at one of the best hotels.

"Suppose we go to the opera to-night?" said Lizzie to the squire, as she sat—all her languor gone—looking out of the window at the stream of life flowing below.

"Just as you like—it's all one to me," said the squire, with most sublime indifference.

"Then the opera be it," said Lizzie, and the opera, accordingly, it was. And a few hours later found them comfortably seated, listening to the music, and gazing on the gayly-attired people around them.

"How delightful this is!" exclaimed Lizzie, her eyes sparkling with pleasure.

"Humph!—delightful! Set of fools! 'All is vanity,' as Solomon says. Wonder who foots the bills for all this glittering and shaking toggery?" grunted the squire.

"I've heard them say that the young *danseuse*, 'La Petite Eaglet,' is going to dance to-night," said Louis. "Everybody's raving about her."

"Why? Is she so beautiful?" inquired Lizzie.

"No, I believe not; it's because she dances so well," replied Louis.

At this moment the curtain arose, a thunder of applause shook the house, and La Petite Eaglet herself stood before them. A little straight, lithe figure, arrayed in floating, gauzy robes of white silver tissue, and crowned with white roses—a small, dark, keen, piquant face—bright, roguish eyes, that went dancing like lightning around the house. Suddenly her eye fell on our party from St. Mark's; a slight start and a quick removal of her eyes followed. The applause grew deafening as the people hailed their favorite. She bowed. The music struck merrily up, and her tiny feet went glancing, like rain-drops, here and there. She seemed floating in air, not touching the ground, as she whirled, and flew, and skimmed like a bird in the sunshine. The squire was dizzy—absolutely dizzy—looking at her. His head was going round, spinning like a top, or like her feet, as he gazed. Lizzie and Louis were entranced, but Archie, after the first glance, sat with dilating eyes and parted lips—incredulous, amazed, bewildered—with a look of half-puzzled, half-delighted recognition on his face.

Still the little dancer whirled and pirouetted before them ; and when she ceased a shout of applause thundered through the building, shaking it to its center Flowers, wreaths, and bouquets fell in showers around her ; ladies waved their handkerchiefs and clapped their little hands in the excitement of the moment. The opera-going world seemed to have gone mad. And there stood the little Eaglet, bowing to the delighted audience, the very impersonification of self-possession and grace.

Suddenly, rising as if to speak, she removed the crown of roses from her head. There was a profound, a dead silence, where lately all had been uproar. Every eye was bent in wonder—every neck was strained to see what she was about to do.

Taking one step forward, she fixed her eyes on the box occupied by the squire and his family. Every eye, as a matter of course, turned in that direction likewise. Raising the wreath, she threw it toward them, and it alighted in triumph on the brow of the squire.

In a moment she was gone. Up sprang Archie, quite regardless of the thousands of eyes upon him, and waving his cap in the air above his head, he shouted, in wild exultation :

"I knew it ! I knew it ! *It's our Gipsy !—it's Gipsy Gower !*"

CHAPTER XVII.

GIPSY'S RETURN TO SUNSET HALL.

> "This maiden's sparkling eyes
> Are pretty and all that, sir ;
> But then her little tongue
> Is quite too full of chat, sir."—MOORE.

HE effect of Archie's announcement on our party may be imagined. Lizzie uttered a stifled shriek and fell back in her seat ; the squire's eyes protruded until they seemed ready to burst from their sockets ; Louis gazed like one thunder-struck, and caught hold of Archie, who seemed inclined to leap on the stage in search of his little lady-love.

"Let me go into the green-room—let us go before she leaves," cried Archie, struggling to free himself from the grasp of Louis.

The crowd were now dispersing ; and the squire and his party arose and were borne along by the throng, headed by Archie, whose frantic exertions—as he dug his elbows right and left, to make a passage, quite regardless of feelings and ribs—soon brought them to the outer air ; and ten minutes later—the squire never could tell how—found them in the green-room, among painted actresses and slip-shod, shabby-looking actors.

Archie's eyes danced over the assembled company, who looked rather surprised, not to say indignant, at this sudden entrance, and rested at last on a straight, slight, little figure, with its back toward them. With one bound he cleared the intervening space betwixt them, and without waiting to say "by your leave," clasped her in his arms, and imprinted a kiss upon her cheek.

"Dear me, Archie, is that you? Take care! you're mussing my new dress dreadfully!" was the astoundingly cool salutation, in the well-known tones of our little Gipsy.

"Oh, Gipsy, how *could* you do it? Oh, Gipsy, it was *such* a shame," exclaimed Archie, reproachfully.

At this moment she espied Louis advancing toward her, and accosted him with:

"How d'ye do, Louis?—how's Celeste and Minnette, and Mignonne, and all the rest? Pretty well, eh?"

"Gipsy! Gipsy! what a way to talk after our long parting," said Louis, almost provoked by her indifference. "You don't know how we all grieved for you. Poor Mrs. Gower has become quite a skeleton crying for her 'monkey.'"

"Oh, poor, dear aunty! that's too bad now. But here comes Guardy and Lizzie. I don't think Guardy was breaking his heart about me anyway! He looks in capital condition yet."

At this moment the squire came over with Lizzie leaning on his arm.

"Hallo! Guardy, how are you? How did you like the opera?" exclaimed Gipsy, in the same tone she would have used had she parted from him an hour before.

"Oh, Gipsy! you little wretch you! I never thought it would come to this," groaned the squire.

"No, you thought I wasn't clever enough! Just see how easy it is to be deceived! Didn't I dance beautifully, though, and ain't I credit to you now? I'll leave it to Archie here. Aunt Lizzie, I'll speak to you as soon as I get time. Here comes old Barnes, the manager, to know what's the matter."

"Oh, Gipsy, you'll come home with us, my love, you really must," exclaimed Lizzie.

"Couldn't, aunty, by no manner of means," replied Gipsy, shaking her head.

"But I'll be shot if you *don't*, though," shouted the squire, "so no more about it. Do you think I'm going to let a ward of *mine* go with a gang of strolling players any longer ?"

"I'm no ward of yours, Squire Erliston ; I'm my own mistress, thanks be to goodness, free and independent, and so I mean to stay," exclaimed Gipsy, with sparkling eyes.

"But, oh, my dear ! my *dear* Gipsy, do come home with us to-night," pleaded Lizzie, taking her hand.

"You will, Gipsy, just for to-night," coaxed Louis. And : "Ah, Gipsy, *won't* you now ?" pleaded Archie, looking up in her saucy little face, with something very like tears shining in his usually merry blue eyes.

"Well—maybe—just for to-night," said Gipsy, slowly yielding ; "but mind, I must go back to-morrow."

"And may I be kicked to death by grasshoppers, if ever I *let* you go back," muttered the squire to himself.

"Here comes the manager, Mr. Barnes," said Gipsy, raising her voice; "these are my friends, and I am going home with them to-night."

"You'll be back to-morrow in time for the rehearsal ?" inquired Mr. Barnes, in no very pleased tone of .voice.

"Oh, yes, to be sure," said Gipsy, as she ran off to get her hat and cloak.

"*We'll see about that !*" said the squire, inwardly, with a knowing nod.

Gipsy soon made her appearance. A cab was in waiting, and the whole party were soon on their way to the hotel.

"And now, tell us all your adventures since the night you eloped from Sunset Hall," said Louis, as they drove along.

"By and by. Tell me first all that has happened at St. Mark's since I left—all about Celeste, and the rest of my friends."

So Louis related all that had transpired since her departure—softening, as much as he could, the outrageous conduct of Minnette.

"Poor Celeste!" exclaimed Gipsy, with glowing cheeks and flashing eyes. "Oh, don't I wish I'd only been there to take her part! *Wouldn't* I have given it to Minnette—the ugly old thing!—beg pardon, Archie, for calling your cousin names."

"Oh, you're welcome to call her what you please, for all I care," replied Archie, in a nonchalant tone. "I'm not dying about her."

"There's no love lost, I think," said Louis, laughing.

By this time they had reached the hotel. Lizzie took Gipsy to her room to brush her hair and arrange her dress, and then led her to the parlor, where the trio were waiting them.

"And now for your story!" exclaimed Archie, condescendingly pushing a stool toward Gipsy with his foot.

"Well, it's not much to tell," said Gipsy. "After leaving *you*, Guardy, that night, in an excessively amiable frame of mind, I went up to my room and sat down to deliberate whether I'd set fire to the house and burn you all in your beds, or take a razor and cut *your* windpipe, by way of letting in a little hint to be more polite to me in future."

"Good Lord! I just thought so!" ejaculated the horrified squire.

"Finally, Guardy, I came to the conclusion that I would do neither. Both were unpleasant jobs—at least they would have been unpleasant to you, whatever they might have been to me, and would have taken too much time. So I concluded to let you burden the earth a little longer, and quote Solomon for the edification of the world generally, and in the meantime to make myself as scarce as possible ; for I'd no idea of staying to be knocked about like an old dishcloth. So I got up, took my last supply of pocket-money, stole down to the stables, mounted Mignonne, and dashed off like the wind. Poor Mignonne ! I rather think I astonished him that night, and we were both pretty well blown by the time we reached Brande's Tavern.

"There I took breakfast, left Mignonne—much against my will—jumped into the mail-coach, and started for the city. Arrived there, I was for awhile rather at a loss in what direction to turn my talents. My predominant idea, however, was to don pantaloons and go to sea. Being determined to see the lions, while I staid, I went one night to the play, saw a little girl dancing, and—Eureka ! I had discovered what I was born for at last ! '*Couldn't* I beat that ?' says I to myself. And so, when I went home, I just got up before the looking-glass, stood on one toe, and stuck the other leg straight out, as she had done, cut a few pigeon-wings, turned a somerset or two, and came to the conclusion that if I didn't become a *danseuse* forthwith, it would be the greatest loss this world ever sustained—the fall of Jerusalem not excepted. To a young lady of my genius it was no very difficult thing to accomplish. I went to see Old Barnes, who politely declined my services. But I wasn't going 'to give it up so, Mr. Brown,' and, like the widow in the Scripture, I gave him no peace, night or day, until he accepted my services. Well, after that all was plain sailing enough. Maybe I didn't astonish the world by the rapidity with which my continuations went up and down. It was while there I wrote that letter of consolation to Aunty Gower, by way of setting your minds at ease. Then we went to Washington, then to New York, and everywhere I 'won golden opinions from all sorts of people,' as Shakespeare, or Solomon, or some of them old fellows says. I always kept a bright lookout for you all, for I had a sort of presentiment I'd stumble against you some day. So I wasn't much surprised, but a good pleased, when I saw Guardy's dear old head protruding, like a huge overboiled beet, from one of the boxes to-night. And so—*Finis!*"

"Gipsy," exclaimed Archie, "you're a regular specimen of Young America! You deserve a leather medal, or a service of tin plate—you do, by Jove!"

"'Pon honor, now?"

"Oh, Gipsy, my love, I'm very sorry to think you could have degraded yourself in such a way!" said Lizzie, with a shockingly shocked expression of countenance.

"Degraded, Aunt Lizzie!" exclaimed Gipsy, indignantly. "I'd like to know whether it's more degrading to earn one's living, free and merry, as a respectable, 'sponsible, danceable dancer, as Totty would say, or to stay depending on any one, to be called a beggar, and kicked about like an old shoe, if you didn't do everything a snappish old crab of an old gentleman took into his absurd old head. I never was made to obey any one —and what's more, I won't neither. There, now!"

"Take care, Gipsy; don't make any rash promises," said Archie. "You've got to promise to 'love, honor, and obey' *me*, one of these days."

"Never-r-r! Obey *you*, indeed! Don't you wish J may do it?"

"Well, but, my love," said Lizzie, returning to the charge, "though it is too late to repair what you have done, you must be a dancing-girl no longer. You must return home with us to Sunset Hall."

"Return to Sunset Hall! Likely I'll go there to be abused again! Not I, indeed, Aunt Lizzie; much obliged to you, at the same time, for the offer."

"And I vow, Miss Flyaway, you *shall* go with us—there!"

"And I vow, Guardy, I *sha'n't* go with you—there!"

"I'll go to law, and *compel* you to come. I'm your rightful guardian!" said the squire, in rising wrath.·

"Rightful fiddlesticks! I'm no ward of yours; I'm Aunty Gower's niece; and the law's got nothing to do with me," replied Gipsy, with an audacious snap of her fingers; for neither Gipsy nor the boys knew how she was found on the beach.

"And is that all the thanks you give me for offering to plague myself with you, you ungrateful little var- mint?"

"I'm *not* ungrateful, Squire Erliston!" flashed Gipsy —a streak of fiery red darting across her dark face. "I'm *not* ungrateful; but I *won't* be a slave to come at your beck; I *won't* be called a beggar—a pauper; I *won't* be told the workhouse is my rightful home; I *won't* be struck like a cur, and then kiss the hand that strikes me. No! I'm not ungrateful; but, though I'm only a little girl, I *won't* be insulted and abused for nothing. I can earn my own living, free and happy, without whining for any one's favor, thank Heaven!"

Her little form seemed to tower upward with the con- sciousness of inward power, her eyes filled, blazed, and dilated, and her dark cheek crimsoned with proud defiance.

The squire forgot his anger as he gazed in admiration on the high-spirited little creature standing before him, as haughty as a little empress. Stretching out his arms, he caught her, and seated her on his knee—stroking her short, dancing curls, as he said, in the playful tone one might use to a spoiled baby:

"And can't my little monkey make allowance for an old man's words? You know you were very naughty and mischievous that day, and I had cause to be angry with you; and if I said harsh things, it was all for your good, you know."

"All for my good!—such stuff! I wish you'd put me down. I'm a young lady, I'd have you to know; and I ain't going to be used like a baby, dandled up and down without any regard for my dignity!" said Gipsy, with so indignant an expression of countenance, that Archie—who, as I before mentioned, was blessed with a keen sense of the ludicrous—fell back, roaring with laughter.

"Now, Gipsy, my love, do be reasonable and return home with us," said Lizzie, impatiently.

"I won't, then—there!" said Gipsy, rather sullenly.

But the tears rushed into Lizzie's eyes—for she really was very fond of the eccentric elf—and in a moment Gipsy was off the squire's knee, and her arms round Lizzie's neck.

"Why, aunty, did I make you cry? Oh, I'm so sorry! Please don't cry, dear, *dear* aunty."

"Oh, Gipsy, it's so selfish of you not to return with us, when we are so lonesome at home without you," said Lizzie, fairly sobbing.

"Yes; and poor Mrs. Gower will break her heart

when she hears about it—I know she will," said Louis, in a lachrymose tone.

"And I'll break mine—I know I will!" added Archie, rubbing his knuckles into his eyes, and with some difficulty squeezing out a tear.

"And I'll blow my stupid old brains out ; and *after that*, I'll break my heart, too," chimed in the squire, in a very melancholy tone of voice.

"Well! la me! you'll have rather a smashing time of it if you all break your hearts. What'll you do with the pieces, Guardy ?—sell them for marbles ?" said Gipsy, laughing.

"There! I knew you'd relent ; I said it. Oh, Gipsy, my darling, I knew you wouldn't desert your 'Guardy' in his old age. I knew you wouldn't let him go down to his grave like a miserable, consumptive old tabby-cat, with no wicked little 'imp' to keep him from stagnating. Oh, Gipsy, my dear, may Heaven bless you !"

"Bother! I haven't said I'd go. Don't jump at conclusions. Before I'd be with you a week you'd be blowing me up sky-high."

"But, Gipsy, you know I can't live without blowing somebody up. You ought to make allowance for an old man's temper. It runs in our family to blow up. I had an uncle, or something, that was 'blown up' at the battle of Bunker Hill. Then I always feel after it as amiable as a cat when eating her kittens. 'After a storm there cometh a calm,' as Solomon says."

"Well, maybe there's something in that," said Gipsy, thoughtfully.

"And you know, my love," said Lizzie, "that, though a little girl may be a dancer, it's a dreadful life for a young woman—which you will be in two or three years. No one ever respects a dancing girl ; no gentleman ever would marry you."

·"Wouldn't they, though !" said Gipsy, so indignantly that Archie once more fell back, convulsed. "If they wouldn't, somebody 'd lose the smartest, cleverest, handsomest young lady on this terrestrial globe, though I say it, as 'hadn't oughter.' Well, since you all are going to commit suicide if I don't go with you, I suppose old Barnes must lose the 'bright particular star' of his company, and I must return to St. Mark's, to waste my sweetness on the desert air."

This resolution was greeted with enthusiastic delight by all present ; and the night was far advanced before the squire could part with his "little vixen," and allow her to go to rest.

Old Barnes—as Gipsy called him—was highly indignant at the treatment he had received, and, going to the hotel, began abusing Gipsy and the squire, and everybody else generally ; whereupon the squire, who never was noted for his patience, took him by the collar, and, by a well-applied kick, landed him in the kennel—a pleasant way of settling disputes which he had learned while dealing with his negroes, but for which an over-particular court made him pay pretty high damages.

Three days after, Louis and Archie bade them farewell, and entered college ; and the squire, after a pleasure-trip of a few weeks, set out for St. Mark's.

In due course of time he arrived at that *refugium peccatorum ;* and the unbounded delight with which Gipsy was hailed can never be described by pen of mine.

Good Mrs. Gower could scarcely believe that her darling was really before her ; and it was only when listening to the uproar that everywhere followed the footsteps of the said darling, that she could be convinced.

As for Celeste, not knowing whether to laugh or cry

with joy, she split the difference, and did both. Even
Miss Hagar's grim face relaxed as Gipsy came flashing
into their quiet cottage like a March whirlwind, throwing everything into such "admired disorder," that it generally took the quiet little housekeeper, Celeste, half a
day to set things to rights afterward.

And now it began to be time to think of completing
the education of the two young girls. Minnette had left
for school before the return of Gipsy, and it became
necessary to send them likewise. Loath as the squire was
to part with his pet, he felt he must do it, and urged Miss
Hagar to allow Celeste to accompany her.

"Gipsy will defend her from the malice of Minnette,
and the two girls will be company for each other," said
the old man to the spinster. "Girls *must* know how to
chatter French, and bang on a piano, and make worsted
cats and dogs, and all *such!* So let little Snowdrop, here,
go with my monkey, and I'll foot the bill."

Miss Hagar consented ; and a month after found our
little rustic lasses—our fair "Star of the Valley" and
our mountain fairy, moving in the new world of boarding-school.

CHAPTER XVIII.

ARCHIE.

"His youthful form was middle size,
  For feat of strength or exercise
    Shaped in proportion fair ;
And dark-blue was his eagle eye,
And auburn of the darkest dye
  His short and curling hair.
Light was his footstep in the dance,
  And firm his stirrup in the lists,
And oh ! he had that merry glance
That seldom lady's heart resists."—SCOTT.

IVE years passed. And the children, Gipsy and Celeste, we can never see more ; for those five years have changed them into young ladies of seventeen. Strange to say, neither Louis nor Archie has met Minnette, Gipsy, or Celeste, since the time they parted to go to college : and with all the change that years have made in their appearance, it is doubtful whether they would even recognize one another now, if they met.

The way of it was this : Louis and Archie, after the life and excitement of the city, began to think that Sunset Hall was an insufferably dull place ; and with the usual fickleness of youth, instead of going home to spend their vacation, invariably went with some of their schoolfellows. This troubled the old squire. very little ; for without Gipsy, in the quiet of Sunset Hall, he was falling into a state of stupid apathy, and gave Master Louis *carte blanche* to go where he pleased. Lizzie was too indolent to trouble herself much about it, and as she generally went on a visit to New York every winter, she contented herself with seeing her son and heir then, and knowing he was well. As for Gipsy and Celeste, their faithless boy-lovers seemed to have quite outgrown their early affection for them.

Then, when the time came for them to graduate, and make choice of a profession, Squire Erliston found that young Mr. Oranmore would neither be doctor, lawyer, nor clergyman ; nor even accept a post in the army or navy.

" Why not," said the squire, during an interview he had with him ; " what's your objection ?"

" Why, my dear grandfather," replied Louis, " you should have too much regard for your suffering fellow-mortals to make a doctor of me. As for being a lawyer, I haven't rascality enough for that *yet ;* and I've too much respect for the church to take holy orders. Neither does the camp nor forecastle agree with me. I have no particular love for forced marches or wholesale slaughter ; nor do I care over much for stale biscuit, bilge-water, and the cat-o'-nine-tails ; so I must e'en decline all."

" Then what in the name of Heaven *will* you be ?" exclaimed the squire.

" An artist, sir ; an artist. Heaven has destined me for a painter. I feel something within me that tells me I will yet win fame and renown. Let me go to Europe— to Germany and Italy, and study the works of the glorious old masters, and I will yet win a name you will not blush to hear."

" Glorious old fiddlesticks ! Go, if you like, but I never expected to find a grandson of mine such a fool ! The heir of Mount Sunset and its broad lands, the heir of Oranmore Hall, and old Mother Oranmore's yellow guineas, can do as he pleases, of course. Go and waste your time daubing canvas if you will, I'll be hanged if *I* care !"

Therefore, six months before the return of the girls from school, Louis, accompanied by a friend, sailed for Europe without seeing them.

"And you, sir," said the squire, turning to Archie; "are *you* going to be a fool and turn painter, too?"

"No, sir," replied Master Archie; "I'm not going to be a fool, but I'm going to be something worse—a knave; in other words, a lawyer. As for painting, thank fortune, I've no more talent for it than I have for turning milliner, beyond painting my face when acting charades."

So Archie went to Washington, and began studying for the bar.

Gipsy, who was a universal favorite in school, began, for the last few years, to copy the example of the boys, and spend her vacations with her friends. Minnette and Celeste always returned home; for Minnette, cold, and reserved, and proud, was disliked and feared by all; and though Celeste was beloved by everybody, duty and affection forbade her to leave Miss Hagar for her own pleasure.

Our madcap friend, Gipsy, had lost none of her wicked nor mischief-loving propensities during those years. Such a pest and a plague as she was in the school, driving teachers and pupils to their wits' end with her mad pranks, and yet liked so well. There was usually a downright quarrel, about the time of the holidays, to see who would possess her; and Gipsy, after looking on and enjoying the fun, would, to the surprise and chagrin of all, go with some one who least hoped for the honor.

Gipsy was spending the winter with a school-friend, Jennie Moore, at Washington. The three girls, whose united fortunes are the subject of this history, had graduated; Minnette, with the highest honors the school could give; Celeste, with fewer laurels, but with far more love; and Gipsy—alas, that I should have to say it!—

most wófully behind all. The restless elf *would* not study—was *always* at the foot of her class, and only laughed at the grave lectures of the teachers ; and yawned horribly over the rules of syntax, and the trying names in her botany. So poor Gipsy left little better than when she entered.

The folding-doors of Mr. Moore's spacious drawing-room were thrown open, blazing with light and radiant with brilliantly-dressed ladies. Miss Jennie had resolved that the first ball should surpass anything that had taken place that winter. All the *elite* of the city, wealth, beauty, fashion, gallantry, and talent, were mingled in gay confusion. There were soft rustling of silks, and waving of perfumed handkerchiefs, and flirting of fans, and flirting of *belles ;* and bright ladies cast killing glances from their brilliant eyes ; and gentlemen bowed and smiled, and paid compliments, and talked all sorts of nonsense, and

> " All went merry as a marriage bell."

Near the upper end of the room the belle, *par excellence*, seemed to be ; for in her train flowed all that were wittiest, and gayest, and loveliest there. Whenever *she* moved, a throng of admirers followed ; and where the laughter was loudest, the mirth highest, the crowd greatest, there might you find the center of attraction, this belle of whom I am speaking.

And yet she was not beautiful ; at least, not beautiful when compared with many there who were neglected for her. She is floating now in a gay waltz round the room with a distinguished foreigner, and " I will paint her as I see her."

A small, slight, straight, lithe figure, airy and bird-like in its motions, skimming over the floor without seeming to touch it; never at rest; but quick, sudden, abrupt, and startling in all its motions, yet every motion instinct, glowing with life. A dark, bright, laughing little face, that no one knows whether it is handsome or not, it is so radiant, so bewitching, so sparkling, so full of overflowing mirth and mischief. Short, crisp black curls, adorning the sauciest little head in the world; wicked brown eyes, fairly *twinkling* with wickedness; a rosy little mouth, that seemed always laughing to display the little pearly teeth. Such was the star of the evening. Reader, do you recognize her?

As she seated herself after the dance, tired and a little fatigued, Jennie Moore, a pretty, graceful girl, came up to her, saying, in a low voice:

"Oh, Gipsy, I have a stranger to introduce to you—a most *distinguished* one. One of the cleverest and most talented young lawyers in Washington."

"Distinguished! Now, I'm tired to death of 'distinguished' people; they're all a set of bores—ugly as sin and pedantic as schoolmasters. Don't stare—it's a fact!"

"Oh, but Mr. Rivers is not; he is young, handsome, agreeable, witty, a regular lady-killer, and worth nobody knows how much."

"Mr.—worth what?" exclaimed Gipsy, springing to her feet so impulsively that her friend started back.

"Why, what's the matter?" said Jennie in surprise.

"Nothing! nothing!" said Gipsy, hastily. "*Who* did you say it was?"

"Mr. Archibald Rivers, student-at-law."

"Jennie, they say I've changed greatly of late. Do you think I look anything like I did when you first saw me?"

"Why, not much. You were a tawny little fright

then ; you're *almost* handsome now," said the candid Jennie.

"Then he won't know me. Jennie, will you oblige by introducing Mr. Rivers to me under an assumed name?"

"Why——"

"There! there! don't ask questions ; I'll tell by and by. Go and do it."

"Well, you have always some new crotchet in your crotchety little head," said Jennie, as she started to obey.

In a few moments she reappeared, leaning on the arm of the "distinguished" Mr. Rivers. Our Archie has not changed as much as Gipsy has done during these years, save that he has grown taller and more manly-looking. He has still his frank, handsome, boyish face ; his merry blue eye and boisterous manner, a *little* subdued.

The indistinct tone in which Miss Moore introduced him prevented him from catching the name, but he scarcely observed ; and seeing in the young lady, whose lips were now pursed up and whose eyes were cast modestly on the floor, a shrinking, bashful girl, he charitably began to draw her out.

"There is quite an assembly here this evening," was his original remark, by way of encouraging her.

"Yes, sir," was the reply, in a tone slightly tremulous, which *he* ascribed to maiden bashfulness.

"What a delightful young lady your friend, Miss Moore, is," continued Archie.

"Yes, sir."

"There are a great many beautiful ladies in the room."

"Yes, sir."

"Confound her!" muttered Archie, "can she say

nothing but '*Yes, sir ?*' But the most beautiful lady present is by my side," he continued, aloud, to see how she would swallow so palpable a dose of flattery.

"*Yes, sir !*"

"Whew ! if that's not cool ! I wonder if the girl's an idiot !" thought Master Archie. Then, aloud : "Do you know you're very beautiful ?"

"Yes. I know it."

A stare of surprise followed this answer. Then he continued :

"You are a most bewitching young lady ! Never was so much charmed by anybody in my life !"

"Sorry I can't return the compliment."

"Hallo !" thought Archie, rather taken aback. "She's not such a fool as I took her to be. What do you think of that lady !" he added, pointing to a handsome but dark-complexioned girl, whom report said would one day be Mrs Rivers.

"Oh ! I don't think her pretty at all—she's such a *gipsy.*"

Archie gave a little start at the name. Poor Gipsy ! he had quite forgotten her of late.

"Do you know," he said, "I once had a little friend called Gipsy ? Your words recalled her to my memory. You remind me of her, somehow, only you are hand-somer. She was dark and ugly."

"Indeed ! Did you like her ?"

"Ye-e-e-s—a little," said Archie, hesitatingly ; "she was a half-crazy little thing—black as a squaw, and I don't think I was very fond of *her*, but she was *very* fond of me."

"Indeed, sir !" said the young lady, a momentary flash gleaming from her dark eyes ; "she must have been a bold girl, rather, to let you know it."

"She was bold—the boldest girl ever I knew, with nothing gentle and womanly about her whatever."

"What did you say her name was?"

"Gipsy—Gipsy Gower. You seem interested in her."

"I am, sir—I know her."

"*You do?*" cried Archie, aghast.

"Yes, sir; but I like her no more than you do. She was a rough, uncouth savage, detested by every one who knew her. I had the misfortune to be her room-mate in school, and she used to bore me dreadfully talking about her gawky country friends, particularly some one whom she called *Archie.*"

"Yes? What used she to say about him? She liked him, didn't she?" said Archie, eagerly.

"Why, *no;* I should say not. She used to say he was a regular fool—always laughing. She said she never knew such a greeny in all her life."

Mr. Rivers suddenly wilted down, and hadn't a word to say. Just at that moment a party of Gipsy's friends came along, and it was:

"Oh, Gipsy! Gipsy! Oh, Miss Gower! we've been searching all over for you. Everybody's dying of the blues, because you are absent. Do come with us!"

Archie leaped from his seat as though he had received a bayonet thrust. Gipsy rose, saying, in a low, sarcastic voice, as she passed him:

"Remember me to Gipsy when you see her. Tell her what I said about Archie," and she was gone.

During the remainder of the evening the "distinguished" Mr. Rivers looked about as crestfallen as a young lawyer possessed of a large stock of native impudence could well do. There he stood and watched Gipsy, who had never been so magnetic, so bewitching, so entrancing in her life before. Never by chance did

she look at him ; but there was scarcely another masculine head in the room she had not turned.

"Confound the little witch !" muttered Master Archie,
" no wonder she called me a fool ! But who the deuce
would ever think of finding little Gipsy Gower in one
of the belles of Washington ? Had it been Celeste, now,
I should not have felt surprised. And who would ever
think that yonder dazzling, brilliant, magnetic girl was
the little shy maiden who, ten minutes ago, sat beside
me with her demure '*yes, sir !*' Well, she seems to be enjoying herself anyway. So, Miss Gipsy, I'll follow your
example and do the same."

For the remainder of the evening Archie threw himself into the gay throng with the evident determination
of enjoying himself or dying in the attempt. And more
than one fair cheek flushed, and more than one pair of
bright eyes grew brighter, as their owner listened with
downcast lashes and smiling lips to the gallant words of
the handsome young lawyer. He was, if not *the* handsomest, at least *one* of the handsomest, men in the room ;
and

> "Oh ! he had that merry glance,
> That seldom lady's heart resists."

And eclipsed belles raised their graceful heads in
triumph to find the bewildering Gipsy had no power
over him. But if they had known all, they would have
found that those " merry glances " were not for them,
but to pique the jealousy of the evening star.

Ere the company dispersed he sought out Gipsy, who
withdrawing herself from the revelers, stood, silent and
alone, by the window.

"Gipsy !" he said, gently.

" Mr. Rivers !" she said, drawing herself up.

"Forgive me, Gipsy, for what I said."

8*

"I have nothing to forgive! I rather think we are quits!" replied Gipsy, coolly.

"Well, make up friends with me, and be a little like the Gipsy I used to know."

"What! like that black little squaw—that bold, ugly, half-crazy thing? You astonish me, Mr. Rivers!"

"Yes, even so, Gipsy; you know it's all true; and I'll be the same 'regular fool, always laughing.' Then shake hands and call me Archie, as you used to."

"Well, now, I don't know," said Gipsy—"I don't *think* I ought to forgive you."

"Don't think about it, then, Nonsense, Gipsy—you know you're to be my little wife!"

She laughed and extended her hand, though her dark cheek grew crimson.

"Well, there, I forgive you, Archie. Will that do? And now let us go into the supper-room, for I'm starving. One of my early habits I have not outgrown—and that is, a most alarming appetite."

"Now I shall have her all to myself for the rest of the evening," thought Archie, as he stood beside her, and watched triumphantly the many savage and ferocious glances cast toward him by the gentlemen.

But Archie found himself slightly mistaken; for Gipsy, five minutes later, told him to be off—that he was an old bore, and not half as agreeable as the most stupid of her beaus. Then laughing at his mortified face, she danced and flirted unmercifully, leaving Mr. Rivers to think she was the most capricious elf that ever tormented a young lawyer.

Every day for a week after he was a constant visitor at Mr. Moore's. And every day for a week he went away as he came, without seeing Gipsy. She was always out riding, or driving, or "not at home," though he could see her plainly laughing at him at the window.

The willful fairy seemed to take a malicious delight in teasing the life out of poor Archie. Evening after evening she accepted the escort of a handsome young English baronet, Sir George Stuart, the most devoted of all her lovers—leaving Archie to bear it as he pleased. And between jealousy, and rage, and mortification, and wounded pride, Mr. Rivers had a hard time of it. It *was* too bad to see his own little Gipsy—his girlish lady-love —taken from him this way without being able to say a word against it.

So Archie fell a prey to "green and yellow melancholy," and never saw the stately young nobleman without feeling a demoniacal desire to blow his brains out ; and nothing prevented him from doing it but the becoming respect he had for the laws of his country.

One morning, however, for a wonder, he had the good fortune to find Gipsy alone in the parlor, looking perfectly charming in her becoming *deshabille*.

"How did you enjoy yourself last night at Mrs. Greer's ball ? I saw you there with that fool of a baronet," said Archie, rather savagely.

"I enjoyed myself very well, as I always do. And I must beg of you not to speak of Sir George in that way, Mr. Rivers. I won't allow it."

"Oh, you won't !" sneered Archie. "You seem to think a great deal of him, Miss Gower."

"Why, *of course I do !* He's *so* handsome—so perfectly gentlemanlike—so agreeable, and so—everything else. He's a real love of a man."

"Oh ! the deuce take him !"

"Why, Mr. Rivers !" said Gipsy, with a very shocked expression of countenance.

"Gipsy, be serious for once. I have had something to say to you this long time, but you have been so precious careful to keep out of my sight, I've had no chance to say it.   Gipsy, do you *love* Sir George Stuart ?"

" Why, Archie ! *to be sure* I do."

" Oh-h-h !" groaned Archie.

" What's the matter ?—got the toothache ?"

" Oh, dear, no.   I have the heart-ache !"

" Sorry to hear it.   Better go to Deep Dale and consult Doctor Spider about it."

" Will you come with me ?"

" I've no objection.   I'm going home to-morrow, and I'd just as lief have you for an escort as any one else."

" Then you are not going to be married to Sir George Stuart, Gipsy ?" exclaimed Archie, eagerly.

" Why, not just now, I think."

" Gipsy, would you marry me ?"

" Well, I wouldn't mind, if nobody better offers."

" Oh, Gipsy ! be serious ; don't laugh at me now. You know you promised, when a little girl, to be my little wife.   Will you, *dear* Gipsy ?"

" There—gracious me ! you're treading on Sambo's toes."

A howl from an unfortunate black pug dog testified to the truth of this remark.

" Men are such awkward creatures ! Poor Sambo ! did he hurt you ?" said Gipsy, stooping and caressing the ugly little brute.

" Oh, saints and angels ! only hear her. She will drive me mad—I know she will. Here I offer her my heart, and hand, and fortune (though I don't happen to have such a thing about me), and she begins talking about Sambo's toes. That girl will be the death of me. And when I die I'll charge them to place on my tombstone, 'Died from an overdose of a coquette.' "

And Master Archie stamped up and down, and flung

his coat-tails about with an utterly distracted expression of countenance.

"Why, what nonsense are you going on with there?" inquired Gipsy, pausing in her task of comforting Sambo, and looking at him in surprise.

"Nonsense!" exclaimed Archie, pausing before her, and throwing himself into a tragic attitude. "Infatuated girl! the heart you now cast from you will haunt you in the dead hours of the night, when everything (but the mosquitoes) is sleeping; it will be ever before you in your English home, when you are the bride of Sir George (confound him!) Stuart; it will——"

But Master Archie could proceed no further; for Gipsy fell back in her chair, fairly screaming with laughter. Archie made a desperate effort to maintain his gravity, but the effort proved a failure, and he was forced to join Gipsy in an uproarious peal.

"Oh, dear!" said Gipsy, wiping her eyes, "I don't know when I have laughed so much."

"Yes," said Archie, in high dudgeon—"pretty thing to laugh at, too! After breaking my heart, to begin grinning about it. Humph!"

"You looked so funny—you looked——"

Gipsy's voice was lost in another fit of laughter.

"Come, now, Gipsy, like a good girl, don't laugh any more; but tell me, *will* you marry me—will you be my wife?"

"Why, yes, you dear old goose, you! I never intended to be anything else. You might have known that I'd be your wife, without making such a fuss about it," said Gipsy.

"And Sir George, Gipsy?"

"Oh, poor fellow, I gave him his *coup de conge* last night, and he set out for England this morning."

"Oh, Gipsy, my dear, you're a pearl without price!" exclaimed Archie, in a rapture.

"Glad to hear it, I'm sure. And now *do* go away, Archie, and don't bother me any longer ; for I must pack up my things and start for home to-morrow."

"You little tyrant ! Well, I am to accompany you, mind."

"Just as you please—only *do* leave me."

"Little termagant ! Accept this ring as a betrothal gift."

"Well, there—put it on, and for goodness' sake clear out."

With a glance of comical despair, Mr. Rivers took his hat and quitted the house.

CHAPTER XIX.

GIPSY'S DARING.

" It is a fearful night ; a feeble glare
Streams from the sick moon in the overclouded sky,
The ridgy billows, with a mighty cry,
Rush on the foamy beaches wild and bare.
What bark the madness of the waves will dare !"
—BYRON.

IPSY was once more at Sunset Hall. Archie had escorted her home and then returned to Washington. He would have mentioned their engagement to the squire, and asked his consent to their union, but Gipsy said :

"No, you mustn't. I hate a fuss ; and as I don't intend to be married for two or three years yet, it will be time enough to tell them all by and by."

So Archie, with a sigh, was forced to obey his capricious little love and go back, after making her promise to let him come down every month and see her; for she wouldn't write to him—it was "too much bother."

It began again to seem like old times at St. Mark's. There was Gipsy at Sunset Hall, keeping them all from dying of torpor, and astonishing the whole neighborhood by her mad freaks. There was Minnette—the proud, cold, but now beautiful Minnette—living alone at Deep Dale; for the doctor had gone from home on business. There was sweet Celeste, the Star of the Valley, in her little cottage home—the fairest, loveliest maiden the sun ever shone upon.

It was a lovely May morning. The air was made jocund with the songs of birds; the balmy breeze scarce rippled the surface of the bay, where the sunshine fell in golden glory.

Through the open doors and windows of Valley Cottage the bright May sunbeams fell warm and bright; they lingered in broad patches on the white floor, and touched gently the iron-gray locks of Miss Hagar, as she sat knitting in her leathern chair in the chimney-corner, as upright and gray as ever. Years seemed to pass on without touching her; for just as we first saw her at Lizzie Oranmore's bridal, the same does she appear to-day.

In the doorway stands a young girl, tall and graceful, dressed in soft gray muslin, fastened at her slender waist by a gold-colored belt. *Can* this young lady be our little, shy Celeste? Yes; here is the same superb form, the same dainty little head, with its wealth of pale-gold hair; the same clear, transparent complexion; the soft, dove-like eyes of blue; the broad, white queenly forehead; the little, rosy, smiling mouth. Yes, it is Celeste—celestial, truly, with the promise of her childhood more than fulfilled. The world and its flatterers —and she has heard many—have had no power to spoil her pure heart, and she has returned the same gentle, loving Celeste—the idol of all who know her, radiating light and beauty wherever she goes, a very angel of charity to the poor, and beloved and cherished by the rich. More hearts than Celeste likes to think of have been laid at her feet, to be gently and firmly, but sadly, refused ; for that sound, unsullied heart has never yet been stirred by the words of man.

She stood in the doorway, gazing with parted lips and sparkling eyes on the balmy beauty of that bright spring morning, with a hymn of gratitude and love to the Author of all this beauty filling her mind.

Suddenly the sylvan silence of the spot was broken by the thunder of horse's hoofs, and the next instant Gipsy came bounding along upon the back of her favorite Mignonne.

"Good-morning, dear Gipsy," said Celeste, with her own bright smile, as she hastened to open the gate for her. "Have you been out, as usual, hunting this morning ?"

"Yes, and there are the spoils," said Gipsy, throwing a well-filled game-bag on the ground. "I come like a true hunter—a leal knight of the gay greenwood—to lay them at the feet of my liege lady. I fancied a canvas-back duck and a bright-winged partridge would not come amiss this morning. I know my gallop has made me perfectly ravenous."

"You shall have one of them presently for breakfast," said Celeste, calling Curly, their little black maid-of-all-work. "Tie Mignonne there, and come in."

"By the way, Celeste, you don't seem to think it such an appalling act to shoot birds now as you used to," said

Gipsy, springing from her horse; "it was once a crime of the first magnitude in your eyes."

"And I confess it seems a needless piece of cruelty to me still. I could scarcely do it if I were starving, I think."

"You always were—with reverence be it spoken—rather a coward, Celeste. Do you remember the day I shot the bird that Louis saved for you, and you fell fainting to the ground?" said Gipsy, laughing at the remembrance.

"Yes, I remember. I was rather an absurd little thing in those days," said Celeste, smiling. "How I *did* love that unlucky little bird!"

"Oh! that was because Louis gave it to you. There! don't blush. Apropos of Louis, I wonder where he is now?"

"In Rome, I suppose; at least Mrs. Oranmore told me so," replied Celeste.

"Yes; when last we heard from him he was studying the old masters, as he calls them—or the old grannies, as Guardy calls them. I shouldn't wonder if he became quite famous yet, and—oh, Celeste! where did you get that pretty chain and cross?" abruptly asked Gipsy, as her eye fell on the trinket.

"A present," said Celeste, smiling and blushing.

Gipsy's keen eyes were fixed on her face with so quizzical an expression, that the rose-hue deepened to crimson on her fair cheek as they passed into the house. And Gipsy went up and shook hands with Miss Hagar, and seated herself on a low stool at her feet, to relate the morning's adventures, while Celeste laid the cloth and set the table for breakfast.

After breakfast Gipsy rode off in the direction of Deep Dale. On entering the parlor she found Minnette sitting reading.

Minnette—now a tall, splendidly developed, womanly girl, with the proud, handsome face of her childhood—rose and welcomed her guest with cold courtesy. The old, fiery light lurked still in her black eyes; but the world had learned her to subdue it, and a coldly-polite reserve had taken the place of the violent outburst of passion so common in her tempestuous childhood.

"Don't you find it horribly dull here, Minnette?" said Gipsy, swallowing a rising yawn.

"No," replied Minnette; "I prefer solitude. There are few—*none*, perhaps—who sympathize with me, and in books I find companions."

"Well, I prefer less silent companions, for my part," said Gipsy. "I don't believe in making an old hermit or bookworm of myself for anybody."

"Every one to her taste," was the cold rejoinder.

"When do you expect your father home?" inquired Gipsy.

"To-night."

"Then he'll have a storm to herald his coming," said Gipsy, going to the window and scanning the heavens with a practiced eye.

"A storm—impossible!" said Minnette. "There is not a cloud in the sky."

"Nevertheless, we shall have a storm," said Gipsy. "I read the sky as truly as you do your books; and if he attempts to enter the bay to-night, I'm inclined to think that the first land he makes will be the bottom."

Minnette heard this intelligence with the utmost coolness, saying only:

"Indeed! I did not know you were such a judge of the weather. Well, probably, when they see the storm coming, they will put into some place until it is over."

"If they don't, I wouldn't give much for their chance

of life," said Gipsy, as she arose to go ; "but don't worry, Minnette—all may be right yet."

Minnette looked after her with a scornful smile. Fret ! She had little intention of doing it ; and five minutes after the departure of Gipsy she was so deeply immersed in her book as to forget everything else.

As the day wore on and evening approached, Gipsy's prophecy seemed about to prove true. Dark, leaden clouds rolled about the sky ; the wind no longer blew in a steady breeze, but howled in wild gusts. The bosom of the bay was tossing and moaning wildly, heaving and plunging as though struggling madly in agony. Gipsy seized her telescope, and running up to one of the highest rooms in the old hall, swept an anxious glance across the troubled face of the deep. Far out, scarcely distinguishable from the white caps of the billows, she beheld the sail of a vessel driving, with frightful rapidity, toward the coast—driving toward its own doom ; for, once near those foaming breakers covering the sunken reefs of rocks, no human being could save her. Gipsy stood gazing like one fascinated ; and onward still the doomed bark drove—like a lost soul rushing to its own destruction.

Night and darkness at last shut out the ill-fated ship from her view. Leaving the house, she hastily made her way to the shore, and standing on a high, projecting peak, waited for the moon to rise, to view the scene of tempest and death.

It lifted its wan, spectral face at last from behind a bank of dull, black clouds, and lit up with its ghastly light the heaving sea and driving vessel. The tempest seemed momentarily increasing. The waves boiled, and seethed, and foamed, and lashed themselves in fury against the beetling rocks. And, holding by a projecting cliff, Gipsy stood surveying the scene. You might have thought her the spirit of the storm, looking on the tempest she had herself raised. Her black hair and thin dress streamed in the wind behind her, as she stood leaning forward, her little, wild, dark face looking strange and weird, with its blazing eyes, and cheeks burning with the mad excitement of the scene. Down below her, on the shore, a crowd of hardy fishermen were gathered, watching with straining eyes the gallant craft that in a few moments would be a broken ruin. On the deck could be plainly seen the crew, making most superhuman exertions to save themselves from the terrible fate impending over them.

All in vain! Ten minutes more and they would be dashed to pieces. Gipsy could endure the maddening sight no longer. Leaping from the cliff, she sprang down the rocks, like a mountain kid, and landed among the fishermen, who were too much accustomed to see her among them in scenes like this to be much startled by it now.

"Will you let them perish before your eyes?" she cried, wildly. "Are you men, to stand here idle in a time like this? But with the boats, and save their lives!'

"Impossible, Miss Gipsy!" answered half a dozen voices. "No boat could live in such a surf."

"Oh, great heaven! And must they die miserably before your very eyes, without even making an effort to save them?" she exclaimed, passionately, wringing her hands. "Oh, that I were a man! Listen! Whoever will make the attempt shall receive five hundred dollars reward!"

Not one moved. Life could not be sacrificed for money.

"There she goes!" cried a voice.

Gipsy turned to look. A wild, prolonged shriek of mortal agony rose above the uproar of the storm, and the crew were left struggling for life in the boiling waves.

With a piercing cry, scarcely less anguished than their own, the mad girl bounded to the shore, pushed off a light *batteau*, seized the oars, and the next moment was dancing over the foaming waves.

A shout of fear and horror arose from the shore at the daring act. She heeded it not, as, bending all her energies to the task of guiding her frail bark through the tempestuous billows, she bent her whole strength to the oars.

Oh! surely her guardian angel steered that boat on its errand of mercy through the heaving, tempest-tossed sea! The salt spray seemed blinding her as it dashed in her face; but on she flew, now balanced for a moment on the top of a snowy hill of foam, the next, sunk down, down, as though it were never more to rise.

"Leap into the boat!" she cried, in a clear, shrill voice, that made itself heard, even above the storm.

Strong hands clutched it with the desperation of death, and two heavy bodies rolled violently in. The weight nearly overset the light skiff; but, bending her body to the oars, she righted it again.

"Where are the rest?" she exclaimed, wildly.

"All gone to the bottom. Give me the oars!" cried a voice.

She felt herself lifted from where she sat, placed gently in the bottom of the boat, and then all consciousness left her, and, overcome by the excitement, she fainted where she lay.

When she again opened her eyes she was lying in the arms of some one on the shore, with a circle of troubled, anxious faces around her. She sprang up wildly.

"Are they saved?" she exclaimed, looking around.

"Yes; thanks to your heroism, our lives are preserved," said a voice beside her.

She turned hastily round. It was Doctor Nicholas Wiseman. Another form lay stark and rigid on the sand, with men bending over him.

A deadly sickness came over Gipsy—she knew not why it was. She turned away, with a violent shudder, from his outstretched hand, and bent over the still form on the sand. All made way for her with respectful deference; and she knelt beside him and looked in his face. He was a boy—a mere youth, but singularly handsome, with a look of deep repose on his almost beautiful face.

"Is he dead?" she cried, in a voice of piercing anguish.

"No; only stunned," said the doctor, coming over and feeling his pulse.

"Take him to Sunset Hall, then," said Gipsy, turning to some of the men standing by.

A shutter was procured, and the senseless form of the lad placed upon it, and, raising it on their shoulders, they bore him in the direction of the old mansion-house.

Doctor Wiseman went toward his own home. And Gipsy, the free mountain maid, leaped up the rocks, feeling, for the first time in her life, sick and giddy. Oh! better, far better for her had they but perished in the seething waves!

CHAPTER XX.

THE SAILOR BOY'S DOOM.

" With gentle hand and soothing tongue
    She bore the leech's part ;
And while she o'er his sick bed hung
    He paid her with his heart."—SCOTT.

HE sunshine of a breezy June morning fell pleasantly into the chamber of the invalid. It was a bright, airy room—a perfect paradise of a sick chamber—with its snowy curtained bed, its tempting easy-chair, its white lace window curtains fluttering softly in the morning air. The odor of flowers came wafted through the open casement ; and the merry chirping of a bright-winged canary, hanging in the sunshine, filled the room with its cheerful music.

Reclining in the easy-chair, gazing longingly out at the glorious sunshine, sat the young sailor whose life Gipsy had saved. His heavy dark hair fell in shining waves over his pale, intelligent brow ; and his large blue eyes had a look of dreamy melancholy that few female hearts could have resisted.

Suddenly his eye lighted up, and his whole face brightened, as a clear, sweet voice, singing a gay carol, met his ear. Gipsy still retained her old habit of singing as she walked ; and the next moment the door opened, and she stood, like some bright vision, before him, with cheeks glowing, eyes sparkling, and her countenance bright and radiant from her morning ride ; her dark purple riding-habit setting off to the best advantage her straight, slight; rounded form ; and her jaunty riding-hat, with its long, sweeping, sable plume, giving her the air of a young mountain queen, crowned with vitality, and sceptered with life and beauty.

"Oh, I have had such a charming canter over the hills this morning," she cried, with her wild, breezy laugh. "How I wished you had been well enough to accompany me. Mignonne fairly flew, leaping over yawning chasms and rocks as though he felt not the ground beneath him. But I am forgetting—how do you feel this morning?"

"Much better, sweet lady. Who could be long ill with such a nurse?" he replied, while his fine eyes lit up with admiration and gratitude.

Gipsy, be it known, had installed herself as the nurse of the young sailor; and, by her sleepless care and tender nursing, had almost restored him from death to life. And when he became convalescent, she would sit by his bedside for hours, reading, talking, and singing for him, until gratitude on his part ripened into fervent love; while she only looked upon him as she would on any other stranger—taking an interest in him only on account of his youth and friendliness, and because she had saved his life.

"Well, I'm glad to hear it, I'm sure! I want you to hurry and get well, so you can ride out with me. Are you a good horseman?"

"Yes, I think so," he said, smiling.

"Because, if you're not, you mustn't attempt to try our hills. It takes an expert rider, I can tell you, to gallop over them without breaking his neck."

"Yet *you* venture, fairest lady."

"*Me?* Ha, ha! Why, I've been on horseback ever since I was two years old. My horse is my other self. I could as soon think of living without laughing as without Mignonne."

"Then, sweet lady, you will kindly be my teacher in the art of riding."

"Oh, I wouldn't want better fun ; but look here, Mr. Danvers, don't be ' sweet lady'-ing me ! I ain't used to it, you know. People generally call me 'Monkey,' 'Imp,' 'Torment,' 'Wretch,' and other pet names of a like nature. But if you don't like any of them, call me Gipsy, or Gipsy Gower, but don't call me 'sweet lady' again. You see, I never could stand nicknames."

"And may I ask you why you have received those names?" inquired the young midshipman (for such he was), laughing.

"Why, because I *am* an imp, a wretch, and always was—and always will be, for that matter. I believe I was made to keep the world alive. Why, everybody in St. Mark's would be dead of the blues if it weren't for me."

"Yes ; I have heard of some of your wild antics. That good old lady, Mrs. Gower, was with me last night, and we had quite a long conversation about you, I assure you."

"Poor dear aunty, she's at her wits' end, sometimes, to know what to do with me. And, by that same token, here she comes. Speak of somebody, and he'll appear, you know."

Mrs. Gower opened the door, flushed and palpitating with her walk up-stairs. Poor Mrs. Gower was "waxing fat" with years ; and it was no easy task for her to toil her way up the long staircase of Sunset Hall.

"Oh, Gipsy, my dear !" she exclaimed, all in a glow of pleasurable excitement, "guess who's come !"

"Who, who ?" cried Gipsy, eagerly.

"Archie !"

Up sprang Gipsy, flew past Mrs. Gower, and was down the stairs in a twinkling.

9

"Archie! who the deuce is he?" thought the young midshipman, with a jealous twinge.

"You seem to have brought Miss Gower pleasant news," he remarked, by way of drawing her out, after he he had answered her inquiries about his health.

"Why, yes, it's natural she should be glad to meet her old playmate," replied the unsuspecting old lady.

"Ah! her old playmate. Then she has known him for a long time?"

"Yes; they were children together, grew up together, and were always fond of one another. It has always been my dearest wish to see them united; and I dare say they will be yet."

The youth's face was turned to the window as she spoke, or good Mrs. Gower might have been startled by his paleness. As he asked no more questions, the worthy old lady began to think he might wish to be left to himself; so, after a few general directions to be sure and take care of himself and not catch cold, she quitted the room.

Meantime, Archie and Gipsy were holding a very animated conversation in the parlor below. Archie was relating how he had undertaken a very important case, that would call him from home for four or five months; and that, when it was over, he would be rich enough to set up an establishment for himself, and return to St. Mark's to claim his little bride.

"And now, Gipsy," he concluded, "what mischief have you been perpetrating since I saw you last? Who have you locked up, or shot, or ran away with since?"

In reply, Gipsy related the story of the wreck, and went into ecstasies on the beauty of Mr. Harry Danvers, U. S. N. Archie listened with a savage frown, that grew perceptibly more savage every moment. Gipsy saw it, and maliciously praised him more and more.

"Oh, Archie, he's the handsomest fellow I ever met. So agreeable and polite, with such a beautiful, melancholy countenance!"

"Oh, curse his melancholy countenance!"

"For shame, sir! How can you speak so of my friends? But it's just like you. You always were a cross, disagreeable old thing—now then!"

"Yes; I'm not such a sweet seraph as this agreeable and polite young son of Neptune," said Mr. Rivers, with a withering sneer. "Just let me catch sight of his 'beautiful, melancholy countenance,' and maybe I'll spoil its beauty for him."

"Now, Archie, you're real hateful. I'm sure you'll like him when you see him."

"Like him! Yes, I'd like to blow his brains out."

"No, you mustn't, either; he's too handsome to be killed. Oh, Archie, when he laughs he looks so charming!"

"Confound him! *I'll* make him laugh on the other side of his mouth!" growled the exasperated Archie.

"He's got *such* a sweet mouth and *such* lovely white teeth!" continued the tantalizing fairy.

"I wish he and his white teeth were at the bottom of the Red Sea!" burst out Archie, in a rage.

"Why, Mr. Rivers, you're positively jealous!" said Gipsy, looking very much surprised indeed.

"Jealous! Yes, I should think so. You are enough to drive any one jealous. Suppose I began raving about young ladies—their 'melancholy countenances,' and 'sweet mouths,' and 'white teeth,' and all such stuff—how would you like it, I want to know?"

"Why, I shouldn't care."

"You wouldn't? Oh, Jupiter Olympus! Only hear

that!" exclaimed Archie, striding up and down in a towering passion. "That shows all you care about *me!* Going and falling in love with the first old tarry sailor you meet! I won't endure it! I'll blow my brains out—I'll——"

"Well, don't do it in the house, then. Pistols make a noise, and might disturb Mr. Danvers."

Archie fell into a chair with a deep groan.

"There, don't look so dismal. I declare, you give me a fit of the blues every time you come to see me. Why can't you be pleasant, and laugh?"

"Laugh!" exclaimed poor Archie.

"Yes, *laugh!* I'm sure you used to be forever grinning. Poor, dear Mr. Danvers is sick, yet *he* laughs."

"Mr. Danvers again!" shouted Archie, springing to his feet. "May Lucifer twist Mr. Danvers' neck for him! I won't stay another minute in the house. I'll clear out, and never see you more. I'll never enter your presence again, you heartless girl!"

"Well, won't you take a cup of coffee before you go?" said Gipsy, with her sweetest smile.

"Hallo, Jupiter! Jupiter, I say, bring round my horse. And now, most faithless of women, I leave you forever. Life is now a blank to me; and, ere yonder sun sets, I shall be in eternity."

"Is it possible? Won't you write when you get there, and let me know if it's a good place for lawyers to settle in?"

Oh! such a groan as followed this! Casting a tragical look of despair at Gipsy, who sat smiling serenely, Archie rushed from the house.

Ten minutes later he was back again. Gipsy had stretched herself on a sofa, and was apparently fast asleep.

"Heartless girl!" exclaimed Archie, shaking her; "wake up, Gipsy!"

"Oh! is it you?" said Gipsy, drowsily opening her eyes. "What did you wake me up for? I thought you had started on your journey to eternity."

"Gipsy, shall I go?"

"Just as you please, Archie—only let me go to sleep, and don't bother me."

"Oh, Gipsy!—you cruel coquette! won't you bid me stay?"

"Well, *stay*, then! I wish to goodness you wouldn't be such a pest."

"Gipsy, tell me—do you love me or Mr. Danvers best?"

"I don't love either of you—there, now! And I tell you what, Archie Rivers, if you don't go off and let me get asleep, I'll never speak to you again. Mind that!"

With a deep sigh, Archie obeyed, and walked out of the room with a most dejected expression of countenance. No sooner was he gone than Gipsy sprang up, and, clapping her hands, danced round the room—her eyes sparkling with delight.

"Oh, it's such fun!" she exclaimed. "Poor, dear Archie!—if I haven't made him a victim to the 'green-eyed monster!' Mr. Danvers, indeed! As if that dear, good-natured Archie wasn't worth all the Mr. Danvers that ever adorned the quarterdeck! Oh! won't I flirt, though, and make the 'distinguished Mr. Rivers' so jealous, that he won't know whether he's standing on his head or his heels! If I *am* to settle down into a humdrum Mrs. Rivers some day, I'll have as much frolic as I can before it. So, Master Archie, look out for the 'wrath that's to come;' for your agonies won't move me in the least."

And never did any one keep her word more faithfully

than Gipsy. During the fortnight that Archie was to stay with them she flirted unmercifully with the handsome young midshipman, who was now able to ride out, quite unconscious of all the hopes she was rousing in his bosom. Poor Gipsy! little did she dream that, while she rode by his side, and bestowed upon him her enchanting smiles, and wore the colors he liked, and sang the songs he loved, to torment the unhappy Archie, that he, believing her serious, had already surrendered his heart to the bewitching sprite, and reposed in the blissful dream of one day calling her his!

Archie Rivers *was* jealous. Many were the ferocious glances he cast upon the young sailor; and many and dire were his threats of vengeance. But Gipsy, mad girl, only listened and laughed, and knew not that *another* pair of ears heard those threats, and would one day use them to her destruction.

But matters were now drawing to a crisis. The young midshipman was now quite restored to health, and found himself obliged to turn his thoughts toward his own home. Archie's fortnight had elapsed; but still he lingered—too jealous to leave while his rival remained.

One bright moonlight night the three were gathered in the cool, wide porch in front of the mansion. Gipsy stood in the doorway—her white dress fluttering in the breeze—binding in her dark, glossy curls a wreath of crimson rosebuds, given her a few moments previous by Mr. Danvers. All her smiles, and words, and glances were directed toward him. Archie was apparently forgotten.

"Please sing one of your charming songs, Miss Gipsy; this is just the hour for music," said Mr. Danvers.

"With pleasure. What shall it be?—your favorite?"

inquired Gipsy, taking her guitar and seating herself at his feet.

"If you will be so good," he replied, his eyes sparkling with pleasure at her evident preference.

Archie's brow grew dark. He hated the sailor's favorite song, because it *was* his favorite. This Gipsy well knew ; and her brown eyes twinkled with mischief, as she began, in her clear, sweet voice :

> "'Sleeping, I dream, love—I dream, love, of thee ;
> O'er the bright waves, love, floating with thee ;
> Light in thy soft hair played the soft wind,
> Fondly thy white arms around me were twined ;
> And as thy song, love, swelled o'er the sea,
> Fondly thy blue eyes beamed, love, on me.'"

She hesitated a moment, and looked up in his face, as though really intending the words for him. He was bending over her, pale and panting—his blue eyes blazing with a light that brought the crimson blood in a rosy tide to her very temples. She stopped abruptly.

"Go on !" he said, in a low voice.

She hesitated, glanced at Archie, and seeing the storm-cloud on his brow, the demon of mischief once more conquered her better nature, and she resumed :

> "'Soon o'er the bright waves howled forth the gale,
> Fiercely the lightning flashed on our sail ;
> And as our frail bark drove through the sea,
> Thine eyes, like loadstones, beamed, love, on me.
> Oh, heart, awaken !—wrecked on lone shore,
> Thou art forsaken !—dream, heart, no more.'"

Ere the last words were uttered, Archie had seized his hat and rushed from the house ; and Danvers, forgetting everything save the entrancing creature at his feet, clasped her suddenly in his arms, and passionately exclaimed :

"Oh, Gipsy! my love! my life, my beautiful mountain sprite!—can you, will you love me?"

With a wild, sharp cry of terror and anger, she broke from his arms, and sprang back, with flashing eyes.

"Back, sir, back!—I command you! How *dare* you attempt such a liberty with me?"

How beautiful she looked in her wrath, with her blazing eyes, and crimson cheeks, and straight little form drawn up to its full height, in surprise and indignation.

He stood gazing at her for a moment—amazed, thunder-struck at the change. Then, seeing only her enchanting beauty, he took a step forward, threw himself at her feet, and broke forth passionately:

"Gipsy, I love you—I worship you. Have you been mocking me all this time?—or do you love me, too?"

"Rise, sir! I have neither been mocking you, nor do I love you! Rise! rise! Kneel not to me!"

"And I have been deceived? Oh, falsest of false ones! why did you learn me to love you?"

"Mr. Danvers, don't call me names. As to the learning you to love *me*, I never attempted such a thing in my life! I'd scorn to do it," she said, indignantly; but even while she spoke, the blood rushed in a fiery torrent to her face, and then back to her heart, for she thought of all the encouragement her merciless flirtation must have given him.

"You did, Gipsy, you know you *did!*" he vehemently exclaimed. "Every encouragement that could be given to a lover, you gave to me; and I—fool that I was—I believed you, never dreaming that I should find a flinty, hardened flirt in one whom I took to be a pure-hearted mountain maiden."

Had Gipsy felt herself innocent of the charge, how indignantly she would have denied it. But the consciousness of guilt sent the crimson once more to her brow, as she replied in a low, hurried tone :

" Mr. Danvers, I have done wrong ! Forgive me ! As heaven is my witness, I dreamed not that you cared for me. It was my mad, wild love of mischief brought all this about. Mr. Danvers, it is as yet a secret, but Mr. Rivers is my betrothed husband. Some fiend prompted me to make him jealous, and to accomplish that end I—I blush to say it—flirted with you ; alas, never dreaming you thought anything of it. And now that I have acknowledged my fault, will you forgive me, and—be my friend ?"

She extended her hand. He smiled bitterly, and passed her without touching it. Then leaving the house, he mounted his horse and galloped furiously away. Prophetic, indeed, were the words with which her song had ended—words that came pealing through the dim aisles of the forest after him, as he plunged frantically along :

> "Oh, heart, awaken !—wrecked on lone shore,
> Thou art forsaken !—dream, heart, no more !"

Gipsy stood still in the porch, cold and pale, awaiting his return. But though she waited until the stars grew dim in the sky, he came not. Morning dawned, and found her pale with undefined fear, but still he was absent.

After breakfast, Archie came over, still angry and sullen, after the previous night's scene, to find Gipsy quieter and more gentle than he had ever seen her before in her life.

"I wish he would come ! I wish he would come !" cried her wild, excited heart, as she paced up and down, until her eyes grew bright and her cheeks grew burning hot, with feverish watching and vague fear.

9*

"You look ill and excited, Gipsy. A canter over the hills will do you good," said Archie, anxiously.

She eagerly assented, and leaping on Mignonne's back, dashed away at a tremendous pace, yet could not go half quick enough to satisfy her restless longing to fly, fly, she knew not where.

"Where are you going, Gipsy?" cried Archie, who found some difficulty to keep up with the break-neck pace at which she rode.

"To the Black Gorge," was her reply, as she thundered over the cliff.

"Why, Gipsy! what possesses you to go to that wild place?" said Archie, in surprise.

"I don't know—I feel as if I must go there! Don't talk to me, Archie! I believe I'm crazy this morning!"

She flew on swifter than ever, until they reached the spot—a huge, black, yawning gulf among the hills. She rode so close to the fearful brink that Archie's heart stood still in horror.

"Are you mad, Gipsy?" he cried, seizing her bridle-rein and forcing her back. "One false step, and your brains would be dashed out against the rocks."

But, fixing her eyes on the dark chasm, she answered him only by a wild, prolonged shriek, so full of piercing anguish that his blood seemed curdling in his veins, while, with bloodless face and quivering finger, she pointed to the gulf.

He leaped from his horse and approached the dizzy edge. And there a sight met his eyes that froze his heart with horror.

"Great God!" he cried, springing back, with a face deadly white. "A horse and rider lie dead and mangled below!"

A deadly faintness came over Gipsy; the ground seemed reeling around her, and countless stars danced before her eyes. For a moment she was on the verge of swooning, then by a powerful effort the tide of life rolled back, and she leaped from her horse and stood by his side.

"It is impossible to reach the bottom," cried Archie, in a voice low with horror. "A cat could hardly clamber down those perpendicular sides."

"I can do it, Archie; I often went up and down there when a child," exclaimed Gipsy; and ere Archie could restrain her, the fearless girl had caught hold of a stunted spruce tree and swung herself over the edge of the appalling gorge.

Archie Rivers scarcely breathed; he felt as though he scarcely lived while she rapidly descended by catching the matted shrubs growing along its sides. She was down at last, and bending over the mangled form below.

"Gipsy! Gipsy! do you recognize him?" cried Archie.

She looked up, and he saw a face from which every trace of life seemed to have fled.

"Yes," she replied, hoarsely. "*It is Danvers!* Ride—ride for your life to Sunset Hall, and bring men and ropes to take him up!"

In an instant he was in the saddle, and off. In less than an hour he returned, with half the population in the village after him, whom the news of the catastrophe had brought together.

Ropes were lowered to Gipsy, who still remained where Archie had left her, and the lifeless form of the young man drawn up. Gipsy, refusing all aid, clambered up the side, and the mournful cavalcade set out for Sunset Hall.

He was quite dead. It was evident he had fallen, in the darkness, into the gorge, and been instantly killed. His fair hair hung, clotted with blood, round his forehead : and a fearful gash in the temple showed the wound whence his young life had flowed away. And Gipsy, feeling as though she were his murderess, sat by his side, and, gazing on the still, cold form, shed the first bitter tears that had ever fallen from her eyes. By some strange coincidence, it was in that self-same spot the dead body of Barry Oranmore had been found.

Poor Gipsy ! The sunshine was fast fading out of her sky, and the clouds of fate gathering thick and fast around her. She wept now for another—knowing not how soon she was to weep for herself.

CHAPTER XXI.

THE SPIDER WEAVES HIS WEB.

" A fearful sign stands in thy house of life—
An enemy—a fiend lurks close behind
The radiance of thy planet. Oh, be warned !"
—COLERIDGE.

" And now a darker hour ascends."—MARMION.

WEEK after the event recorded in the last chapter Archie went back to the city. Before he went, he had obtained a promise from Gipsy—who had grown strangely still and gentle since the death of Danvers—to become his wife immediately upon his return ; but, with her usual eccentricity, she refused to allow him to make their engagement public.

" Time enough by and by," was still her answer ; and Archie was forced to be content.

Gipsy was, for a while, sad and quiet, but both were

foreign to her character ; and, with the natural buoyancy of youth, she shook off her gloom, and soon once more her merry laugh made music through the old house.

Doctor Nicholas Wiseman sometimes made his appearance at Sunset Hall of late. Lizzie was suffering from a low fever ; and as he was the only physician in St. Mark's, he was called in.

As he sat one day in the parlor at luncheon with the squire, Gipsy came tripping along with her usual elastic step, and touching her hat gallantly to the gentlemen, ran up to her own room. The squire's eyes followed her with a look of fond pride.

"Did you ever see such another charming little vixen?" he asked, turning to the doctor.

"Miss Gower's certainly an extraordinary young lady," said the doctor, dryly. "I have often been surprised, Squire Erliston, that you should treat your housekeeper's niece as one of your own family."

"She's not my housekeeper's niece," blurted out the squire ; "she was——"

He paused, suddenly recollecting that the discovery of Gipsy was a secret.

"She was what?" said the doctor, fixing his keen eyes on the old man's face.

"Well, hang it, Wiseman, I suppose it makes no difference whether I tell *you* or not. 'Gipsy is not Mrs. Gower's niece : she is a foundling."

"Yes," said the doctor, pricking up his ears.

"Yes, last Christmas Eve, just seventeen years ago, Mrs. Gower, returning from A——, found Gipsy lying on the beach, near the south end of the city."

Long habit had given Dr. Wiseman full control over his emotions, but now the blood rushed in a purple tide to his sallow face, as he leaped from his chair and fairly shouted :

" *What!* "

" Eh? Lord bless the man!—what's the matter?" said the squire, staring at him until his little fat eyes seemed ready to burst from their sockets.

"What did you say?—found her on the beach on Christmas Eve, seventeen years ago?" said the doctor, seizing him fiercely by the arm, and glaring upon him with his yellow eyes.

"Yes, I said so. What in the name of all the demons is the matter with you?" roared the squire, shaking him off. "What do *you* know about it?"

"Nothing! nothing! nothing!" replied the doctor, remembering himself, and sinking back in his chair. "Pray, go on."

The squire eyed him suspiciously.

"My dear sir," said the doctor, every trace of emotion now passed away, "forgive my violence. But, really, the story seemed so improbable——"

"Improbable or not, sir," interrupted the squire, angry at being doubted, "it's true as Gospel. It was a snowy, unpleasant night. Mrs. Gower and Jupiter were returning from the city, and took the shore road in preference to going over the hills. As they went along, Mrs. Gower was forced to get out on account of the dangerous road; and hearing a child cry, she stooped down, and found Gipsy lying wrapped up in a shawl, in the sand. Well, sir, *my* housekeeper, as a matter of course—being a humane woman—brought the child (which could not have been a week old) home, and gave it her name. And *that*, sir, is the history of Gipsy Gower, let it seem ever so improbable."

Like lightning there flashed across the mind of the doctor the recollection of the advancing sleigh-bells which had startled him from the beach. This, then, was the secret of her disappearance! This, then, was

the child of Esther Erliston and Alfred Oranmore!
This wild, untamed, daring elf was the heiress, in her
mother's right, of all the broad lands of the Erlistons.
She had been brought up as a dependent in the house of
which she was the rightful heiress: and the squire
dreamed not that his "monkey" was his grandchild!

Thoughts like these flashed like lightning through
the mind of Dr. Wiseman. The sudden, startling discovery bewildered him; he felt unequal to the task of
conversing. And making some excuse, he arose abruptly, entered his gig, and letting the reins fall on his
horse's neck, allowed him to make the best of his way
home; while, with his head dropped on his breast,
he pondered on the strange disclosure he had just
heard.

No one living, it was evident, knew who she was,
save himself. What would old Dame Oranmore say
when she heard it? Wretch as he was, he found himself
forced to acknowledge the hand of a ruling Providence
in all this. The child who had been cast out to die had
been nurtured in the home that was hers by right. By
his hand the mother had perished; yet the heroism of
the daughter had preserved his worthless life.

"What use shall I make of this· discovery?" he
mused, as he rode along. "How can I turn it to my
own advantage? If I wish it, I can find little difficulty
in convincing the world that she is the rightful heiress
of Mount Sunset, instead of Louis Oranmore. But how
to do it, without implicating myself—that's the question.
There was no witness to the death-bed scene of Esther
Erliston; and I can assert that Madam Oranmore caused
me to remove the child, without mentioning the mother
at all. I can also easily feign some excuse for leaving
her in the snow—talk about my remorse and anguish at
finding her gone, and all that. Now, if I could only get

this hare-brained girl securely in my power, in such a way as to make her money the price of her freedom, I would not hesitate one moment about proclaiming it all. But how to get her in my power—she is keen and wide-awake, with all her madness, and not half so easily duped as most girls of her age   Let me think !"

His head fell lower, his claw-like harrds opened and shut as though clutching some one, his brows knit in a hard knot, and his eyes seemed burning holes in the ground, with their wicked, immovable gaze.

At last, his mind seemed to be made up.   Lifting his head, he said, with calm, grim determination :

"Yes, my mind is made up ; that—girl—shall—be—my—WIFE !"

Again he paused.   His project, when repeated aloud, seemed so impossible to accomplish that it almost startled him.

"It may be difficult to bring about," he said, as if in answer to his momentary hesitation.   "No doubt it will ; but, nevertheless, it shall, it will, it *must* be done !   Once her husband, and I shall have a legal right to everything she possesses.   The world need not know I have made the discovery until after our marriage ; it shall think it is for love I marry her.   Love!—ha, ha, ha !   Just fancy Dr. Wiseman, at the age of fifty-nine, falling in love with a chit of a girl of seventeen !   Well, I shall set my wits to work ; and if I fail to accomplish it, it will be the first time I have ever failed in aught I have undertaken. She calls me a spider ; let her take care lest she be caught—lest her bright wings are imprisoned in the web I will weave.   Her opposition will be fierce and firm ; and, if I have studied her aright, she can only be conquered through those she loves.   That she loves that whipper-snapper of a nephew of mine, I have long known ; and yet that very love shall make her become my wife. And so my bright little Gipsy Gower—or Gipsy Oranmore—from this day forth you are mine !"

———

"Look here, aunty," said Gipsy, following Mrs. Gower, as she wandered through the house, brush in hand, "what brings that old spider here so often of late? He and Guardy appear to be as thick as two pickpockets—though, a few years ago, Guardy detested the sight of him. They are for everlasting closeted together, plotting something. Now, aunty, it looks suspicious, don't it ?"

"I am afraid Dr. Wiseman is drawing your guardian into some rash speculation," said Mrs. Gower. "The squire is always muttering about 'stocks,' and 'interest,' and such things. I am afraid the doctor is using him for his own purposes. Heaven forgive me if I wrong him !"

"Wrong him! I tell you, aunty, that Spider's a regular snake. I wouldn't trust him as far as I could see him. He has a way of looking at me that I don't half like. Whenever I'm in the room he stares and stares at me, as if I were some natural curiosity. Perhaps he's falling in love with me. There! I tell you what, aunty—I've just hit the right thing in the middle —he's meditating whether or not he'll raise me to the dignity of Mrs. Spider Wiseman—I know he is !" exclaimed Gipsy, laughing, little dreaming how near she had stumbled to the truth.

"Nonsense, child. A man of Dr. Wiseman's age and habits has little thought of taking a wife, much less such a wild one as you. I hope it may all turn out well, though I have my doubts."

"So have I," said Gipsy ; "and I'm going to keep a bright lookout for breakers ahead. If that yellow old ogre tries to bamboozle poor, dear, simple Guardy, he'll find himself in a worse scrape than when I saved him from drowning. I know I was born to be a knight-errant, and protect innocent old men, and astonish the world generally. And now I must run up stairs, and see if I can do anything for poor little Aunt Liz."

While Gipsy was conversing with Mrs. Gower, a dialogue of a different nature was going on in the parlor betwixt the squire and the doctor.

Artfully had Dr. Wiseman's plans been laid, and skillfully were they executed. With his oily, persuasive words, and flattering tongue, he had got the squire completely and irrecoverably in his power, in order that the hand of his ward might be the price of his freedom.

Dr. Wiseman knew the squire always had a mania for speculating. Taking advantage of this, he entrapped him into investing in some mad scheme, which failed, as the doctor well knew it would, leaving the squire hopelessly in debt. Of all his creditors he owed the doctor himself the most; for that obliging man had insisted on lending him large sums of ready money. And now the time of payment was at hand, and where should he obtain the money?

Squire Erliston was rich—that is, the estate of Mount Sunset was in itself a princely fortune; but this was to descend to his grandson; and the squire had too much pride to allow it to go to him burdened with debt. Neither could he mortgage any part of it to pay off the debt. He felt that his heir ought not to suffer for his own madness. Besides, he did not wish his grandson to know how egregiously he had allowed himself to be duped by a set of sharpers. Therefore he now sat listening to the doctor, half-stupefied at learning the extent of his losses—the amount of debts which he had no means of paying; while the doctor condoled with him outwardly, and chuckled inwardly at the success of his plans.

"Moore, to whom you are indebted to the amount of

twenty thousand dollars, even goes so far as to threaten law proceedings if he is not immediately paid," said the doctor, continuing the conversation.

The squire groaned.

"I told him it might not be convenient for you to meet so many heavy liabilities at once : but he would not listen to reason—said he would give you a week to deliberate, and if at the end of that time the money was not forthcoming, your *rascality*, as he termed it, should be openly proclaimed to the world, and the law would force you to pay."

"Oh, Lord !" said the squire, writhing inwardly.

"His intention, without doubt, is to obtain a claim on Mount Sunset ; and, your other creditors joining him, the whole estate will finally become theirs."

"Never !" shouted the squire, leaping fiercely to his feet. "I will shoot every villain among them first ! Mount Sunset has been in our family for years, and no gang of swindlers shall ever possess it."

. "My dear sir," said the doctor, soothingly, "do not be excited. It is useless, and will only make matters worse. You see you are completely in their power, and there is no possible hope of escape. In spite of all you can do, I fear Mount Sunset will be theirs, and you and your family will be turned out upon the world, comparatively speaking, beggars."

The unhappy squire sank back in his chair ; and, covering his face with his hands, writhed and groaned in mental torture.

"Your only course now," continued the merciless doctor, fixing his snake-like eyes with lurking triumph on his victim, "is to write to your grandson, confess all to him, and bring him home. He is an artist of some note, they say. Most probably, therefore, he will be able to support you—though it may seem strange to him first to work for his living."

" Work for his living !" shouted the squire, maddened by the words. "Louis Oranmore work for his living ! No, sir ! he has not sunk so low as that yet. If need be, he has the property of his grandmother Oranmore still remaining."

" The property of Mrs. Oranmore will not be his until her death, which may not be this ten years yet. She is hard and penurious, and would hardly give him a guinea to keep him from starving. Besides, would *you*, Squire Erliston, live on the bounty of Mrs. Oranmore ?" said the doctor, with a sarcastic sneer.

"No, sir ; I would die of starvation first !" replied the squire, almost fiercely. "But she, or some one else, might lend me the money to pay off these accursed debts."

"Not on such security as you would give, Squire Erliston," said the doctor, calmly. " In fact, my dear sir, it is useless to think of escaping your fate. Mount Sunset *must* be given up to satisfy these men !"

"Oh, fool ! fool ! fool !—miserable old fool that I was, to allow myself to be so wretchedly duped !" groaned the squire, in bitter anguish and remorse. "Better for me had I never been born, than that such disgrace should be mine in my old age ! And Louis !— poor Louis ! But I will never see him again. If Mount Sunset be taken from me it will break my heart. Every tree and picture about the old place is hallowed by the memory of the past ; and now that I should lose it through my own blind, miserable folly ! Oh ! woe is me !" And, burying his great head in his hands, the unhappy old man actually sobbed outright.

Now had the hour of Dr. Wiseman's triumph come ; now was the time to make his daring proposal. Awhile he sat gloating over the agonies of his victim ; and then, in slow, deliberate tones, he said :

"But in all this darkness, Squire Erliston, there still remains one ray of light—*one* solitary hope. What would you do if I were to offer to cancel what you owe me, to pay off all your other debts, and free you once more ?"

"Do !" exclaimed the squire, leaping in his excitement from the chair. "*Do*, did you say ? I tell you, Dr. Wiseman, there is nothing under heaven I would *not* do. But you—you only mock me by these words."

"I do not, Squire Erliston. On one condition your debts shall every one be paid, and Mount Sunset still remain yours."

"And that condition ! For Heaven's sake name it !" cried the squire, half maddened by excitement.

"Will you agree to it ?"

"Yes, though you should even ask my life !"

"*That* would be of little service to me," said the doctor, with a dry smile. "No ; I ask something much easier."

"For Heaven's sake name it !" exclaimed the squire, wildly.

"It is——"

"What ?"

"*The hand of your ward, Gipsy Gower.*"

The squire stood like one transfixed with amazement, his eyes ready to shoot from his head with surprise and consternation. And calmly before him sat the doctor, his leathern countenance as expressionless as ever.

"*What* did you say ?" said the squire, at length, as though doubting the evidence of his senses.

"My words were plainly spoken. I will free you from all your debts on condition that you bestow upon me in marriage the hand of your young ward, Gipsy Gower."

"But—Lord bless me! my *dear* sir, what in the world can *you* want with that chit of a child—that mad girl of the mountains—for a wife?" exclaimed the squire, still aghast.

"I *want* her, let that suffice," said the doctor, with a frown. "Do you agree to this proposal?"

"Why, *I'm* willing enough, but *she*—oh, Dr. Wiseman, the thing is hopeless—she'd never consent in this world. She can be as obstinate as a little mule when she likes. 'When a woman won't, she won't, and there's the end on't,' as Solomon says."

"You must make her."

"Me! Why, she doesn't mind *me*——"

"Squire Erliston," angrily broke in the doctor, "listen to me; either you lose Mount Sunset and are publicly disgraced, or you will compel this girl to marry me. Do you hear?"

"There! there! don't be hasty! I'll do what I can. It won't be my fault if she don't. But who'd ever think of *you* wanting to marry little Gipsy. Well, well, well, 'Wonders will never cease,' as Solomon says."

"You can explain the matter to her—urge her by her gratitude, her love for you, to consent," said the doctor; "try the sentimental dodge—commands in this case will be worse than useless. Enlist the women on your side; and above all things keep it a profound secret from Archibald Rivers and Louis Oranmore. If none of your arguments move her, I have still another in reserve that I know will clinch the business. Give her no rest, day or night, until she consents; and if she complains of cruelty, and all that, don't mind her. All girls are silly; and she, being half-crazy, as she is, it seems to me the greatest favor you can do her is to marry her to a man of sense and experience like myself. Keep in mind what you lose by her refusal, and what you gain by her consent. If she will not marry me, I will add my claims to those of your other creditors, and no earthly power will be able to save you from total ruin," said the doctor, with grim, iron determination.

"She shall consent ! she shall—she *must!*" said the squire, startled by his last threat ; "she shall be your wife, that is settled. I think I can manage her, though it *will* be a desperate struggle."

"I shall force myself into her presence as little as possible," said the doctor, calmly ; "she has no particular love for me as yet, and it will not help on my case. Mind, I shall expect you will use all your energies, for our marriage must take place in a month at farthest," said the doctor, as he arose, and, with a last expressive glance at his victim, withdrew.

CHAPTER XXII.

FETTERS FOR THE EAGLET.

"I'm o'er young, I'm o'er young—
I'm o'er young to marry yet.
I'm o'er young ; 'twould be a sin
To take me from my mammy yet."—BURNS.

"GIPSY, my dear, come here and sit beside me. I have something very important to say to you," said the squire, as, half an hour later, he caught sight of Gipsy, running, singing, down stairs.

"Why, Guardy, what's the matter? You look as

solemn as a coffin," said Gipsy, coming in and sitting down on a stool at his side.

"Gipsy, marriage is a solemn subject."

"Shockingly solemn, Guardy. And who are you thinking of marrying?"

"I'm thinking of marrying you——"

"Marrying *me?* Oh, Jerusalem! Well, if aunty consents, I'm willing. La! won't it be fun? Just fancy Louis calling me grandmother! Ha, ha!"

"Hush, you chatterbox—don't interrupt me. As I was saying, I have been thinking of marrying you to some discreet, sensible man. You are too wild and giddy, and you must get married and settle down."

"Just so, Guardy; I've been thinking of it myself."

"Now, there's Doctor Wiseman, for instance. He'd be an excellent husband for you. He's a pleasant gentleman, possessing many sound, sterling qualities, learned, and not bad looking——"

"Exactly, Guardy—useful as well as ornamental. For instance, he'd do to put in a corn-field to scare away the crows."

"Don't be impertinent, Miss Gower! Doctor Wiseman is a serious man, self-balanced and grave——"

"Grave! I guess so! He always reminds me of death and his scythe whenever I see him."

"Silence, and listen to me! Now what objection could you possibly make to Doctor Wiseman as a husband?"

"As a husband? Ha, ha, ha! Why, Guardy, you don't mean to say that that yellow-skinned, spindle-shanked, dwarfed old ogre, with one leg in the grave, and the other over the fence, is thinking of marrying—do you?"

"Hold your tongue, or you'll lose it, you little wretch!

Doctor Wiseman is no old ogre, but a dark-complexioned——"

"Saffron, saffron, Guardy! Tell the truth, now, and shame your master. Isn't it saffron?"

"I'll brain you if you don't stop! A man can't get in a word edgeways with you. Dr. Wiseman, minx, has done you the honor to propose for your hand. I have consented, and——"

But the squire broke off suddenly, in a towering rage —for Gipsy, after an incredulous stare, burst into a shout of laughter that made the house ring. Pressing her hands to her sides, she laughed until the tears ran down her cheeks ; and, at last, unable to stop, she rolled off her seat on to the floor, and tumbled over and over in a perfect convulsion.

"Oh, you little aggravation! *Will* you stop?" cried the squire, seizing her by the shoulder, and shaking her until she was breathless.

"Oh, Guardy, that's too good! Marry me? Oh, I declare, I'll split my sides!" exclaimed Gipsy, going into another fit of laughter, as she essayed in vain to rise.

"Gipsy Gower! Cease your folly for a moment, and rise up and listen to me," said the squire, so sternly that Gipsy wiped the tears from her eyes, and pressing her hands to her sides, resumed her seat.

"Gipsy, I do not wish you to consider me a boaster, but you know I have done a great deal for you, brought you up, educated you, and intended leaving you a fortune at my death——"

"Thank you, Guardy ; couldn't you let me have part of it now?"

"Silence, I tell you! Gipsy, this is what I *intended* doing ; but, child, I have become involved in debt. Mount Sunset will be taken from me, and you, and Louis, and the rest of us will be beggars."

Up flew Gipsy's eyebrows, open flew her eyes, and down dropped her chin, in unfeigned amazement.

"Yes," continued the squire, "you may stare, but it's true.   And now, Gipsy, since you told me you were not ungrateful—now is the time to prove it, by saving me and all your friends from ruin."

"*I* save you from ruin?" said Gipsy, staring with all her eyes, and wondering if "Guardy" was wandering in his mind.

"Yes, *you*.   As I told you, I am involved in debt, which it is utterly impossible for me to pay.   Now, Doctor Wiseman, who has fallen in love with my fairy, has offered to pay my debts if you will marry him.   Don't laugh, *don't*, as I see you are going to do—this is no time for laughter, Gipsy."

"Oh, but Guardy, that's too funny !   The idea of me, a little girl of seventeen, marrying a man of sixty— 'specially such a man as Spider Wiseman !   Oh, Guardy, it's the best joke of the season !" cried Gipsy, bursting into another immoderate fit of laughter.

"Ungrateful, hard-hearted girl !" said the squire, with tears actually in his stormy old eyes ; " this is your return for all I have done for you !   You, the only living being who can save those who have been your best friends from being turned out of the old homestead, instead of rejoicing in being able to do it, you only laugh at him in scorn, you—" the squire broke down fairly here.

Never had the elf seen the usually violent old man so moved.   A pang shot through her heart for her levity ; and the next moment her arms were round his neck, and her white handkerchief wiping away the tears of which he was ashamed.

"Dear—*dear* Guardy, I'm so sorry !   I never thought you felt so bad about it.   I'll do anything in the world to help you; I'm not ungrateful. What do you want me to do, Guardy?"

"To save me, by marrying Doctor Wiseman, my dear."

"Oh, Guardy, oh, *Guardy!* You surely weren't serious in proposing *that?*" exclaimed Gipsy, really astonished.

"Serious? Alas! I was never so serious before in my life. You will do this, Gipsy?"

"Oh, Guardy! Marry *him?* Heaven forbid!" exclaimed Gipsy, with a violent shudder.

"Then you will let us all be turned out from the old roof-tree—out into the world to die; for, Gipsy, if the old place is taken from me, I should break my heart through grief!"

"Oh, Guardy, it won't be so bad as that! Surely *something* can be done? How much do you owe?"

"More than I dare mention. Child, nothing can be done to save us unless you consent to this marriage."

"Oh! that is too horrible even to think of. Can you not write to Louis? I'm sure he could do something to save us."

"No, he could do nothing; and he must never know it at all. Even supposing he could, before a letter could reach him we would be publicly disgraced—I should be branded as a rogue, and turned out of doors to die. No, Gipsy, unless you consent, before the week is out, to become the bride of Doctor Wiseman, all hope will be over. And though afterward, by some hitherto unheard-of miracle, the property should be restored to us, I should not live to see it; for if you persist in refusing, Gipsy, I will die by my own hand, sooner than live to be branded like a felon. And Lizzie and Mrs. Gower, who love you so well, how do you think they could live, knowing that all had been lost through your ingratitude! Louis, too, your foster-brother, how will he look on the girl whose obstinacy will make him a beggar ? Consent and all will be well, the gratitude and love of an old man will bless you through life ; *refuse*, and my death will be on your soul, haunting you through all your cheerless, unblessed life."

With all the eloquence and passion of intense selfishness he spoke, while each word burned into the heart and soul of his listener. She was pacing up and down the floor, half-maddened by his words, while the word *ingratitude* seemed dancing in living letters of fire before her.

"Oh ! what shall I do ? What shall I do ?" she cried, wringing her hands wildly.

"Let me advise you ; I am older and have had experience, and a claim on your obedience. Marry Doctor Wiseman ; he is, I know, somewhat older than you, but you *need* a man of age and wisdom. He is rich, and loves you ; and with him, conscious that you have done your duty, you will be blessed by God, and be happy."

"Happy !" she broke in, scornfully, "and with him ! Happy !"

"It is the first favor I ever asked of you, Gipsy, and I know you will not refuse. No one must know of it, not one, save Lizzie and Mrs. Gower. You must not breathe it to a living soul, save them."

"Guardy, there is some guilt or mystery connected with this debt. What is it ?"

"I cannot tell you now, child ; when you have obeyed me, I will. Come, Doctor Wiseman will be here for your answer to-morrow. Shall I tell him you have consented ?"

"Oh ! no, no ! no, no ! Good heavens !" she cried, shudderingly.

"Gipsy! Gipsy! consent. I implore you, by all you hold dear on earth, and sacred in heaven, to consent!" he said, with wild vehemence.

"Oh! I cannot! I cannot! I *cannot!* Oh, Guardy, do not urge me to this living death," she cried passionately.

"Then you can see me die, child. This, then, is your gratitude!" he said, bitterly.

"Oh, Guardy, you will not die! I will work for you—yes, I will toil night and day, and work my fingers to the bone, if need be. I can work more than you would think."

"It would be useless, worse than useless. I should not live to make you work for me. Refuse, if you will, and go through life with the death of a fellow-creature on your soul."

"Oh! I wish I had never been born," said Gipsy, wringing her pale fingers in anguish.

"Consent! consent! Gipsy, for my sake! For the sake of the old man who loves you!"

She did not reply; she was pacing up and down the room like one half-crazed, with wild, excited eyes, and flushed cheeks.

"You do not speak. 'Silence gives consent,' as Solomon says," said the squire, the ruling habit still "strong in death."

"Let me think! You must give me time, Guardy! I will go to my room now, and to-morrow you shall have my answer."

"Go, then; I know it will be favorable. I dare not think otherwise. To-morrow morning I will know."

"Yes, to-morrow," said Gipsy, as she left the room and fled wildly up stairs.

"To-morrow," said the old sinner, looking after her. "And what will that answer be? 'Who can tell what a day may bring forth?' as Solomon says."

CHAPTER XXII.

THE BIRD CAGED.

"Lay on him the curse of a withered heart,
  The curse of a sleepless eye ;
Till he wish and pray that his life would part,
  Nor yet find leave to die."—Scott.

ORNING came. The squire sat in the breakfast parlor, impatiently waiting for the coming of Gipsy. He waited in vain. The moments flew on ; still she came not.

Losing patience at last, he caught the bell-rope and rang a furious peal. Five minutes after the black face and woolly head of Totty appeared in the door-way.

"Totty, where's your young mistress?"

"Here!" answered the voice of Gipsy herself, as she stood, bright and smiling, behind Totty.

Somehow, that smile alarmed the old man, and he began trembling for the decision he had so anxiously been expecting.

"Well, come in. Clear out, Totty. Now, Gipsy, your decision."

"Now, Guardy, wait until after breakfast. How is any one to form an opinion on an empty stomach, I'd like to know? There, don't get into a fidget about it, as I see you're going to do, because it's no use."

"But, Gipsy, tell me—will it be favorable?"

"That depends upon circumstances. If I have a good appetite for my breakfast I may probably be in good-humor enough to say ·yes to everything you propose ; if not, I tremble for you, Guardy. Visions of blunt pen-knives and bulletless pistols flash in 'awful array' before my mind's eye. Shall I ring the bell for Aunty Gower?"

"I suppose so," growled the old man ; "you are as contrary as Balaam's ass."

"Guardy, look out ! Don't compare me to any of your ancestors."

At this moment Mrs. Gower entered, followed by Lizzie, now an invalid, wrapped up in numberless shawls, until she resembled a mummy.

The squire had informed them both, the night before, . how matters stood ; and they glanced anxiously at Gipsy, as they entered, to read, if possible, her decision in her countenance. Nothing could they guess from that little dark, sparkling face, as vivacious and merry as ever.

When breakfast was over Mrs. Gower and Mrs. Oranmore quitted the room, leaving Gipsy alone with the squire.

"Now, Gipsy, now," he exclaimed, impatiently.

"Guardy," said Gipsy, earnestly, "all last night I lay awake, trying to find out where my path of duty lay ; and, Guardy, I have come to the conclusion that I cannot add to your sin, if you have committed one, by a still greater crime. I cannot perjure myself, before God's holy altar, even to save you. Guardy, I always loathed and detested this man—this Dr. Wiseman·; and now I would sooner die by slow torture than be his wife. Your threat of suicide I know you will not fulfill—'twas but idle words. But even had you been serious, it would be all the same ; for sooner than marry that man I would plunge a dagger into my own heart and let out my life's blood. I do not speak hastily, for I have done that which I seldom do—thought before I spoke. If we really, as you say, become poor, I am willing to leave my wild, free life, my horses, hounds, and the 'merry greenwood,' to become a toiling kitchen brownie for your sake. Do not interrupt me, Guardy ; nothing you can say can change my purpose. I am not ungrateful, but I cannot commit a crime in the face of high heaven, even for the sake of those I love best. Tell my decision to Dr. Wiseman. And now, Guardy, this subject must be forever dropped between us, for you have heard my ultimatum."

And without waiting for the words that were ready to burst forth, she arose, bent her graceful little head, and walked out of the room.

As she went up-stairs, on her way to her own room, she passed Lizzie's chamber. Mrs. Oranmore caught sight of her through the half-opened door, and called her.

"Gipsy, my love, come in here."

Gipsy went in. It was a pleasant, cheerful room, with bright pictures on the walls, and rich crimson damask hangings in the window. 'Lizzie Oranmore, as she lies on her lounge, enveloped in a large, soft shawl, is not much like the Lizzie, the bright little coquette, we once knew. A pale, faded creature she is now, with sallow cheeks, and thin, pinched face.

"Well, my dear," said Mrs. Oranmore, anxiously, "papa has mentioned this shocking affair to me. What has been your answer to Dr. Wiseman's proposal ?"

"Oh, aunty, what could it be but *no ?* You didn't suppose I'd marry that ugly old daddy-long-legs, did you ? Why, aunty, when I get married—which I never will if I can help it—for I would be ever free—it must be to a lord, duke, or a Sir Harry, or something above the common. Just fancy such a little bit of a thing like me being tied for life to a detestable old Bluebeard like Spider. Not I, indeed!" said the elf, as she danced around the room and gayly sang :

> " An old man, an old man, will never do for me,
>   For May and December can never agree."

"But Gipsy, my dear, do you not know that we are to be turned out, if you refuse?" said Lizzie, in blank dismay.

" Well, let us be turned out, then. I will be turned out, but I won't marry that old death's-head. I'm young and smart, and able to earn my own living, thank goodness!"

"Oh, ungrateful girl, will you see me die? For, Gipsy, if I am deprived now, in my illness, of the comforts to which I have always been accustomed, I shall die."

"Oh, no, you won't, aunty. I don't think that things are as bad as Guardy makes them appear ; and, even if they were, Dr. Wiseman, old wretch as he is, would let you remain."

"No, he would not, child; you don't know the revengeful disposition of that man. Oh, Gipsy, by the momory of all we have done for you, I beseech you to consent !"

" Aunty, aunty, I cannot ; it is too dreadful even to think about. Oh, aunty, I cannot tell you how I loathe, abhor, and detest that hideous old sinner !"

"Gipsy, that is wrong—that is sinful. Dr. Wiseman is a highly respectable gentleman—rather old for you, it is true—but of what difference is a few years? He is rich, and loves you well enough to gratify your every wish. What more would you have ?"

10*

"*Happiness*, aunty. I should be utterly miserable with him."

"Nonsense, child, you only think so. It is not as if you were older, and loved somebody else. People often marry those they don't care about, and grow quite fond of them after a time. Now, I shouldn't be surprised if you grew quite fond of Dr. Wiseman by and by."

. Gipsy laughed her own merry laugh again as she heard Lizzie's words.

"Oh, Gipsy, you thoughtless creature! is this your answer to my petition?" said Lizzie, putting her handkerchief to her eyes. "Leave me, then. I will not long survive your ingratitude ; but, mark me, your name will become a by-word, far and near, and descend to posterity branded with the disgrace of your ungrateful conduct. Go—leave me! Why should you stay to witness the misery you have caused?"

Poor Gipsy ! how these reproaches stung her. She started to her feet, and began pacing the floor rapidly, crying wildly :

"Oh, Heaven help me! I know not what to do! I wish I were dead, sooner than be branded thus as an ingrate !"

Lizzie's sobs alone broke the stillness of the room. At last, unable to endure them longer, she rushed out and sought refuge in her own chamber. As she entered she saw Mrs. Gower seated by the window—a look of trouble and sadness on her usually happy, good-natured face.

"Oh ! aunty, what *shall* I do? Oh ! aunty, I am going crazy, I think !" cried Gipsy, distressedly, half maddened by the sight of Lizzie's tears.

"My dear, it is very plain what you must do. You must marry Dr. Wiseman," said Mrs. Gower, gravely.

"Oh ! aunty, have you turned against me, too? Then

I have no friend in the wide world ! Oh! I wish—*I wish* I had never been born !"

"My love, don't talk in that way ; it is not only very foolish, but very sinful. Dr. Wiseman is certainly not the man I would wish to see you married to ; but, you perceive, there is no alternative. Gipsy, I am getting old, so is the squire ; Mrs. Oranmore is ill, and I do not think she will live long. Will you, therefore, allow the old man and woman—who love you above all human beings—and a poor, weak invalid, to be turned upon the charity of the cold world to die ? Gipsy, you know if we could save you from misery, we would coin our very hearts' blood to do it."

"And, oh, aunt ! could there be greater misery for me than that to which you are urging me ?"

"You talk like the thoughtless girl you are, Gipsy. How often, for wealth or social position merely, or to raise their friends from want, do young girls marry old men ! Yet, *you* refuse to save us from worse than want, from disgrace and death—yes, *death !* I know what I am saying, Gipsy—you obstinately refuse. Gipsy, my child, for my sake do not become such a monster of ingratitude, but consent."

"Oh, aunty ! leave me. I feel as if I were going mad ! Every one in the world seems to have turned against me—even *you !* Oh, aunty, dear, good aunty ! don't talk to me any more ; my very brain seems on fire."

"Yes ; your cheeks are burning, and your eyes are like fire—you are ill and feverish, my poor little fairy. Lie down, and let me bathe your head."

"No, no, aunty, don't mind. Oh ! what matter is it whether I am ill or not ? If it wasn't for you, and Guardy, and all the rest, I feel as if I should like to lie down and die !"

"My own little darling, you must not talk of dying; every one has trouble in this world, and you cannot expect to escape!"

"Yes; I know, I know! Hitherto, life has been to me a fairy dream; and now this terrible awakening to reality! Life seemed to me one long, golden summer day; and now—and now——"

"You are excited, love; lie down, and try to sleep—you talk too much."

"Yes, I know; I always did talk too much; but I do not think I will ever talk much again. Oh, aunty! I have heard of the heart-ache, but I never knew what it was before!"

"My love, you must not feel this so deeply. How wild your eyes are! and your hands are burning hot! Do lie down, and try to rest."

"Rest! rest! Shall I ever find rest again?"

"Of course you will, my dear. Now what shall I tell the squire is your decision about this? I promised him to talk to you about it."

"Oh, aunty, don't—*don't!* Leave me alone, and let me think—I cannot talk to you now!"

"Shall I bring you up ice for your head, my dear?"

"No, no; you have already brought ice for my heart, aunty—that is enough."

"You talk wildly, love; I am afraid your mind is disordered."

"Don't mind my talk, dear aunty, I always was a crazy, elfish changeling, without a heart, you know. Nobody minds what I say. Only leave me now; I will be better by and by."

With a sigh Mrs. Gower left the room. It was strange that, loving her poor little fay as she did, she should urge her to this wretched marriage; but the squire had talked and persuaded her until he brought her to see the matter with his eyes. And poor Gipsy was left alone to pace up and down the room like one deranged, wringing her hands, while her cheeks and eyes burned with the fire of fever.

"Oh, if Archie would only come!" was the wild cry of her aching heart, as she walked restlessly to and fro.

But Archie was away; she knew not even his present address, and she was left to battle against the dark decree of fate alone.

"I will seek Dr. Wiseman; I will beg, I will implore him to spare me, and those who would have me make this fatal sacrifice. Surely his heart is not made of stone; he cannot resist my prayers!"

So, waiting in her room until she saw him ride up to the Hall, she descended the stairs and entered the parlor, where he and the squire sat in close conversation together, and formally desired the honor of a private interview.

He arose, and, bowing, followed her into the drawing-room. Motioning him to a seat she stood before him, her little form drawn up to its full height, her defiant, dark eyes fixed on his repulsive face with undisguised loathing.

"Dr. Wiseman," she began, "I have heard of this proposal which you have honored me by making. Believe me, I fully appreciate the honor you have done me"—and her beautiful lip curled scornfully—"even while I must decline it. A silly little girl like me is unworthy to be raised to the dignity of the wife of so distinguished a gentleman as Dr. Wiseman!"

The doctor acknowledged the compliment by a grave bow, while Gipsy continued:

"My guardian has informed me that, unless I consent to this union, he will lose Mount Sunset, be reduced to poverty, and, consequently, die, he says. You, it seems, will prevent this, if I marry you. Now, Dr. Wiseman, knowing this marriage is not agreeable to me, I feel that you will withdraw your claim to my hand, and still prevent Guardy from being reduced to poverty!"

"Miss Gower, I regret to say I cannot do so. Unless you become my wife, I shall be obliged to let the law take its course ; and all that Squire Erliston has told you will prove true."

"Dr. Wiseman, you will not be so cruel? I beg—I implore you to prevent this catastrophe!"

"I will, with pleasure, Miss Gower, if you will be my wife."

"That I can never be, Dr. Wiseman ! I would not, to save my head from the block, consent to such a thing ! What in the name of heaven can make a man of *your* age wish to marry a silly little thing like me ?"

"*Love*, my pretty mountain sprite," replied the doctor, with a grim smile—"*love !* Years do not freeze the blood, nor still the heart of man !"

"Then, sir, if you love me, renounce all claim upon my hand, and save my guardian from impending ruin !"

"That I can never do !"

"Be it so, then, Dr. Wiseman. To you I will plead no more. Let us be turned out ; I would die a death of lingering starvation sooner than wed with a cold-blooded monster like you !" exclaimed Gipsy, her old fiery spirit flashing from her eyes and radiating her face.

"And will you see those you love die, too ?"

"Yes, even so ; sooner than realize the living tomb of a marriage with you !"

"Ha ! ha ! ha ! All very fine and affectionate, my dear ; yet, marry me you *shall !*"

"Marry you ? Not if I die for it !" flashed Gipsy, with blazing eyes.

"That we shall see presently. I think I have an argument in reserve that will bend your high spirit. You love Archie Rivers?"

"That is no business of yours, Dr. Wiseman!"

"No; no farther than that I am glad of it. Now, Gipsy Gower, I swear by all the heavens contain, unless you marry me, *he shall die on the scaffold!*"

"*What?*" gasped Gipsy, appalled by his low, fearful tone, even more than by his words.

"I say there is but one alternative; marry me, or see him die on the scaffold!"

"Ha! ha! that's excellent. Are you going to hang him, Dr. Wiseman?" mocked Gipsy.

"Laugh, girl; but beware! It is in my power to bring his head to the halter!"

"Where, if everybody had their dues, yours would have been long ago."

"Take care, madam; don't carry your taunts too far —even my forbearance has its limits!"

"That's more than can be said of your manners!"

The doctor's sallow visage blanched with anger; but, subduing his wrath, he said :

"I can accuse him of the murder of young Henry Danvers, who was so mysteriously killed. There is circumstantial evidence against him strong enough to convict him in any court of justice in the world!"

"Archie kill Danvers? Why, you horrid old monster, you! Ain't you afraid of the fate of Ananias and his better half, who never told half such a lie in their lives?"

"Lie or not, girl, it can be proved that he killed him. Listen, now," said the doctor, while his repulsive face lighted up with a look of fiendish exultation. "Archibald Rivers loved *you*—that was plain to every one. This Danvers came along and fell in love with you, too —that, likewise, can be duly proved. Your preference for the young sailor was observable from the first. Rivers was jealous, and I know many who can prove he often uttered threats of future vengeance against the midshipman. On the night of the *murder*, Archie was observed riding from here, in a violent rage. Half an hour afterward the sailor went for a ride over the hills. I can *swear* that Archie Rivers followed him. I know he was not at home until late. Most probably, therefore, he followed Danvers, and murdered him treacherously. Jealousy will make a man do almost anything. In a court of justice, many more things than this can be proved ; and if he dies on the scaffold, his blood will be upon your head."

Gipsy stood listening to his terrible words with blanched face, livid lips, and horror-stricken eyes. For a moment he thought she would faint. The very power of life seemed stricken from her heart ; but, by a powerful effort, she aroused herself from the deadly faintness creeping over her, and exclaimed, in a voice low with unspeakable horror :

" Fiend—demon incarnate ! would you perjure your own soul ! Would you become the murderer of your own nephew ?"

" Murderer, forsooth ! Is that what you call legal justice ?"

" It would not be legal justice ! Doctor Wiseman, I tell you, if you say Archie Rivers killed Danvers, you lie ! Yes, meanest of vile wretches, I tell you, you lie !"

He leaped to his feet, glaring with rage, as though he would spring upon her, and rend her limb from limb. Before him she stood, her little form drawn up to its full height, defiant and daring—her dark face glaring with scorn and hatred. For a moment they stood thus —he quivering with impotent rage—she, proud, defying, .

and fearless. Then, sinking into his seat, he said, with stern calmness :

"No—I will restrain myself ; but, daring girl, listen to me. As sure as yonder heaven is above us, if you refuse, so surely shall Squire Erliston and all belonging to him be turned from their home—to die, if they will ; and Archibald Rivers shall perish by the hand of the hangman, scorned and hated by all, and knowing that you, for whom he would have given his life, have brought him to the scaffold. Gipsy Gower, his blood will cry for vengeance from the earth against you !"

He ceased. There was a wild, thrilling, intense solemnity in his tone, that made the blood curdle. One look at his fiendish face would have made you think Satan himself was before you.

And Gipsy ! She had dropped, as if suddenly stricken by an unseen hand, to the floor ; her face changed to the ghastly hue of death, the light dying out in her eyes : her very life seemed passing away from the blue, quivering lips, from which no sound came ; a thousand ages of suffering seemed concentrated in that one single moment of intense anguish.

But no spark of pity entered the heart that exulted in her agony. No ; a demoniacal joy flashed from his snake-like eyes as he beheld that free, wild, untamed spirit broken at last, and lying in anguish at his feet.

"This struggle is the last. Now she will yield," was his thought, as he watched her.

"Gipsy !" he called.

She writhed at the sound of his voice.

"Gipsy !" he called again.

This time she looked up, lifting a face so like that of death that he started back involuntarily.

"What ?" she asked, in a low, hollow voice of despair.

"Do you consent?"

She arose, and walked over until she stood before him. Appalled by her look, he arose in alarm and drew back.

"Consent!" she repeated, fixing her wild eyes on his frightened face ; "yes, I consent to the living death of a marriage with you. And, Dr. Wiseman, may my curse and the curse of Heaven cling to you like a garment of fire, now and forevermore, burning your miserable soul like a flame in this life, and consigning you to everlasting perdition in the next! May every torture and suffering that man can know follow the wronged orphan's curse! In this life I will be your deadliest enemy, and in the next I will bear witness against you at the throne of God! To your very grave, and beyond, my undying hatred and revenge for the wrong you have done me shall be yours ; and now I wish you joy of your bride!"

She passed from the room like a spirit ; and Dr. Wiseman, terrified and appalled, sank into a chair, with the vision of that death-like face, with its blazing eyes and wild, maniac words and wilder stare, haunting him until he shuddered with superstitious terror.

"What a wife I will have!" he muttered ; "a perfect little fiend. Mount Sunset will be dearly enough purchased with that young tempest for its mistress. The fiery spirit of the old Oranmores runs in her veins—that's certain. And now, as there is nothing like striking the iron while it's hot, I'll go and report my success to that old dotard, the squire, and have the wedding-day fixed as soon as possible."

CHAPTER XXIV.

MAY AND DECEMBER.

"She looked to the river—looked to the hill—
　And thought on the spirit's prophecy;
Then broke the silence stern and still:
　'Not you, but Fate, has vanquished me.'"
LAY OF THE LAST MINSTREL.

"CELESTE, Celeste! do not leave me. Oh! all the world has left me, and will you go, too? This heart—this restless, beating heart—will it never stop aching? Oh, Celeste! once I thought I had no heart; but by this dull, aching pain where it should be, I know I must have had one some time. Stay with me, Celeste. You are the only one in the world left for me to love now."

Gipsy—small, fair and fragile, with her little wan face and unnaturally lustrous eyes—lay moaning restlessly on her low couch, like some tempest-tossed soul quivering between life and death. Like an angel of light, by her side knelt Celeste, with her fair, pitying face and her soft blue eyes, from which the tears fell on the small brown fingers that tightly clasped hers.

"Dear Gipsy, I will not leave you; but you know you must get up and dress soon."

"Oh, yes; but not yet. It is so nice to lie here, and have you beside me. I am so tired, Celeste—I have never rested since I made that promise. It seems as if ever since I had been walking and walking on through the dark, unable to stop, with such an aching here."

And she pressed her hand to the poor quivering heart

that was fluttering to escape from the heavy chain fate
was drawing tighter and tighter around it.

"What can I do for you, Gipsy?" said Celeste, stooping and kissing her pale lips, while two pitying drops
fell from her eyes on the poor little face below her.

"Don't cry for me, Celeste. I never wept for myself
yet. Sing for me, dear friend, the 'Evening Hymn' we
used to sing at the Sisters' school, long ago."

Forcing back her tears, Celeste sang, in a voice low
and sweet as liquid music :

> "Ave sanctissima !
>   We lift our souls to thee—
> Ora pro nobis,
>   Bright star of the sea !
> Watch us while shadows lie
>   Far o'er the waters spread ;
> Hear the heart's lonely sigh—
>   Thine, too, hath bled !"

Gipsy listened, with her eyes closed, an expression
of peace and rest falling on her dark, restless face, until
Celeste ceased.

"   h, Celeste, I always feel so much better and happier when you are with me—not half so much of a heartless imp as at other times," said Gipsy, opening her
eyes. "I wish I could go and live with you and Miss
Hagar at Valley Cottage, or enter a convent, or anywhere, to be at peace. While you sang I almost fancied
myself back again at school, listening to those dear,
kind sisters singing that beautiful 'Evening Hymn.'"

She paused, and murmured, dreamily :

> "Watch us while shadows lie
>   Far o'er the waters spread ;
> Hear the heart's lonely sigh—
>   Thine, too, hath bled !"

"Dear Gipsy, do not be so sad. Our Heavenly
Father, perhaps, has but sent you this trial to purify your

heart and make it His own. In the time of youth and happiness we are apt ungratefully to forget the Author of all good gifts, and yield the heart that should be His to idols of clay. · But in the days of sorrow and suffering we stretch out our arms to Him ; and He, forgetting the past, takes us to his bosom. And, dearest Gipsy, shall we shrink from treading through trials and sufferings in the steps of the sinless Son of God, to that home of rest and peace that He died to gain for us ?"

Her beautiful face was transfigured, her eyes radiant, her lips glowing with the fervor of the deep devotion with which she spoke.

"I cannot feel as you do, Celeste, said Gipsy, turning restlessly. "I feel like one without a light, groping my way in the dark—like one who is blind, hastening to my own doom. I cannot look up ; I can see into the dark grave, but no farther."

"Light will come yet, dear friend. Every cloud has its silver lining."

"Never for me. But, hark ! What is that ?"

Celeste arose, and went to the window.

"It is the carriages bringing more people. The parlors below are full. You must rise, and dress for your bridal, Gipsy."

"Would to heaven it were for my burial ! I am *so* tired, Celeste. *Must* I get up ?"

"Yes, dear Gipsy ; they are waiting for you. I will dress you myself," said Celeste, as Gipsy, pale, wan, and spirituelle, arose from her couch, her little, slight figure smaller and slighter than ever.

Rapidly moved the nimble fingers of Celeste. The dancing dark locks fell in short, shining curls around the superb little head, making the pale face of the bride look paler still by contrast. Then Celeste went into her wardrobe and brought forth the jewels, the white vail, the orange blossoms, and the rich robes of white brocade, frosted with seed pearls, and laid them on the bed.

"What is that white dress for?" demanded Gipsy, abruptly, looking up from a reverie into which she had fallen.

"For you to wear, of course," replied Celeste, astonished at the question.

"A white dress for me! Ha! ha! ha!" she said, with a wild laugh. "True, I forgot—when the ancients were about to sacrifice a victim, they robed her in white and crowned her with flowers. But I will differ from all other victims, and wear a more suitable color. *This* shall be my wedding-dress," said Gipsy, leaving the room, and returning with a dress of *black* lace.

Celeste shrank back from its ominous hue with something like a shudder.

"Oh, not in black! Oh, Gipsy! any other color but black for your wedding. Think how you will shock every one," said Celeste, imploringly.

"Shock them! Why, Celeste, I've shocked them so continually ever since I was a year old, that when I cease to shock them they won't know Gipsy Gower. And that reminds me that after to-day I will be 'Mad Gipsy Gower' no longer, but Mrs. Doctor Nicholas Wiseman. Ha! ha! ha! Wiseman! how appropriate the name will be! Oh! *won't* I lead him a life—*won't* I make him wish he had never been born—*won't* I teach him what it is to drive a girl to desperation? He thinks because I am a little thing he can hold me up with one hand—and, by the way, Celeste, his hands always remind me of a lobster's claw stuck into a pump-handle—that he can do what he pleases with me. We'll see! Hook my dress, Celeste. It's a pity to keep my Adonis waiting, and disappoint all these good people who have come to see the fun."

"Dear Gipsy, do not look and talk so wildly. And pray, take off that black dress, and wear any other color you wish. People *will* talk so, you know."

"Let 'em talk then, my dear. They'll only say it's one of Gipsy's whims. Besides, it will shock Spider, which is just what I want. He'll get a few more shocks before I have done with him, I rather think. Hook my dress, Celeste."

With a sigh at the elf's perversity, Celeste obeyed ; and with a sad face, watched the eccentric little bride shake out the folds of her black robe, and fasten a dark crimson belt around her waist.

"Now, if I had a few poppies or marigolds to fasten in my hair, I'd look bewitching ; as I haven't, these must do." And with a high, ringing laugh, she twined a dark, purplish passion-flower amid her shining curls. "Now for my rouge. I must look blooming, you know—happy brides always should. Then it will save me the trouble of blushing, which is something I never was guilty of in my life. No, never mind those pearls, Celeste ; I fear Dr. Wiseman might find them brighter than my eye, which would not do by ' no manner of means.' There ! I'm ready. Who ever saw so bewildering a bride ?"

She turned from the mirror, and stood before Celeste, her eyes shining like stars, streaming with an unnaturally blazing light, the pallor of her face hidden by the rouge, the dark passion-flower drooping amid her curls, fit emblem of herself. There was an airy, floating lightness about her, as if she scarcely felt the ground she walked on—a fire and wildness in her large, dark eyes that made Celeste's heart ache for her. Very beautiful she looked, with her dark, oriental face, shaded by its sable locks, the rich, dark dress falling with classic elegance from her round, little waist. She looked, as she stood, bright, mocking, defiant, scornful—more like some fairy changeling—some fay of the moonlight—than a living creature, with a woman's heart. And yet, under that daring, bright exterior, a wild, anguished heart lay crushed and quivering, shedding tears of blood, that leaped to the eyes to be changed to sparks of fire.

"Let us go down," said Celeste, with a sigh.

"Yes, let us go. Do you know, Celeste, I read once of a man whom the Indians were going to burn to death at the stake, and who began cursing them when they led him there for making him wait so long. Now I feel just like that man; since I *am* to be doomed to the stake—why, the sooner the torture is over the better."

She looked so beautiful, so bewitching, yet so mocking and unreal, so like a spirit of air, as she spoke, that, almost expecting to see her vanish from her sight, Celeste caught her in her arms, and gazed upon her with pitying, yearning, love-lit eyes, from which the tears were fast falling.

"Don't cry for me, Celeste; you make me feel more like an imp than ever. I really think I must be a family relation of the goblin page we read about in the 'Lay of the Last Minstrel,' for I feel like doing as he did, throwing up my arms, and crying, 'Lost!' I'm sure that goblin page would have made his fortune in a circus, since his ordinary mode of walking consisted of leaps of fifty feet high or so. Crying still, Celeste! Why, I thought I'd make you laugh. Now, Celeste, if you don't dry your eyes, I'll go right up to where Aunty Gower keeps prussic acid for the rats, and commit suicide right off the reel. I've felt like doing it all the time lately, but never so much so as when I see you crying for me. Why, Celeste, I never was worth one tear from those blue eyes, body and bones. What's the use of anybody's grieving for a little, mad, hare-brained thing like me? *I'll* do well enough; I'll be perfectly happy—see if I don't! It will be such glorious fun, you know, driving Spider mad! And, oh, *won't* I dose him! Tra! la, la, la, la, la!" and Gipsy waltzed airily around the room.

At this moment there came a knock at the door. Celeste opened it, and Mrs. Gower, in the well-preserved silk and lace cap she had worn years before to Lizzie Oranmore's wedding, stood in the doorway.

"Oh, Celeste! why don't you hurry? Where is Gipsy? Oh, good gracious, child! not dressed yet? What on earth have you been doing? The people have been waiting these two hours, almost, in the parlors! Do hurry, for mercy sake, and dress!"

"Why, aunty, I *am* dressed. Don't you see I am all ready to become Mrs. Wiseman?"

"But my *dear* child, that black dress——"

"This black dress will do very well—suits my complexion best, which is rather of the mulatto order than otherwise; and it's a pity if a blessed bride can't wear what she likes without such a fuss being made about it. Now, aunty, don't begin to lecture—it'll only be a waste of powder and a loss of time; and I'm impatient to arrive at the place of execution."

Mrs. Gower sank horrified into a chair, and gazed with a look of despair into the mocking, defiant eyes of the elfin bride.

"Oh, Gipsy! what ever will the people say? In a *black dress!* Good heavens! Why, you'll look more like the chief mourner at a funeral than a bride! And what will Dr. Wiseman say?"

"Oh, don't, aunty! I hope he'll get into a passion, and blow me and everybody else up when he sees it!" cried Gipsy, clapping her hands with delight at the idea.

"Oh, dear! oh, dear! did any one ever know such a

strange girl? Just to think of throwing aside that beautiful dress that your guardian paid a small fortune for, for that common black lace thing, the worst dress you have!"

"Aunty—see here!—you may have this 'beautiful dress' when you get married. You're young, and good-looking, and substantial, too, and I shouldn't wonder if you had a proposal one of these days. With a little letting down in the skirt, and a little letting out in the waist——"

"Gipsy, hush! How can you go on with such non-sense at such a time? Miss Pearl, can you not induce her to take off that horrid black dress?"

"I think you had better let her wear it, madam. Miss Gower will not be persuaded."

."Well, since it must be so, then come. Luckily, everybody knows what an odd, flighty thing Gipsy is, and therefore will not be so much surprised."

"I should think the world would not be surprised at anything I would do since I have consented to marry that hideous orang-outang, that mockery of man, that death's-head, that 'thing of legs and arms,' that——"

"Hush! hush! you little termagant! What a way to speak of the man you are going to promise to 'love, honor, and obey,'" said the profoundly shocked Mrs. Gower.

"*Love, honor, and obey!* Ha, ha, ha! Oh, won't I though, with a vengeance! Won't I be a pattern wife! You'll see!"

"What do you mean, child?"

"Nothing, aunty," said Gipsy, with a strange smile, "merely making a meditation. Here we are at the stake at last, and there I perceive Reverend Mr. Goodenough ready to act the part of executioner; and there, too, is Dr. Wiseman, the victim—who, as he will by and by find out, is going to prove himself most decidedly a silly man to-day. Now, Gipsy Gower, you are going to create a sensation, my dear, though you are pretty well accustomed to that sort of thing."

They had reached the hall by this time, where Dr. Wiseman, Squire Erliston, and a number of others stood. All stared aghast at the sable robes of Gipsy.

"Oh? how is it? Why, what is the meaning of this?" demanded the squire, in a rage.

"Meaning of what, Guardy?"

"What do you mean, miss, by wearing that black frock?"

"And what business is it of yours, sir?"

"You impudent minx! Go right up stairs and take it off."

"I won't do anything of the kind! There now! Anybody that doesn't like me in this can let me alone," retorted Gipsy.

A fierce imprecation was on the lips of the squire, but Dr. Wiseman laid his hand on his arm, and said, in his oiliest tones:

"Never mind her, my dear sir; let her consult her own taste. I am as willing my bride should wear black as anything else; she looks bewitching in anything. Come, fairest lady."

He attempted to draw her arm within his, but she sprang back, and transfixing him with a flashing glance, she hissed:

"No; withered be my arm if it ever rests in yours! Stand aside, Dr. Wiseman; there is pollution in the very touch of your hand."

"You capricious little fairy, why do you hate me so?"

"Hate! Don't flatter yourself I hate you, Dr. Wiseman—I despise you too much for that," she replied, her beautiful lip curling scornfully.

"Exasperating little dare-devil that you are!" he exclaimed, growing white with impotent rage, "take care that I do not make you repent this."

"You hideous old fright! do you dare to threaten now?"

"Yes, and dare to perform, too, if you do not beware. Keep a guard on your tongue, my lady, or you know who will suffer for it."

The fierce retort that hovered on the lip of Gipsy was checked by their entrance into the drawing-room. Such a crowd as was there, drawn together for miles around by the news of this singular marriage. All shrank back and looked at one another, as their eyes fell on the ominous garments of the bride, as she walked in, proudly erect, beside her grim bridegroom.

"Beauty and the Beast!" "Vulcan and Venus!" "May and December!" were the whispers that went round the room as they appeared.

The Rev. Mr. Goodenough approached, and the bridal party stood before him—the doctor glancing uneasily at his little bride, who stood with her flashing eyes riveted to the floor, her lips firmly compressed, proud, erect and haughty.

The marriage ceremony commenced, and Mr. Goodenough, turning to the doctor, put the usual question :

"Nicholas Wiseman, wilt thou have Aurora Gower, here present, to be thy wedded wife, to have and to hold, for better for worse, for richer, for poorer, in sickness and health, until death doth you part?"

"Yes," was the reply, loud, clear, and distinct.

Turning to the bride the clergyman demanded ;

"Aurora Gower, wilt thou have Nicholas Wiseman,

here present, to be thy lawful husband, to have, and to hold?" etc.

A loud, fierce, passionate "*No!*" burst from the lips of the bride. Dr. Wiseman saw her intention, and was immediately seized with a violent fit of coughing, in which her reply was drowned.

The mockery of a marriage was over, and Nicholas Wiseman and Aurora Gower were solemnly pronounced "man and wife."

A mocking smile curled the lips of the bride at the words, and she turned to receive the congratulations of her many friends, to bear all the hand-shaking, and hear herself addressed as "Mrs. Wiseman."

"Now, beautiful fairy, you are my own at last. You see fate had decreed it," said the doctor, with a grim smile.

"And bitterly shall you repent that decree. Do you know what I was doing when I stood up before the clergyman with you?"

"No, sweet wife."

"Well, then, listen. I was vowing and consecrating my whole life to one purpose—one aim; and that is *deadly vengeance against you* for what you have done. Night and day, sleeping or waking, it shall always occupy my thoughts, and I will live now only for revenge. Ha! I see I can make your saffron visage blanch already, Dr. Wiseman. Oh! you'll find what a happy thing it is to be married. Since I must go down, I shall drag down with me all who have had part or share in this, my misery. You, viper, ghoul that you are, have turned my very nature into that of a fiend. Dr. Wiseman, if I thought, by any monstrous possibility, you could ever go to heaven, I would take a dagger and send my own soul to perdition, sooner than go there with you."

There was something in her words, her tone, her face, perfectly appalling.   Her countenance was deadly white, save where the rouge colored it, and her eyes. Oh! never were such wild, burning, gleaming eyes seen in any face before. He cowered from her like the soul-struck coward that he was ; and, as with one glance of deadly concentrated hate she glided from his side and mingled with the crowd, he wiped the cold perspiration off his brow, and realized how true were the words oft quoted :

" Hell has no fury like a woman scorned,"

and began to fear that, after all, Mount Sunset was purchased at a dear price.

* * *

CHAPTER XXV.

ARCHIE'S LOST LOVE.

" Be it so ! we part forever—
   Let the past as nothing be ;
Had I only loved thee, never
   Hadst thou been thus dear to me.

" More than woman thou wast to me—
   Not as man I looked on thee ;
Why, like woman, then, undo me ?
   Why heap man's worst curse on me ?"—Byron.

T was the evening of Gipsy's wedding-day— a wet, chilly, disagreeable evening, giving promise of a stormy, tempestuous night—fit weather for such a bridal !

Lights were already gleaming in the cottages of the villagers. and the large parlor of the " Inn of St. Mark's" was crowded—every one discussing the surprising wedding up at the Hall, and wondering what Miss Gipsy would do next—when, as James says, "a solitary horseman might have been seen," riding at a break-neck pace toward Deep Dale. The house looked dreary, dark, and dismal—unlighted save by the glare from one window. Unheeding this, the "solitary horseman" alighted, and giving his horse to the care of the servant, ran up the stairs and unceremoniously burst into the parlor, where Minnette Wiseman sat reading alone. All her father's entreaties and commands to be present at his wedding were unheeded. She had heard the news of his approaching marriage with the utmost coolness—a stare of surprise from her bright black eyes being the only outward emotion it caused.

"Why should I go to see you married?" was her impatient reply to his stern commands. "I care nothing for Gipsy Gower, nor she for me. You can be married just as well without me. I won't go!"

Therefore she sat quietly reading at home while the nuptial revelry was at its height in Sunset Hall, and looked up, with an exclamation of surprise, to see our traveler standing before her.

"Archie! what in the world brought *you* here?" she exclaimed, rising, and placing a chair for him before the fire.

"Rail-cars part of the way, steamer next, and, finally, my horse."

"Don't be absurd. Why have you come to Saint Mark's? No one expected you here these three months."

"Know it, coz. But I've found out I am the luckiest dog in creation, and ran down here to tell you and *another* particular friend I have. I suppose you have heard of Uncle John Rivers, my father's brother. Yes! Well, about four months ago he returned from Europe, with one hundred and fifty thousand dollars and the consumption. Though he never had the honor of my acquaintance, he knew there existed so distinguished an individual, and accordingly left the whole of his property to me ; and a few weeks after, gave up the ghost. You see, therefore, Minnette, I'm a rich man. I've pitched law to its patron saint, the—hem !—and started off down here post-haste to marry a certain little girl in these diggin's, and take her with me to see the sights in Europe."

"My dear cousin, I congratulate you. I presume Miss Pearl is to be the young lady of your choice."

"No ; Celeste is too much of an angel for such a hot-headed scamp as I am. I mean another little girl, whom I've long had a *penchant* for. But where's your father?"

Minnette laughed sarcastically.

"Getting married, I presume. This night my worthy parent follows the Scriptural injunction, and takes unto himself a wife."

"Nonsense, Minnette !—you jest."

"Do I ?" said Minnette, quietly. "I thought you knew me well enough now, Archie, to know I never jest."

"But, Minnette, it is absurd. Dr. Wiseman married in his old age. Why, it's a capital joke." And Archie laughed uproariously. "Who is the fortunate lady that is to be your mamma and my respected aunt?"

"Why, no other than that little savage, Gipsy Gower."

Had a spasm been suddenly thrust into Archie's heart, he could not have leaped more convulsively from his seat. Even the undaunted Minnette drew back in alarm.

"What did you say?" he exclaimed, grasping her

arm, unconsciously, with a grip of iron. "To whom is he to be married?"

"To Aurora Gower. What do you mean, sir? Let go my arm."

He dropped it, staggered to a chair, dropped his head in his hands, and sat like one suddenly struck by death.

"Archie, what *is* the matter?" said Minnette, looking at him in wonder. "Was Gipsy the one you came here to marry?"

"Minnette! Minnette! it cannot be true!" he exclaimed, springing to his feet, without heeding her question. "It is absurd—monstrous—*impossible!* My wild, free, daring Gipsy would never consent to marry a man she abhorred. For Heaven's sake, Minnette, only say you have been jesting!"

"I have spoken the truth," she answered, coldly. "My father this morning married Aurora Gower!"

"Great heavens! I shall go mad! What in the name of all the saints tempted her to commit such an act?"

"I know not. Most probably it is one of her strange freaks—or, perhaps, she thinks papa rich, and married him for his money. At all events, married him she has; her reasons for doing so I neither know nor care for."

"Heaven of heavens! Could Gipsy—she whom I always thought the pure, warm-hearted child of nature—commit so base an act? It cannot be! I will *never* believe it! By some infernal plot she has been entrapped into this unnatural marriage, and dearly shall those who have forced her rue it!" exclaimed Archie, treading up and down the room like one distracted.

"You always *thought* her simple and guileless; I always *knew* her to be artful and ambitious. She has not

11*

been entrapped. I have heard that she laughs as merrily as ever, and talks more nonsense than she ever did before in her life—in short, appears perfectly happy. She is too bold and daring to be entrapped. Besides, what means could they use to compel her? If she found them trying to tyrannize over her, she would run off as she did before. Nonsense, Archie! Your own sense must tell you she has married him willingly."

Every word was like a dagger to his heart. He dropped into a chair, buried his face in his hands, and groaned.

"Oh, Gipsy! Gipsy!—lost to me forever. What are wealth and honor to me now! For you I toiled to win a home and name, believing you true. And thus I am repaid for all. Oh, is there nothing but treachery and deceit in this world? Would to heaven," he added, springing fiercely up, and shaking back his fair, brown hair, "that the man she has wedded were not an old dotard like that. I would blow his brains out ere another hour."

"My father will, no doubt, rejoice to find his years have saved his life," said Minnette, in her customary cold tone. "Pray, Mr. Rivers, be more calm; there is no necessity for all this excitement. If Aurora Gower has deserted you for one whom she supposed wealthier, it is only the old story over again."

"The old story!" exclaimed Archie, bitterly. "Yes, the old story of woman's heartlessness and treachery, and man's blind self-deception. Be calm! Yes; if you had told me she whom I love above all on earth was dead, and in her grave, I might be calm; but the wife of another, and that *other*"—he paused, and ground his teeth with impotent rage.

"Well, since it is so, and cannot be helped, what's the

use of making such a time about it?" said Minnette, impatiently, taking up her book and beginning to read.

Archie glanced at the cold, stone-like girl before him, whose very calmness seemed to madden him ; then, seizing his hat, he rushed from the room, exclaiming :

"Yes, I will see her—I will confront her once more, accuse her of her deceit and selfishness, and then leave the country forever."

He was out of the house in an instant ; and in five minutes was galloping madly through the driving wind and rain, unheeded and unfelt, now toward Mount Sunset Hall.

The numberless blazing lights from the many windows illumined his path before it ; the sound of revelry was wafted to his ears by the wind, making him gnash his teeth in very rage.

He reached the mansion, threw the reins to one of the many servants standing in the court-yard ; and all wet and travel-stained, pale, wild, and excited as he was, he made his way through the wondering crowd, that involuntarily made way for him to pass ; and

> "So boldly he entered the Netherby Hall,
>   Among bridesmen, and kinsmen, and brothers and all.
>   But ere he alighted at Netherby gate,
>   The bride had consented—the gallant came late."

Heeding not the many curious eyes bent upon him, still he strode on, until he stood within the crowded drawing-room.

Amid all that throng his eye saw but one face, beheld but one form. Standing near the upper end of the room was Gipsy—*his* Gipsy once—looking far more beautiful than he had ever seen her before, and flirting with all her might with a dashing lieutenant.

Having gained her point, to be married in black, she

had exchanged her dismal robes for the gorgeous wedding-dress that fell around her in folds of light. Pearls flashed amid her raven curls, gleamed in her ears, shone on her white arms, and rose and fell on her restless bosom. She needed no rouge, for her cheeks were vivid crimson, her lips red and glowing, her eyes outshining the jewels she wore. Never had Gipsy been so lovely, so bewildering, so intoxicating before.

The very sight seemed to madden Archie. To see her there in all her dazzling beauty, the wife of another, laughing and talking as gayly as though *he* had never existed, nearly drove him to desperation. Striding through the crowd of gay revelers, who drew back in alarm from his wild, pale face and fierce eyes, he advanced through the room, and stood before the bride.

There was an instantaneous hush through the room. Dr. Wiseman, already sullen and jealous, sprang up from the distant corner to which he had retreated, but did not venture to approach.

Gipsy's graceful head was bent in well-affected timidity as she listened to the gallant words and whispered compliments of the gay young officer, when, suddenly looking up, she beheld a sight that froze the smile on her lip, the light in her eye, the blood in her veins, the very life in her heart. Every trace of color faded from her face, leaving her white as the dead ; her lips parted, but no sound came forth.

"So, Mrs. Wiseman, I see you recognize me !" he said, with bitter sarcasm. "Allow me to congratulate you upon this joyful occasion. Do not let the recollection that you have perjured yourself to-day before God's minister, mar your festivity to-night. No doubt the wealth for which you have cast a true heart aside, and wedded a man you loathe, will make you completely happy. As I leave America forever to-morrow, I wished to offer my congratulations to the 'happy pair' before I went. I was fool enough, at one time, to believe the promises you made me ; but I did not then know 'how fair an outside falsehood hath.' Farewell, Mrs. Wiseman ! you and I will never meet again. All your treachery, all your deceit, your heartlessness, is known to me, and I will never trouble you more !"

He turned, left the house, sprang on his horse, and was out of St. Mark's ere any one had recovered from their astonishment and stupefaction sufficiently to speak.

He heard not, as he rode along, the wild, piercing cry of anguish that broke from the lips of the bride, as she fell senseless to the ground. He knew not, as he stood on the deck of the steamer, next morning, bound for "merrie England," that the once free, wild, mountain huntress, the once daring, defying Gipsy, lay raving and shrieking in the wild delirium of brain fever, calling always in vain for him she had lost. They had caught the young eaglet, and caged it at last; but the free bird of the mountains lay wounded and dying in their grasp.

CHAPTER XXVI.

LOUIS.

A look of pride, an eye of flame ;
A full-drawn lip that upward curled ;
An eye that seemed to scorn the world."—SCOTT.

IT was a merry morn in June, many months after the events related in the last chapter. A brief retrospective glance it is necessary to take ere we proceed.

For many long weeks after the fatal night of her marriage, Gipsy lay hovering between life and death ; and Celeste came, with her loving heart, and gentle voice, and noiseless footstep, and, unheeding rest or sleep, nursed the poor, pale, crazed little bride back to life. No one else would Gipsy have near her—not even Aunty Gower ; and a physician from the city attended her—for the very mention of her detested bridegroom threw her into hysterics. But, notwithstanding all their care, long months passed away ere Gipsy was well again, and Celeste, worn and wearied, but uncomplaining, permitted to return to the peaceful solitude of Valley Cottage.

Dr. Wiseman had not yet breathed a syllable of Gipsy's parentage. He could not do so during her illness ; and when she recovered, he wished a decent interval of time to elapse ere he made it known, lest the world should suspect his previous knowledge of it had caused him to marry her. Besides, he found there was no cause to hurry ; for, during Gipsy's illness, the squire had invited him to shut up his house at Deep Dale, and

bring Minnette with him, to reside at Sunset Hall. To
this the doctor eagerly assented ; and having, with some
trouble, prevailed upon Minnette to accompany him,
Deep Dale was rented, and the doctor and his daughter
became domesticated at Mount Sunset Hall.

Nearly nine months had elapsed. Gipsy—now as
well as ever, and more daring and mischievous even
than before—had just set herself to work to begin ful-
filling the vow she had made, and soon succeeded in
driving the doctor nearly wild. Though he had merely
married her for her money, he had, as time passed on,
learned to love her with a strange, selfish, absorbing
passion ; and the more she mocked, and scorned, and
laughed at him, the more infatuated he grew. The wil-
ful elf kept her husband in a constant state of panic and
terror, running into the greatest dangers with the utmost recklessness, and often barely escaping with her
life. Out all hours of the day and night, sometimes not
coming home until morning, it is not to be wondered at
that she kept the whole household in alarm. Often after
midnight, going out to search for her, they would find
her riding among the rocks, or, having tied up Mignonne, she would be discovered asleep in some grotto or
cavern. Then her flirting ! The doctor was madly
jealous, and not without reason. There was not a man
under thirty, if at all presentable, but the reckless girl
had flirted unmercifully with, in a way that would have
completely destroyed the reputation of any other woman,
but which was merely noticed by the remark that it was
"just like Gipsy ;" and her maddest actions were listened to with a smile and a stare of astonishment, and a
"wonder what she'll do next ?" Poor, half-crazed little
Gipsy ! The real goodness of her nature was too ap-
parent to all through her outward recklessness to make
them suspect her of evil.

St. Mark's had become a much gayer place than when we first knew it. Many new families had moved hither from the city; and balls, and parties, and sleigh-rides in winter, and picnics, and excursions, and soirees, in summer, became all the rage; and the leader of all these was the "merry little Mrs. Wiseman," as these new-comers called her. And no one, to see her entering heart and soul into these festivities, would ever dream of the miserable secret weighing on her mind, or the still untamed, restless heart that struggled to find forgetfulness in constant gayety.

They had never heard of Archie since his departure, save once through Louis, who, in one of his letters, spoke of having met him in Paris. No one mentioned his name at Sunset Hall. Gipsy especially, even in the remotest way, never alluded to him; and the good, obtuse family began to hope she had quite forgotten him.

And now we have come back to that merry morn in June with which this chapter opened. Gipsy, arrayed in a tasteful riding-habit, which she held up with one hand, while in the other she held a silver-mounted riding-whip, stood in the breezy park, watching her horse, that was neighing impatiently to be off. Mrs. Gower stood behind her, looking troubled and anxious.

"My dear Gipsy," she was saying, "I wish you would not go out this morning. What will people say to see you out riding, and your husband having fallen from his horse, and broken two of his ribs and his leg, last night?"

"I wish it had been his neck!"

"Oh, child! don't say such sinful, wicked things. Of course, I know you don't mean them; but then it's very wrong."

"I don't care, aunty; I *do* wish it—there! I don't see what possesses him to cumber the earth so long. If he doesn't give up the ghost soon, I'll administer a dose of hemp some night—for I do believe his destiny is hanging. If there ever was a neck made for a rope, it's his—just the shape for it. Jupe, mind what you're at there. Don't let Mignonne get all over dust."

"Gipsy, you will stay?"

"I *won't* stay, aunty—not if it were Dr. Wiseman's neck, instead of his ribs, that was broken. Oh, yes, I would, too ; I'd stay home then for joy. I'm off now. Good-bye. If his worship becomes extinct during my absence, just send for me, and I'll shed a few tears, and everything will go off in fashionable style."

And, laughing at Mrs. Gower's scandalized face, Gipsy leaped on her horse and rode off.

As she ascended the hills behind Mount Sunset she beheld, opposite to her, a horseman with his back toward her, standing silent and motionless, gazing upon Sunset Hall.

"I wonder who he is?" thought Gipsy. "A handsome fellow, I should say, for his form is superb. Wonder if he knows he's standing on my favorite point of view? Well, as I've no notion of surrendering my rights to him or any one else, I'll just give him a hint to get out of that." And, suiting the action to the words, Gipsy shouted, as she reined up her horse : "Hallo, sir !"

The horseman was still gazing like one entranced. He evidently did not hear her.

"I say, sir !" again called Gipsy.

Still no answer.

"Well, whoever you are," soliloquized Gipsy, "you're mighty polite to refuse answering a lady. I'll try again. Look here, sirrah, will you?"

He did not move.

"Well, 'pon my honor, that's decidedly cool !" said

Gipsy. "So you won't pretend to notice me, eh? Very well, sir; we'll see whether you'll pay more attention to a lady than this."

And Gipsy drew a pistol from her belt, took deliberate aim, and fired.

It was well she doubted not her own skill; it was well she had a steady hand and eye; for the bullet passed through the crown of his hat, scarcely two inches above the temple.

With an exclamation of surprise and anger, the stranger turned round, and likewise drew a pistol. His eye wandered over the scene; but he could see no one but a young girl, who was coolly reloading her pistol, as if about to send a second ball in the same direction.

"Good-morning, madam. Did you see any one fire just now," said the stranger, in a most musical voice, as he rode toward her.

"Yes, sir, *I* fired it," replied Gipsy, impudently.

"*You* did!" said the stranger, with a stare of surprise; "and may I ask, madam, if it was your intention to shoot me?"

"Of course it was! My aim was unfortunately taken a little too high. If you'll just stand there again, I'll try another shot," replied Gipsy gravely.

Again the stranger stared, as though doubting the sanity of his companion. There was no idiocy, however, in the bright, keen eyes, twinkling with suppressed mirth, that were now lifted to his; and, taking off his hat, the stranger pointed to the hole, saying:

"On the whole, I think I have no particular fancy for being made a target of—especially for so good a shot as you. May I ask the name of the fair amazon I have been fortunate enough to meet?"

"You must be a stranger here not to know it. I have

several names ; the last and least of which is—Mrs. Wiseman.   And yours ?"

" Louis Oranmore, very much at your service," he answered, with a courtly bow.

"Oh !"   Such a stare as he got from those bright eyes
—such a quick flush of delight as overspread the pretty
face beneath him—such a keen scrutiny as his face un-
derwent at that moment.   He noticed it, without pre-
tending to do so ; but there was an ill-repressed smile of
amusement hovering about his finely-chiseled lip.   Yet
it was evident he did not recognize her.

The handsome, impetuous boy had grown into a tall,
elegant, princely-looking man.   His complexion, darkened by foreign suns to a clear, manly olive, was shaded
by a profusion of jet-black curling hair.   His fine dark
eyes were bright, clear, almost piercing ; his upper lip
was shaded by a black mustache, but it did not conceal
its scornful upward curve.   Pride and passion, genius
and unbending will were written in every lineament of
that irresistibly handsome face ; yet there was at times a
winning softness in it, particularly when he smiled.   He
still bore a strong likeness to his dead father, save that
Louis was much handsomer.   There was something
grand and noble in his tall yet slight figure, mingled
with an ease and grace of manner that bespoke his acquaintance with polished society.   His voice, that could
at times ring with the clarion tones of command, never
addressed a woman without being modulated to the softest and most musical of sounds.   Such had our old favorite Louis become—very little like the Louis we once
knew, we must own—very little like the guileless, innocent Louis, this gay young man of pleasure.

Perhaps something of all this was floating through
the mind of Gipsy ; for in spite of the admiration that

shone in her now radiant face, she finished her scrutiny with a sigh.

"Well, fair lady, do you find me so very hideous that you thus turn away?" he asked, fixing his deep, dark eyes in evident amusement on her face.

Gipsy would have blushed had she known how ; but it was something she knew very little about, so she merely answered :

"Well, I think I have seen persons almost as frightful looking as you before. You are a stranger here, I presume?"

"Yes ; though this is my native village, yet I have been absent for many years in Europe. May I ask if you are acquainted with the inmates of Sunset Hall yonder?"

"Yes ; I've seen them."

"Are they all well?"

"Why, yes, I believe so ; all but Spi—I mean Dr. Wiseman."

"Dr. Wiseman ! What has he to do there ?—he does not belong to the family."

"Yes, he does."

"*What?*"

"He married a ward of Squire Erliston's—Gipsy—something, I think they called her. Gow—Gow—Gower, I believe, was the name—and then, with his daughter, came there to live."

"Why, is it possible? Has little Gipsy Gower married that old man—old enough to be her grandfather ?" exclaimed Louis, in unbounded amazement.

"Yes."

"Well, after that, nothing will surprise me. And Archie never mentioned a word of it," said Louis, in a sort of soliloquy ; "and my—and Mrs. Oranmore, how is she?"

"Pretty well.   She has not been very strong lately."

"Poor mother !   And the squire ?"

"Is quite well."

"You reside in St. Mark's, I presume ?"

"Why, yes.   Nonsense, Louis ! Don't you know me ?"

"Hallo !   No, it's not ; yes, it is, though ; it's Gipsy Gower, is it not ?" cried Louis.

"No, sir.   Mrs. Nicholas Wiseman, if you please," said Gipsy, drawing herself up.

"My dear little Gipsy, I am delighted to meet you again.   How handsome you have grown !   Allow me to embrace my little playmate ?"

Accepting his salute with saucy cordiality, Gipsy turned her horse's head in the direction of the Hall.

"Tell me now, Louis, what brings you home so suddenly ?" asked Gipsy.

"Why, to confess the truth, I grew tired of sight-seeing, and began to feel homesick for the old, familiar faces ; so, wishing to surprise you all, I started without sending you word, and here I am.   But, Gipsy, whatever possessed you to marry that old man ?"

"*Love*, of course.   People always marry for love, you know."

"Pshaw !   Gipsy, I know better than that.   Why did you jilt poor Archie?   I met him in Paris, half crazy, one would imagine.   He answered my questions rationally enough, until we came to speak of you, when he burst forth into a torrent of invectives against flirts and deceivers in general, and then seized his hat and fled from the room, leaving me to conjecture as best I might his meaning.   Come, Gipsy, own up, are you not the cause of all this frenzy ?"

Gipsy's face had grown very pale ; her eyes were bent

on the ground, her lips firmly compressed, as she answered, in a low, hurried voice :

"Louis, don't talk to me on this subject. I am wicked and wretched enough the best of times, but I always feel like a perfect fiend when this subject is mentioned. Suffice it for you to know that fate had decreed I should wed Dr. Wiseman ; no earthly power could have prevented it, therefore I became his wife."

"Did they dare to force you ?" exclaimed Louis, with a kindling eye. "If so——"

"No, no, Louis ; I could have refused if I would. Don't mention this subject more. See, there is the old hall ; and there at the gate stands Minnette Wiseman, *my* daughter now, you know. Is she not a beautiful girl ?"

"Beautiful indeed !" exclaimed Louis, enthusiastically, pausing involuntarily to gaze upon her.

Splendid indeed looked Minnette. Her dress of black (she always wore black) fluttering in the morning breeze, and confined at the slender waist by a dark crimson belt. Her long, shiny blue-black hair was twined in classic braids around her superb head. Her glorious black eyes were fixed on the glancing waters of the bay, and no June rose ever bloomed a more brilliant crimson than the hue of her cheek. She might have been an Eastern queen—for her beauty was truly regal, with her dark, oriental face, and splendid Syrian eye ; but there was too much fire and passion in her nature, and too few womanly traits and feelings.

"Oh, Minnette, guess who's come !" cried Gipsy, riding up to where she stood.

"Who?" said Minnette, breathlessly, as her eye fell on Louis.

The next moment she started convulsively ; the blood rushed in torrents to her brow. *She* had recognized him, though Gipsy had not.

"It's Louis," said Gipsy—"Louis Oranmore! Come, Louis! come! Miss Minnette. I am going up to the house to tell them you have come."

She was off like a flash, up the lawn, and in the house, while Louis leaped from his horse, and with courtly grace raised Minnette's hand to his lips; while she, pressing her hand to her heart, that beat and throbbed as though it would force its way to him, strove to return his salutation. It was a strange thing to see the cold, marble-like Minnette so moved.

"How everything has changed since I left home!" said Louis; "the place itself seems changed, and you more than all. I left you a little girl, thoughtful beyond your years, and I return to find you——"

"The most beautiful woman my eyes ever rested on," he would have said, but she raised her head, and something in the expression of her face checked him.

No marble ever was whiter or more cold, as she said:

"Yes, all has changed, and none more so than your former *favorite*, Celeste."

"Ah! little Celeste—how is she? I had forgotten to ask for her. I trust she is well?"

"I presume so. I know nothing to the contrary."

"I remember her a lovely child; I suppose she is an equally lovely girl?" said Louis, carelessly.

A scorching, scathing glance shot from the lightning eyes of Minnette; but, without answering him, she turned away, and walked steadily into the house.

"Strange, incomprehensible girl!" said Louis, looking in surprise after her. "How that flashing glance reminds me of the Minnette of other days! Have I said anything to offend her, I wonder? Heigho! what a radiant creature she is, to be sure! What would not some of the gay court beauties I know give for that superb form and glorious face! Well, I must not fall in love with her, however, if I can help it. Here comes that airy little mountain sprite, Gipsy ! and now for my lady mother !"

"Come, Louis, come !" she cried, darting in again.

Louis followed her as she led the way to his mother's chamber. Then opening the door, she ushered him in, and closing it after her, immediately retreated.

Lizzie sat in an easy-chair, a crimson shawl wrapped around her, her eyes bright, her pale cheeks flushed with expectation. She arose at his entrance, and the next moment was clasped in his arms, while their mutual exclamations were :

"My dear Louis !"

"My dearest mother !"

There was a moment's silence ; then Lizzie raised her head and surveyed him from head to foot, her face sparkling with pride and admiration.

"How tall you have grown ! and how handsome you are !—handsome enough for a king, I think, Louis !" she said, delightedly.

"Are kings handsomer than other people, my dear mother ?" he said, with a smile.

"Why, I suppose so ; I never saw one. You are the very image of your poor dead father, too ! Dear me ! what an age it seems since we parted last !" said Lizzie, sinking back in her seat, with a sigh.

"I am sorry to find you so ill, mother," said Louis, gazing sadly into her thin, pale face, from which the bright glow was fast fading.

"Oh, I am always worse in the spring than at any other time. In a month or two I will be quite a different-looking individual," said Lizzie, hopefully.

An hour passed away, and then there came a tap at the door. Louis arose and opened it, and beheld Gipsy.

"Well, Louis, if you're done talking to your mother,

you'd better come down and see Guardy. He's just woke up, but he doesn't know yet you've come," said Gipsy.

Louis went down stairs, taking half the staircase at a bound in his haste. Pushing open the parlor door, he unceremoniously entered the presence of the squire, who, after his old habit, lay in a lounging chair, with his feet stretched upon another, smoking his pipe with the benign air of a man at peace with himself and the rest of mankind.

At the abrupt entrance of Louis he looked up with a start, and muttered something suspiciously like an oath at seeing a tall, dark foreigner—as he supposed him to be—standing before him.

"Eh? who the deuce—I beg your pardon, sir, sit down," said the squire, staring with all his eyes.

"Do you not know me, my dear grandfather?" said Louis, advancing with extended hand.

"Why! Lord bless me, if it is not Louis Oranmore," said the squire, jumping up, "with as much hair on his face as a chimpanzee monkey has on its body. Bless my heart! this *is* a surprise! When did you get home? Eh, when did you come?"

"About an hour ago, sir."

"And you're Louis? Well, well! Why, you weren't as high as that when you left," holding his hand about three inches from the ground, "and here you come back as tall as a lamp-post, with mustache enough for a shoe-brush, and dressed like a Spanish grandee. 'All's vanity,' as Solomon says. Well, and how did you get on with those old humbugs you went off to see—eh?"

"What old humbugs, sir?"

"Pooh! you know very well—the old masters."

"Oh! I flatter myself I have seen them to some purpose," said Louis, laughing; "but, to change the subject,

I perceive you have made a few changes in the domestic economy of Sunset Hall during my absence."

"Why, yes, my boy ; a few, a few ! Gipsy's married to the old doctor, and didn't want to, cither ; but we coaxed her round and took her while she was ' in the humor,' as Solomon says."

"I trust, sir, Gipsy was not *compelled* to marry this old man ?" said Louis, with a darkening brow.

"Pooh ! pshaw ! of course not ! Married him of her own free will—just like Gipsy, always doing what nobody would expect ; ' women are like mules,' as Solomon says—want them to go one way, and they'll be sure to go t'other," said the squire, uneasily, evidently anxious to change the subject. "Have you seen old Wiseman and his daughter since your return ?"

"I have not seen the doctor, but his daughter I have. She is a most beautiful girl," replied Louis.

"Bah ! 'All that glitters is not gold,' as Solomon says. She's a proud, sullen, conceited minx, *that's* what she is—never likcd her. And mind, my young jacka-napes, you mustn't go and fall in love with her. You must look out for an heiress ; not a girl like her, without a cent to bless herself with."

"I thought the doctor was rich," said Louis.

"So he is ; but stingy—infernally stingy ! Won't give her a copper till his death !"

"Well, sir, I have no present intention of falling in love with her or any one else ; but if I had, Minnette Wiseman would be just the girl for me. She is hand-some, refined, intellectual, as any one can tell from her conversation. What more would a man have ?"

"Stuff ! moonshine ! 'Fine words butter no par-snips,' as Solomon says. She wants the *gilt*—the money, my boy. Love in a cottage sounds very fine, but come to real life and see what it is. No, sir ; I will never hear to your marrying a poor girl—never! The heir of Erliston and Oranmore must find an heiress for a wife. No matter about love, you know ; money's the thing. 'When poverty comes in at the door love flies out of the window,' as Solomon says."

CHAPTER XXVII.

LOVE AT FIRST SIGHT.

"Oh, her smile it seemed half holy,
    As if drawn from thoughts more fair
Than our common jestings are ;
    And if any painter drew her,
He would paint her, unaware,
    With a halo round her hair."
                    —E. B. BROWNING.

 WEEK had passed away at Mount Sunset Hall since the arrival of Louis.

It had been a week of unremitting storm. Rain, rain, rain, from morning till night, and from night to morning, without ceasing.

No one could go abroad in such weather ; so the arrival of Louis remained a secret in the neighborhood. It is true, Gipsy, who feared storm no more than sunshine, would have ridden forth, but preparations were being made for a grand party at the mansion, in honor of Louis' arrival, and she was forced to stay at home to assist. The whole household, with the exception of Louis and Minnette, were pressed into the business. Even Lizzie sat in the dining-room and stoned raisins, and sorted fruit, and pickles, and preserves, and looked over dresses, and laces, and muslins, and flowers, with unabated zeal. Gipsy might have been seen flying about in calico long-shorts from morning till night, entering heart and soul into the excitement. Jupiter and Mrs. Gower were sent to the city for "things," and the squire was continually blowing and blustering about, and overseeing all in general.

Minnette was too indolent to have anything to do with it, and so was left to herself—and Louis. That young gentleman, seeing how busy all were, gravely offered his services in the kitchen, saying, with the assistance of Totty, he had no doubt but he would learn how to wash dishes and make himself useful in time. His offer, however, like the manuscripts often sent to publishers, was "respectfully declined," and he and Minnette being thus thrown together, became, during the week of the storm, the best of friends—perhaps something more.

Their mornings were usually spent in the library, she embroidering while he read aloud poetry—dangerous occupation for a young and handsome man. Then he had such long stories and anecdotes to tell her, of his travels, of his "hair-breadth escapes by flood and field;" and it *did* flatter his vanity a little to see the work drop unnoticed from her hand, her cheek flush or pale, her breath come quick and short at his words. Their afternoons were mostly devoted to music; she seated at the piano playing and singing his favorite songs, chiefly old Scotch and German love ditties, which he liked better than Italian songs or opera music, in spite of his usually fashionable taste. And Minnette— wild, passionate girl that she was—who can tell the tumultuous thoughts that set her heart throbbing so fast, or brought so vivid a crimson to her blooming cheek, as he bent over her, entranced—his dark, glossy locks mingling with hers? Perhaps he did not exactly make love to her, but he was too thorough a man of the world not to perceive that she loved him, as only one of her fiery, passionate nature can love. The proud, haughty girl, who had all her life been a marble statue to others, was gentle and timid as a child before him. And he—I cannot excuse him—but though he loved her not he liked this devoted homage, this fiery heart he had tamed and won ; and by his manner, almost unconsciously, led her to believe her love was returned. For the first time in her life, she was supremely happy, yielding herself, without restraint, to the intoxicating spell of his eye and voice.

Gipsy's keen eyes saw all this, too—saw it with regret and apprehension, and with instinctive dread.

"Minnette's marble heart had been changed to quivering flesh at last," was her soliloquy. "She *loves* him, and (it is the old story) he *likes* her. Heaven forbid he should trifle with her ! for woe to you, Louis Oranmore, if the unchained force of Minnette's lion-passions is aroused. Better for you you had never been born, than that the mad love of her tiger heart should turn to still madder hate. She can never make him or any one else happy ; she is too fierce, too jealous, too exacting. I wish she had never come here. I will ride over to-night or to-morrow, and bring Celeste here ; when he sees *her*, I know he can never love Minnette. It may not be too late yet to remedy the evil. The love of Celeste would ennoble him—raise him above the earth, that of Minnette will drag him down, down, to darkness and doom. I must prevent it."

Too late ! too late ! Gipsy. The evil has been done that can never be remedied. The "marble-heart" is awakened from its long repose at last.

The cards of invitation had been sent out for miles around. Early in the evening of the day appointed

Gipsy ordered the carriage and drove to Valley Cottage. Miss Hagar, gray, grim, and unchanged, stiff and upright as ever, sat (as usual) knitting in the chimney-corner. A perfect bower of neatness was that little cottage —outside almost hidden in its wealth of vines and leaves— inside, bright with cleanliness, and odoriferous with the perfume of flowers that came drifting in through the white draped windows and open door. And there, sitting by the window in her neat-fitting muslin dress, bright, sunshiny, and smiling, sat sweet Celeste, the " Star of the Valley," celebrated for her beauty for miles around.

"Ah, Miss Hagar! how d' ye do? Pleasant day," said Gipsy, flashing in after her old fashion. "Celeste, throw down that sewing, and come right off to the Hall with me ; I want you."

"Oh! really, my dear Gipsy, you must excuse me," smiled Celeste ; "I am making this dress for poor old Widow Mayer, and must finish it to-night. So I cannot possibly go."

"Now, that's just like you, Celeste—always sewing, or sitting up, or writing letters, or reading the Testament to some poor old unfortunate, instead of taking any pleasure for yourself. I declare you ought to be a Sister of Charity, at once ! But you sha'n't work yourself to death for any one ; so come along. I'll send the old lady over, to-morrow, every dress I have, sooner than want you to-night."

"But Miss Hagar, Gipsy ; it is not right for me to leave her alone. She is so lonesome without me."

"No, she's not. You're glad to get rid of her ; ain't you, Miss Hagar ?"

"I should be pleased to have her go. It is right she should enjoy herself with the rest of the young folks," said Miss Hagar.

"There! you hear that? Now you go and get ready!"

" But really, dear Gipsy——"

" Now, none of your 'dear Gipsy-ing' me! I won't listen to another word! You *must* come; that's the whole of it," said Gipsy, seizing the work, and throwing it into a corner, and pulling the laughing Celeste by main force from the room.

"But, Gipsy, why are you so anxious for me to go with you to-night?" said Celeste, when they had reached her chamber.

"Oh, because I have my *raysons* for it," as little Pat Flynn says. "Now I want you to look your very prettiest to-night, Celeste. In fact, you must be perfectly irresistible."

"I am afraid you are going to play me some trick, Gipsy!" said Celeste, smiling and hesitating.

"Oh! honor bright! Come, hurry up! Put on your white muslin; you look better in it than anything else."

"Besides being the best dress I have," said Celeste, as she took it down; for the cottage maiden. always dressed with the utmost plainness and simplicity.

"I'll run out and gather you some rosebuds for your hair," said Gipsy, as Celeste began to dress.

"But, indeed, Gipsy, I am not accustomed to be so gayly attired," said Celeste, anxiously.

"Nonsense! what is there gay in a few white rosebuds, I'd like to know? You *shall* wear them," said Gipsy, hurrying from the room.

Half an hour later and Celeste's toilet was complete. Very lovely she looked in her simple white robe, fastened at her slender waist by a blue ribbon, her shining hair of pale gold falling like a shower of sunlight over her beautifully white and rounded neck, and wreathed with moss roses. Her fair, rose-tinted face, with its deep, blue eyes, shaded by long, sunny lashes ; her red, smiling lips ; her softly flushed cheeks, and broad, transparent forehead, bright with youth, and goodness, and loveliness !

" Why, Celeste, you are radiant to-night—lovely, bewitching, angelic !" exclaimed Gipsy, gazing upon her in sort of rapture.

" Nonsense, dear Gipsy !" said Celeste, smiling, and blushing even at the words of the little hoyden. " Are you, too, becoming a flatterer ?"

" Not I ; I would scorn to be ! You know I never flatter, Celeste ; but you seem to have received a baptism of living beauty to-night."

Celeste very well knew Gipsy never flattered. Candor was a part of the elf's nature ; so, blushing still more, she threw a light shawl over her shoulders, and entered the sitting-room. Both girls took leave of Miss Hagar, and entered the carriage, that whirled them rapidly in the direction of Mount Sunset.

" Gipsy, I know you have some design in all this ?" said Celeste, as they drove along.

" Well ; suppose I have ?"

" Why, I shall be tempted to take it very hard indeed. Why have you brought me here, Gipsy ?"

" Well, to meet a friend. There now !"

" Who is it ?"

" Sha'n't tell you yet. Here we are at home."

Celeste glanced from the window, and saw the court-yard full of carriages, the hall illuminated, and throngs of people pouring in.

" Is it possible, Gipsy, this is a large party ?"

" Yes ; just so, my dear."

" Oh, Gipsy ! it was too bad of you to entrap me in this way !" said Celeste, reproachfully.

" Fiddle ! it's a great thing to go to a party, ain't it ?

Come, jump out, and come up to my dressing-room; I have a still greater surprise in store for you."

Celeste passed, with Gipsy, through a side door, and both ran, unobserved, up to her room. Then—after an hour or so, which it took Gipsy to dress, both descended to the saloon, where the dancing was already at its height.

Their entrance into the crowded rooms produced a decided sensation. Gipsy, blazing with jewels, moved along like a spirit of light, and Celeste, in her fair, moonlight beauty, looking like some stray angel newly dropped in their midst..

Gipsy led her guest to the upper end of the room, under a raised arch of flowers that filled the air with fragrance.

"Stay here until I come back for you," she whispered, as she turned, and disappeared among the throng.

Flitting hither and thither like a sunbeam, she paused until she discovered Louis, with Minnette leaning on his arm, calling up the smiles and blushes to her face at his all-powerful will.

"Louis! Louis! come with me! I want you a moment. You'll excuse him, Minnette, will you not?" said Gipsy.

"Oh, certainly!" said Minnette, with a radiant look, little dreaming for what purpose he was taken from her.

Passing her arm through his, Gipsy led him to where he could obtain a full view of Celeste, without being seen by her.

"Look!" she said, pointing.

He looked, started suddenly, and then stood like one transfixed, with his eyes riveted to the glorious vision before him.

She stood under the flowery canopy, robed in white, crowned with roses, leaning against a marble statue of

12*

Hebe, herself a thousand times lovelier than that exquisitely sculptured form and face. This was his ideal, found at last—this the face and figure that had haunted, his dreams all his life, but had never been found before; just such an angelic creature he had striven all his life to produce on canvas, and always failed. He stood motionless, enchanted, drinking in to intoxication the bewildering draught of her beauty.

"Louis," said Gipsy, laying her hand on his arm.

He heard not, answered not; he stood gazing like one chained to the spot.

"Louis," she said in a louder tone.

Still she was unheeded,

"Louis, you provoking wretch!" she said, giving him a shake.

"Well?" he said, without removing his dazzled eyes from the vision before him.

"What do you think of her? Is she not lovely?"

"Lovely!" he repeated, rousing himself from the trance into which he had fallen. "Gipsy, she is *divine*. Do not praise her beauty; no words can do it justice."

"Whew!—caught already! There's love at first sight for you."

"Gipsy, who is she—that vision of light—my life-dream—that I have found at last?"

"Then you don't know her? Bless your dear, innocent heart! that's Celeste—your 'Star of the Valley,' you know!"

"Yes, yes! I recognize her now—my Star of the Valley, rightly named. Would she *were* mine!" he added, in a lower tone.

"Shall I present you?"

"Does she know I am here?"

"No; I didn't tell her a word about it."

"Then leave me. I will present myself."

"All right ; that'll save me some trouble ; and I hear somebody over there singing out for Mrs. Wiseman. So *au revoir*, and Cupid be with you !"

And, laughingly, Gipsy glided away, and Louis went up and stood before Celeste.

She looked up with a start, to find the handsomest man she had ever seen in her life standing before her, gazing upon her with such a look of intense admiration in his deep, dark eyes, that the blood rushed to her cheek, and the white lids dropped over the shrinking blue eyes. Another moment, and both her hands were clasped in his ; while he cried, in a voice that was low, but full of passion :

"Celeste ! Celeste ! little sister !—do you not know me ?"

"Louis !" broke from her lips, in a wild exclamation of joy.

"Yes, sweet sister, your boy-friend, Louis, home again."

"Oh, Louis, I am *so* glad !" she said, lifting her cloudless blue eyes to his, radiant with delight.

"Then you have not forgotten me ? I feared you had," he said, bending over her, and holding fast the little hand that lay imprisoned in his.

"Forget you !—oh, no," she said, her heart fluttering wildly that moment against a little golden cross—*his* parting gilt, which had lain on her bosom all those years.

There was a look of eager delight on his face at her words. She saw it, and grew embarrassed. Withdrawing her hand from his, she said, in a more composed voice :

"When did you arrive ?"

"About a week ago. I would have gone to see you,

but the weather was so disagreeable," he replied, with a pang of regret and remorse for his neglect.

"Yes, so it was," said Celeste, sincerely; for, having no morbid self-love to be wounded, his excuse seemed the most natural thing in the world.

"And how is my old friend, Miss Hagar?" he asked, drawing her arm within his, and leading her toward the conservatory, now almost deserted.

"Oh, quite well. She will be delighted to see you."

"May I go and see her to-morrow, sweet Celeste?"

"Certainly you may. We will *both* be very glad to see you," answered Celeste, delightedly.

"She is certainly a paragon of simplicity. No woman of the world would say that," thought Louis, as he glanced at her eager, happy face.

An exclamation from Celeste attracted his attention. He looked up. Right before him stood Minnette, with her glittering black eyes fixed upon them with a look so fierce, so flamingly jealous, that he started back.

"Why, Minnette, what is the matter? Are you ill?" asked Celeste, in alarm.

She would have turned away without answering; but the dark eye of Louis was upon her, and she replied, coldly:

"I am perfectly well. Excuse me; I fear I have interrupted a pleasant *tete-a-tete.*"

And, with one fierce, scorching glance at Celeste, she turned, and hurried away.

Celeste shuddered; something in the dark, passionate face of Minnette frightened her. Her companion perceived it—well he understood the cause; and with matchless tact he drew her mind from the subject to fix it on himself.

During the evening he devoted himself assiduously to Celeste. With her he danced; on his arm she leaned in the promenade ; by his side she sat at table. Standing alone and neglected by herself, Minnette saw it all ; and, had looks power to kill, those flaming glances of fire would have stricken her rival dead.

It was near morning when the party broke up. Celeste—who always shared Gipsy's room when at the Hall—sought her couch, and soon closed her weary blue eyes in blissful slumbers.

That night, in the dreams of Louis, the dark, resplendent face of Minnette was forgotten for a white-robed vision with a haunting pair of blue eyes. And Minnette—in the calm light of the stars, she trod up and down her apartment until morning broke over the hill-tops, with a wild anguish at her heart she had never before known.

CHAPTER XXVIII.

"THE OLD, OLD STORY."

" I have loved thee, thou gentlest, from a child,
    And borne thine image with me o'er the sea—
    Thy soft voice in my soul ! Speak ! oh, yet live for me !"
                                                —HEMANS.

GAY party gathered around the breakfast-table at Sunset Hall the next morning.

There was Mrs. Oranmore—fair, fragile, but still pretty ; then Mrs. Gower, over-shadowing the rest with her large proportions until they all shrank into skeletons beside her, with the exception of the squire, who was in a state of roaring good humor. There was Mrs. Doctor Nicholas Wiseman—our own little Gipsy—as usual, all life, bus-

tle and gayety, keeping up a constant fire of repartee —
laughing and chatting unceasingly, poor little elf! to
drown thought.

Then there was Louis—gay, gallant and handsome—
setting himself and everybody else at ease by his stately
courtesy and polished manners. By his side sat our
favorite Celeste, fair and fresh, and bright as a rosebud,
smiling and blushing at the compliments showered upon
her. And last, there sat Minnette, pale, and cold, and
silent, with the long, black lashes falling over her eyes
to hide the dusky fire that filled them.

"I wish you would stay all day with us, Celeste,"
said Mrs. Oranmore. "I always feel twice as well when
I can look upon your bright face. It seems to me you
must have drank at the fountain of beauty and youth."

"In that I agree with you, madam," said Louis.

Minnette bit her lip till the blood started.

"Oh! I really cannot stay, Mrs. Oranmore," said
Celeste, blushing vividly. "Miss Hagar is always very
lonely during my absence ; and besides——"

"You are engaged to make gowns and nightcaps for
all the old women of the parish! I know all about it,"
broke in Gipsy. "Formerly *I* used to be prime favorite
in St. Mark's ; but since our return from school I am
thrown aside like an old shoe, to make room for your
ladyship. I'll leave it to the world in general if I
wasn't quoted as an oracle on every occasion. There
wasn't a baby spanked, nor an old dress turned upside
down, but I was consulted about it. Now, just look at
the difference ; it's Miss Celeste here, and Miss Celeste
there, and Miss Celeste everywhere ; while I'm nothing
but a poor, dethroned, misfortunate little wretch! I
won't put up with it—I just won't. I'll leave it to my
daughter-in-law over there, if it isn't unbearable."

"Ha, ha, ha! What do you say, Miss Wiseman?" said the squire, laughing.

"I know nothing about it," coldly replied Minnette.

"And care less, I suppose," said Gipsy. "That's just the way! Even my own children treat me with disrespect. Well, never mind; perhaps the tables will turn yet."

"I am to attend you home, am I not, Celeste?" said Louis, in a low voice, as they arose from the table.

"I am sure I do not know. I suppose you may, if you wish," she replied, ingenuously.

"Oh, go, by all means," said Gipsy, who overheard them. "Anything to keep them away from Minnette," she muttered inwardly.

Accordingly, shortly after the carriage was brought round. Louis handed Celeste in, took the reins, and drove off, unconscious that Minnette, from her chamber window, was watching them, with a look that would have appalled him had he seen it.

That drive home—to what an unheard-of length was it prolonged! Had he been training his horses for a funeral, Louis could not have driven them slower. He had so many things to tell her; wild yet beautiful German legends—of the glorious skies of glorious Italy—of the vine-clad hills of sunny Spain—of gay, gorgeous Paris—and of the happy homes of "merrie England." And Celeste, lying back among the cushions, with half-closed eyes, drank in his low-toned, eloquent words— listened to the dangerous music of his voice—with a feeling unspeakably delicious, but hitherto unknown. She saw not the burning glances of his dark eyes, as they rested on her fair face, but yielded herself up to his magnetic influence without attempting to analyze her feelings.

They reached Valley Cottage all too soon. Louis handed her out, and entered the cottage after her.

Miss Hagar sat in her old seat, as though she had never moved from it.

"Good-morning, dear Miss Hagar," said Celeste, kissing her so affectionately that Louis inwardly wished he could become an old woman forthwith. "See—I have brought a stranger home with me."

Louis stood smiling before her. She raised her solemn, prophetic gray eyes to his face, with a long, earnest gaze.

"Louis Oranmore!" she exclaimed — "welcome home!"

He raised the withered hand she extended so respectfully to his lips that a radiant glance of gratitude from the blue eyes of Celeste rewarded him.

How that morning slipped away, Louis could never tell ; but seated, talking to Miss Hagar, with his eyes fixed on the rosy fingers of Celeste flying with redoubled velocity to make up for what was lost, he "took no note of time," until the little clock on the mantel struck two.

"By Jove! so it is!" exclaimed Louis, horrified at his prolonged visit. "What will they think of me at home ?"

"Stay and take dinner with us," said Miss Hagar, hospitably.

He hesitated, and glanced at Celeste.

"Pray do," she said, lifting her sunshiny face with an enchanting smile.

Inwardly rejoicing, he consented ; and the long summer afternoon vanished as the morning had done—unnoticed.

"I fear your cottage is enchanted, Miss Hagar," he said, laughingly, as he at last arose to go ; "I find it next to impossible to tear myself away from it. Or perhaps there is some magnet concealed that keeps people here against their will."

Miss Hagar smiled good-humoredly, and invited him to repeat his visit—an invitation, it is unnecessary to say, the young gentleman condescended to accept.

Celeste accompanied him to the door. As they passed out, he said :

" On this very spot we parted years ago. Do you remember that parting, Celeste ?"

" Yes," she said, softly, while her fair face grew crimson as she remembered how wildly she had wept and clung to his neck then.

He read what was passing in her mind, and smiled slightly.

" Your farewell gift, that shining ring of gold, I have kept ever since, as a talisman against all evil," he said, with a slight twinge of conscience as he remembered where it was—at the bottom of one of his trunks, with some scores of other tresses, severed from other fair heads, their owners long since forgotten.

" I am glad you did not forget me during your absence," said Celeste, feeling very much confused, and not knowing very well what she was expected to reply.

" Forget you, Celeste ! Who could ever do so after beholding you once ?" Then, seeing how painfully she was embarrassed, he turned gayly away, saying : " Good-bye, fairest Celeste ! When shall we meet again ?"

" I know not. Next Sunday, at church, perhaps."

" As if I could exist so long without seeing my fair Star of the Valley ! May I not come to-morrow, Celeste ?"

" Yes, if you will bring Gipsy."

" Oh, never mind Gipsy ! 'She will most probably be ' over the hills and far away' long before I open my eyes on this mortal life in the morning. Therefore, to-morrow will behold me once more by the side of my liege lady."

And bowing lightly, he sprang into the saddle and galloped off, followed by Celeste's eyes until he was out of sight.

The gloaming was falling when he reached Sunset Hall. He entered the parlor. It was dark and untenanted, save by a slender, black-robed figure, seated by the window, as motionless as a statue. It was Minnette —her white hands clasped tightly together, and resting on the window-sill, her forehead leaned upon them, her long black hair falling in disorder over her shoulders.

A pang of remorse shot through his heart at the sight of that despairing figure. He went over and laid his hand gently on her arm.

" Minnette !" he said, softly.

At the sound of that loved voice, at the touch of that dear hand, she started up, and, flinging back her long hair, confronted him, with such a white, haggard face, such wild, despairing eyes, that involuntarily he started back.

"Dear Minnette, what is the matter ?" he said, gently taking her hand.

She wrenched it from his grasp, with a bitter cry, and sinking back into a seat, covered her face with her hands.

"Minnette, are you ill ? What is the matter ?" he asked, afraid to accept the answer that his own heart gave.

"The matter !" she cried, bitterly. "Oh, you may ask ! *You* do not know. *You* were not by my side from morning till night, whispering your wily words into my ear, until this fair, this angelic, Celeste came ! *You* do not know what it is to have led a cold, loveless life, until some one came and won all the wealth of love that had all your days lain dormant, and then cast it back as a worthless gift at your feet! *You* do not know what it 'is to discover first you have a heart by its aching! Oh, no! All this is unknown to you. 'Ill!'"

She laughed wildly.

"Minnette! Minnette! do not talk so passionately! In the name of heaven, what have I done?"

"Done!" she repeated, springing fiercely to her feet. "No need to ask what you have done! Was not this heart marble—harder than marble—ay, or granite—till you came? Did you not read it as you would an open book? Did you not strike the rock with a more powerful wand than that of Moses, and did not all the flood of life and love spring forth at your command? You never said in so many words: 'I love you.' Oh, no—you took care not to commit yourself; but could I not read it in every glance of your eye. Yes, deny it if you will, you *did* love me, under this fair-faced seraph—this 'stray angel,' as I heard you call her—came, and then, for the first new face, I was cast aside as worthless. I was too easy a conquest for this modern hero; and for this artful little hypocrite—for her pink cheeks, her blue eyes, and yellow hair—the heart that loves you ten thousand times more than she can ever do, is trampled under foot! But I tell you to beware, Louis Oranmore; for if I am a 'tigress,' as you often called me in my childhood, I can tear and rend in pieces all those who will cause my misery."

She looked like some beautiful fiend, in her fierce outburst of stormy passion; her face livid, save two dark purple spots on either cheek; her eyes flaming, blazing; her lips, white; her wild black hair falling like a vail of darkness around her white face.

"Minnette—*dear* Minnette!"—like a magic spell his low-toned words fell on her maddened spirit—"you are

mistaken. I never loved you as you fancy ; I admired
your beauty. I might have loved you, but I well knew
the fierce, jealous nature that lay smoldering in your
heart, under the living coals of your passions. Minnette,
the woman I love must be gentle and *womanly*, for that
means all ; the fawn, not the lioness, suits me. Ex-
tremes meet, they say ; and my own nature is too hot,
passionate, and fiery, ever to mate with a spirit like to
itself. In Celeste, gentle, tender, and dove-like—sit
still, Minnette, you *must* hear me out." He held her
down, writhing in anguish, by the force of his stronger
will. "In her, I say, I find all that I would ask of a
woman. Therefore my heart was drawn toward her.
Had I found the same qualities in you, I would have
loved you, instead of her. And now, dear Minnette, forgive me if I have occasioned you pain ; but for your
own peace of mind, it was necessary that I should tell
you this."

She was quivering, writhing in intense anguish,
crouching in her seat in a strange, distorted attitude of
utter despair. His eyes were full of deep pity as he
gazed upon her.

"Minnette, do you forgive me?" he said, coming
over and trying to raise her head.

"Oh, leave me—leave me !" was her reply, in a voice
so full of intense suffering that he started.

"Only say you forgive me."

"Never ! May God never forgive me if I do !" she
cried, with such appalling fierceness that he quailed before her. "Leave me, I tell you !" she cried, stamping
her foot, "leave me before I go mad !"

He quitted the room : and Minnette was alone, with
her own uncontrolled passions for company. The agony
of ages seemed to be concentrated into those moments ;

every fiber of her heart seemed tearing from its place, and lay quivering and bleeding in her bosom.

———

Weeks passed. Day after day found Louis at Valley Cottage, reading and talking, or walking with Celeste. And she—there was no mistaking that quick flushing, that involuntary smile, that sudden brightening of the eye, at the sound of his footstep or the tones of his voice. Yes, the Star of the Valley was wooed and won. And all this time Minnette sat in her own room, alone, wrapped in her own gloomy thoughts as in a mantle—the same cold, impassible Minnette as ever. Yet there was a lurid lightning, a blazing fire, at times, in her eye, that might have startled any one had it been seen.

One bright moonlight night in July Louis and Celeste were wandering slowly along the rocky path leading to the cottage. Even in the moonlight could be seen the bright flush that overspread her fair face, as she listened, with drooping head and downcast eyes, to his low, love-toned words.

"And so you love me, my sweet Celeste, better than all the world?" he asked softly.

"Oh, yes!" was the answer, almost involuntarily breathed.

"And you will be my wife, Celeste?"

"Oh, Louis! Your grandfather will never consent."

"And if he does not, what matter?" cried Louis, impetuously. "I am my own master, and can marry whom I please."

"Louis—Louis! do not talk so. I would never marry you against his will."

"You would not?"

"No, certainly not. It would be wrong, you know."

"Wrong ! How would it be wrong, Celeste ? I am sure my mother would not object ; and as for him, what right has he to interfere with my marriage ?"

"Oh, Louis ! you know he has a guardian's right—a parent's right—to interfere. Besides," she added, blushing, "we are both too young to be married. Time enough these seven years."

"Seven years !" echoed Louis, laughing ; " why, that would be as bad as Jacob and—Rachel. Wasn't that the name ? Come, my dear Celeste, be reasonable. I cannot wait seven years, though very likely you could. During all those long years of absence the remembrance of you has cheered my loneliest hours. I looked forward impatiently to the time when I might return and see my Star of the Valley again. And now that I have come, you tell me to wait seven years ! Say, Celeste, may I not ask my grandfather—and if he consents, will you not be mine ?"

"I don't know—I'll think about it," said Celeste, timidly.

"And I know how that thinking will end. Here we are at the cottage. Good-night, my little white dove ! To-morrow I will see you, and tell you his decision."

One parting embrace, and he turned away. Celeste stood watching him until he was out of sight, then turned to enter the cottage. As she did so, an iron grasp was laid on her shoulder, and a hoarse, fierce voice cried :

"Stop !"

Celeste turned, and almost shrieked aloud, as she beheld Minnette standing like a galvanized corpse before her.

CHAPTER XXIX.

THE RIVALS.

"All other passions have their hour of thinking,
And hear the voice of reason. This alone
Breaks at the first suspicion into frenzy,
And sweeps the soul in tempests."—SHAKESPEARE.

FOR a moment the rivals stood silently confronting each other—Celeste pale and trembling before that dark, passionate glance; Minnette white and rigid, but with scorching, burning eyes.

"Minnette, what is the matter?" said Celeste, at last finding voice. "Good heavens! you look as though you were crazed."

"Crazed!" hissed Minnette through her teeth. "You consummate little hypocrite! Your conduct, no doubt, should make me very cool and composed. Girl, I say to you, beware! Better for you you had never been born, than live to cross my path!"

Her voice was hoarse with concentrated passion—her small hands clenched until the nails sank into the quivering flesh. With a shudder, Celeste covered her face in her hands to shut out the scathing glance of those dark, gleaming eyes.

"Oh, Minnette!—dear Minnette!—do not look at me so. Your eyes kill me," she said, with a shiver.

"Would to Heaven they could!" fiercely exclaimed Minnette.

"Oh, Minnette! what have I done? If I have injured you, I am very sorry. Indeed, indeed, it was unintentional. I would sooner die than have any one hate me!" said Celeste, clasping her hands imploringly.

"Injured me!" almost shrieked Minnette, clutching her arm so fiercely, that Celeste cried out with pain. "Injured me, did you say? Yes—the greatest injury one woman can ever do another you have done me. From early childhood you have crossed my path, and, under your artfully assumed vail of simplicity, won the love of the only being under heaven I ever cared for—won him with your silly smiles, your baby face, and cowardly tears; you, a poor, nameless beggar—a dependent on the bounty of others. *Hate you!*—yes, from the first moment I beheld you, I hated you with an intensity you can never dream of until you feel the full weight of my vengeance; for I tell you I will be avenged; yes, I would peril my own soul, if by so doing I could wreak still more dire revenge on your head. I tell you, you began a dangerous game when you trifled with me. I am no sickly, sentimental fool, to break my heart and die—no; I shall drag down with me all who have stood in my way, and then die, if need be, gloating over the agonies I have made them suffer. Beware, I tell you; for no tigress, robbed of her young, can be fiercer than this newly awakened heart!"

She hurled Celeste from her, as she ceased, with such violence, that she reeled and fell; and, striking her head against a projecting stone, lay for some minutes stunned and motionless. A dark stream of blood flowed slowly from the wound; and Minnette stood gazing upon it with a fiendish smile on her beautiful face. Slowly, and with difficulty, Celeste arose—pressing her handkerchief to her face to stanch the flowing blood; and, lifting her soft, pitying eyes to the wild, vindictive face above her, she said:

"Minnette, I forgive you. You are crazed, and know

not what you do. But, oh! Minnette, you wrong me. I never intentionally injured you—never, as heaven is my witness! I have tried to love you as a sister always. Never, never—by word, or thought, or deed—have I willingly given you a moment's pain. I would sooner cut off my right hand than offend you. Oh, Minnette! can we never be friends?"

"Friends!" repeated Minnette, with a wild laugh; "yes, when the serpent dwells with the dove; when the tiger mates with the lamb; when two jealous woman love each other—then we will be friends. Perjure yourself not before me. Though an angel from heaven were to d scend to plead for you, I would neither forgive you nor believe your words."

"What have I done to make you hate me so?"

"You brazen hypocrite! do you dare to ask me what you have done? *He* did, too! A precious pair of innocents, both of you!" said Minnette, with her bitter, jeering laugh. "Little need to tell you what you have done. Did you not win the love of Louis Oranmore from me by your skillful machinations? He loved me before he saw you. You knew it; and yet, from the very first moment you beheld him, you set to work to make him hate me. Do not deny it, you barefaced, artful impostor! Did I not hear you both to-night?—and was not the demon within me prompting me to spring forward and stab you both to the heart? But my vengeance, though delayed, shall be none the less sure, and, when the time comes, woe to you and to him; for if I must perish, I shall not perish alone."

During this fierce, excited speech—every word of which had stabbed her to the heart—Celeste had staggered against a tree; and, covering her face with her hands, stood like one suddenly pierced by a sword; every word burned into her very brain like fire, as she stood like one fainting—dying. By a great effort, she crushed back the flood of her emotions; and when Minnette ceased, she lifted up her face—pale as death, but firm and earnest.

" Minnette Wiseman," she said, in a voice of gentle dignity, so unusual to her that the dark, passionate girl gazed on her in astonishment, " as heaven hears me, I am guilty of none of these things of which you accuse me. If Louis Oranmore loved you, I knew it not, or I would not have listened to him; if he won your heart, I dreamed not of it, or he should never have won mine. I thought you loved no one but yourself. I never— never dreamed you cared for him. For all the misery he has caused us both, may heaven forgive him, as I do ! If he loved you first, you have a prior claim to his heart. I will tell him so to-morrow, and never listen to him more."

She strove to speak calmly to the end ; but at the last her voice died away in a low tone of utter despair.

" Bah ! your acting disgusts me !" exclaimed Minnette, contemptuously. " Do you not suppose I can see through this vail with which you would blind my eyes ? You will tell him to-morrow, forsooth ! Yes, you will tell him I came here to abuse you, and strike you, and load you with vile epithets, and with what saint-like patience you bore them. You will represent yourself as such an injured innocent, and I as a monster of cruelty ; you will tell him, when I smote you on one cheek, how you turned the other. Faugh ! do not make me despise you as well as hate you."

" You cannot despise me, Minnette ; you know you cannot," said Celeste, with something like indignation in her gentle voice, as her truth-beaming eye met undauntedly the flashing orbs before her. " You know I have spoken the truth. You know in your own heart I am no hypocrite. Hate me if you will—I cannot prevent you ; but you shall not despise me. I have never intentionally wronged you, and I never will. If Louis Oranmore loves you as you say, I wish you both all happiness. I shall no longer stand between you and his heart."

"Oh ! wonderful heroism !" cried Minnette, in bitter mockery. " You can well afford to say you give him up, when you know he loves me no longer ; when you know you have surely and unalterably won him to yourself. Well do you know this pretended self-denial of yours will elevate you a thousand times higher still in his estimation, and make him love you far more than ever before. Oh ! you have learned your trade of deception well. Pity all cannot see through it as I do. Think not to deceive me as you have done so many others ; I, at least, can see your shallow, selfish, cold-blooded heart."

" I will not stay to listen to your words, Minnette ; they are too dreadful. Some day, perhaps, you will discover how you have wronged me. I am not deceiving you ; he *must* give me up if what you say be true. I will even go away if you wish it—anywhere, so that you may be satisfied. I will write and tell him, and never see him more, if that will satisfy you." Her voice faltered a little, but she went on ; " I will do anything— anything, Minnette, if you will only not call me such terrible things. It is fearful—horrible, to be hated so without cause."

Minnette did not speak, but glared upon her with her burning, flaming eyes. Two dark purple spots—now fading, now glowing vividly out—burned on either cheek ; otherwise, no snow-wreath was ever whiter than her face. Her teeth were set hard ; her hands tightly clenched ; her dark brows knit, as though about to spring upon the speaker and rend her to pieces She made one step toward her. With a piercing cry of terror, Celeste sprang away, darted through the garden gate, flew up the narrow path, burst into the cottage, closed and bolted the door, and sank, panting and almost fainting, on the ground.

"Good heavens! child, what is the matter?" asked Miss Hagar, rising, in alarm.

"Oh! save me—save me from her!" was all Celeste could utter.

"Save you from whom? Who are you speaking of? Who has frightened you so?" inquired Miss Hagar, still more astonished.

Celeste slowly rose from the ground, without speaking. Consciousness was beginning to return, but she was still stunned and bewildered.

"Merciful Father!" cried Miss Hagar, as Celeste turned toward the light, "what has happened?"

And truly she might exclaim, at beholding that deadly pale face—those wild, excited eyes—the disheveled golden hair—the blood-stained, and torn and disordered dress.

"Nothing! oh, nothing, nothing!" said Celeste, passing her hand slowly over her eyes, as if to clear away a mist, and speaking in a slow, bewildered tone.

"But, child, there is something the matter!" insisted Miss Hagar. "You look as though you were crazed, and your face is stained with blood."

"Is it? I had forgotten," said Celeste, pushing her hair vacantly off her wounded forehead. "It is nothing at all, though. I do not feel it."

"But how did it happen?"

"Oh!—why, I was frightened, and ran, and fell," said Celeste, scarcely knowing what she said.

"What was it frightened you?" pursued Miss Hagar, wondering at her strange manner.

Celeste, without reply, sank upon a seat and pressed her hands to her throbbing temples to collect her scattered thoughts. She felt sick and dizzy—unable to think and speak coherently. Her head ached with the intensity of her emotions; and her eyes felt dry and burning. Her brow was hot and feverish with such violent and unusual excitement. Her only idea was to get away—to be alone—that she might collect her wandering senses.

"Miss Hagar," she said, rising, "I cannot tell you what has happened. I must be alone to-night. To-morrow, perhaps, I will tell you all."

"Any time you please, child," said Miss Hagar, kindly. "Go to your room by all means. Good-night."

"Good-night!" said Celeste, taking her lamp and quitting the room.

She staggered as she walked. On reaching her room she set the lamp on the table, and entwined her arms above her head, which dropped heavily upon it. Unaccustomed to excitement of any kind, she felt more as if heart and brain were on fire. Loving Louis with the strong affection of her loving heart, the sudden disclosure and jealous fury of Minnette stunned and stupefied her for a time. So she lay for nearly an hour, unable to think or realize what had happened—only conscious of a dull, dreary pain at her heart. Then the mist slowly cleared away from her mental vision—the fierce words of Minnette danced in red, lurid letters before her eyes. She started to her feet, and paced her chamber wildly.

"Oh! why am I doomed to make others miserable?" she cried, wringing her hands. "Oh, Louis, Louis! why have you deceived me thus? What have I done that I should suffer such misery? But it is wrong to complain. I must not, will not murmur. I will not reproach him for what he has done, but try to forget him. May he be as happy with Minnette as I would have striven to render him! To-morrow I will see him, and return all the gifts cherished for his sake; to-morrow I will bid him a last adieu; to-morrow—but, oh! I cannot—I cannot!" she exclaimed, passionately. "I cannot see him and bid him go. Oh, Father of the fatherless! aid me in my anguish!"

She fell on her knees by the bedside, and a wild, earnest prayer broke from her tortured lips.

By degrees she grew calm; her wild excitement died away; the scorching heat left her brain, and blessed tears came to her aid. Long and bitterly she wept; long and earnestly she prayed—no longer as one without hope, but trustful and resigned, bending her meek head to the blow of the chastening rod.

She arose from her knees, pale, but calm and resigned.

"I will not see him," she murmured. "Better for us both I should never see him again! I will write—I will tell him all—and then all that is past must be forgotten. In the creature I was forgetting the Creator; for the worship of God I was substituting the worship of man; and my Heavenly Father, tempering justice with mercy, has lifted me from the gulf into which I was falling, and set me in the narrow way once more. Henceforth, no earthly idol shall fill my heart; to Him alone shall it be consecrated; and I will live on in the hope that there is yet 'balm in Gilead' for me."

It was very easy to speak thus, in the sudden reaction from despair to joy—very easy to talk in this way in the excitement of the moment, after her heart had been relieved by tears. She thought not of the weary days and nights in the future, that would seem to have no end, when her very soul would cry out in wild despair for that "earthly idol" again.

And full of her resolution, with cheeks and eyes

glowing with the light of inspiration, she sat down at the table, and, drawing pen and paper before her, began to write.

A long, earnest, eloquent letter it was. She resigned him forever, bidding him be happy with Minnette, and forget and forgive her, and breathing the very soul of sisterly love and forgiveness. Page after page was filled, while her cheek flushed deeper, and her eyes grew brighter, and her pen flew on as if inspired.

There, in the holy seclusion of her chamber, in the solemn stillness of night, she made the total renunciation of him she loved best on earth, scarcely feeling now she had lost him, in the lofty exaltation of her feelings.

It was finished at last. The pen dropped from her hand, and she arose to seek for the few gifts he had ever given her. A little golden locket, containing his likeness and a lock of his hair ; her betrothal-ring ; and the oft-mentioned gold cross. That was all.

She opened the likeness, and through all her heroism a wild, sharp thrill of anguish pierced her heart, as she gazed on those calm, beautiful features. The sable ring of hair twined itself round her fingers as though unwilling to leave her ; but resolutely she replaced it, and drew off the plain gold circlet of their betrothal, and laid them side by side. Then her cross—it had never left her neck since the night he had placed it there. All the old tide of love swelled back to her heart as she gazed upon it. It seemed like rending her very heart-strings to take it off.

"I cannot ! I cannot !" was her anguished cry, as her arm dropped powerless on the table.

"You must ! you must ! it is your duty !" cried the stern voice of conscience ; and, with trembling fingers and blanched lips, the precious token was removed and laid beside the others.

Then, sealing them up, with one last, agonizing look, such as we might bestow on the face of a dear friend about to be consigned to the grave, she sealed and directed the packet, and then threw herself on her bed and pressed her hands over her eyes to hide out the face of her dead.

But in spite of sorrow, sleep *will* visit the afflicted, and a bright morning sunbeam fell like a halo on her pale face, calm in sleep, and on the golden eyelashes, still wet with undried tear-drops.

That same broad July sunbeam fell on Minnette lying prone on her face in the damp pine woods, her long, black hair and dark garments dropping with the soaking dew. The dark, lonely woods had been her couch the livelong night.

* * *

CHAPTER XXX.

GIPSY HUNTS NEW GAME.

" And by the watch-fire's gleaming light,
  Close by his side was seen
A huntress maid in beauty bright
  With airy robes of green."—SCOTT.

T was early afternoon of that same day on which the events related in the last chapter occurred. Squire Erliston, in after-dinner mood, sat in his arm-chair ; Louis lay idly on a lounge at a little distance, and Gipsy sat by the window, yawningly turning over a volume of prints. Mrs. Oranmore, swathed in shawls, lounged on her sofa, her prayerbook in her hand, taking a succession of short naps.

It was the squire's custom to go to sleep after dinner; but now, in his evident excitement, he seemed quite to forget it altogether.

"Yes, sir," he was saying to Louis, "the scoundrel actually entered the sheriff's house through the window, and carried off more than a hundred dollars, right under their very noses. It's monstrous!—it's outrageous! He deserves to be drawn and quartered for his villainy! And he will be, too, if he's taken. The country 'll soon be overrun with just such rascals, if the scoundrel isn't made an example of."

"Of whom are you speaking, papa?" inquired Lizzie, suddenly walking up.

"Of one of Drummond's negroes—a perfect ruffian; Big Tom, they call him. He's fled to the woods, and only makes his appearance at night. He stabbed young Drummond himself; and since then, he's committed all sorts of depredations. Simms, the sheriff, came down yesterday with constables to arrest them; and during the night, the scoundrel actually had the audacity to enter the sheriff's window, and decamped with a hundred dollars before they could take him. He met one of the constables in the yard as he was going out. The constable cried 'murder,' and seized him; but Big Tom—who is a regular giant—just lifted him up and hurled him over the wall, where he fell upon a heap of stones, breaking his collar-bone, two of his legs, 'and the rest of his ribs,' as Solomon says. The constable's not expected to live; and Big Tom got off to his den in safety with his booty."

"Why do they not scour the woods in a body?" inquired Louis.

"So they did; but—bless your soul!—it's like looking for a needle in a hay-stack—couldn't find him anywhere."

"Oh! it was capital fun!" said Gipsy, laughing, "it

13*

reminded me of 'hide-and-go-seek' more than anything else. Once or twice they caught sight of me through the bushes, and taking me for poor Tom, came pretty near firing on me. Simms made them stop, and called to me to surrender to the law, or I'd repent it. Accordingly, I surrendered, and rode out, and—my goodness!—if they didn't look blue when they saw me! I burst right out laughing in their face, and made Simms so mad that I guess he wished he had let his men shoot me. Oh! didn't I have a jolly time, though! I took them, by various artifices, miles out of their way—generally leaving them half-swamped in a bog, or in some pathless part of the woods—until Simms lost all patience, and swore till he was black in the face, and rode home in a towering passion, all covered with mud, and his fine city clothes torn to tatters. Ha, ha, ha! I guess I enjoyed it, if they didn't."

"As mischievous as ever!" exclaimed the squire. "Pretty way, that, to treat the officers of the law in the discharge of their duty! How will you like it, if that black demon comes here some night, and murders us all in our beds?"

Lizzie uttered a stifled shriek at the idea.

"I'm sure I'll be glad of it, if he only murders Spider first, and so save me the trouble," said Gipsy.

"You're an affectionate wife, 'pon my word," muttered Louis.

"Yes; but it's just like the diabolical young imp," growled the squire.

"Thank you — you're complimentary," muttered Gipsy.

"Mind you," continued the squire, "while Big Tom's at liberty you must leave off your rides through the woods and over the hills—because he might be the death of you at any moment."

"More likely I'd be the death of him. I never was born to be killed by a ruffian."

"No ; for if the gallows had its dues——"

"You wouldn't be here to-day," interrupted Gipsy.

"Come—don't interrupt me, young woman. I positively forbid you or any one in this place riding out while Big Tom's roaming about."

"That's right, Guardy—show your authority. Nothing like keeping it up, you know. And now, as I'm off to give Mignonne an airing, I'll think of your commands by the way."

And the disobedient elf arose to leave the room.

"But, my dear, tantalizing little coz, it really is dangerous," interrupted Louis. "If you were to encounter this gigantic negro, alone, it would be rather a serious affair, I'm afraid."

"Bother !" exclaimed the polite and courteous Mrs. Wiseman. "Do you s'pose I'm afraid—Gipsy Gower afraid ! Whew ! I like that ! Make your mind easy, my dear Louis. I could face a regiment on Mignonne's back without flinching."

And Gipsy darted off to don her riding-habit, singing as she went :

> "Some love to roam
> O'er the dark sea foam,
> Where the shrill winds whistle free ;
> But a chosen band
> In the mountain land,
> And a life in the woods for me."

Ten minutes afterward they saw her ride out of the court-yard at her usual furious rate, and dash away over the hills, where she was speedily out of sight.

Gipsy must have had some of the Arab in her nature ; for she spent almost her whole life on horse-back. She heeded not the flight of time, as she thundered along, riding in the most hazardous places—sometimes narrowly escaping being dashed to pieces over precipices—sometimes leaping yawning chasms that would make many a stout hunter's head giddy. The excitement was a part—a necessity—of her nature. The almost stagnant life in the village would have driven the hot-headed, impetuous girl wild, but for the mad excitement of the chase. Brave as a young lioness—bold and free as the eagle of her native mountains—she scorned fear, and sought danger as others do safety. She knew it was putting her head into the lion's mouth to venture alone into this wild, unfrequented region, within arm's length of a desperate villain, hunted down like a furious beast ; yet the idea of not venturing here never once entered her mad little head.

It was growing dark before Gipsy began to think of turning her steps homeward. Reluctantly she turned her horse's head, and set out for Mount Sunset—half regretting she had met with no adventure worth relating on her return.

As she rapidly galloped along she discovered she had ridden much farther than she had intended, and that it would be late ere she reached the hall. The dim starlight alone guided her path ; for the moon had not yet risen. But Mignonne was so well accustomed to the road that he could have found his way in the dark ; and Gipsy rode on gayly, humming to herself a merry hunting-chorus.

Suddenly a gleam of light from between the trees flashed across their path. Mignonne, like his mistress, being only a half-tamed thing at best, reared suddenly upright, and would have dashed off at headlong speed, had not Gipsy held the reins with a grasp of iron. Her strength was wonderful for a creature so small and slight ; but her vigorous exercise had given her thews and muscles of steel. Mignonne felt he was in the hand of a master-spirit, and after a few fierce bounds and plunges, stood still and surrendered.

Rapidly alighting, Gipsy bound her horse securely, and then stole noiselessly through the trees. The cause of the light was soon discovered; and Gipsy beheld a sight that, daring and fearless as she was, for a moment froze the very blood in her veins.

A small semicircle was before her, in the center of which the remains of a fire still glowed, casting a hot, reddish glare around. By its lurid light the huge figure of a gigantic negro, whose hideous face was now frightfully convulsed with rage. On her knees at his feet was a woman, whom he grasped with one hand by the throat, and with the other brandished over her head a long, murderous knife. The sight for a moment left Gipsy's eyes, and her very heart ceased beating. Then, with the rapidity of lightning, she drew a pistol, aimed and fired.

One second more and she would have been too late. With the shriek of a madman the huge negro leaped into the air, and bounded to where she stood. She turned to fly, but ere she had advanced a yard she was in the furious grasp of the wounded monster. His red eyes were like balls of fire, he foamed, he roared with rage and pain, as with one huge hand he raised the slight form of Gipsy to dash out her brains.

In that moment of deadly peril the brave girl was as cool and self-possessed as though she were seated in safety in her guardian's parlor. A gleaming knife was stuck in his belt. Quick as thought she drew it out, and, concentrating all her strength, she plunged it in his breast.

The hot blood spurted in a gush up in her face. Without a cry the ruffian reeled, his hand relaxed, and

Gipsy sprang from his grasp just as he fell heavily to the ground.

Gipsy staggered against a tree, with a deadly inclination to swoon coming over her. She covered her face with her hands to hide the ghastly form of the huge negro, lying weltering in his own blood before her. She had taken a life; and though it was done in self-defense, and to save the life of another, it lay on her heart like lead.

The thought of that other at length aroused her to action. Darting through the trees she approached the fire. The woman lay on the ground, senseless, and half strangled. The firelight, as it fell upon her, showed the face and form of an old woman, upward of fifty, poorly clad, and garments half torn off in the scuffle.

The sight restored Gipsy to her wonted composure. Kneeling down, she began chafing the old woman's hands and temples with an energy that soon restored her to consciousness. She opened her eyes and glared for a moment wildly around; then, as consciousness returned, she uttered shriek upon shriek, making the forest resound.

"Stop your screaming," said Gipsy, shaking her in her excitement. "You're safe enough now. Stop, will you. I tell you you're safe."

"Safe!" repeated the woman, wildly. "Oh, that drefful nigger——"

"He won't hurt you any more. Stop your noise, and get up, and come with me!" said Gipsy, impatiently.

"Oh! Lor' a massey! I can't git up. I'm all out o' j'int. I'm dead entirely!" groaned the woman.

"Then I shall leave you here," said Gipsy, rising.

"Oh, don't leave me!—don't, for God's sake! I'd

die o' fear !" screamed the woman, grasping Gipsy's dress.

"Then, you stupid old thing, get up and come along," cried Gipsy, losing all patience, as she seized her with no gentle hand, and pulled her to her feet.

"Where 'll I go ?" said the poor old creature, trembling with mortal terror, evidently as much afraid of the fierce little Amazon before her, as of the huge negro.

"This way," said Gipsy, pulling her along to where stood her horse. "Now, get up there, and put your arms around my waist, and hold on for your life."

"Oh! dear me! I never rid a horseback in my life, and I'll fall off—I know I will!" said the old woman, wringing her hands in fresh distress.

"Well, I can't help it ; you'll have to make the attempt, or stay here till I reach St. Mark's, and rouse up the people. Which will you do ?"

"Oh! I dassent stay. I'll go 'long with you, somehow."

"Very well. Up with you then," said Gipsy, almost lifting her into the saddle. "Now, I'll get on before you, and mind, if you don't hold on well, you'll never reach the village alive."

With the clutch of mortal fear, the old lady grasped Gipsy round the waist, and held on for dear life, until Mount Sunset was gained, when, more dead than alive, she was assisted to alight, and consigned to the care of the servants.

Louis, who had just returned from his interview with Celeste, was in the parlor with the squire, meditating how he should make his proposal, when Gipsy, pale, wild, and disordered, her hair disheveled, and her garments dyed with blood, burst in upon them, electrifying them with amazement.

Great was their consternation as they listened to the

rapidly-told tale.   There was no time left to congratulate
her on her narrow escape, for she impetuously commanded Louis to mount immediately and take three or
four of the servants to bring away the body.

With a rapidity almost as great as her own, her coun-
sels were obeyed, and Gipsy, with Louis beside her,
started back to the scene of the catastrophe, followed by
four of the servants.

They reached the spot at last, and Gipsy drew back
in dismay as she discovered the body was gone.

"Who can have carried it off?" she exclaimed,
aghast.

"I rather think he has carried himself off," said
Louis, who had been attentively examining the ground.

"Oh, impossible!   He was dead, I tell you—just as
dead as ever he could be," said Gipsy.

"Well, dead or not, he has made his escape," said
Louis.   "See, the grass is dyed with blood all along,
showing the way he has gone.   Come, the trail is plain
enough, let us follow it."

All dismounted and followed Louis.   Not far had
they to go, for lying by the fire was the burly form of
the negro.   He had evidently, with much difficulty,
dragged himself thus far, and then sank down exhausted.
He rolled his glaring eyes fiercely on the faces bending over him, and gnashed his teeth in impotent rage as
he saw Gipsy.

"Thank God! I have not killed him!" was her first
fervent ejaculation.   Then, while Louis and the servants began making a sort of litter, she knelt beside
him, and strove to stanch the flowing blood, undeterred
by the wild, ferocious glare of his fiery eyes.

"Now, Tom, look here," said Gipsy, as she composedly went on with her work, "there's no use in your
looking daggers at me that way, because it don't alarm

me a bit. You needn't be mad at me either, for though I fired on you first, it was to save the life of an old woman, who might have been a loss to the world ; and if I made use of your knife afterward, it was to save the life of Mrs. Doctor Nicholas Wiseman, who would have been a greater loss still. So you see I couldn't help myself, and you may as well look at the matter in the same light."

By this time the rest came back with a sort of litter ; and groaning and writhing with pain, the heavy form of the wounded giant was lifted on their shoulders, and borne toward the village, where it was consigned to the care of the sheriff, who was thunderstruck when he heard of Gipsy's daring.

On their return to Sunset Hall, they learned from the old woman, who seemed threatened with a severe illness, how it had all occurred.

She was a " poor, lone woman," she said—a widow, named Mrs. Donne, living by herself for ten odd years, in a little cottage beyond St. Mark's.

She was reputed to be rich—a rumor she never contradicted, as it made her neighbors treat her with distinction, in the hope that she would remember them in her will.

Big Tom, hearing the rumor, and believing it, came to her cottage, and demanded money. She had none to give him, and told him so, which exasperated him beyond measure. He threatened to kill her if she persisted in refusing, and gagged her to stifle her cries. Then, finding her still obstinate, he carried her off with him to the spot where Gipsy had found them, and again offered her her life if she would deliver up her money. Still she was forced to refuse, and maddened with rage and disappointment, he was about to murder her, when Gipsy providentially appeared, and saved her life.

Not without many interruptions was this story told; and ere it was concluded, Mrs. Donne was in a high fever. Gipsy installed herself as nurse, and listened in wonder and surprise to her raving of infants left to perish in snow-storms, and her wild words of sorrow and remorse for some past crime.

CHAPTER XXXI.

CELESTE'S TRIAL.

"This morn is merry June, I trow,
　The rose is budding fain;
But she shall bloom in winter snow,
　Ere we two meet again.
He turned his charger as he spoke,
　Upon the river shore;
He gave the reins a shake, and said,
　Adieu forevermore,
　　My love!
Adieu forevermore."

"MARRY Celeste Pearl!— a girl without a farthing! a beggar! a foundling! I'm astonished, thunderstruck, *speechless*, sir, at your audacity in proposing such a thing! I *have* objections, sir—most *de*-cided objections, sir! Don't ever let me hear you mention such a thing again!"

And Squire Erliston stamped up and down, red with rage and indignation.

Louis stood with darkening brows, flashing eyes, and folded arms, before him—outwardly quiet, but compressing his lips to keep down the fiery tide of his rising passion.

"What are your objections, sir?" he asked, with forced calmness.

"Objections! Why, sir, there's so many objections that I can't enumerate them. First place, she hasn't a cent; second, nobody knows who or what she is; third, she'll never do for my granddaughter-in-law. Therefore, sir, please drop the subject; I never want to hear anything more about it—for I shouldn't consent if you were to plead on your knees. The girl's a good girl enough in her place, but she won't do for the wife of Louis Oranmore. What, sir, consent that you, the heir to the richest landed estate this side the north pole, should marry a poor, unknown beggar-girl, who has lived all her life on the charity of others! No, sir, never!" said the squire, furiously, flinging himself into his chair, and mopping his inflamed visage.

The face of Louis was white with suppressed rage, and with an expression of ungovernable anger, he burst from the room. In his fierce excitement he saw not whither he went, until he ran full against Totty, who was entering, with a letter in her hand.

"Lor', Mas'r Lou, how you scare me! You like to knock me upside down. Hi! here's a 'pistle for you, what Curly, old Miss Ager's gal, brought over, an' told me her young Miss 'Sless sent you."

"From Celeste," exclaimed Louis, snatching it from her hand and tearing it open. His gifts fell to the floor; and scarcely able to believe his senses, he read its contents—his brow growing darker and darker as he read. He crushed it fiercely in his hand as he finished, and paced up and down the long hall like a madman.

"And such is woman's love!" he exclaimed, with a scornful laugh. "She gives me up, and bids me be happy with Minnette.   What drove that jealous girl to love me ; and to make Celeste believe I loved her first ? Everything seems to cross my path—this mad girl's passion, and my grandfather's obstinate refusal.   Well, she shall be mine, in spite of fate.   I will marry her privately, and take her with me to Italy.   Yes, that is the only plan.   I will ride over to the cottage, and obtain her consent ; and then, let those I leave behind do as they will, my happiness will be complete."

So saying, he quitted the house, mounted his horse, and rode rapidly toward the cottage.

Celeste was in the garden, binding up a broken rosebush—looking paler, but lovelier than ever. She uttered a half-stifled cry as she saw him, and the last trace of color faded from her face as he leaped from his horse and stood beside her.

"Celeste, what means this ?" he demanded, impetuously.   "Do you really believe this tale told you by Minnette ?"

"Oh, Louis, is it not true ?" exclaimed Celeste, clasping her hands.

"True !   Celeste, Celeste ! do you take me to be such a villain ?   As heaven hears me, I never spoke a word of love to her in my life !"

This was true in the letter, but not in the spirit.   He had never *spoken* of love to Minnette, but he had *looked* it often enough.

"Thank heaven !" exclaimed Celeste, impulsively, while she bowed her face in her hands and wept.

"Dear Celeste," said Louis, drawing her gently toward him, " do you retract those cruel words you have written ?   You will not give me up, will you ?"

"Oh, no ! not *now*," replied Celeste, yielding to his embrace.   "Oh, Louis, what do you suppose made Minnette say such dreadful things to me last night ?"

"Because—I beg you will not think me conceited, dearest—she fancies she loves me, and is jealous of you. Perhaps, too, she thinks if I did not love you, I might return her affection ; and the only way to end her chimerical hopes is by our immediate union. Say, dear love, when will you be mine?"

"Oh, Louis! I do not know," said Celeste, blushing scarlet. "I do not want to be married so soon, and —you must ask your grandfather."

"I have asked him, dearest."

"And he——"

"*Refused!* I knew it would be so. He is obstinate and eccentric. But, Celeste, his refusal need make no difference to us."

She raised her blue eyes to his face, with a look of unconcealed wonder.

"We can be privately wedded, and I will take you with me to Europe, where we will reside until I have succeeded in pacifying the squire with my course."

She stood before him, looking calmly and gravely in his face. His voice was low, but full of passion, and he saw not that earnest, sorrowful gaze.

"Say, Celeste—dearest Celeste—do you consent?" he asked, his eyes filled with fire, as he strove to clasp her. She shrank away, almost in fear, and pushed back his hands.

"Oh, Louis! don't, don't," she cried, sadly.

"But you will consent? you will go with me?" he said, eagerly, passionately.

"Oh, no, no!—no, no! I cannot—it is impossible."

"Impossible! *Why*, Celeste?"

"It would be wrong."

"Wrong! Because an old man object to your want of fortune, it would be wrong to marry me. Nonsense, Celeste!"

"It would be wrong to disobey your grandfather, Louis."

"Not in a case like this, Celeste. I am not bound to obey him when he is unreasonable."

"He is not unreasonable in this, Louis. It is very reasonable he should wish you to marry one your equal in wealth and social position."

"And would *you* have me marry for wealth and social position, Celeste?" he asked, reproachfully.

"Oh! no, no! Heaven forbid! But I would not marry you against his will. We can wait—a few years will not make much difference, dear Louis. We are both young, and can afford to be patient."

"Patience! Don't talk to me of patience!" he exclaimed, passionately. "You never loved me; if you had you would not stand thus on a little point of decorum. You are your own mistress—you have no parents to whom you owe obedience; my mother is willing enough, and yet, because an old man objects to your want of money, you stand there in your cold dignity, and exhort me to be patient and wait. Celeste, I *will not* wait. You *must* come with me to Italy!"

But she only stood before him, pale and sad, but firm and unyielding.

Long and eloquently he pleaded, passionately and vehemently he urged her, but all in vain. She listened and answered by silence and tears, but steadily and firmly refused to consent.

"Well, Celeste, will you come?" he asked, at length, after a long and earnest entreaty.

"Louis, I cannot. Not even for your sake can I do what my conscience tells me would be wrong. You say your grandfather has no right to control you in your choice of a wife. It may be so; but even in that case I would not marry you against his wishes. Perhaps I am proud and sinful ; but, Louis, I could never enter a family who would not be willing to receive me. Besides, my duty is here with Miss Hagar. If I were to marry you, what would become of her, alone and childless. No, Louis, I am not so utterly selfish and ungrateful. Do not urge me further, as I see you are about to do, for my resolution is unalterable. Yielding as my nature naturally is, I can be firm at times ; and in this case, nothing that you can say will alter my determination."

He stood erect before her, his fine face clouded with anger and mortification.

" This, then, is your last resolve ?" he said, coldly.

" It is. Dear Louis, forgive me if I have caused you pain. Believe me, it has grieved me deeply to be obliged to speak thus," she said, laying her hand upon his arm, and looking up pleadingly, sorrowfully, in his face.

"Oh! do not trouble yourself about grieving me, fair Celeste," he said, scornfully ; the glamour has faded from my eyes, that is all. I fancied you little less than an angel. I was fool enough to believe you loved me well enough to brave even the opinion of the world for my sake. I find you are only a woman, after all, with more pride and ambition than love for me. Well, be it so. I have never sued for the favor of any one yet, and cannot begin now. Farewell, Celeste ; forgive me for trespassing thus long upon your time, but it will be long before it happens again."

He turned away with a haughty bow. She saw he was angry, disappointed and deeply mortified, and tears sprang to her gentle eyes.

" Oh, Louis !" was all she could say, as sobs choked her utterance.

He turned round and stood gazing coldly upon her.

" Well, Miss Pearl," he said, calmly.

"Oh, Louis ! *dear* Louis ! forgive me ! do not be

angry with your Celeste. Oh, Louis ! I am sorry I have offended you."

"I am not angry, Miss Pearl ; only a little disappointed. You have a perfect right to reject me if you choose. My only regret is that I should have troubled you so long. I have the honor to wish you good-day."

And with the last bitter words he sprang on his horse, and in a few minutes was out of sight.

All Celeste's fortitude gave way then ; and sinking on a seat, she hid her face in her hands and wept the bitterest tears she had ever shed in her life. Louis was gone, and in anger, believing her proud, artful, and fickle—perhaps he would love her no more ; and her bosom heaved with convulsive sobs at the thought.

All that day and the next, and the next, Louis came not. How wearily the hours dragged on while she sat listening in vain for his coming. Taking her work, she would sit by the window commanding a view of the road, and strain her eyes in the fruitless endeavor to catch a glimpse of his tall, elegant figure. At every noise she would start convulsively, and a wild thrill would dart through her heart, in the hope that it might be his footsteps. Then sinking back disappointed, she would close her eyes to force back the gathering tears, and strive to keep down the choking sensation that would arise to her throat. And when night fell, and still he came not, unable longer to restrain herself, she would hastily seek her own chamber, and weep and sob until, utterly prostrated in mind and body, the morning would find her pale, ill, and languid, with slow step and heavy, dimmed eyes.

The morning of the fourth day came, and this suspense was growing intolerable. Breakfast had passed untasted, and suffering with a dull, throbbing headache, she was about to quit the room, when the sound of a horse's hoofs thundering down the road made her leap to her feet with a wild thrill of joy that sent new light to her, eyes and new color to her cheeks.

"He is come! he is come!" she exclaimed, rushing to the door. A cry of disappointment almost escaped her, as her eye fell on Gipsy in the act of dismounting.

"Here I am, all alive, like a bag of grasshoppers," exclaimed Gipsy, as, gathering her riding-habit in her hand, she tripped with her usual airy motion up the garden walk. "How have you been this age, Celeste? My stars! how pale you are; have you been ill?"

"I have not been very well for the past week," said Celeste, forcing a smile. "I am very glad to see you. Come in."

Gipsy entered; and having saluted Miss Hagar, threw herself into a chair, and snatching off her hat, began swinging it by the strings. Celeste took her sewing and seated herself by the window.

"Well, I declare! we have had such times up at the Hall this week," said Gipsy. "Have you heard how I captured Big Tom?"

"No," said Celeste, in surprise; whereupon Gipsy related what had occurred, ending with:

"Old Mrs. Donne is still very sick, and raves at an appalling rate about babies, and snow-storms, and all such stuff. Big Tom's in prison, rapidly recovering from his wounds, which is good news for me; for I should be sorry to think I had killed the poor wretch. I should have come over to see you sooner, only Louis is going away, and we've all been as busy as nailers."

"Going away!" echoed Celeste, growing deadly pale.

"Yes; he leaves here to-morrow morning. He is going to Italy, and will not be back for several years.

14

But, my goodness ! Celeste, what's the matter ? You look as though you were going to faint !"

"It's nothing—only a sudden spasm," said Celeste, in a low, smothered voice, dropping her forehead on her hand, while her long, golden ringlets, falling like a vail over her face, hid it from view.

"The notion took him so suddenly," continued Gipsy, "that we have scarcely begun to recover from our astonishment yet. It's no use trying to coax him not to go, for he puts on that iron face of his, and says, ' the thing's decided.' Men of genius always are a queer crotchety set, they say. Thank Minerva, I'm not a genius, anyway—one of that sort's enough in any family. Minnette, too, went off the other day with the Carsons for Washington—good riddance of bad rubbish, I say. So, when Louis goes, I'll be alone in my glory, and you must come over and spend a few days with me. Won't you, Celeste ?"

There was no reply. Gipsy gazed in wonder and alarm at her, as she sat still and motionless as a figure in marble.

"Celeste ! Celeste ! what's the matter ?" she said, going over and trying to raise her head. "Are you sick, or fainting, or what ?"

Celeste looked up, and Gipsy started back as she saw that white, despairing face, and wild, anguished eyes.

"You are ill, Celeste," she said, in alarm. "Your hands are like ice, and your face is cold as death. Come, let me assist you to your room."

"Thank you—I will go myself. I will be better, if let alone," said Celeste, faintly, as she arose to her feet, and, sick and giddy, tottered rather than walked from the room.

Gipsy looked after her, perplexed and anxious.

"Well, now, I'd like to know what all this is about,"

she muttered to herself. "Wonder if Louis' departure has anything to do with it? They've had a quarrel, I suppose, and Louis is going off in a huff. Well, it's none of my business, anyway, so I sha'n't interfere. Louis looked as if he'd like to murder me when I asked him what he was going to do without Celeste, and walked off without ever deigning to answer me. But I guess I ain't afraid of him; and if he hasn't behaved well to poor Celeste, I'll tell him a piece of my mind anyway before he goes." And the soliloquizing Gipsy left the house and rode thoughtfully homeward.

During the rest of that day and night Celeste did not leave her room. Miss Hagar grew anxious, and several times came to her door to beg admittance, but the low voice within always said:

"No, no; not now, I will be better to-morrow—only leave me alone."

And, troubled and perplexed, Miss Hagar was forced to yield. Many times she approached the chamber door to listen, but all within was still as death—not the faintest sound reached her ear.

"Has Miss Celeste left her room yet?" inquired Miss Hagar, the following morning, of her sable handmaid, Curly.

"Laws! yes, missus; she comed outen her room 'fore de sun riz dis mornin': an' I 'clare to goodness! I like to drop when I seed her. She was jes' as pale as a ghos', wid her eyes sunken right in like, an' lookin' drefful sick. She'd on her bunnit and shawl, and tole me to tell you she war a-goin' out for a walk. 'Deed, she needed a walk, honey, for her face was jes' as white as dat ar table-cloff."

"Where was she going?" inquired Miss Hagar, alarmed.

"'Deed, I didn't mind to ax her, 'cause she 'peared in

'stress o' mind 'bout somefin or udder. I looked arter her, dough, an' seed her take de road down to de shore," replied Curly.

Still more perplexed and troubled by this strange and most unusual conduct on the part of Celeste, Miss Hagar seated herself at the breakfast-table, having vainly waited an hour past the usual time for the return of the young girl.

When Celeste left the cottage, it was with a mind filled with but one idea—that of seeing Louis once more before he left. But few people were abroad when she passed through the village ; and descending to the beach, she seated herself behind a projecting rock, where, unseen herself, she could behold him going away.

Out on the glittering waves, dancing in the first rays of the morning sunlight, lay a schooner, rising and falling lazily on the swell. It was the vessel in which Gipsy had told her Louis was to leave St. Mark's, and Celeste gazed upon it, with that passionate, straining gaze, with which one might look on a coffin, where the one we love best is about to be laid. Hours passed on, but she heeded them not, as, seated on a low rock, with her hands clasped over her knees, she waited for his coming.

After the lapse of some time, a boat put off from the schooner, and, propelled by the strong arms of four sailors, soon touched shore. Three of them landed, and took the road leading to Mount Sunset. Half an hour passed, and they reappeared, laden with trunks and valises, and followed by Louis and Gipsy.

He seemed careless, even gay, while Gipsy wore a sad, troubled look, all unused to her. Little did either of them dream of the wild, despairing eyes watching them, as if her very life were concentrated in that agonizing gaze.

"Well, good-bye, *ma belle*," said Louis, with a last embrace. "You perceive my boat is on the shore, and my bark is on the sea, and I must away."

"Good-bye," repeated Gipsy, mechanically.

He turned away and walked toward the boat, entered it, and the seamen pushed off. Gipsy stood gazing after his tall, graceful form until the boat reached the schooner, and he ascended the deck. Then it danced away in the fresh morning breeze down the bay, until it became a mere speck in the distance, and then faded altogether from view.

Dashing away a tear, Gipsy turned to ascend the rocks, when the flutter of a muslin dress from behind a cliff caught her eye. With a vague presentiment flashing across her mind, she approached to see who it was. And there she beheld Celeste, lying cold and senseless on the sand.

CHAPTER XXXII.

"THE QUEEN OF SONG."

"Give me·the boon of love—
    Renown is but a breath,
Whose loudest echo ever floats
    From out the halls of death.
A loving eye beguiles me more
    Than Fame's emblazon'd seal ;
And one sweet note of tenderness,
    Than triumph's wildest peal."—TUCKERMAN.

"RANMORE, my dear fellow, welcome back to Italy!" exclaimed a distinguished-looking man, as Louis—the day after his arrival in Venice—was passing through one of the picturesque streets of that "palace-crowned city."

"Ah, Lugari! happy to see you!" said Louis, extending his hand, which was cordially grasped.

"When did you arrive?" asked the Italian, as, linking his arm through that of Louis, they strolled toward the "Bridge of the Rialto."

"Only yesterday. My longings for Venice were too strong to be resisted ; so I returned."

"Then you have not heard our 'Queen of Song' yet?" inquired his companion.

"No.   Who is she ?"

"An angel ! a seraph ! the loveliest woman you ever beheld !—sings like a nightingale, and has everybody raving about her !"

"Indeed !   And what is the name of this paragon ?"

"She is called Madame Evelini—a widow, I believe —English or American by birth.   She came here as poor as Job and as proud as Lucifer. Now, she has made a fortune on the stage; but is as proud as ever. Half the men at Venice are sighing at her feet; but no icicle ever was colder than she—it is impossible to warm her into love. There was an English duke here not long ago, who—with reverence be it spoken!—had more money than brains, and actually went so far as to propose marriage; and, to the amazement of himself and everybody else, was most decidedly and emphatically rejected."

"A wonderful woman, indeed, to reject a ducal crown. When does she sing?"

"To-night. You must come with me and hear her."

"With pleasure. Look, Lugari—what a magnificent woman that is!"

"By St. Peter! it's the very woman we are speaking of— Madame Evelini herself!" exclaimed Lugari. "Come, we'll join her. I have the pleasure of her acquaintance. Take a good look at her first, and tell me if she does not justify my praises."

Louis, with some curiosity, scrutinized the lady they were approaching. She was about the middle height, with an exquisitely-proportioned figure—a small, fair, but somewhat melancholy face, shaded by a profusion of pale-brown ringlets. Her complexion was exquisitely fair, with dark-blue eyes and beautifully chiseled features. As he gazed, a strange, vague feeling, that he had seen that face somewhere before, flashed across his mind.

"Well, what do you think of her?" said Lugari, rousing him from a reverie into which he was falling.

"That she is a very lovely woman—there can be but one opinion about that."

"How old would you take her to be?"

"About twenty, or twenty-three at the most."

"Phew! she's over thirty."

"Oh, impossible!"

"Fact, sir; I had it from her own lips. Now, I'll present you; but take care of your heart, my boy—few men can resist the fascinations of the Queen of Song."

"I have a counter-charm," said Louis, with a cold smile.

"The memory of some fairer face in America, I suppose. Well, we shall see. Good-morning, Madame Evelini," he said, acknowledging that lady's salutation. "Charming day. Allow me to present to you my friend Mr. Oranmore."

From the first moment the lady's eyes had fallen on the face of Louis, she had gazed as if fascinated. Every trace of color slowly faded from her face, leaving her cold and pale as marble. As his name was uttered she reeled, as if she were faint, and grasped the arm of Lugari for support.

"*Whom* did you say?" she asked, in a breathless voice.

"Mr. Oranmore, a young American," replied Lugari, looking in amazement from the lady to Louis—who, quite as much amazed as himself, stood gazing upon her, lost in wonder.

"Oranmore!" she exclaimed, unheeding their looks—"Oranmore! Surely not Barry Oranmore?"

"That was my father's name," replied the astonished Louis.

A low cry broke from the white lips of the lady, as her hands flew up and covered her face. Lugari and Louis gazed in each other's faces in consternation. She dropped her hands at last, and said, in a low, hurried voice:

"Excuse this agitation, Mr. Oranmore. Can I have the pleasure of a private interview with you?"

"Assuredly, madam," said the astonished Louis.

"Well, call at my residence in the Palazzo B——, this

afternoon. And now I must ask you to excuse me, gentlemen. Good-morning."

She hurried away, leaving the two young men overwhelmed with amazement.

" What the deuce does this mean ?" said Lugari.

"That's more than I can tell. I'm as much in the dark as you are."

"She cannot have fallen in love with him already," said Lugari, in the musing tone of one speaking to himself.

Louis laughed.

"Hardly, I think. I cannot expect to succeed where a royal duke failed."

"There's no accounting for a woman's whims ; and he's confoundedly good-looking," went on Lugari, in the same meditative tone.

"Come, Antonio, none of your nonsense," said Louis. "Come with me to my studio, and spend the morning with me. It will help to pass the time until the hour for calling on her ladyship."

They soon reached the residence of the artist. The door was opened for them by a boy of such singular beauty, that Lugari stared at him in surprise and admiration. His short, crisp, black curls fell over a brow of snowy whiteness, and his pale face looked paler in contrast with his large, melancholy, black eyes.

"Well, Isadore," said Louis kindly, " has there been any one here since ?"

"No, signor," replied the boy, dropping his eyes, while a faint color rose to his cheek, as he met the penetrating gaze of the stranger.

"That will do, then. Bring wine and cigars, and leave us."

The boy did as directed, and hurried from the room.

14*

"Handsome lad, that," said Lugari, carelessly. "Who is he ?"

"Isadore something—I forget what. He *is*, as you say, remarkably handsome."

" He is not a Venetian ?"

" No ; English, I believe. I met him in Naples, friendless and nearly destitute, and took charge of him. Have a glass of wine ?"

Lugari looked keenly in the face of his friend with a peculiar smile, that seemed to say : " Yes—I understand it perfectly ;" but Louis, busy in lighting a cigar, did not observe him.

The morning passed rapidly away in gay conversation ; and at the hour appointed, Louis sat in one of the magnificent rooms of the Palazzo B——, awaiting the entrance of the singer.

She soon made her appearance, quite bewitching in blue silk, but looking paler, he thought, than when he had seen her in the morning.

"I see you are punctual," she said, holding out her hand, with a slight smile. " Doubtless you are at your wits' end trying to account for my singular conduct."

"My only wonder is, madam, how I could have merited so great an honor."

"Ah ! I knew you would say something like that," said the lady. "Insincere, like the rest of your sex. Well, you shall not be kept long in suspense. I have sent for you here to tell you my history."

"Madam !" exclaimed Louis, in surprise.

"Yes, even so. It concerns you more nearly, perhaps, than you think. Listen, now."

She leaned her head in her hand, and, for a moment, seemed lost in thought ; while Louis, with eager curiosity, waited for her to begin.

"I am Irish by birth," she said, at last, looking up ;

"I was born in Galway. My father was a poor farmer, and I was his only child. I grew up a wild, untutored country girl ; and reached the age of fifteen, knowing sorrow and trouble only by name.

" My occupation, sometimes, was watching my father's sheep on the mountain. One day, as I sat merrily singing to myself, a horseman, attracted by my voice, rode up and accosted me. I was bold and fearless, and entered into conversation with him as if I had known him all my life—told him my name and residence ; and learned, in return, that he was a young American of respectable and wealthy connections, who had visited Galway to see a friend.

" From that day forth, he was constantly with me ; and I soon learned to watch for his coming as I had never watched for any one before. He was rash, daring, and passionate ; and, captivated by my beauty (for I *was* handsome then), he urged me to marry him privately, and fly with him. I had never learned to control myself in anything ; and loving him with a passion that has never yet died out, I consented. I fled with him to England. There we were secretly wedded. He took me to France, where we remained almost a year—a year of bliss to me. Then he received letters demanding his immediate presence in America. He would have left me behind him, and returned for me again ; but I refused to leave him ; I therefore accompanied him to his native land, and a few weeks after—one stormy Christmas Eve—my child, a daughter, was born.

"I never saw it but once. The nurse must have drugged me—for I have a dim recollection of a long, long sleep, that seemed endless ; and when I awoke, I found myself in a strange room with the face of a strange woman bending over me. To my wild, bewildered inquiries, she answered, that I had been very ill, and my life despaired of for several weeks; but that I was now recovering. I asked for my husband and child. She knew nothing of them, she said. I had been brought there in a carriage, after night, by a man whose features she could not recognize—he was so muffled up. He had paid her liberally for taking charge of me, and promised to return to see me in a few weeks.

"I was a child in years and wisdom, and suspected nothing. I felt angry at his desertion, and cried like the petted child I was, at his absence. The woman was very kind to me, though I saw she looked upon me with a sort of contempt, the reason of which I did not then understand. Still, she took good care of me, and in a fortnight I was as well as ever.

"One evening, I sat in my room silent and alone (for *I* was not permitted to go out), and crying like a spoiled baby, when the sound of a well-known voice reached my ear from the adjoining room. With a cry of joy, I sprang to my feet, rushed from the room, and fell into the arms of my husband. In my joy at meeting him, I did not perceive, at first, the change those few weeks had made in him. He was pale and haggard, and there was an unaccountable something in his manner that puzzled me. He was not less affectionate; but he seemed wild, and restless, and ill at ease.

"My first inquiry was for my child.

"'It is dead, Eveleen,' he answered, hurriedly; 'and you were so ill that it became necessary to bring you here. Now that you are better, you must leave this and come with me.'

"'And you will publicly proclaim our marriage, and we will not be separated more?' I eagerly inquired.

"He made no answer, save to urge me to make haste. In a few moments I was ready; a carriage at the door. He handed me in, then followed, and we drove rapidly away.

"'Where are we going?' I asked, as we drove along.

"'Back to Ireland; you are always wishing to return.'

"'But you will go with me, will you not?' I asked, in vague alarm.

"'Yes, yes; to be sure,' he answered, quickly. Just then, the murmur of the sea reached my ear; the carriage stopped, and my husband assisted me out.

"A boat was in waiting on the shore. We both entered, and were rowed to the vessel lying in the harbor. I reached the deck, and was conducted below to a well-furnished cabin.

"'Now, Eveleen, you look fatigued and must retire to rest. I am going on deck to join the captain for a few hours,' said my husband, as he gently kissed my brow. His voice was low and agitated, and I could see his face was deadly pale. Still, no suspicion of the truth entered my mind. I was, indeed, tired; and wearily disengaging myself from the arms that clasped me in a parting embrace, I threw myself on my bed, and in a few minutes was fast asleep. My husband turned away and went on deck, and—I never saw him more."

Her voice failed, and her lips quivered; but after a few moments she went on.

"The next morning the captain entered the cabin and handed me a letter. I opened it in surprise. A draft for five thousand dollars fell out, but I saw it not; my eyes were fixed in unspeakable horror on the dreadful words before me.

"The letter was from my husband. He told me that we were parted forever, that he had wedded another bride, and that the vessel I was in would convey me home, where he hoped I would forget him, and look upon the past year only as a dream. I read that terrible letter from beginning to end, while every word burned into my heart and brain like fire. I did not faint nor shriek; I was of too sanguine a temperament to do either; but I sat in stupefied despair; I was stunned; I could not realize what had happened. The captain brought me a newspaper, and showed me the announcement of his marriage to some great beauty and heiress—some Miss Erliston, who——"

"What!" exclaimed Louis, springing fiercely to his feet. "In the name of heaven, of whom have you been talking all this time?"

"Of my husband—of your father—of Barry Oranmore!"

He staggered into his seat, horror-stricken and deadly white. There was a pause, then he said, hoarsely:

"Go on."

"I know not how that voyage passed—it is all like a dream to me. I reached Liverpool. The captain, who had been well paid, had me conveyed home; and still I lived and moved like one who lives not. I was in a stupor of despair, and months passed away before I recovered; when I did, all my childishness had passed away, and I was in heart and mind a woman.

"Time passed on. I had read in an American paper the announcement of my false husband's dreadful death. Years blunted the poignancy of my grief, and I began to tire of my aimless life. He had often told me my voice would make my fortune on the stage. Acting on this hint, I went to London, had it cultivated, and learned music. At last, after years of unremitting application, I made my *debut.* It was a triumph, and every fresh attempt crowned me with new laurels. I next visited France; then I came here; and here I have been ever since. To-day, when I beheld you, the very image of your father as I knew him first, I almost imagined the grave had given up its dead. Such is my story—every word true, as heaven hears me. Was I not right, when I said it concerned you more nearly than you imagined?"

"Good Heaven! And was my father such a villain?" said Louis, with a groan.

"Hush! Speak no ill of the dead. I forgave him long ago, and surely you can do so too."

"Heaven help us all! what a world we live in!" said Louis, while, with a pang of remorse, his thoughts reverted to Celeste; and he inwardly thought how similar her fate might have been, had she consented to go with him.

"And was your child really dead?" he inquired, after a pause, during which she sat with her eyes fixed sadly on the floor. "He may have deceived you in that as in other things."

"I know not," she answered; "yet I have always had a sort of presentiment that it still lives. Oh, if heaven would but permit me to behold her alive, I could die happy!"

Louis sat gazing upon her with a puzzled look.

"I know not how it is," he said, "but you remind me strangely of some one I have seen before. I recognize your face, vaguely and indistinctly, as one does faces they see in dreams. I am *sure* I have seen some one resembling you elsewhere."

"Only fancy, I fear," said the lady, smiling, and shaking her head. "Do you intend hearing me sing to-night?"

"Oh, decidedly! Do you think I would miss what one might make a pilgrimage round the world to hear once?"

"Flattery! flattery! I see you are like all the rest," said Madame Evelini, raising her finger reprovingly.

"Not so, madam; I never flatter. And now I regret that a previous engagement renders it necessary for me to leave you," said Louis, taking his hat and rising to leave.

"Well, I shall expect to see you soon again," she said, with an enchanting smile; and Louis, having bowed assent, left the house; and, giddy and bewildered by what he had just heard, turned in the direction of his own residence.

CHAPTER XXXIII.

A STARTLING DISCOVERY.

" Fixed was her look and stern her air ;
Back from her shoulders streamed her hair ;
Her figure seemed to rise more high ;
Her voice, Despair's wild energy
Had given a tone of prophecy."—MARMION.

WEEKS passed away. Louis became a daily visitor at the Palazzo B——. His growing intimacy with the beautiful "Queen of Song" was looked upon with jealous eyes by her numerous admirers; and many were the rumors circulated regarding her affection for the handsome young American. But Madame Evelini was either too proud or too indifferent to heed these reports, and visited Louis in his studio whenever she pleased, leaving the world to say of her what it listed. Louis, too, was winning fame as an artist, and, next to madame herself, was becoming one of the greatest celebrities in Venice.

"What a handsome boy that attendant of yours is!" said the lady, one day, to Louis, as Isadore quitted the room ; "all who visit you vie with each other in their praises of his beauty."

"Who? Isadore? Yes, he is handsome ; but a most singular youth—silent, taciturn, at times almost fierce, and at others, sullenly morose."

"He seems to have a strong antipathy to ladies, and to me in particular," said Madame Evelini ; "he looks as if he wished to shut the door in my face every time I come here."

"Yes, that is another of his oddities ; in fact, he is quite an unaccountable lad."

"He is very much attached to *you*, at all events. If he were a woman, I should say he is in love with you, and jealous of the rest of us," said madame, laughing. "As it is, it can only be accounted for by ill-nature on his part. Well, adieu !" said madame, rising to take her leave.

Louis soon had a most convincing proof of the lad's attachment. Being detained one evening, by some business, in one of the narrow courts inhabited by the lower class in Venice, he returned with a violent headache. He grew worse so rapidly, that before night he was in a high fever, raving deliriously.

A physician was sent for, who pronounced it to be a dangerous and most infectious fever, and advised his immediate removal to a hospital, where he might receive better attendance than he could in his lodgings. But Isadore positively refused to have him removed, vehemently asserting that he himself was quite competent to take care of him.

And well did he redeem his word. No mother ever

nursed her sick child witn more tender care than he did
Louis. Night and day he was ever by his side, bathing
his burning brow, or holding a cooling draught to his
feverish lips. And though his pale face grew paler day
after day, and his lustrous black eyes lost their brightness with his weary vigils, nothing could tempt him
from that sick room. With womanly care, he arranged
the pillows beneath the restless head of the invalid ;
drew the curtains to exclude the glaring light, totally
unheeding the danger of contagion. With jealous
vigilance, too, he kept out all strangers. Madame Evelini, upon hearing of her friend's illness, immediately
came to see him, but she was met in the outer room by
Isadore, who said, coldly :

"You cannot see him, madame ; the physician has
forbidden it."

"But only for one moment. I will not speak to him,
or disturb him," pleaded Madame Evelini.

"No ; you cannot enter. It is impossible," said Isadore, as he turned and left the room, fairly shutting the
door in her face.

In his wild delirium, Louis talked incessantly of
Celeste, and urged her with passionate vehemence to fly
with him. At such times, the dark brow of Isadore
would knit, and his eyes flash with smoldering fire
beneath their lids. But if his own name was mentioned,
his beautiful face would light up with such a radiant
look of light and joy, that he seemed recompensed for
all his weary watching and unceasing care.

At length, a naturally strong constitution, and the
tender nursing of Isadore triumphed over disease, and
Louis became convalescent. And then he began to
realize all he owed to the boy who had been his guardian-
angel during his illness.

"How can I ever repay you, Isadore ?" he said, one

day, as the youth hovered by his side, smoothing the tossed pillows, and arranging the bed-clothes with a skill few nurses could have surpassed.

"I wish for no return, signor. I am only too happy to have been of service to you," said the boy, dropping his eyes.

"Well, at least, you will find I am not ungrateful. Once I am well, you shall no longer remain a servant. I will place you in a fair way to make your fortune," said Louis.

"Signor, I beg you will not think of such a thing. I have no wish to leave you," said Isadore, in alarm.

"But with me you will only be an obscure servant, while it is in my power to place you in a situation to become honored and wealthy."

"I would rather remain with you."

"Strange boy! Why are you so anxious to stay with me?"

"Because——"

"Well?"

"Because I love you, Signor," said the boy, while his whole face, a moment before so pale, grew vivid crimson.

Louis looked at him in surprise.

"And what have I done for you, that you should love me so?" he asked, at length.

"Do we only love those who have conferred favors upon us, Signor?"

"Well, generally speaking, among men it is so. If you were a woman, now, it would be different," said Louis, laughing.

"Would you love me, if I were a woman?" asked the boy, in a tone so abrupt and startling, that Louis gazed at him in wonder.

"Not more than I do now. One cannot *love* two

women at a time, as you will find out when you grow older."

"Then the signor is already in love?" asked Isadore, raising his dark eyes, now filled with dusky fire.

There was no reply. Louis turned aside restlessly, so that the boy could not see the expression of his face. And Isadore, paler than before, seated himself in silence, and fixed his burning black eyes steadily on the ground.

Louis now rapidly recovered, and in a short time was able to resume his duties. During his first interview with Madame Evelini, she related the scene that had taken place between her and Isadore.

"His motive in keeping me out was certainly other than the physician's commands," she said. "In fact, my dear Louis, I should not be surprised if your Isadore should turn out to be a female in disguise. His conduct savors so strongly of jealousy that I more than half suspect him. Some fiery Italian might have conceived a romantic passion for you, and taken this means of following you. Those hot-blooded Venetians will do such things sometimes."

The words were lightly spoken, but they set Louis to thinking. What if they were true? A number of things, trifling in themselves, rushed on his mind, tending to confirm this opinion. He started up, seized his hat, bade madame a hasty farewell, and started for home, fully resolved to discover immediately whether or not her words were true.

On entering, he found Isadore standing with folded arms, gazing with eyes almost fiendish with hate upon a picture on the easel. It was the portrait of Celeste as a child, standing as when he first beheld her caressing her wounded bird. No words can describe the look of fierce hatred with which the boy regarded it.

"Well, Isadore, you seem struck by that painting. Did you ever see a sweeter face?" asked Louis, pointing to Celeste, but keeping his eyes fixed steadily on the face of the boy.

"Do you love her?" asked Isadore, hoarsely, without looking up.

"Yes, with my whole heart and soul!" replied Louis, fervently.

"Ungrateful wretch!" cried the youth, in a voice of intense passion ; and lifting his head, he disclosed a face so pale, and eyes so full of fire, that Louis started back. "Was it for this that I left home, and country, and friends, that I assumed a disguise like this to follow you? Was it for such a turn as this I risked my life for yours? Was it for words like these I cast aside my pride, and became your menial? Was it not enough for you to call on her unceasingly during your delirium—she who feared the opinion of the world more than she loved you —while I, who braved disgrace and death for your sake, was unnamed and forgotten? Look on me, most ungrateful of men," he continued, almost with a shriek. "Look at me ; and say, do you yet know me?"

He dashed his cap to the ground, and with features convulsed with contending passions, stood before him. Louis looked, turned deadly pale, and exclaimed, in a voice of utter surprise :

"Merciful heaven ! Minnette !"

CHAPTER XXXIV.

LIGHT IN DARKNESS.

" By the strong spirit's discipline—
By the fierce wrong forgiven—
By all that wrings the heart of sin,
Is woman won to Heaven."—WILLIS.

HERE was a moment's profound silence, during which Louis stood like one thunder-struck, and Minnette glared upon him with her fierce black eyes.

"And you have been with me all this time, Minnette, and I knew it not," said Louis, at length.

"No," she said, with a bitter laugh. "You did not know me. Had it been Celeste, do you think you would have recognized her?"

"Minnette, do not look so wildly. Good heaven! who would ever think of seeing you here, and in such disguise?" he added, still scarcely able to realize it was Minnette who stood before him.

"And it was for your sake," she replied, in a voice almost choked by contending emotions.

"For me, for me! wretch that I am!" he said, with bitter remorse. "Oh, Minnette! I am unworthy such devoted love."

Something in his manner inspired her with hope. She clasped her hands, and said, wildly :

"Only say you will not cast me off. Only say you will yet love me, and I will be a thousand-fold repaid for all I have endured for your sake. Oh, Louis! is it for the cold, prudish Celeste you reject such love as mine?"

"We cannot compel our affections, Minnette. Celeste is the only woman who can ever possess my heart ; but you—you shall always be to me as a dear sister. You must throw off this disguise, and return with me home immediately. Your friends shall never know of this—they do not dream you are here; and you will soon learn to look back to this time as a troubled dream, happily past."

" Ha, ha, ha ! You might take me back to America, that I might witness your marriage with Celeste. No, Louis Oranmore, *never* shall *she* enjoy such a triumph ! I have hated her all my life ; and I shall hate her with my last breath. Do you think I could live and survive this disgrace ? You have driven me to madness ; and now behold its fruits."

Her voice was hoarse with concentrated passion ; her eyes burning like fire ; her face ghastly and livid. As she spoke, she drew from within the doublet she wore a gleaming dagger. As the quick eye of Louis saw the motion, he sprang forward and seized her by the wrist. She struggled madly to free herself from his grasp ; and in the struggle the point of the dagger entered her eye.

A torrent of blood flowed over his hands. Shriek after shriek of mortal agony broke from the lips of Minnette. The fatal dagger dropped from the hand of Louis—he staggered back, and stood for a moment paralyzed with horror. Mad with agony, Minnette fled round the room, the blood gushing from her sightless eye and covering her face, her agonizing screams making the house resound. It was an awful, ghastly, appalling spectacle. Louis stood rooted to the ground, unable to remove his gaze from the terrible sight.

Her piercing shrieks soon filled the room. Among the crowd came Lugari, who instantly guessed what had happened. A surgeon was sent for, and poor Minnette, struggling madly, was borne to her room and laid upon her bed. The surgeon, an Englishman, at length arrived ; and Louis, at last restored to presence of mind, speedily expelled the gaping crowd, and shut himself up in his own room, unable to endure the harrowing sight of Minnette's agony. For upwards of two hours he trod up and down, almost maddened by the recollection of the dreadful scene just past. Bitter, indeed, was his anguish and remorse ; in those two hours seemed concentrated ages of suffering.

Suddenly the sound of footsteps announced that the physician was about to take his leave. Hurriedly leaving the room, Louis followed him, scarcely daring to ask the question that hovered upon his lips.

"Tell me !" he exclaimed, vehemently, "is she—will she——"

"No, she will not die," replied the doctor, who knew what he would ask. "The wound is dangerous, but not mortal. She must be taken care of. I will have her immediately removed from here."

"Then she will recover !" said Louis, fervently, "Thank God ! "

" Yes, she will recover," said the doctor, hesitatingly, " but——"

"But what ?" exclaimed Louis, in vague alarm.

." *She will be blind for life !*"

"Great heaven !"

"Her right eye is already gone, and the other, I fear, will never more see the light. Still, you should be grateful that her life will be preserved." And the surgeon took his hat and left.

"Blind ! blind for life !" murmured Louis, in horror ; "a fate worse than death. Oh, Minnette ! Minnette !"

The lingering glory of an Italian sunset was streaming through the open window of the room where Minnette lay. It was a plainly, but neatly furnished room,
in one of the *Scuole*, or benevolent institutions of the
city. Two months had passed since that unhappy day
on which we saw her last. She lies now on the bed, the
sunlight falling brightly on her wan face ; that blessed
sunlight she will never see more. A Sister of Mercy,
with holy face and meek eyes, sits by her side, holding
one of her hands in hers.

And this is Minnette ; this pale, faded, sightless girl,
the once beautiful, haughty, resplendent Minnette ! All
her beauty was gone now ; the glowing crimson of high
health rests no longer on those hollow, sunken cheeks ;
the fierce light of passion will never more flash from
those dimmed orbs ; from those poor, pale lips, bitter,
scathing words can never more fall. But through all
this outward wreck shines a calmer, holier beauty than
ever rested on her face before. In the furnace, she has
been purified ; the fierce, passionate spirit has been subdued by grace ; the lion in her nature has yielded to the
Lamb that was slain ; the wrung, agonized heart has
ceased to struggle, and rests in peace at last.

Not without many a struggle had her wild, fierce
nature yielded to the soothings of religion. Long,
tempestuous, and passionate was the struggle ; and
when her good angel triumphed at last she came, not as
a meek penitent, but as a worn, world-weary sinner,
longing only for peace and rest.

She had not seen Louis during her illness. Often he
came to visit her, but still her cry was : " Not yet ! not
yet !" Her wild, mad love was dying out of her heart,
and with it her intense hatred of Celeste. Her days,
now, were spent in meditation and prayer, or listening
to the gentle, soothing words of Sister Beatrice.

15

"The sun is setting, sister, is it not?" she asked, turning her head towards the windows, as though she still could see.

"Yes; a more glorious sunset I never beheld."

"And I can never see it more; never behold the beautiful earth or sky; never see sun, or moon, or stars again!" said Minnette, in a voice low, but unspeakably sad.

"No, my child, but there is an inward vision that can never be seen with corporeal eyes. Now that those outward eyes are sealed forever, a glimpse of heaven has been bestowed upon you, to lighten the darkness of your life."

"Oh! Sister Beatrice, if I were always with you, I feel I could submit to my fate without a murmur. But when I go out into the world, this fierce nature that is within me, that is subdued but not conquered, will again arise; and I will become more passionate, selfish, and sinful than ever."

"Then why go out into the world any more? Why not enter a convent, and end your days in peace?"

"Oh, sister! if I only might," said Minnette, clasping her hands; "but I, poor, blind, and helpless, what could I do in a convent?"

"You could pray, you could be happy; if you wish to enter, your blindness shall be no obstacle," said Sister Beatrice.

At this moment a servant entered and handed the sister a note, addressed to Minnette. She opened it, and read aloud:

"Every day for a month I have called here, and you have refused to see me. Minnette, I conjure you to let me visit you; I cannot rest until I have seen you, and obtained your forgiveness.   LOUIS."

Minnette's pale face flushed deep crimson, and then grew whiter than before, as she said, vehemently :

"No, I will not ! I will not ! I *cannot* see him more !"

"Why not ?" said Sister Beatrice. "Confess, my child, that vanity still lingers in your heart. You do not wish to see him because you think he will be shocked to find you so changed and altered. Is it not so ?"

"Yes, yes !" replied Minnette, in a fainting voice.

"But this is wrong ; you ought to see him. As you are desirous of taking the vail, it is but right that you should see him, and bid him farewell, and let him inform your friends when he sees them. Come, my dear child, cast out this spirit of pride, and let me admit him, if only for a moment."

There was a fierce struggle in the breast of Minnette. It was but momentary, however, as, shading her face with one hand, she said :

"Be it so ; I will endure the humiliation ; let him come."

Sister Beatrice pressed her lips to the brow of the invalid, and left the room. A moment later, and Louis, pale, thin, and careworn, entered. He started, and grew a shade paler, as his eyes fell on that poor, pale face, robbed of all its beauty, and with a suppressed groan, sank on his knees by the bedside.

"Minnette ! Minnette !" he said, hoarsely. "Can you ever forgive me ?"

The sightless eyes were turned toward him, in the vain effort to see. Alas ! All was darkness. She held out one little, transparent hand, which he took between both of his.

"I have nothing to forgive," she said, meekly. "All that has happened to me I deserved. Do not grieve for me, Louis, you have nothing to reproach yourself with; it was all my own fault."

He bowed his forehead on her hand, and tears, that did honor to his generous heart, fell from his eyes.

"Tell Celeste, when you see her, how sorry I am for all my cruelty and injustice toward her. Ask her to forgive me; she is good and gentle, I feel she will do it. If I only had her pardon, I feel I could die content. And, Oh Louis! when she is happy with you, will you both sometimes think of Minnette, blind, and alone in a foreign land?"

"Oh, *poor* Minnette!" he said, in a choking voice.

"Do not pity me, Louis; I am very happy," but the pale lips trembled as she spoke; "happier than I ever was when I was full of life and health. Oh, Louis, when I look back and think of what I have been—so selfish, and hard-hearted, and cruel—I tremble to think what I might yet have been if God in his mercy had not sent me this affliction. And Celeste; no words can ever tell how I have wronged her. You know how I struck her, in my blind rage, and the angelic patience and forgiveness with which she afterward sought to love me, and make me happy. Oh, Louis! all her sweetness and meekness will haunt me to my dying day."

Her voice faltered, then entirely failed, and for the first time in her life the once haughty Minnette wept.

"Tears are strange visitors to these eyes," she said, with a sad smile; "there may be hope for me yet, since I can weep for the past. Louis, in a few weeks I will enter a convent, and the remainder of my life shall be spent in praying for you and Celeste, and the rest of my friends. And now you must leave me—farewell, a last farewell, *dear* Louis. Tell them all at home how I have learned to love them at last, and ask them to forgive poor Minnette."

He could not speak ; she made a sign for him to go. Raising the thin, pale hand to his lips, and casting one long, last look on the sad, yet peaceful face of the once beautiful Minnette, he quitted the room. And thus they parted, these two, never to meet in life again.

Meantime, we must revisit St. Mark's, and witness the startling events that are bringing matters to a rapid *denouement* there.

----•----

CHAPTER XXXV.

THE DEATH-BED CONFESSION.

" Her wretched brain gave way,
And she became a wreck, at random driven,
Without one glimpse of reason or of Heaven."

T was a bleak, stormy December evening, a week before Christmas. A bright fire was burning in the well-known parlor of Sunset Hall.

In his easy-chair, with his gouty legs, swathed in flannels, reposing on two others, lay our old friend the squire, literally "laid up by the legs." In the opposite corner was Lizzie, dozing, as usual, on her sofa ; while good Mrs. Gower sat with her fat hands folded in her lap, reposing after the cares of the day. Dr. Wiseman had not yet sufficiently recovered from his wounds and bruises to go abroad, and had just retired to his room, while his affectionate spouse was enjoying herself at a grand ball in the village.

The worthy trio had sat in solemn silence for upwards

of an hour, when the door was flung open, and Jupiter rushed in to announce "dat a boy commanded to see ole marster 'mediately."

"To see me?" said the squire, in amazement. "What does he want? I won't see anybody to-night."

"He's got a letter, and says he must d'liver it to-night—it's very important," said Jupiter.

"Humph! well, admit him then. I never can get a minute's peace. 'No rest for the wicked,' as Solomon says. Well, here he comes."

As he spoke, a youth, apparently about sixteen, entered the apartment, bearing every evidence of having journeyed fast.

"You are Squire Erliston, I believe," said the lad, bowing respectfully.

"Well, you may believe it," said the squire, testily; "it's a name I was never ashamed of. What do you want of me at this hour of the night, young man?"

"I have been sent with this letter," said the boy, presenting one; "it's a matter of life and death."

"Matter of life and death! Lord bless me!" exclaimed the astonished squire, "what can it mean? Hand me my spectacles, Mrs. Gower, and put them on my nose, till I overhaul this document. Maybe it contains state-treason, a gunpowder plot or something. 'The pen is mightier than the sword,' as Solomon says; though I'll be shot if I believe it. Solomon didn't know much about swords, and acted queer sometimes—didn't behave well to his wife, they say. Humph! well, here goes."

So saying, the squire opened the letter and began to read. And as he read, his eyes began to protrude, till they threatened to shoot from his head altogether. The letter ran as follows:

"MAGNUS ERLISTON : Come to me immediately—am dying. I have something to tell you of the utmost importance, and I cannot die with it on my conscience. Above all things, do not, for your life, breathe a word of this to Dr. Wiseman. Come instantly, or you may repent it.   MADGE ORANMORE."

"Now, what in the name of Beelzebub does the woman mean?" exclaimed the squire, as he finished reading this. "How does she expect a man to turn out on a December night, with the gout in his legs? I say, youngster, do you know who sent you with this precious letter?"

"Yes, sir ; my mistress, Mrs. Oranmore."

"And what's the matter with her, may I ask?"

"She has been ailing for some time ; and a week ago, her illness took a dangerous turn. The doctors say she has but few days to live, and she seems to be anxious about some secret that preys on her mind. I have not rested day or night since I started for this place. I fear she will not live until I get back, unless you make haste."

"I know not what to do," said the squire, evidently appalled. "I'd like to see the old lady before she leaves this 'vale of tears,' as Solomon says, but how the mischief I'm to go, I can't tell. If she could only put off dying for a month or two, now, I'd go with pleasure, but I suppose she can't conveniently. 'Time and tide wait for no man,' as Solomon says. I mustn't tell old Wiseman, either, it seems—hum-m-m! 'Pon my life, I don't know what to say about it."

All this was muttered in a sort of soliloquy ; and as he ceased, the merry jingle of bells approaching the house saluted his ears. The next moment, Gipsy, wrapped up in shawls, and hoods, and furs, fresh and bright as a daisy, danced into the room, exclaiming :

"Here I am, good folks! The ball was a horrid stupid affair, without a bit of fun, so I thought I'd come home." Here, catching sight of the stranger, Gipsy favored him with a stare of surprise, and was about to leave the room, when the squire called :

"Come back here, monkey ; I'm in a confounded scrape, and I want you to help me out of it."

"All right ; just hint what it is, will you ? and I'll have you out of it in a twinkling."

"Read that," said the squire, placing the mysterious letter in her hand.

Gipsy read it, and then exclaimed :

"Well, there's some mystery here—that's certain. But you can't go, can you, Guardy ?"

"To be sure I can't. You might as well expect Mrs. Gower, there, to dance the double shuffle, as expect me to go on such a journey."

"Well, Spider's not to know of it, and he couldn't go if he did, with his dilapidated continuations ; Aunty Liz can't travel and lie asleep on a sofa at the same time ; and Aunty Gower, poor woman ! can't travel up stairs, under half an hour's panting and groaning ; so none of them can go, *that's* demonstrated—as old Mr. Blackboard used to say. Eh ! Guardy ?"

"Yes, yes. But what's to be done ?"

"Why, it's very clear what's to be done. *I'll* go !"

"*You*," said the squire, with a stare. "What good can you do ?"

"Come, now ! I like that ! I'll leave it to everybody, if I'm not worth the whole of you put together. Ain't I, now ?"

"Mrs. Oranmore won't tell *you* her secret."

"Well, if she don't, she'll lose the wisest, nicest

sensiblest confidante ever anybody had, though I say it. Any way, I'll try ; and if she won't tell, why, she'll have to leave it alone—that's all.   When do you start ?" she asked, turning to the youth.

"Now, if you're ready," replied the lad.

"Yes, I'm ready. How did you come ? by the stage ?"

"No, in a sleigh—it's at the door."

"Well, then, I won't detain you. Good-bye for a week, Guardy ; good-bye, Aunty Gower. Off we go !"

"Hadn't you better stay till morning," said Mrs. Gower, anxiously. "It is too cold and stormy to travel by night."

"And in the meantime this old lady may give up the ghost. No; there's no time to lose; and besides, I rather like the idea of a journey, to vary the monotony of St. Mark's. Good-bye all—I leave you my blessing," said Gipsy, with a parting flourish, as she left the room and took her place by the side of the boy in the sleigh. Nothing remarkable occurred on the journey. Gipsy, comfortably nestled under the buffalo robes, scarcely felt the cold. The next morning they halted at a wayside inn to take breakfast, and then dashed off again.

Owing to the state of the roads it was late in the afternoon when they reached the city ; and almost dark when Gipsy, preceded by her companion, entered the gloomy home of Mrs. Oranmore.

"My stars ! what a dismal old tomb. It really smells of ghosts and rats, and I should not wonder if it was tenanted by both," was Gipsy's internal comment as she passed up the long, dark staircase, and longer, darker hall, and entered the sick-room of Mrs. Oranmore—the longest and darkest of all. Stretched on a hearse-like bed—stiff, stark, and rigid, as though she were already dead—lay Madge Oranmore—her face looking like some

15*

grim, stern mask carved in iron. An old woman, whom the boy addressed as " mother," sat by her side.

The invalid started quickly at the sound of their footsteps ; and seeing the boy, exclaimed, in a faint, yet eager and imperious tone :

" Has he come ?"

" No ; he is ill, and could not come," said Gipsy, stepping forward. " He is unable to walk, so I have come in his stead."

" Who are you ?" demanded Mrs. Oranmore, sharply.

" Well, really, I'd be obliged to anybody who would tell me—at present, it's more than I know. I used to think I was Gipsy Gower—Squire Erliston's ward ; but, of late, I've found out I don't belong to anybody in particular. I was picked up, one night, as if I had been a piece of drift-wood ; and I expect, like Venus, I rose from the sea."

" Girl, have you come here to mock me ?" exclaimed Dame Oranmore, fiercely.

" The saints forbid ! I'm telling you the truth, the whole truth, and nothing but the truth. I was picked up one Christmas eve, nineteen years ago, on the beach, about a quarter of a mile from here ; and—good Heaven ! what's the matter with you ?" exclaimed Gipsy, springing back.

With the shriek of a dying panther, Mrs. Oranmore sprung up in her bed, with her eyes starting from their sockets, as she fairly screamed :

" What ! Heaven of heavens ! did he not drown you ?"

" Why, *no ;* I rather think not—at least, if I ever was drowned, I have no recollection of it. But, my goodness ! don't glare at me so—you're absolutely hideous enough to make every hair on a body's head stand perpendicular, with those eyes of yours."

"How were you saved?" Answer me that! How were you saved?" again screamed the excited woman.

"Well, I don't recollect much about it myself; but Mrs. Gower told me, the other day, that she found me rolled up in a shawl, on the beach, like an Esquimaux papoose asleep in a snow-bank. I haven't any notion who the 'he' is you speak of; but if 'he' left me there to turn into an icicle, I only wish I could see him, and tell him a piece of my mind—that's all."

"And this was Christmas eve, nineteen years ago?" exclaimed Madge Oranmore, breathlessly.

" Yes."

"Great Heaven! how just is thy retribution! And at last, in my dying hour, I behold before me the child of Esther Erliston and Alfred Oranmore!" exclaimed the dying woman, falling back on her pillow, and clasping her hands.

" *What!*" exclaimed Gipsy, springing forward, and seizing her by the arm. "Whose child, did you say I was?"

"The only daughter of Esther Erliston and Alfred Oranmore; and heiress, in your mother's right, of Mount Sunset Hall," replied Mrs. Oranmore.

"And grandchild of Squire Erliston?"

"Yes."

Gipsy staggered back, and covered her face with her hands. Her emotion was but momentary, however; and again approaching the bed, she said, in a tone that was perfectly calm, though her wild, excited eyes spoke a different tale:

"Tell me all about this. How came I to be left to perish on the shore?"

" Leave the room, both of you," said the sick woman, to her attendants. They obeyed. "Now, sit down beside me," she continued, turning to Gipsy; "and tell me, are you married?"

"Yes, they say so—to old Dr. Nicholas Wiseman."

"Great heaven! what did you say?" exclaimed Mrs. Oranmore, in a voice of horror.

"Yes. It's surprising, ain't it, that I married that old man. But that's got nothing to do with your story. Go on," urged Gipsy.

"Child! child!" said the dying woman faintly, "*you have wedded the murderer of your mother.*"

With a low, sharp cry Gipsy sprang to her feet—her countenance blanched to the hue of death.

"Did he know your history?" asked Mrs. Oranmore, breaking the long pause that followed.

"Yes; he heard it a few weeks before we were married," said Gipsy, in a voice that was hoarse and unnatural.

"Then he married you that he might possess Mount Sunset. Oh, the villainy of that wretch! But let him beware! for the day of retribution is at hand."

"Tell me all, from the beginning," said Gipsy, seating herself, and speaking in a tone as stern, and with a face as firm and rigid, as that of the grim invalid herself; but those eyes—those eyes—how they blazed!

There is little need to recapitulate the tale told to Gipsy—she related only what the reader already knows; the death of Esther by *her* instigation, but by *his* hand; and the infant left to perish in the waves.

"I suppose he left you on the shore, thinking the waves would wash you away," concluded Mrs. Oranmore, "when you were providentially saved by the same Almighty power that guarded Moses in his cradle of bulrushes. I supposed you had perished, and so did he; but the agonies of remorse I have suffered for what I have done, I can never reveal. Night and day, sleeping

or waking, the last dying shrieks of Esther Oranmore
have been ringing in my ears. My son married Lizzie
Erliston ; and his violent death was but the beginning
of my living punishment. For *his* son's sake, I have
kept my dreadful secret during life ; but now, at the
hour of death, a power over which I have no control
compels me to reveal all. I am beyond the power of the
law—I go to answer for my crimes at the bar of God ;
therefore, I fear not in making these disclosures. My
hour has come."

"But he shall not escape !" said Gipsy, rising from
the chair, on which she sat as if petrified, while listening
to the story of her birth. " No ! by the heaven above
us both, his life shall pay for this ! Woman," she continued, turning fiercely upon Mrs. Oranmore, "you *shall
not* die until you have done justice to the child of her
you have murdered ! I will send for a magistrate ; and
you must make a deposition of all you have told me to
him. Death shall not enter here yet, to cheat the gallows of its due !"

She sprang to the bell, and rang a peal that brought
all the servants in the house flocking wildly into the
room.

"Go to the nearest magistrate," she said, turning to
the boy who had accompanied her from St. Mark's—
"fly ! vanish ! Tell him it is a matter of life and death.
Go! and be back here in ten minutes, or you shall rue it !"

The boy fled, frightened out of his wits by her fierce
words and looks. Shutting the door in the faces of the
others, Gipsy seated herself ; and setting her teeth hard
together, and clenching her hands, she fixed her eyes on
the floor, and sat as immovable as if turning to stone.
Mrs. Oranmore lay in silence—either not willing or not
able to speak.

Ere fifteen minutes had thus passed, the boy returned, accompanied by a magistrate—a short, blustering, important personage. He bowed to Gipsy—who arose upon his entrance—and began drawing off his gloves, making some remark upon the inclemency of the weather, which she abruptly cut short, by saying:

"This woman is dying, and wishes to make a deposition. Here are writing-materials; sit down and commence—you have no time to spare."

Hurried away by her impetuosity, the little man found himself, before he was aware of it, sitting by the bed-side, pen in hand, writing and listening, with many an ejaculation of wonder, horror, and amazement.

At length the deposition was duly drawn up and signed, and he arose, exclaiming:

"But, good heaven! madam, do you not know, if you survive, you will be arrested too, and——"

"Hush!" said Gipsy, sternly; "she is dying."

"I tell you I did not murder her," she exclaimed, almost springing up in bed; "it was he who gave her the poison! I never did it. Listen! do you not hear her shrieks? or is it not the cries of the fiends I hear already? *He* was afraid. Ha! ha! ha!" she said, with a horrid laugh, "I mocked him until he ventured to do it. He drowned her child, too; he said he did—he threw it into the sea; and dead people tell no tales. Who said it was alive? I will never believe it! It is dead! It is dead!"

She sank back exhausted. The magistrate gazed, white with horror; but Gipsy was calm, stern, and still.

"Look, look! they come for me—their arms are outstretched — they approach — they strangle me. Off, demon—off, I say!" A wild, piercing shriek rang through the house, then she fell back, her jaw dropped, her eyes grew glazed, her face rigid, and Madge Oranmore was dead.

There was a moment's appalled silence. Then the magistrate said :

" Let us leave this dreadful place ; the very air seems tainted with blood."

Without a word, she turned and followed him from the room, and the house. Rejecting all his invitations to let him find lodgings for her in the city during the night, she accompanied him to his office, received a warrant for the arrest of Dr. Wiseman ; and with two constables, set off immediately for Sunset Hall.

------- ♦ -------

CHAPTER XXXVI.

RETRIBUTION.

" Oh, woman wronged can cherish hate
  More deep and dark than manhood may,
And when the mockery of fate
  Hath left revenge her chosen way."
—WHITTIER.

T was the afternoon of the following day. The squire sat alone, muttering to himself : "Singular! most singular! most ex-*cess*-ively singular! wants a private interview, eh! What the dickens can be in old Wiseman's noddle now? Maybe he wants to divorce Gipsy, and marry Lizzie. Ha! ha! ha! that would be a joke. Wonder what old Mother Oranmore wanted? that's another secret. I suppose she told Gipsy and—ha! here's Gipsy herself. 'Speak of Old Nick, and he'll appear,' as Solomon says. Well, what's the news?"

" Where's Dr. Wiseman ?" inquired Gipsy, abruptly.

" Up stairs. He sent down word some time ago,

that he had something important to tell me, and wanted a private interview. Think of that! But what is the matter with you? You look as if you'd been riding on a broomstick all night—as if you were the Witch of Endor, who told King Saul's fortune long ago."

As he spoke, a slow, heavy footstep was heard descending the stairs.

"There's old Wiseman now, pegging along," said the squire. "I never see him walking, since he broke his shin-bone, that he doesn't remind me of Old Nick himself. Now for this wonderful secret of his."

"Guardy, don't mention that I am here," said Gipsy, hurriedly. "I have a project in hand, that I fancy will astonish him a little, by and by."

"Well, be sure you're right, then go ahead, as Solomon says—you always have some project or other in your cranium to bother his brains."

"I fancy I will bother him a little more than usual this time," said Gipsy, with a low, bitter laugh—gliding through one door just as the doctor entered by another.

Dr. Wiseman, thin and attenuated by illness, looked even more ghastly and hideous (if such a thing were possible) than when we saw him last. He advanced, and took a seat near the fire.

"Well, Wiseman, what's this wonderful affair you have to tell me?" said the squire, adjusting himself in his seat to listen.

"It concerns my wife," replied the doctor, slowly.

"Yes, some complaint, I'll be bound! Now, I tell you what, Wiseman, I won't listen to your stories about Gipsy. She has always done what she liked, and she always shall, for what I care. If she likes to enjoy herself, she will, and you nor no one else shall interfere," said the squire, striking. the table with an emphatic thump.

"Don't jump at conclusions so hastily, my dear sir," said the doctor, dryly. "I have no complaint to make of Mrs. Wiseman. It is of her birth and parentage I would speak."

"Her birth and parentage! Is the man mad? Don't you know she's a foundling?" said the squire, staring with all his eyes.

"Yes, but lately I have discovered who she is. You need not excite yourself, Squire Erliston, as I see you intend doing. Listen to me, and I will tell you all about it. The time has come for you to know.

"Perhaps you are not aware that for many years I have been the friend and confidant of Mrs. Madge Oranmore; but so it is. I was bound to her by the strongest ties of gratitude, and willingly served her in all things.

"One Christmas eve, just nineteen years ago, she sent for me in most urgent haste. I followed her messenger, and was shown to the lady's room. There I found an infant enveloped in a large shawl, which she told me I was to consign to the waves—in a word, to drown it. You start, Squire Erliston, but such was her command. She refused to tell me what prompted her to so fiendish an act. I was in her power, and she knew I dared not refuse; I therefore consented——"

"To drown the child?" said the squire, recoiling in horror.

"Listen—I feared to refuse, and promised to do it. I went to the beach, the tide was out; while I stood hesitating, I heard a sleigh approaching. I wrapped the child up closely, and laid it right in their way, and stood aside to watch the event; determined, in case they did not see it, to provide for it comfortably myself. Fortunately, they saw it. A woman who was in the sleigh took it with her—that woman was Mrs. Gower—that child is now my wife."

"Goo-oo-d Lord!" ejaculated the squire, whose mouth and eyes were open to their widest extent.

"When you told me how she had been found, I knew immediately it was the same. I had long felt remorse for what I had done, and I at once resolved to make reparation to the best of my power, by marrying the foundling. This, Squire Erliston, was the secret of my wish to marry Gipsy, which puzzled you so long.

"Still, I was completely ignorant of her parentage. Owing to my accident, I was unable to visit Mrs. Oranmore; but I wrote to her repeatedly, threatening her with exposure if she did not immediately reveal the whole affair. She grew alarmed at last, and sent me a letter that explained all, only begging me not to disgrace her, by letting the world know what she had done. That letter, I regret to say, has been unhappily lost."

"Well!" said the squire, breathlessly, seeing he paused.

"Well, sir, she told me all. My wife is the child of your eldest daughter, Esther, and Alfred Oranmore."

Bewildered, amazed, thunderstruck, the squire sat gazing upon him in a speechless horror.

"The way of it was *this*," continued the doctor, as calmly as though he was ordering him a prescription. "Alfred Oranmore, as you know, was accidentally drowned, leaving his wife in the utmost destitution. Mrs. Oranmore heard of it, and had Esther privately conveyed to her house, while she caused a notice of her death to be published in the papers. What her object was in doing this, I know not. Esther, she says, died in her house. How she came by her death, I cannot even guess. I knew nothing of it at the time, as I told you before. Mrs. Oranmore wished this child removed, that it might not be in the way of her son, Barry; and thinking I was as heartless and cruel as herself, she employed me to drown it. Such, Squire Erliston, is this singular story. I thought it my duty to inform you immediately."

"And Gipsy is my grandchild," said the squire, in the slow, bewildered tone of one who cannot realize what he says.

"Yes; and the rightful heiress of Mount Sunset," said the wily doctor, in a slow, triumphant tone.

"And the avenger of her mother!" cried the voice of Gipsy herself, as she stood before them. "Oh, wonderful Doctor Wiseman! astonishing indeed is thy talent for invention and hardihood. What a strain on your imagination it must have been, to invent such a story! Have you ever heard of the proverb, 'Murder will out,' my lord and master? Ho, there! Burke and Johnston, enter! here is your prisoner!"

She opened the door as she spoke, and the constables entered.

"What in the devil's name means this?" exclaimed the doctor, growing deadly pale.

"Yes, call on your master," mocked Gipsy; "he has stood by you long, but I fear he will not serve you more. Quick, there, Burke! on with the handcuffs. Gently, Doctor Wiseman—gently, my dear sir; you will hurt your delicate wrists if you struggle so. Did any prophetic seer ever foretell, Doctor Wiseman, your end would be by the halter?"

"What means this outrage? Unhand me, villains!" exclaimed the doctor, hoarse with rage and fear, as he struggled madly to free himself from the grasp of the constables.

"Softly, doctor, softly," said Gipsy, in a voice, low, calm, and mocking; "you are *only* arrested for the murder of my mother, Esther Oranmore, just nineteen years ago. Ah! I see you remember it. I feared such a trifle might have escaped your memory!"

The face of the doctor grew perfectly ghastly. He staggered back, and would have fallen, had he not been upheld by one of the men. Gipsy stood before him, with a face perfectly white, save two dark purple spots burning on either cheek. Her wild eyes were blazing with an intense light, her lips wreathed in a smile of exultant triumph; her long hair, streaming in disorder down her back, gave her a look that awed even the constables themselves.

"And now, Doctor Wiseman," she said, in a slow, bitter, but exulting voice, "I have fulfilled my vow of vengeance; my revenge is complete, or will be, when your miserable body swings from the gallows. I see now, your aim in compelling me to marry you; but you have failed. Satan has deserted his earthly representative, at last. No earthly power can save you from hanging now. Away with him to prison! The very air is tainted which a murderer breathes."

The men advanced to bear off their prisoner. At that moment the recollection of the astrologer's fell prediction flashed across his mind. Word for word it had been fulfilled. Before him, in ghastly array, arose the scaffold, the hangman, his dying agonies, and the terrible hereafter. Overcome by fear, horror, and remorse, with a piercing shriek of utter woe, the wretched man fell senseless to the floor.

"Take him away," said Gipsy, sternly, turning aside with a shudder of disgust; "my eyes loathe the sight of him!"

They bore him away. Gipsy stood at the window listening, until the last sound of the carriage died away in the distance; then, abruptly turning, she quitted the room, leaving the squire stunned, speechless, and bewildered by the rapidity with which all this had taken place.

CHAPTER XXXVII.

ANOTHER SURPRISE.

" No heiress art thou, lady, but the child
Of one who's still unknown."

REAT was the excitement and consternation which the news of Dr. Wiseman's crime and arrest created in St. Mark's and the neighboring city. The peculiar and romantic circumstances attending it, imperfectly known as they were, the respectability of the parties implicated, the high standing of the prisoner in society—all contributed to add to the general interest of the case.

The rapid and exciting events, the startling discovery that Gipsy was his grandchild, so confounded and bewildered the squire, who was never noted for the brightness of his intellect, that it completely upset his equilibrium ; and his days were passed alone, smoking and staring stupidly at every one he saw. As for Lizzie, she was too feeble and languid either to feel horror or surprise, and a faint stare and shiver was the only effect the news produced upon her. Mrs. Gower groaned in spirit over the depravity of mankind in general, and Dr. Wiseman in particular; and generally passed her days in solemn exhortations to the servants, to be warned by his fearful example, and mend their ways.

On Gipsy, therefore, all the business of the household devolved. A great change had come over the elf; her laughing days seemed passed ; and quietly establishing herself as mistress of the household, she issued her orders with a quiet dignity and calm authority, that commanded obedience and respect. She wrote to Louis, informing him of all that had occurred, and desiring him to return home immediately.

The only moments of relaxation which Gipsy ever allowed herself were her visits to Valley Cottage, listening to the gentle words of Celeste—"dear Celeste," as Gipsy called her. Day by day she had grown paler and frailer, her step had lost its airy lightness, her cheeks no longer wore the hue of health ; but no complaint ever passed her lips. Gipsy often passed her nights at the cottage, feeling it a comfort to pour her troubles into the sympathizing ears of her friend. And Celeste would forget her own sorrow in soothing and consoling the poor, half-crazed little elf.

Miss Hagar, whose health had for some time been failing, was now unable to leave her bed. Fearing the shock might prove fatal, Celeste had taken care she should not hear of her brother's arrest. As for Minnette, no one knew where she was ; and, indeed, few cared— for her hard, selfish nature had made her disliked by all.

One evening, Mrs. Gower sat in one of the upper chambers conversing with Mrs. Donne, whose life, it will be remembered, Gipsy saved. That worthy old lady was still an inmate of Sunset Hall, and unwilling to leave her comfortable quarters while suffering with the "rheumatiz." In the confusion and excitement following the arrest, she had been almost totally neglected, and had as yet no opportunity of learning the particulars. Providentially encountering Mrs. Gower, when really dying of curiosity, she began plying her with questions ; and the worthy housekeeper, delighted to find so attentive a listener, sat down, and with much gravity began narrating .the whole affair, while the attention of her auditor deepened every moment.

"Laws a massy 'pon me!" exclaimed Mrs. Donne, as she ceased; "was she picked up on the beach, Christmas eve, nineteen years ago?"

"Yes; astonishing, isn't it?"

"'Stonishing! I guess so!" said Mrs. Donne; "if you knew what I do, you'd say so."

"Why, what do you know? *do* tell me," said Mrs. Gower, whose curiosity was aroused.

"Well, I don't mind if I do; though I did intend to carry the secret to the grave with me. But as I couldn't help it, they can't do nothing to me for losing the child.

"On the very night you speak of, Christmas eve, nineteen years ago, I was brought by a young man to a house in the distant part of the city to nurse a woman and child. The young man was tall, and dark, and powerful handsome, but sort o' fierce-looking; and she—oh, she was the loveliest creature I ever laid my eyes onto! She was nothin' but a child herself, too, and a furriner, I suspect, by her tongue.

"Well, I staid there 'long with her, till nigh onto midnight; and then I wrapped myself up to come home. As I was going out, he called on me to stop. So I sat down to listen, and he told me, if I'd take the child home with me, and take care on't, he'd pay me well. I had neither chick nor child of my own, besides being a widder, and I took him at his word. He gave me a purse with a good round sum of money in it, on the spot, and promised me more.

"I took the little one, wrapped it up in my shawl, and set out for home.

"On the way I got tired; and when I reached the beach, I sat down to rest. Two or three minutes after, there was a great cry of fire. I became frightened;

dropped the baby in my confusion ; wandered off I know not how ; and when I came back, not long afterward, it was gone.

"Well, I 'clare to man ! I was most crazy. I hunted up and down the beach till nigh mornin', but I could see no signs of it ; and I supposed the tide carried the poor little thing away. I was dreadfully sorry, you may be sure ; but as it couldn't be helped, I thought I'd make the best of it, and say nothing about it. So when the young man came, I told him it was doing very well. And he never asked to see it, but gave me some money, and went away.

"For some time after he continued sending me money ; but he soon stopped altogether, and I never heard from either of them more."

"Did you ever find out his name?" inquired Mrs. Gower.

"Yes. One day he dropped his handkerchief, going out. I picked it up, and his name was written on it in full : it was, *Barry Oranmore !*"

"Barry Oranmore !" repeated Mrs. Gower, thunderstruck.

"Yes, that was his name ; and they were the handsomest pair ever I saw. I'm sure I'd know either of 'em again, if ever I saw them."

Much agitated, Mrs. Gower arose, and going to where she had laid the miniature she had found on his neck when dead, she handed it to Mrs. Donne. That personage seized it, with a stifled shriek, as she exclaimed :

"My goodness gracious ! it's the picter of the lady I 'tended. I'd know that face anywhere."

"Oh ! dear ! dear ! dear ! what *would* Miss Lizzie say if she heard this?" ejaculated Mrs. Gower, holding up her hands. "And the child, poor thing ! are you sure it was drowned?"

"Well, no; I ain't to say *sure;* but it's most likely. It was an odd-looking little thing, too, with a nat'ral mark, like a red cross, right onto its shoulder, which is something I never seed on any baby before."

But to the surprise of Mrs. Donne, Mrs. Gower sprang panting to her feet, and grasped her by the arm, exclaiming:

"On which shoulder was that mark? Say on which shoulder!"

"On the left. Laws a massy 'pon me! what's the matter?" said the astonished Mrs Donne.

"Good heavens! Can the child she speaks of have been——"

"Who's?" inquired Mrs. Donne, eagerly.

Before Mrs. Gower could reply, she heard Gipsy's foot in the passage. Going out, she caught her by the arm and drew her into the room. Then before the young lady could recover from her astonishment at this summary proceeding, she had unfastened her dress, pulled it down off her left shoulder, and displayed a *deep-red cross.*

Recovering herself, Gipsy sprang back, exclaiming indignantly:

"What in the name of all that's impolite, has got into you, Aunty Gower? Pretty work this, pulling the clothes off a lady's back without even saying, by your leave."

But Mrs. Donne had seen the mark, and fell back, with a stifled cry.

"That's it! that's it exactly! She's the child saved, after all."

"Why, whose child am I *now?*" said the astonished Gipsy.

"Can you describe the shawl the child you speak of

was wrapped in ?" inquired Mrs. Gower, without giving her time to answer Gipsy's question.

"Yes, that I can—it was my own wedding shawl, as my blessed husband, who is now an angel up above, bought for me afore we were married. It was bright red with a white border, and the letters J. D. (which stands for Jane Donne) in one corner, and the letters J. D. (which stands for *James* Donne) in t'other," replied Mrs. Donne, with animation.

Mrs. Gower sank into a seat and covered her face with her hands ; while Gipsy stood gazing from one to the other in the utmost perplexity.

"What does all this mean ?" she asked, at length.

Without replying, Mrs. Gower left the room, and presently re-appeared with a faded crimson shawl, which she spread upon the bed. Mrs. Donne uttered a cry of joy when she saw it.

"Sakes alive ! that is the very one. Where on earth did you get it ?"

"Wrapped around the child."

"Aunty, pray tell me what in the world does all this mean ?" exclaimed Gipsy.

For reply, Mrs. Gower briefly narrated what had been told her by Mrs. Donne. The surprise of Gipsy may be imagined, but her surprise scarcely equaled her pleasure.

"Thank God !" she fervently exclaimed, as Mrs. Gower ceased, "then I have *not* married the murderer of my mother—that thought would have rendered me wretched to my dying day. My mother, then, may be living yet, for all you know."

In her exultation Gipsy first rode over to tell Celeste, then coming home she seated herself and wrote the following letter to Louis :

"SUNSET HALL, ST. MARK'S,
December 23, 18—.

"DEAR LOUIS: In my last I told you I was the child of your Aunt Esther, and Alfred Oranmore; since then I have discovered we were mistaken. My father and yours, Louis, were the same—who my mother was, I know not; but Aunty Gower has shown me a likeness found on my father's neck when dead, representing a young and lovely girl, who must have been my mother; for though the picture is fair, and I am dark, yet they say they can trace a strong resemblance between us. It seems I was taken away by the nurse the night of my birth, and left on the shore, where aunty found me. What has become of their infant is yet unknown, but it may be it, too, was saved, and will yet be found. How singularly things are turning out! Who would ever think we were brother and sister? Do hasten home, dear Louis, more hearts than one are longing for your coming. I have a thousand things yet to tell you, but you know I hate writing, so I will wait until I see you. Your affectionate *sister*, GIPSY."

CHAPTER XXXVIII.

THE HEIRESS OF SUNSET HALL.

> " A perfect woman, nobly planned,
>   To warm, to comfort, and command ;
>   And yet a spirit still and bright,
>   With something of an angel light."—WORDSWORTH.

HE darkened rooms, the hushed footfalls, the whispered words, the anxious faces, betoken the presence of sickness. Like some long, dark effigy, Miss Hagar lies on her bed, prostrated in body and mind, and sick unto death. By her side sits Celeste, in a quiet dress of soft gray, her golden hair lying in bands on her fair cheeks, pale and thin with long days and nights of unceasing watching.

Never had the tender love and cherishing care of the young girl been so manifested as in the sick-room of her benefactress. Night and day, like some angel of mercy, she hovered over the couch of the invalid— ready at the slightest motion to hold the cup to her parched lips, or bathe her burning brow. Nothing could induce her to leave her side, save, when tired Nature could watch no longer, she sought her couch to catch a few moments' sleep. And Miss Hagar, with the usual fretful waywardness of illness, would have no one near her but Celeste. Gipsy had offered her services as assistant nurse, but was most promptly rejected.

" I want Celeste. Where is Celeste ?" was ever the cry of the invalid.

It was the second week of Miss Hagar's illness. For days she had been raving deliriously, recognizing no one, not even Celeste. Toward the close of the tenth day she grew worse, and the doctor pronounced the crisis of her disease at hand.

Evening was approaching, the evening of a bleak January day. The snow was falling drearily without; and the cold wind wailed and moaned around the lonely house. The fire, burning low in the grate, cast a red, fitful, uncertain light through the room, giving everything an unearthly, spectral appearance. Celeste sat by the window, her chin resting on her hand, her eyes fixed on the desolate prospect without, her mind and heart far away—far away. Her face was wet with tears, but she knew it not; sobs, long and deep, that she struggled in vain to repress, swelled her bosom. Never in her life had she felt so utterly desolate; yet a sort of awe mingled with her tears, as she felt herself in the presence of death.

Night fell in storm and darkness. In the deep gloom, nothing could be discerned save the white; unearthly light of the drifting snow. Celeste arose, drew the curtain, lit a small lamp, and was about to resume her seat, when she heard her name pronounced by the lips of the invalid.

In a moment she was bending over her. Reason had returned to its throne; and for the first time in many weeks, Miss Hagar recognized her.

"Thank God!" exclaimed Celeste, joyfully. "Dear Miss Hagar, do you not know me?"

"Certainly, Celeste," said the invalid, passing her hand across her eyes, as if to clear away a mist. "I have been ill, have I not?"

"Yes; but now you will recover. I feared you would never speak to me more; but now you will get well, and we will be happy together once more."

"No, child, I will never get well. Something here

tells me that I am called," said Miss Hagar, solemnly, laying her hand on her heart. "I am sinking fast, and perhaps I may never see the morning dawn. I wish I could see them all before I die. Send for my brother and Archie Rivers, and little Gipsy, and Minnette! Poor Minnette! I have been harsh to her sometimes, I am afraid; and I would ask her pardon before I depart. Why don't you send for them, Celeste?"

What should she do? What ought she to say? How could she tell her what had happened?

"Dear Miss Hagar," she said, gently, "neither the doctor, nor Minnette, nor Archie, are at home. But if you will see Gipsy, I will go for her."

"All gone! all gone!" murmured the sick woman, feebly, "scattered far and wide. But you, Celeste, you have stood by me through all; you have been the staff and comfort of my old age. May God bless you for it! Truly has he said: 'Cast thy bread upon the waters, and it shall return unto thee after many days.' But, child, have you never wondered who you were; have you never wished to know who were your parents?"

"Oh, yes, often!" replied Celeste, eagerly, "but I knew, when the proper time came, you would tell me; so I never asked."

"Well, that time has come at last. It is but little I can tell; for I neither know who you are, nor what is your name. The way you came under my care is simply this:

"One night, as I was returning home from the village, at an unusually late hour, a little girl came running out from a wretched hovel, and begged me to enter with her, for her aunty, as she called her, was dying. I went in, and found an old woman lying on a heap of rags and straw, whose end was evidently at hand. I did what I could for her; but I saw she was sinking fast. Her whole care seemed to be for her little girl, who crouched at the foot of the bed, weeping bitterly. In her anxiety for her, she seemed to forget her own sufferings.

"'What will she do when I am gone? Who will protect her and care for her in this selfish world?"

"'Is she an orphan?" I asked.

"'That I do not know. The child is a foundling, and no relation to me; but I love her as though she were my own child. Oh! what will become of her when I am gone?"

"'And have you no clue to her birth?'

"'None. One Christmas eve, about twelve years ago, my husband was caught in a storm coming from A——. As he was hurrying along by the shore road, he saw a sleigh in advance of him, and hastened on in hopes to overtake it. In his hurry his foot struck against something on the ground, and he stumbled and fell. As he arose, he turned to examine it; and judge of his surprise at finding it to be a young infant, wrapped in a long shawl, and sweetly sleeping. In his astonishment he stood rooted to the ground, unable to move, and the sleigh passed on, and was soon out of sight. It was evident to him that the inmates of the sleigh had either left it there to perish, or it had accidentally fallen out. In either case, the only thing he could do was to take it home, which he did; and handed it to me, half frozen, the next morning. Our own little girl was dead; and this child seemed so like a god-send to fill her place, that I received it with joy, and resolved to adopt it, if its parents never claimed it. For months we lived in the constant dread that it would be taken from us; but years passed on, and no inquiry was ever made concerning it. We named her Celeste; for there was something truly celestial in her sweet, angel-like face, and loving nature; and never did parents love any only child as we did her.

" ' We were in very comfortable circumstances then ; but when Celeste was about eight years old, my husband died ; and after that everything seemed against us. We got poorer and poorer ; and I was forced to take in sewing, to keep us from starving. For nearly four years I worked at this, stitching away from daylight till dark ; and then scarcely able to keep soul and body together. Celeste assisted me nobly ; but at length my health began to fail, and I resolved to leave the city. My husband's friends had formerly resided here, and I was in hopes of finding them ; but when I came, I learned that they were all gone. Last night I was taken dangerously ill ; and now I feel that I am dying ; and my poor Celeste will be left utterly friendless and alone. She is beautiful, as you see ; and what her fate may be, should she live to grow up, I dare not think of. My poor, poor Celeste !'

" The deep affliction of the dying woman, and the heartfelt grief of the child, touched me deeply. I resolved that the poor orphan should not be left to struggle alone through the world. I was not rich, but still I was able to provide for her. In a few brief words I told her my resolution ; and never shall I forget the fervent gratitude that beamed from the dying eyes, as she listened.

" ' May God forever bless you !' she exclaimed, 'and may the Father of the fatherless reward you for this !'

" That night she died ; and next day she was buried at the expense of the parish. I took you home ; and since then you have been my sole earthly joy, Celeste ; and now that I am dying, I leave you, as a legacy, your history. Perhaps some day you may yet discover your parents, if they live."

Utterly exhausted, Miss Hagar's lips ceased to move. During all the time she had been speaking, Celeste had remained as if riveted to the spot, with an emotion unnoticed by Miss Hagar. Her pale face grew whiter and whiter, her eyes were slowly dilating, her lips parted; until, when the spinster ceased, her head dropped on her hands, while she exclaimed, half aloud:

"Can I believe my ears? Then I am that other child left to perish on the beach that stormy Christmas Eve. Good heavens! Can it be that I am the child of Esther Erliston? Have I discovered who I am at last?"

"What are you saying there?" said Miss Hagar, feebly.

"Miss Hagar!" exclaimed Celeste, starting with sudden energy to her feet, "I am going to Sunset Hall, for Squire Erliston. You must repeat this story to him; it concerns him more than you are aware of, and will clear up a mystery he cannot now penetrate."

"As you please, child," said Miss Hagar, too weak to resist; "but you will not stay long?"

"No; I will be back in less than an hour," replied Celeste, whose cheeks were now flushed, and her eye burning with excitement, as she seized her cloak and hood, and hurried into the kitchen.

Curly, their only servant, was dozing in her chair by the hearth. Rousing her up, Celeste sent her in to watch with her patient until her return.

"Remember you must not fall asleep until my return; I will be back very shortly," said the young mistress, as she tied on her mantle.

"But laws! misses, you ain't a goin' out in de storm to-night!" said Curly, opening her eyes in wonder.

"Yes, I must, for an hour or so. Secure the door, and do not leave Miss Hagar until I come back," said Celeste, as she opened the door.

A blinding drift of snow met her in the face; a fierce gust of wind pierced through her wrappings, and sent the embers on the hearth whirling redly through the room. It required all her strength to close the door after her, but she succeeded, after two or three efforts, and stepped out into the wild wintry storm.

At length St. Mark's was reached ; and looking up, she could see the welcome lights of Sunset Hall streaming redly and warmly on the cold, drifting snow. Elevated above the village, its windows glowing with light, it looked the very picture of a home of ease and luxury.

The sight imparted new energy to her drooping limbs ; and hurrying still more rapidly forward, in five minutes more she stood before the astonished inmates of the hall, all white with falling snow.

For a wonder Gipsy was at home. She sat gazing into the glowing fire—a sad, dreamy look on her usually bright, dark face—her little hands folded listlessly in her lap, thinking of one far away ; the squire, utterly disregarding all the laws of etiquette, was smoking his pipe placidly in his arm-chair ; and Mrs. Gower sat dozing in the chimney corner ; Lizzie had been driven to her chamber by the choking fumes of the tobacco.

"Good Heavens ! Celeste ! what has happened ? What has brought you out to-night in this storm ?" exclaimed Gipsy, springing in dismay to her feet, as Celeste—her garments covered with snow-flakes—stood before them, like a moving frost-maiden.

The squire, equally dismayed, had taken his pipe from his mouth, and sat staring at her in utter bewilderment ; while Mrs. Gower, roused from her slumbers, arose from her seat, and drew her over to the fire.

"No, thank you, Mrs. Gower, I cannot sit," said Celeste, hurriedly. " Miss Hagar is dying, and has an important revelation to make to you, sir. It is necessary you should hear it. Will you accompany me back ?" she said, turning to the squire.

" Dying ! important revelations ! Lord bless me !"

ejaculated the squire ; "won t it do to-morrow ?" he added, as a wild blast made the windows rattle. " I don't care about venturing out in this storm."

"You shall go, Guardy," said Gipsy, rising impetuously, "and I'll go, too. Sit down and warm yourself, Celeste—we'll be ready in five minutes. Aunty Gower, please ring for Jupe. Pity if you can't venture out in the storm, when Celeste has walked here in it to tell you. Jupe," she added, as that sable individual entered, " be off and bring round the carriage, and don't be longer than five minutes, at your peril! Here, Totty ! Totty ! bring down my hood, and mantle, and furs ; and your master's hat, gloves, and greatcoat. Quick, there !"

Utterly bewildered by the rapidity with which these orders were given, the squire, unable to resist, found himself enveloped in his fur-lined greatcoat, seated in the carriage, between the two girls, ere he found voice to protest against such summary proceedings.

The fierceness of the storm, which increased in violence, precluded the possibility of entering into conversation ; and the explanation was, therefore, of necessity, deferred until they stood safely within the cozy kitchen of Valley Cottage.

In a few brief words, Celeste gave them to understand that it concerned that " other child," left that eventful Christmas eve on the bleak stormy beach. This was sufficient to rivet their attention ; and the squire, in his anxiety and impatience, forced his way into the sick-room, and stood by the bed-side of Miss Hagar.

"Sorry to see you so sick, Miss Hagar ; 'pon my life I am. I never expected to see you confined to your bed. Celeste—Miss Pearl, I mean—has told me you have something of the greatest importance to communicate to me."

"I do not see how it can possibly concern you,

Squire Erliston," said Miss Hagar, faintly; "but since it is Celeste's desire, I have no objection to relate to you what I have already told her. Oh!" said the sufferer, turning over with a groan.

"Curly, leave the room," said Gipsy, who now entered : while Celeste tenderly raised the head of the invalid, and held a strengthening draught to her lips. Brokenly, feebly, and with many interruptions did the dying woman repeat her tale. Wonder, incredulity, and amazement were alternately depicted on the countenances of the squire and Gipsy, as they listened. She ceased at last ; and totally exhausted, turned wearily aside.

"Then you, Celeste, are that child. You are the heiress of Sunset Hall ! Wonderful ! wonderful !" ejaculated Gipsy, pale with breathless interest.

"And my grandchild !" said the squire, gazing upon her like one bewildered.

"Hush !" said Celeste, in a choking voice, "she is dying."

It was even so. The mysterious shadow of death had fallen on that grim face, softening its gaunt outline into a look of strange, deep awe. The eyes had a far-off, mystic gaze, as if striving to behold something dim and distant.

All had fallen on their knees, and Celeste's choking sobs alone broke the silence.

The sound seemed to disturb Miss Hagar. She turned her face, with a troubled look, on the grief-bowed head of the young girl.

"Do not weep for me, Celeste, but for yourself. Who will care for you when I am dead?"

"I will !" said the squire, solemnly ; "she is my own flesh and blood, and all that I have is hers. She is the long-lost, the rightful heiress of Mount Sunset Hall."

A smile of ineffable peace settled on that dying face. "Then I can go in peace," she said ; "my last care is gone. Good-bye, Celeste. God bless you all ! Tell my brother I spoke of him ; and ask Minnette to forgive me. Minnette—Minnette——"

The words died away. She spoke no more. Her long, weary pilgrimage was over, and Miss Hagar was at rest.

"Don't cry—don't cry," said the squire, dashing a tear from his own eyes, as he stooped over the grief-convulsed form of Celeste. "She's gone the way of all flesh, the way we must all go some day. Everybody must die, you know ; it's only natural they should. 'In the midst of death we are in life,' as Solomon says."

CHAPTER XXXIX.

"LAST SCENE OF ALL."

" Then come the wild weather, come sleet, or snow,
We will stand by each other, however it blow—
Oppression, and sickness, and sorrow, and pain,
Shall be to our true love as links to the chain."
—LONGFELLOW.

WO months have passed away. It is a balmy, genial day in March. Never shone the sun brighter, never looked St. Mark's fairer ; but within Sunset Hall all is silent and gloomy. The very servants step around on tiptoe, with hushed voices and noiseless footfalls. The squire is not in his usual seat, and the parlor is tenanted only by Gipsy and Celeste. The former is pacing up and down the room, with a face almost deadly pale, with sternly-compressed lips, and sad, gloomy eyes. Celeste is kneeling like one in prayer, her face buried in her hands; she, too, is pale with awe and horror. To-day, Dr. Wiseman *dies on the scaffold.* They needed no evidence to condemn him. Fear seemed to have paralyzed his cowardly soul, and he confessed all; and from the moment he heard his sentence, he settled down in a stupor of despair, from which nothing could arouse him.

The sound of carriage-wheels coming up the avenue roused them both, at last. Celeste sprang to her feet, and both stood breathless, when the door opened, and Squire Erliston entered.

"Well?" came from the eager lips of Gipsy.

"All is over," said the squire, gloomily, sinking into a seat. "I visited him in prison, but he did not know me—he only stared at me with a look of stupid imbecility. I could not arouse him for a long time, until, at last, I mentioned your name, Gipsy; then he held out his arms before him, as well as his chains would allow, and cried out, in a voice of agony I will never forget: 'Keep her off! keep her off! she will murder me!' Seeing I could do nothing for him, I came away; and in that state of stupid insensibility, he was launched into eternity."

Celeste, sick and faint with terror, sank into a seat and covered her face with her hands, and Gipsy shuddered slightly.

"And so he has perished—died in his sins," she said, at last. "Once, I vowed never to forgive him; but I retract that oath. May heaven forgive him, as I do! And now, I never want to hear his name again."

"But Minnette, where can she be? Who will tell her of this?" said Celeste, looking up.

"It is most strange what can have become of her," said the squire. "I have spared no pains to discover her, but, so far, all has been in vain. Heaven alone knows whether she is living or dead."

"It is like her usual eccentricity," said Gipsy. "I know

not where she is, yet I feel a sort of presentiment we will meet her again."

*   *   *   *   *   *

"Gipsy, come here," called good Mrs. Gower, one day, about a fortnight after, as that young lady passed by her room on her way down stairs.

"Well, what is it?" said Gipsy, entering, and standing with her back to the door.

"Just look at this likeness; have you ever seen anybody like it?"

Gipsy took it, and looked long and earnestly.

"Well," said she, at length, "if I were a little less tawny, and had blue eyes and yellow hair, I should say it looked remarkably like myself—only I never, the best of times, had such a pretty face.'

"Well, I was just struck by its resemblance to you. I think it must be your mother's picture."

"My mother's picture! My dear Aunty Gower, whatever put such an absurd notion into your head?"

"Because I am quite sure it is. Its very resemblance to you proves this; besides, I found it on your poor father's neck when he was dead."

"It is a sweet face," said Gipsy, heaving a wistful little sigh. "Who knows whether the original be living or dead? Oh, Aunty Gower! it may be that I still have a mother living in some quarter of the globe, who is ignorant she yet has a daughter alive. If I could only think so I would travel the world over to find her."

At this moment Totty burst into the room, her black face all aglow with delight.

"Oh, misses! Oh, Misses Sour! Oh, Misses Gipsy! guess who's 'rived," she breathlessly exclaimed.

"Who? who?" exclaimed both, eagerly.

"Young Marse Louis! he's down in de parlor wid——"

But without waiting to hear more, Gipsy sprang from

the room, burst into the parlor, and beheld Louis standing in the middle of the floor, and the living counterpart of the picture she had just seen, leaning on his arm !

"Gipsy ! my sister !" he exclaimed, but before he could advance toward her, a wild, passionate cry broke from the lips of the strange lady, as she sprang forward, and clasped the astonished Gipsy in her arms.

"My daughter ! my daughter !" she cried, covering her face with burning kisses.

Gipsy grew deadly pale ; she strove to speak ; but wonder and joy chained her ever-ready tongue.

"She is your mother, Gipsy," said Louis, answering her wild look. "I leave her to explain all to you ; your letters first revealed all to me. But Celeste—where is she ?"

"In the drawing-room, reading," was the reply.

He hastily quitted the room, and noiselessly opened the drawing-room door ; Celeste was there, but not reading. She was lying on a lounge, her face hidden in the cushions, her hands clasped over her eyes to repress her falling tears, her heart yearning for the living and the dead. Her thoughts were of him she believed far away ; what were wealth and honors to her, without him ? Her tears fell fast and faster, while she involuntarily exclaimed : "Oh, Louis, Louis ! where are you now ?"

"Here, by your side, Celeste, never to leave it more !" he answered, folding her suddenly in his arms.

> "'Twas his own voice, she could not err !
> Throughout the breathing world's extent
> There was but *one* such voice for her—
> So kind, so soft, so eloquent."

With a wild cry, she unclasped her hands from her eyes and looked up—looked up to encounter those dear, dark eyes, she had never expected to see more.

Great was the surprise of everybody, at this double arrival ; and many were the explanations that followed.

There was Louis, who had to explain how he had met Madame Evelini, and how he had learned her story ; and how, on reading Gipsy's account of the tale told by Mrs. Donne, he had known immediately who was her mother. Then, though the task was a painful one, he was forced to recur to the fate of Minnette, and set their anxiety as rest about her. She had gone to Italy with some friends, he said ; he met her there, and learned from her she was about to take the vail, and there they would find her, safe. Then Gipsy had to recount, at length, all that had transpired since his departure—which was but briefly touched upon in her letters..

It was a strange meeting, when the two living wives of the dead husband stood face to face. Lizzie, too listless and languid to betray much emotion of any kind, listened with faint curiosity ; but tears sprang into the eyes of Madame Evelini, as she stooped to kiss the pale brow of the little lady. She refused to be called Mrs. Oranmore ; saying that Lizzie had held the title longest, and it should still be hers.

"And now there is one other matter to arrange," said Louis, taking the hand of Celeste ; "and that is, your consent to our union. Will you bestow upon me, sir, the hand of your grandchild ?"

"To be sure, I will," said the squire, joyfully. "I was just going to propose, myself, that we should end the play with a wedding. We've all been in the dismals long enough, but a marriage will set us all right again. Come here, you baggage," turning to Celeste, who was blushing most becomingly ; "will you have this graceless scamp, here, for your lord and master? He needs somebody to look after him, or he'll be running to Timbuctoo, or Italy, or some of those heathenish places, tomorrow or next day—just as he did before. Do you consent to take charge of him, and keep him in trim for the rest of his life?"

"Yé-es, sir," said Celeste, looking down, and speaking in the slow, hesitating tone of her childhood.

"Hooray! there's a sensible answer for you. Now I propose that the wedding takes place forthwith. Where's the good of losing time? 'Never delay till to-morrow what you can do to-day,' as Solomon says. What's your opinion, good folks?"

"Mine's decidedly the same as yours, sir," said Louis, promptly.

"Then suppose the affair comes off to-morrow," said the squire, in a business-like tone.

"Oh! no, no!" said Celeste, with such a look of alarm, that the others laughed outright; "a month—two months—"

"Nonsense," said the squire, gruffly, "two months indeed—no, nor two weeks, either. Next Thursday, at the furthest. You can have all your trumpery ready by that time."

"You will have to yield, Celeste," said Gipsy. "Just see how imploringly Louis looks!"

"That's too soon," said Celeste, still pleading for a reprieve. "I never could be ready——"

"Yes, you could," cut in Gipsy. "I'll engage to have everything prepared; and, like Marshal Ney, when I enter the field, the battle is won. Now, not another word. Louis, can't you make her hold her tongue? My dear mother, you must try your eloquence."

"You will have to yield, my dear," said Madame, smiling; "there is no use attempting to resist this impetuous daughter of mine."

"Of course there's not, said Gipsy—"everybody does as I tell them. Now, Louis, take the future Mrs. Oranmore out of this. Aunty Gower and I have got to lay our heads together (figuratively speaking); for on our shoulders, I suppose, must devolve all the bother and bustle of preparation."

Gipsy was in her element during the rest of the week.

The wedding was to be private—the recent death of Miss Hagar and Dr. Wiseman rendering the country fashion of a ball in the evening out of the question ; but still they had a busy time of it in Sunset Hall. It was arranged that the newly-wedded pair should go abroad immediately after their marriage, accompanied by Gipsy and her mother.

The wedding-day dawned, bright and beautiful, as all wedding-days should. Celeste wished to be married in the church, and no one thought of opposing her will. Gipsy stood beside her, robed in white ; and if her face rivaled in pallor the dress she wore, it was thinking of her own gloomy bridal, and of him who had bade her an eternal farewell that night. Mrs. Gower was there, looking very fat, and happy, and respectable, in the venerable brown satin, that was never donned save on an occasion like the present. Lizzie was there, too, supported by Madame Evelini, and looking less listless and far more cheerful than she had been for many a day. There was the squire, looking very pompous and dogmatical, waiting to give the bride away, and repeating, inwardly, all the proverbs he could recollect, by way of offering up a prayer for their happiness. There was Louis, so tall, and stately, and handsome, looking the very happiest individual in existence. And lastly, there was our own Celeste—our "Star of the Valley"— sweeter and fairer than ever, with her blushing face, and drooping eyes, and gentle heart fluttering with joy and happiness.

The church was crowded to excess ; and a universal buzz of admiration greeted the bridal pair, as they entered. Beneath the gaze of a hundred eyes they moved up the aisle, and

> "Before the altar now they stand—the bridegroom and the bride;
> And who can tell what lovers feel in this, their hour of pride."

A few words and all was over; and leaning on the arm of the proud and happy Louis, Celeste received the congratulations of her friends.

Breakfast awaited them on their return to the hall. Immediately after, they were to start for Washington; but before departing, Celeste, turning to Louis, said:

"Before I go, I would visit the grave of poor Miss Hagar. Come with me."

It was not far from Sunset Hall. A white marble tombstone marked the spot, bearing the inscription:

SACRED TO THE MEMORY

OF

HAGAR WISEMAN.

And underneath were the words:

> "Blessed are the dead who die in the Lord."

Tears fell fast from the eyes of Celeste, as she knelt by that lonely grave; but they were not all tears of sorrow.

———

"And this is Venice! Bless me! what a queer-looking old place!" exclaimed Gipsy, lying back amid the cushions of a gondola. "How in the world do they manage to make everything look so funny? This gondola, or whatever they call it, is quite a comfortable place to go to sleep in. I'll bring one of them home to sail on the bay—I will, as sure as shooting. Maybe it won't astonish the natives, slightly. Well this *is* a nice climate, and no mistake. I don't think I'd have any objection to pitching my tent here, myself. What's this the poet says—

> "If woman can make the worst wilderness dear,
> Think, think what a heaven she would make of this 'ere !"

"Oh, what a shame ! to parody the 'Light of the Harem,'" said Celeste, laughing. "But here we are, on land."

It was the day after their arrival in Venice ; and, now, under the guidance of Louis, they were going, in a body, to visit Minnette.

They reached the convent, and were admitted by the old portress—who, as if it were a matter of course, ushered them into the chapel and left them.

For a moment, the whole party stood still in awe. The church was hung with black, and dimly lighted by wax tapers. Clouds of incense filled the air, and the black-robed figures of the nuns looked like shadows, as they knelt in prayer. Many strangers were present, but a deep, solemn hush reigned around.

The cause of all this was soon explained. At the foot of the altar, robed in her nun's dress, the lifeless form of one of the sisterhood lay in state. The beautiful face, shaded by the long, black vail, wore an expression of heavenly peace ; the white hands clasped a crucifix to the cold breast. A nun stood at her head, and another at her feet—holding lighted tapers in their hands—so still and motionless, that they resembled statues.

It was Minnette ! Their hearts almost ceased to beat, as they gazed. The look of deep calm—of child-like rest —on her face, forbade sorrow, but inspired awe. More lovely, and far more gentle than she had ever looked in life, she lay, with a smile still wreathing the sweet, beautiful lips. The blind eyes saw at last.

Suddenly, the deep, solemn stillness was broken, by the low, mournful wail of the organ ; and like a wild cry, many voices chanted forth the dirge :

> "Dies irae, dies illa
> Solvet saeclum in favilla.
> Pie Jesu Dominie,
> Dona eis requiem."

Not one heart there, but echoed the burden of the grand old hymn :

> "Lord of mercy—Jesus blest,
> Grant thy servant light and rest !"

" Let us go—this scene is too much for you," said Louis, as Celeste, clung, pale and trembling, to his arm. And together they quitted the convent.

They were followed by one, who, leaning against a pillar, had watched them intently all the time. He stepped after them into the street ; and Louis, suddenly looking up, beheld him.

"Archie !" he cried, in a tone of mingled amazement and delight.

A stifled shriek broke from the lips of Gipsy, at the name. Yes, it was indeed our old friend Archie—no longer the laughing, fun-loving Archie of other days, but looking pale, and thin, and almost stern.

" O, *dear* Archie ! how glad I am to see you again !" exclaimed Celeste, seizing one of his hands, while Louis wrung the other ; and Gipsy drew back, turning first red, and then pale, and then red again. Madame Evelini, alone, looked very much puzzled what to make of the whole affair.

"Surely; you have not forgotten your old friend, Gipsy ?" said Louis, at last, stepping aside and placing them face to face.

" I am happy to meet you again, Mrs. Wiseman," said Archie, bowing coldly.

" Well, if you *are*," said Louis, looking at him with a doubtful expression, "your looks most confoundedly belie your words. Let me present you to Madame Evelini, Mrs. Wiseman's mother."

" Her mother !" cried the astonished Archie.

" Why, yes. Surely, you don't mean to say you have not heard of the strange events that have lately taken place at St. Mark's ?"

" Even so ; I am in a state of most lamentable ignorance. I pray you, enlighten me."

" What ! have you not even heard that your uncle—Dr. Wiseman—and Miss Hagar were dead ?"

" Dead !" said Archie, starting, and looking at Gipsy, whose face was now hidden by her vail.

" Yes ; but I see you know nothing about it. Come home with us, and you shall hear all."

" Yes, do," urged Celeste ; " Louis and I will be delighted to have you join us."

" Louis and *I*," repeated Archie, rather mischievously ; " then I perceive I have the honor of addressing Mrs. Oranmore."

Of course, Celeste laughed and blushed, according to the rule in such cases. But the scene they had just witnessed had saddened the whole party ; and the journey back was performed in silence. Gipsy was the gravest of all ; and, leaning back in the gondola, with her vail over her face, she never condescended to open her lips, save when directly addressed ; and then her answers were much shorter than sweet.

But when they went home, to their hotel, and everything was explained, and he had learned how Gipsy had been forced into a marriage she abhorred, and the terrible retribution that befell the murderer, matters began to assume a different appearance. Mr. Rivers had long been of the opinion that " it is not good for man to be alone," and firmly believed in the scriptural injunction of becoming a husband of one wife ; and concluded, by proposing in due form to Gipsy—who, after some pressing, consented to make him happy.

"But not till we go home," was the reply to all his entreaties. "I'm just going to get married at dear old St. Mark's, and no place else ; and give Aunty Gower a chance to give her brown satin dress another airing—as ours is likely to be the last wedding at Sunset Hall for some time, unless guardy takes it into his head to get married. Now, you needn't coax ; I won't have you till we get home, that's flat." And to this resolution she adhered, in spite of all his persuasions.

The bridal tour was, of necessity, much shortened by the desperate haste of Archie—who, like the man with the cork leg, seemed unable to rest in any place ; and tore like a comet through Europe, and breathed not freely until they stood once more on American soil.

And three weeks after, a wedding took place at St. Mark's, that surpassed everything of the kind that had ever been heard of before. Good Aunty Gower was in ecstasies ; and the squire, before the party dispersed, full of champagne and emotion, arose to propose a toast.

"Ladies and fellow-citizens : On the present interesting occasion, I rise to "—here the speaker took a pinch of snuff—"I rise to "—here a violent sneeze interrupted him, and drew from him the involuntary remark : "Lord ! what a cold I've got !—as I was saying, I rise to propose the health and happiness of the bride and bridegroom ;" (cheers) "like the flag of our native land, long may they wave !" (desperate cheering). "Marriage, like liberty, is a great institution ; and I would advise every single man present to try it. If he has heretofore given up the idea, let him pluck up courage and try again. 'Better late than never,' as Solomon says."

THE END.